Copyright © Tom Field

Tom Field has asserted
Designs and Patents Act 1988 to be identified as the
author of this work.

This is a work of fiction. Names, characters, businesses, places, events and incidents are either the products of the author's imagination or used in a fictitious manner. Any resemblance to actual persons, living or dead, or actual events is purely coincidental except in the case of historical facts.

Registered IP rights number 4928420270

This book is sold subject to the condition that it shall not, by way of trade or otherwise, be lent, re-sold, hired out or otherwise circulated in any form of binding or cover other than that in which it is published and without a similar condition including this condition being imposed on the subsequent purchaser.

Contact details for the author can be found on

www.therealtomfield.com

On Twitter @therealtomfield

Facebook: Therealtomfield

E-mail: therealtomfield@hotmail.com

# VOLUME 1

## PART FIVE

Warlord

*For Bridgid McCaig*

*Forever my big sister*

*They marched the villagers out onto the dusty square which acted as the focal point for their community.*

*Everyone was there. The men, women, and children, who lived in fear of the moment that the soldiers would visit them and accuse them of crimes they had not committed.*

*That moment had come today.*

*They were made to line up, the men to the left, the women to the right, and the children in the middle. The soldiers walked up and down the lines making sure that no one spoke.*

*A loud rumble filled the distance, and five open top vehicles came into view, and everyone promptly, and sensibly, looked down at the floor as now was not the time to make eye contact. By the time the vehicles had pulled to a stop twenty feet away from them, every one of the villagers was kneeling on the floor, an order given by the soldiers to show respect to their king.*

*Samson Simone stepped out of his vehicle and walked across to where the men were lined up, and looked at them with contempt. One of the men dared to look up at him and so he removed his gun from his holster and shot the man in the head. He died instantly.*

*A woman on the other side screamed and so he walked across to her and kicked her, hard in the face, his huge, military grade boots destroying her face upon impact.*

*Everyone else continued looking at the floor.*
*'Prepare the boys,' he barked.*

*His soldiers marched across to where the children were kneeling and screamed at all the boys to stand on their feet. The boys responded quickly, almost as if they were playing a game, and they were all upright in a matter of seconds.*

*Simone studied them, most of the boys looked under the age of ten, apart from two boys who were much taller than the rest of the group. He stamped across the dirt and looked closer at them.*

*They were definitely too old.*

*He pulled his gun out of the holster once more and shot the two boys he did not need in the head from close range. The rest of the children did not make a sound. They were too afraid.*

*'You are now enlisted to my army,' he said loudly, pacing up and down as he spoke, fixing his eyes firmly on the terrified boys, 'And to prove your loyalty to me, I am going to give you your first command,' he added, looking for a reaction that would indicate the slightest sign of disobedience in his new charges.*

*All of the boys stood still. No tears, no noise and no movement.*

*'Bring them over,'* he barked as he strode across to where the men were kneeling.
*The soldiers shuffled the boys over, prodding them in the back with their machine guns which had been willingly supplied by the C.I.A., and the boys lined up in front of their grandfathers, fathers, brothers, uncles and cousins.*

*The soldiers relinquished their machine guns, placing them in the hands of the boys and then they pulled out their own handguns from their holsters, and to a man, planted the barrels of their weapons firmly against the back of the heads of the boys.*

*'You are with my army, or you are my enemy,'* Simone shouted, his deep, hollow voice echoing around the square, *'I will count to three. On three, those of you that fail to pull your trigger and kill the men in front of you will die, and so will your mothers and sisters. If you show your loyalty and kill the man before you, your women will live and you will be welcomed into my army with open arms.'*

*The boys, the majority of them eight or nine years old, felt the tears filling their eyes.*

*'Do it Sadio, save your sister and mother,'* one desperate father whispered to his son, who had been unfortunate enough to be lined up in front of his own father.

*'One, two, three,'* Simone shouted, without a pause or build-up. He didn't want to drag this out; they had three

*other villages to visit that day as part of their latest recruitment drive.*

*On three, all but one of the boys fired their machine guns at the men kneeling in front of them, the kick of the guns sending over half of the small, weak boys onto the floor. The nine year old boy, who could not bring himself to kill his father, had been shot in the back of his head by his charge before the echo of the gunfire had drifted away.*

*'You have proved your worth,' Simone shouted, 'Welcome to my army. Load them up.'*

*The boys were all marched to the waiting trucks and loaded onto them in silence. There were twenty seven of them, all of them in tears and struggling not to let the soldiers see their devastation and tiny, broken hearts.*

*The women and girls watched the trucks roll out of sight, their sons and brothers gone forever.*

*The soldiers lined up in front of Simone, awaiting their next command, excitement building among them, hoping that their reward would be fitting for the recruitment of twenty seven new warriors. He walked across to his waiting jeep, climbed in and his driver started the engine.*

*'You have one hour. Rape and enjoy the women and girls, and then burn their village and their bodies to the ground,' he shouted, and then Samson Simone was gone.*

# ONE

**Boston - Massachusetts**

The Optician walked through Boston common looking like any other tourist, strolling across the small bridges and casually gazing all around, soaking up the history of the famous patch of land. He walked past the statue of Paul Revere and stopped for a moment. Revere was an integral part of American history, and every kid, in every school, knew who he was. For a moment, he realised how insignificant and lonely his life was, despite the fact that he had given his country as much service as Revere, and probably had as much impact through the political disasters that he had prevented over the past eight years. Perhaps being a silversmith who was a good horse rider was more glamourous than being the best sniper that the world never knew existed, he thought to himself.

He had taken the unusual step of getting to Boston before Ryan Ward. It was the first time that he had ever not flown somewhere on the same jet as him while assisting him in an unofficial mission, even though Ward was oblivious to the fact that the co-pilot, who flew on every flight with him, was one of his closest friends in the world. But Ryan Ward had no idea who The Optician really was or what he looked like.

He was here because he had something personal to take care of. He was heading across the common to Marlborough Street, to pay a ghost from his past a visit.

## Washington D.C.

To Centrepoint, The Optician was his eleventh man. And in his fifty one years he had never known anyone as extraordinary as him, despite being in overall control of both the C.I.A and MI6, even though he was not officially recorded as being affiliated to either agency. But everyone in the murky world of the security services knew who he was by name.
And so did the politicians, including Presidents and Prime Ministers, and they were all terrified of him. His secrets could destroy both Britain's and Americas standing on the worldwide stage.
His real name was Paul. J. McNair and he had spent a lifetime taking care of the problems which troubled governments on both sides of the Atlantic. It was he who made the tough decisions, and cleaned up the messes that the politicians weren't willing to risk their political futures over. He had control of the most elite group of lethal, highly trained and supremely intelligent assassins that did what he ordered without question or fear. They were simply known as the 'Deniables'.
He had been taken aback when The Optician had requested alternative travel arrangements be made for him, an hour before Ward was due to arrive in Boston, and it had been the first time in the twelve years that he

had been his most devoted foot soldier that he had asked him for anything. He resisted the temptation to enquire why, but the question was still burning away inside of him when his phone rang. He recognised the number immediately.

The White House was calling.

'Hello?'

'Please hold for the Vice President,' the voice on the end of the line declared.

He didn't like the Vice President. Recent events had actually made him despise him, but he had used the situation to his own advantage, and he was now speaking to him from a position of power, and the Vice president was just going to have to suck it up.

'Hello McNair', the Vice President said, trying to sound like he was a friend, rather than the quivering politician who was petrified of what he held over him that he really was, but failing miserably.

'What do you want? I'm busy,' he replied, trying to sound as disinterested as he possibly could.

'I know, and I will try not to keep you too long, but I have a message from the President himself,' the Vice president replied, sounding as pathetic as McNair knew he was.

'What is it?' he asked, now using a civilised tone without realising so.

'Obviously he doesn't want this to go any further, and he wants it entirely off the books, which is why I offered to call you, as we have a mutual respect for each other,' he began, a comment that had him rolling his eyes at just how pathetic the Vice President really was, 'But it's a delicate subject and I am not sure exactly how to

approach it,' he continued, waiting for him to coax whatever it was he had to say out of him.
So he remained silent.
After well over ten seconds, and a pause which was long enough to become embarrassing, rather than uncomfortable, he eventually spoke,
'It's about Samson Simone.'
Centrepoint smiled to himself. He had been waiting for the call for the past two days and he was surprised that it had taken this long.
Samson Simone was a warlord. He led a large army in the parts of the Sudan where no one ventured. Unfortunately it was the part of Sudan that gave the big American companies access into Africa, and in turn, all of the natural resources that were available. The C.I.A had armed Simone, and provided the arms and mercenaries to enable him to overthrow the previous warlord who had become too comfortable, and had lost his ruthless edge, which resulted with him leaving the fighting to the American companies and the mercenaries they employed, rather than do it himself. But Simone had decided that he no longer wanted to be at the beck and call of the C.I.A and so he was shutting them out completely, and the American financiers, who were bankrolling all of the elected criminals, or Senators as they were more commonly known, wanted him brought back under control.
Ward had just been involved in a mission where he had discovered the extent of the American involvement in Sudan, and he knew that the power brokers on Capitol Hill would be desperate to get him to sort the mess out. Unofficially of course.

'What about him?' Centrepoint eventually asked.
'The President is aware that we can't send any special forces teams into Sudan, and after the mess that the C.I.A have made of it over there in the first place, he wants them kept well away from the God forsaken place, so he has requested that you solve the problem,' the Vice President replied.
'Solve it how?'
'By removing Simone from power.'
'And replacing him with who?'
'There is a man called Phillipe Bassong. He has already agreed to let us carry out our activities down there, unopposed, if we put him in power.'
'It's a suicide mission. I'd be mad to send a team down there. The people we have aren't superhero's' Centrepoint replied, laughing as he spoke.
'The British guy you sent to deal with my little misdemeanour was most certainly a superhero,' the Vice President replied, referring to his brief encounter with Ward.
'And what is the President offering me in return?'
'What do you want?'
Centrepoint smiled to himself, if the leader of the most powerful nation on earth had to make a deal with him and he had sent his sidekick to broker it, he knew without a doubt that he held all the cards.
And if he could convince Ryan Ward to accept the mission, he would become more powerful than even he had ever anticipated.

### 184 Marlborough Street - Boston

The Optician walked slowly down Marlborough Street. It was one of the most elegant residential areas of Boston, the tree lined streets giving the place a secluded feel, even though it was only a stone's throw from the common and the throngs of tourists itself. He reached number '184' and stopped outside for a moment. It was a simple building, built out of red brick in a simple square shape with no roof. There were steps that led up to the entrance door of the building, and he climbed them in four big strides. He quickly scanned the buzzers, and found the name that he wanted and pushed twice.
A few seconds later, a breathless voice said, 'Hello?'
For a few moments, he felt the urge to turn and walk away.
'Hello?' the voice repeated.
'I need to talk to you,' he said.
There was silence for a moment, and then the voice said, 'I always knew you would find me one day,' and the buzzer sounded before the door lock released.
He pushed through the door and saw the apartment that he wanted at the end of the hallway. He approached it with purpose and knocked twice.
He could hear shuffling behind the door, and after what seemed like an age, the door opened.
A man stood in front of him, it was hard to gauge his size because he was doubled over, wheeling an oxygen tank beside him, which fed a tube to a mask around his neck.
He looked pathetic.
Without waiting for an invitation to come in, he stepped past him and walked through into the lounge. The place

stank of stale cigarettes. He sat down on a battered old sofa and scanned around him, noticing the ashtrays that seemed to be placed three feet apart throughout the room, all overflowing with discarded cigarette ends.
The man eventually made his way into the room and sat on an old chair opposite him.
As he studied him, for a moment, The Optician thought he saw a brief sparkle in his eyes.
'My friend,' The Optician began, 'Gave me back my family, you know, the other three children that you deserted,' he added slowly, shaking his head as he spoke.
The man didn't speak; instead he pulled his oxygen mask up to his face, fitted it, and took a few long, deep breaths before sliding it down again.
And so he continued,
'They have all done extremely well, you have grandchildren that any man would be proud of and those kids all have parents who are balanced, of good moral standing and loving.'
The man went to speak but he raised his hand to stop him,
'In simple terms, they are all good people. You left us to fend for ourselves and disappeared. What sort of man does that?'
'Back then, I wasn't the same man that I am today,' the man quickly said through short breaths, 'If I could turn back the clock, I would do it all differently,' he added.
'But you can't, can you?'
The man looked at the floor.
'But I'm not here to talk about them, they are all better off without you. I'm here to talk about me.'

'Look around,' the man said, 'I think that God issued the appropriate punishment, don't you?'

The Optician scanned the room. The place was disgusting. If there was a God he thought to himself, he got this one right.

But he knew there was no such thing as God.

'The same friend, the one who gave me back the family you deserted, has a saying. He says that every action has a consequence. He's right. Now you look around.'

The man scanned the room. The Optician immediately noticed that he had the same mannerisms as him in the way that he moved his head, and this unnerved him for a few seconds, before he said,

'You have a beautiful family, a large family, and you are here all alone. That's the consequence of your actions.'

'Don't think that I don't regret what I was back then every day of my life,' the man replied solemnly.

The Optician ignored him,

'I know you are dying and that you have very little time left. So as I said, I want to talk about me. Do you know what I do for a job?' he asked.

'Looking at you, something manual, like a construction worker?'

The Optician smiled,

'More like demolition,' he said, for his own amusement.

The man nodded.

'Do you know what happened after you left? Do you know what happened to me and to mom? I know that social services contacted you about taking us back and you did not even respond. I've seen the files.'

The man looked shamefully down at the floor, answering the question without speaking.

'I turned out pretty well under the circumstances,' he continued, 'I had a good career in the military, now I work for the government as a consultant and I have finally found my family, and I have friends who are a second family to me. But I had to see you, to tell you something, before you die.'

The man looked at him. There was something about this son he never knew, something in his eyes that frightened him,

'What exactly do you do for the government?' he asked nervously.

'I kill people,' he answered without a pause, 'Bad people, people who do bad things, especially to kids. And I'm rich, very rich, but I don't care for money. Had you of done the right thing all of those years ago, stayed with your family and raised us, like any decent man would have, then things may have turned out very differently for me.'

'What do you mean, you kill people?'

The Optician was among the most feared and revered men on the planet to those who moved in the Special Forces world, everyone had heard of him and everyone was afraid of him.

Really afraid of him.

'I mean exactly that. And I'm good at it. I have an ability to stay awake for days. That comes from a childhood of first, not sleeping at night because you deserted us, and secondly, because of the bad things that sick men did to me because I had no dad to protect me. So, I guess I should thank you for that,' he said, without once taking his stare away from the man's eyes.

'I'm sorry,' was all the man could muster as a reply.

'I don't want an apology, that's not what I'm here for.'
The man looked confused.
'That would make me too predictable,' The Optician continued, 'And that's one thing I am not.'
'So what do you want?'
'I want to tell you that I forgive you, simple as that. I want nothing from you. And let's face it,' he said, before pausing and looking around the filthy room, 'There isn't anything that you have to give me.'
'Why?' the man asked.
'Because I know you will be dead within a month. I have thought about killing you before, but that would do me no good. You aren't my father, you never were. I've seen what a real father and son bond looks like,' he replied, thinking about Martin McDermott and his son Paul, mercenaries, who lived an unconventional life, 'So when they put you in the ground in a few short weeks, and no one is there and you are all alone, just ask yourself one thing. Who lost the most, us or you?'
Tears started to roll down the man's cheeks.
The Optician stood up.
'Please, stay a little longer,' the man begged, 'I want to know more about the others.'
'They forgive you too. That's all you need to know,' he said as he brushed past him, taking one last look at the sorry excuse of a man beneath him as he walked out of the apartment.
When he got outside, he inhaled a long, deep breath and then exhaled slowly. As the air left his lungs, he felt a weight leave his shoulders. He didn't feel any sadness, he didn't feel any regret, and he didn't feel any anger. He felt a peace that he had never felt before.

He headed back towards the common to position himself as close to the statue of Paul Revere as he could, so that he could follow Ward to wherever he would need him to be.
Because protecting Ryan Ward was what he did.

# TWO

**Adiela - Sudan**

The main route down to conflict torn South Sudan was through Adiela. And Samson Simone now controlled the area with an iron clad fist. It was a crucial point of access, feeding into South Sudan, into DR Congo, through Zambia and Botswana, and eventually into South Africa. The American companies needed safe passage through this route to enable them to transport all of the heavy equipment that they needed to tap into the natural resources on offer throughout Africa. Simone would arrange access through the other countries after he had been paid accordingly. But now he wasn't playing ball. The Chinese and Russian's had been sniffing around, and word had got back to Washington D.C. that his loyalty was no longer to the C.I.A who had put him in power. The oil, diamonds and natural gas throughout the region was worth billions to the large companies, and it had been made abundantly clear to the corrupt politicians that unless order was restored, sponsorship and donations would stop immediately.
Samone stepped out of his jeep and into his palatial mansion. In truth, it wasn't much grander than the mid-range houses that you would find in Miami. But everything was relative. Compared to the majority of the people who lived in the region, those with no running water or electricity, his home was the house of a king. It was built from bricks that had been made by the villagers who lived forty miles away. They had to dig the clay by hand, mould them into brick shapes, and after drying

them in the sun, fired them in crude kilns made out of a coke base and casing slabs. Samone had made the villagers transport the bricks by wheelbarrow the thirty miles to his land until he was satisfied that he had enough bricks to build his new home. Eleven men were killed during the construction of the house, just because he wasn't satisfied with the progress that was being made. It had six bedrooms and outside, a giant patio that looked out across his immaculate grounds. They were grounds which were cared for by a team of nine men, not cared for with love, but out of fear. There was one room in the house that everyone called his 'Special room'. He referred to it as his command centre.

All of the servants lived at the back of the compound in filthy quarters. The women that he had allowed to live and keep their children were expected to work twenty hours a day, and regularly exposed to rape and beatings by his men.

It really was a living hell.

'Bring her to me now,' Simone barked at Hamid Jaffar, his right hand man and most trusted lieutenant, as he paced up and down in his command centre, 'And bring her children with her.'

Jaffar scurried out, after aiming an obedient nod at Simone.

Five minutes later, Lisa Badri was pulled through the door by her wrists.

'Sit!' Simone demanded.

Lisa pulled out a chair from under the long, dark oak table which was the centrepiece of the room.

'Not there!' Simone screamed, 'On the floor.'

Like an obedient dog, Lisa tucked the chair back under the table, ensuring that it was perfectly lined up with the rest of the furniture, clearly with her fear of antagonising Simone even further than he already appeared to be, at the forefront of her mind, and she sat down on the floor in front of him. She crossed her legs and rested her hands on her knees.

'You stole from me?' Simone asked, as he turned his back on her and walked over to the window to take in the view of his garden.

She said nothing, unsure if she was permitted to speak, or if Simone was asking a question or making a statement, so in the end, she decided that silence would annoy him less.

'And now you think it is acceptable to ignore me,' he said, still with his back to her.

'Am I permitted to address you sir?'

'Yes.'

'I took some scraps of food that were intended for the waste bin or the dogs. If I knew you would think of it as stealing master, I would not have done it. My devotion to you is the only faith I have.'

Simone turned around and looked at her.

'My dogs come before you. Why do you think you are more important than them?' he replied, slowly and deliberately stepping towards her as he spoke.

'I will never do that again master,' Lisa said nervously, 'I now know my place, and will never think for myself again.'

'Your place should be with the dogs. Do you think that is fair? You deprive them of their food so perhaps you should go and live with them?'

'If that is what you decide, I will do whatever you say.'
They were interrupted by the screams behind them and Jaffar walked in, pulling two boys, dressed only in shorts, by the hair.
Lisa put her hand to her mouth.
'Are these the dogs you stole from me to feed?' Simone asked, pointing at the two terrified young boys.
Kamal Badri was nine years old. He had lived in a small village sixty miles outside of Adiela with his father Suleyman, mother Lisa, and younger brother Abdo up until two months ago, when Simone and his men had rolled into the village and loaded all of the boys, and a select few of the women, onto a truck and driven them to the palace. He had watched as his father was shot dead by another boy from the village called Okot, after Simone's men had lined them all up in front of the men, and told them that if they did not pull the trigger, they and their mothers and sisters would die. The only consolation was that fate had decided that he was standing opposite Okot's father, and so he felt that retribution had been issued. He was a slight boy, deprived of food and sleep, and malnutrition was setting in on both him and his younger brother, who was seven years old.
Jaffar released his grip on the boys and slapped them hard around the head with his open palm,
'Sit!' he demanded, trying his best to replicate the exact mannerisms of Simone.
The boys stepped forward and sat beside their mother, taking up the same crossed leg position and resting their hands on their knees.
Simone looked down at them with contempt,

'What's your name?' he asked, pointing at Abdo.
'Abdo.'
Abdo what?'
'Abdo Badri.'
'Abdo Badri what?'
'Master.'
'How old are you?' Simone asked.
'Seven master.'
'Is your mother a thief?'
Abdo glanced at his mother, unsure how to answer. Even at seven years old, he understood very clearly that saying the wrong thing would result in angering Simone and then subsequently, their deaths. He knew that they were nothing more than slaves to him.
'What about you?' Simone asked, pointing at Kamal, 'Are you afraid to answer me?'
Since his father had died, even at the tender age of nine, when most kids in the western world are just refining the most basic social skills and starting to play without their parents standing ten feet away, watching lovingly over them to ensure that they come to no harm, Kamal had been left with no choice but to assume the role of the man of the family, and so he replied firmly and with clarity,
'I think that she made a mistake master.'
Simone smiled at him,
'Finally, someone with some courage,' he said.
Kamal looked at the floor.
'Are you the head of the family now?' Simone asked.
'Yes master.'
'So you are responsible for her actions?'

'I am responsible for my own actions master,' Lisa interrupted, her maternal instinct to protect her son kicking in and far outweighing her fear of the horrendous outcome to their predicament that she was playing over and over in her mind.

Simone stepped forward and when he reached her, he jerked his foot forward and kicked her in the face, the toe cap of his solid boot making contact with her nose, the loud crack indicating that it was unlikely that any bone had survived the impact.

She let out a scream and threw her hands to her nose, and the blood started to seep through her fingers immediately.

'I will ask again, are you responsible for her actions?' Simone asked, paying no attention to Lisa, who was now coughing as the sheer volume of blood was making it hard for her to breathe.

Kamal and Abdo both glanced at their stricken mother. Abdo started to silently cry, the tears rolling down his cheeks steadily.

'Yes master, I am,' was all that Kamal could manage to say, his need to protect his mother from anymore strikes, greater than his desire to try and calculate what the right reply would be.

'Then it is only fair that you deal with this thief.'

'She will not do it again master.'

'No she won't. What do you think would be a fitting punishment?'

'A week without food?' Kamal asked, desperately hoping that Simone would agree with him.

'Not sufficient. There is only one suitable punishment,' Simone replied, 'Stand up,' he demanded, waving his hand in an upward motion at the frightened boy.
He stood up.
'Come here and quickly.'
Kamal hesitantly stepped over to Simone.
'You have shown bravery in speaking up. We can make a warrior of you yet,' he said and patted him on the shoulder.
For a brief moment, Kamal felt that he had said the right thing.
And then Simone spoke,
'So to make the step up to warrior, you will take my gun,' he said, pulling his handgun from his holster and weighing it in his hands, 'And shoot the thief right now.'
Kamal started shaking.
'I mean right now,' Simone said, laying the handgun flat on his palm and extending his hand for Kamal to take.
'But she didn't know it was stealing,' he pleaded.
'You have three seconds to take the gun or I will kill her, and then you two sons of a thief.'
'Do it Kamal,' Lisa pleaded.
Abdo's silent tears became wails and Simone glared at him in disgust,
'Quiet you coward!' he shouted.
'Please Kamal, do it now, save your brother,' Lisa begged, taking her hands away from her nose and placing them in the preying position as she started to rock backwards and forwards.
'Three seconds,' Simone said, as a sickening grin spread across his face, and his eyes widened, the excitement of

seeing if the young boy could do it washing over him to such an extent that he found himself becoming aroused. Kamal reluctantly, took the gun, pointed it at his mother, closed his eyes, turned his head away and pulled the trigger.

Nothing happened.

Simone burst out laughing, a loud, terrifying noise that echoed around the room.

Kamal forced a smile.

Lisa smiled, Abdo stopped crying and for a moment, and calm seemed to wash over the room.

And then Simone took the gun from Kamal, pulled a magazine from the pocket of his combat jacket and inserted it slowly into the handle, and then offered it back for the boy to take,

'Now do it properly,' he demanded.

'I shall not,' Kamal defiantly said.

'Please Kamal, do it,' Lisa shouted.

Kamal dropped his hands to his side and bit his lip.

So Simone pointed the gun at his younger brother, the fail, seven year old boy who had not lived long enough to harm or hurt anyone, and pulled the trigger.

The bullet smashed into the centre of his tiny chest and forced him back, his head smashing heavily onto the tiled floor as it made contact.

Lisa screamed and lunged for her youngest son, pawing at him, desperately trying to get some life back into him, placing her hand hard against the small hole in the centre of his chest that was losing blood at an alarming rate.

But it was pointless.

Simone laughed again, enjoying the desperation that was echoing through Lisa's screams.

Until he got bored, just three seconds later.
He shoved Kamal hard in the back and he fell forwards, landing hard onto his mother and his dead little brother. He raised the gun and fired four shots into Kamal's back, one of the bullets going right through him and hitting Lisa in the arm.
He died instantly.
She put one arm around each of her precious children, trying to hug the smallest bit of air back into them.
Simone stepped forward and stood over her,
'That's what happens when you steal from me,' he spat, and because you deprived my dogs of their scraps, you must pay,' he added.
'Go to hell!' Lisa wailed.
'You first.'
He lifted his gun and shot her four times in the chest. The blood spraying out of her as each bullet hit.
He lowered his gun and smiled, satisfied that the thief had got her just rewards,
'Hamid,' he said to Jaffar, 'Get some women here to clean up this mess.'
Jaffar nodded.
'And then cut their bodies up and feed them to the dogs, they must be hungry,' he added, before turning his back and walking over to the giant window once more to take in the splendour of his immaculate grounds.

# THREE
**Logan International Airport – Boston**

'So this Wei guy, do you really think that he will show up in person?' Mike Lawson asked.

Mike Lawson was a former British SAS Sargent. But that's not all that he was. Lawson was born with the good looks that most people could only dream of. He was six feet four, possessed the most stunning, powerful physique, and there were very few women in the world who were not instantly attracted to him, and he had the most remarkable, sparkling blue eyes that everyone got lost in.

But Lawson was also one of the most efficient killing machines on the planet. He now worked with Ryan Ward as part of his most secretive team.

Ward himself was a handsome man, but next to Lawson, he looked like average Joe, and women never noticed him.

They had landed in Boston to attend a meeting with a guy named Zhang Wei.

Ward's partner, Eloisa, had given him the intelligence report on Wei after his vile business had been brought to her attention through her work in child protection at the United Nations in New York. It was a continuing theme of their relationship that Eloisa would ask him to deal with someone who abused children on a large scale, and on each previous occasion, he had eliminated the target and destroyed their operation.

The guy they had come to meet was called Zhang Wei. He was a forty two year old Chinese national who had settled in the Chinatown district of Boston. Officially, he ran a business that was made up of four restaurants, but they were simply in existence just to launder the money that his evil trade generated. His real business was bringing in young girls from poverty stricken areas of China, and selling them to paedophile's who kept them for as long as they wanted them, or they became too old for their perverted and sick minds. Wei would offer a better life to the poor children whose parents saved desperately to pay the extortionate fees that he charged to bring them into America. Those fees were dwarfed by the money that he would charge by selling the children to sick paedophiles, but greed always took hold of people like Wei, and he had a scam going that after the children reached a certain age, an age where they lost their appeal to the sick animals who brought them, he would buy them back at a huge reduction and sell them on as slaves.

Wei had a partner, a woman called Yang Li, who was equally as involved as him. Ward had been surprised to see how beautiful and eloquent she looked, when he read through the file that Eloisa had provided, and it was just another reminder to him, that in the world that he moved in, appearances were deceptive.

Nicole-Louise and Tackler, his digital masterminds in New York, had established that Li seemed to be making the greatest amount of money from the operation, and after they had trawled the dark web and eventually made contact with Wei, they had set up a meeting. They said that they needed to see the goods before any purchase would take place and they arranged a meeting at 1:00pm, next to the statue of Paul Revere in Boston Common, and then they would be taken on the short walk across the common to Chinatown.

They had created an authentic looking digital footprint for Ward in the name of Reece Weldon, a perverted investment banker. It showed that he lived in London, and a check on his passport showed that he was a regular visitor to China, Cambodia and Thailand, all the hotbeds for the paedophiles, which gave his cover some authenticity. They created a similar, but less comprehensive footprint for Lawson's cover, showing that he was Ward's bodyguard. A necessity after he had received death threats after an investment plan he sold, robbed people of millions of dollars. A name search on Google would confirm all of this.

The arrangement was that they were in Boston to buy two twelve year old girls.

'Do you think they will both show?' Lawson asked.

'Concentrate Mike, they will probably send people there early to make sure that we are genuine customers. I doubt the boss will want to be hanging around waiting for us to turn up,' Ward replied, rolling his eyes at what to him, was a dumb question.

Lawson looked at his watch; it was fifty minutes away from the meeting time,

'I'm pretty sure we are safe, they wouldn't risk shooting up the place in broad daylight,' he said.

Ward smiled to himself.

'Even if they do, our friend will see to them before they get one shot off.'

Lawson nodded.

Ward pulled out his cell phone and pressed speed dial,

'Have you just arrived?' The Optician asked as he answered.

'Yes. You?'

'No, I got here a while ago; I had some personal business to take care of.'

This took Ward by surprise. He knew The Optician better than anyone. He had managed, with Tackler's help, to find The Optician's estranged family and put them back in touch with each other. He knew of no other personal issues that he had.

'So you've killed some bad people I take it?' Ward asked in a tone that was similar to another guy asking if his friend has had a couple of beers today.

'I don't want to talk about it my friend.'

Once again, Ward was taken by surprise, and he noticed a tone to The Opticians voice that was different to what he normally heard during the verbal sparring that was their standard form of communication.

Theirs was an unusual relationship, because despite being what they both considered each other's closest friend, they had never met.

At least in Ward's mind they hadn't.

'Are you at the common yet?' he asked, dropping the subject immediately. He knew that if The Optician wanted to talk, he would instigate the conversation.

'I got here an hour ago. They have sent five guys. I've looked at all of them carefully through my scope, and they all appear unarmed, although they probably have knives with them as a minimum.'

'They will be taking us somewhere close to the common, which should be within walking distance, but if they spring a surprise and put us into a vehicle, do you have transport?' Ward asked.

The Optician snorted down the line,

'What a dumb question,' he said and the line went dead.

Ward looked across at Lawson.

'What?' Lawson asked.

'I'm spending way too much time with you,' he replied and started heading across to the Ford Taurus that The Old Man had provided for them, leaving Lawson looking bemused and wondering what he had done wrong this time.

**Boston Common – Boston**

Forty five minutes later, they were standing in front of the statue of Paul Revere.

Ward took a moment to take in the meaning of the statue. He found it ironic that Revere had warned against the British coming, and yet here he was, a British guy, and he was generally the first person that the American government turned to when they had a problem that needed solving.

He wondered if Revere would approve of him. His thoughts were broken when Lawson said,

'What's your favourite Chinese food?'

He chose to ignore him.

To his right, he noticed two Asian looking guys staring across at them, and directly in front of him, partially hidden by Revere's statue, there were two more. That meant there was one more guy, but as hard as he scanned the area, he could not see him, all he could see were the tourists and locals, busy scurrying to wherever they were going.

'You need to come with me,' a soft voice said.

He spun around and looked straight down at a young girl. She was of Asian origin and couldn't have been any older than ten. He felt an anger wash over him that for a moment made him want to kill the four guys that he had spotted for using a small child to do their dirty work. They were nothing but cowards he thought to himself. He smiled at her,

'Where are the men that are with you?' he asked.

She turned without replying and started heading up the path in the direction of Chinatown. He noticed the other four guys walk around behind them as they started to follow her, and when they reached the end of the path, the girl approached a cop and said something that he couldn't hear to him.

'Are you Weldon?' the cop asked him.

He nodded and noticed that he wore a badge with 'Harris' printed on it.

He looked Lawson up and down and then did a double take on his face again and snorted.

Lawson smiled. He was used to the look of contempt from some men; he knew his looks made them feel inadequate.

'Follow me and don't say a word,' the cop said, and he took the girls hand and headed towards the large buildings that had come into view.

'Let me kill him,' Lawson whispered as they walked ten feet behind them.

Ward nodded,

'But I want you to beat him to death.'

## Chinatown – Boston

Ten minutes later they were standing inside Wei's restaurant, staring at an empty table after being instructed to wait.
'What's your role in this?' Ward nonchalantly asked the cop.
'No questions,' he replied curtly.
'Something vexes you?' Lawson asked innocently.
The cop ignored him and Ward smiled.
'Sorry for the delay gentlemen,' a female voice said from behind them, 'Please take a seat,' she added, as she stepped in front of them and sat down at the empty table which had been the focus of their attention for the last few minutes.
Ward had studied her pictures in the file that Eloisa had given him and he had noted how attractive she looked. But in the flesh, it was plainly obvious that the pictures did not do her justice.
Yang Li was stunning, among the prettiest women that he had ever seen in his life, and she carried herself with grace and elegance. In her smart skirt and perfectly fitted blouse, which complimented her figure perfectly, she looked more like a lawyer than a child trafficker. He glanced at Lawson to see if there was any reaction from him.
But there was nothing. She was just another run of the mill woman to him, he thought to himself.
He sat down at the table and Lawson chose to stay where he was. The cop nodded at him, indicating for him to sit,

but he simply ignored him, and the cop eventually just shook his head.

A moment later, the door at the far end of the restaurant opened and a small Asian guy stepped through it, followed by six other men. He approached the table without speaking and sat down,

'Hello Mr Weldon, I'm Zhang Wei,' he said without making any eye contact with Ward at all.

He studied him for a few seconds. He looked at least fifteen years older than the woman he was sitting next to and it most definitely looked like they didn't belong together. Her grace and elegance did not match his haggard and dishevelled look.

The six men circled the table, each standing about ten feet back, so that they would not be seen to be listening into the conversation. The cop pulled up a chair at the table next to them, looking around the room, appearing decidedly disinterested.

'Do you have the money?' Wei asked.

'Not without seeing the goods,' Ward replied.

'They are out the back in a store room.'

This instantly gave Ward a problem. He wasn't banking on Wei having the children in the restaurant and he needed to get them outside so that The Optician could do what he did best.

'We aren't stupid,' Lawson suddenly said from behind him, 'You think we are dumb enough to walk in here with close to one hundred thousand dollars?' he added as he moved towards the table.

The cop stood up.

'My job is to protect Mr Weldon. So that's what I do. The money is no more than two hundred feet from this

building, but we aren't dumb enough to be sitting here with it where you could just take it. I see you have a lot of muscle here, you could just take it,' he added looking at the six guys and the cop.
Ward inwardly smiled, Lawson was on the ball.
Wei smiled,
'You've just confirmed your authenticity to me Mr Weldon,' Wei said, 'What shall we do first, the money or the girls?'
'I want to check my purchase first.'
'Follow me,' Wei said as he stood up and headed towards the door that he had entered through, the six guys who accompanied him earlier immediately jumped into a single file line and followed him.
Yang Li looked at Lawson,
'Would you like to stay here with me and share a drink?'
'You aren't my type,' he replied as he joined Ward in following Wei through to the back, 'You aren't pretty enough.'
Inside the kitchen, Wei opened a large door next to a chiller, and swung it wide open.
'Here they are,' he said to Ward, beckoning with his hand or him to take a look.
Ward stepped forward.
He saw two young children, both sitting on chairs, like they had been told off by a teacher and they were sitting there in silence.
He smiled at them and they clasped their hands together in a praying motion and bowed their heads. It was a surreal situation, but he comforted himself with the fact that they looked to be a lot more cared for than a lot of the children than he had rescued from a life of misery.

But he had seen enough,
'OK Mr Wei, I'm satisfied, let's go and get your money.'

# FOUR

**Adiela - Sudan**

Yury Glushakov poured himself a drink from the expensive looking decanter that Simone kept in his command centre.
Glushakov was one of the most trusted and prominent operatives from Russia's SVR.
And he was brutal. Political correctness and liberalisation had never reached as far as Russia and at home or abroad, they believed that they had no equal. The western spies, while equally as capable, were governed by so many rules and accountable to the politicians.
In Russia, they had no accountability for those who worked for the SVR, a product of Vladimir Putin's former employment as a spy, and they believed that they were the most lethal spy agency in the world.
They had an arrogance gained from the fact that they had no idea that the American and British governments had assembled their own branch of unique and secret operatives, of which Ryan Ward was the most revered.
The SVR was Russia's equivalent of the C.I.A. and MI6. It was the agency responsible for all foreign intelligence operations abroad, and most of the operatives lived deep, undercover lives in their country of allocation. Like all premier intelligence and security agencies, recruitment was carried out at the premier universities, mostly targeting students in the final year of their studies, their degrees being awarded without ever being completed, and they tended to hand pick only those that were

aesthetically pleasing on the eye and had a confidence to them.
Glushakov had been in Sudan for the past four years and he hated the place. He was handsome and approachable, and he had spent the first three years instigating contact with Simone on behalf of the Russian government and in the last year his charm, and the Russian money, had convinced Simone to part company with the C.I.A's support and switch to the Russians.
'Have you told the Americans that you no longer require their services?' Glushakov asked Simone as he put the tumbler to his lips and sipped the obscenely expensive brandy.
'I made the call three days ago. I've been busy getting new recruits and I have ignored their calls back to me so far.'
'Perhaps it would be wise to talk to them so that there is no misunderstanding that their access and involvement is revoked immediately?' Glushakov said, relaying the message that Moscow had been delivering to him non-stop over the past few days, 'And as soon as you have done that, we can begin our new arrangement and make the first payment.'
Simone looked at him. He didn't much care for this Russian man, to him, they were all the same, American, Russian, Chinese and even the Germans and French, who were going behind the backs of their European partners. They all wanted to rape the continent of Africa and didn't care how it got done. Greed was now the overriding factor that they all adhered to.
But the Russians were willing to pay more for his help, and so right now, he didn't care about the political

yardage they were trying to claim, Glushakov was his best friend.

'I will call them now,' he replied and picked up the receiver of the phone on his desk and dialled his contact in Washington D.C.

Glushakov watched as Simone put the receiver to his ear. He felt his palms sweating slightly and he breathed in deeply. He felt good, he would soon be out of this hellhole of a continent and he allowed himself the pleasure of starting to dream about where he would be placed for his next assignment. He hoped it would be somewhere cold.

His thoughts were interrupted by Simone raising his voice,

'Your threats have no impact on me,' he said loudly, 'You are not stupid enough to try and change my mind through force. Firstly, you do not possess the people brave enough or strong enough to step into Sudan, and secondly, what you did was illegal and if the international community got wind of it, your nation would be as guilty of war crimes as me.'

Whatever the response was from the person on the end of the line, it amused Simone a great deal because he let out a long, loud throaty laugh which echoed around the room. Eventually he stopped laughing and said,

'Then I suggest that you contact all of the money men in those big companies, because from this moment, there will be no safe passage and no access into South Sudan,' and he slammed the phone down.

'They weren't too pleased?' Glushakov asked.

'Who cares?' Simone replied, 'Pay your money today and the route is now yours.'

## Chinatown – Boston

Ward had calculated that The Optician would have been in position virtually as soon as they had entered the restaurant. But as he walked back outside into the street, he felt uneasy. Firstly about the fact that there were a lot of people about, and secondly, because he had no idea where Lawson was leading them too, or if indeed, he himself knew where he was going. Lawson seemed to be striding forward with purpose, the cop no more than three feet behind him, matching him stride for stride, Wei by Ward's side next in line, and when he glanced behind him, he saw that Wei's six men were ten feet behind at the rear, walking side by side forming a barrier so that no one could get close to Wei.
He smiled and then told himself that he really had to get out of the habit of underestimating Lawson so frequently.
He now knew exactly what was going to happen and where Lawson was taking them to.
Which was more than Lawson knew until he saw it, a fact confirmed to Ward when he suddenly veered off to the right and headed towards an entrance ramp that led off of the street and down to an underground car park.
'The money is in my car,' Lawson shouted over his shoulder to no one in particular.
They reached the top of the ramp and started to walk down.

One of The Optician's greatest skills was his ability to think like the operatives that he spent his life protecting. When he had watched Ward and Lawson being led into Wei's restaurant by the cop, he had scanned the area and spotted the car park immediately. He knew that Ward would want to get them off the street, away from the risk of any innocent people getting injured, and so he had immediately climbed the fire escape of the building opposite and managed to position himself on a balcony three floors up, directly opposite the car park entrance, elevated about forty feet.

He had a perfect view of the group as they started to descend the ramp.

His job was to eliminate Wei's protection and that was all. He knew that Ward would want to engage in a conversation once he was alone with Wei before he killed him, he always did, and it was one of the many things that he admired about him so much. He thought of his father for a brief moment, and how his words would have hurt him equally as much as his bullets could, and how this was something that Ward had taught him during their time together.

He watched through his scope as the six guys that Wei had following them reached the top of the ramp and turned in a neat line, swinging around from left to right, almost like a synchronised swimming team, and then all pulled handguns out from their waistbands, as you would expect even less than competent protection to do when being led off of the street.

And then time stood still for him, like it always did.

In a micro second, he pictured two scenarios. Shooting the guys with his eyes shut, simply because asking him

to shoot six guys who were all lined up neatly from under a hundred feet away, with their backs to him, was like asking a weightlifter to lift two soda cans above his head, or to try and kill all six of them with only five bullets.
He decided that the second option would make his trip to Boston more entertaining and offer him some light relief after his visit to his father.
And he knew exactly how he was going to do it.
He just had to decide who out of the six guys would be the most impulsive shooter.
And he decided it would be the third guy in from the left. He would just have to make sure that his first shot was very precise.
Which he knew it would be.
He took aim and squeezed the trigger softly, the 7.62mm bullet sailed through the air and caught the guy standing furthest to the left on the right hand side of his skull, his head veered violently to the left and smashed hard into the cheek of the guy standing next to him, and he stumbled behind him through the weight of the impact, as he was meant to, just as The Optician fired another shot which hit the guy standing furthest to the right in the centre of his skull and blew his head apart. His legs collapsed and he stumbled forward and before he had hit the ground, the guy next to him took a bullet in identical fashion and he was falling in sync with his friend.
Three bullets.
Three dead.
The third guy from the left spun around, raised his handgun and fired off a shot, which hit the guy who was falling next to him directly on his temple and blew a two

inch hole in the side of his head, and covered him in a thick spray of blood immediately.
Three bullets.
Four dead.
Without pausing, he fired off the last two shots at the two guys left standing in the middle, and scored a direct hit in the centre of their foreheads, his favourite shot, and four seconds after he had caressed his trigger for the first time, all six guys were dead.
Five bullets.
Six dead.

A split second after the guy third from the left had shot his friend in the temple, Ward, Lawson, Wei and the cop had spun around. The cop reached for his handgun and before he could get a grip on it, Lawson had unleashed a solid jab which caught him full on the nose, and his legs buckled.
Being hit by Lawson was similar to being hit by a train. As the cop landed hard on the floor, he bent down and took the handgun from him.
Wei stood still, frozen in fear.
'Get up!' Lawson shouted.
The cop got to his feet uneasily
'What's your name?'
Ward stifled a laugh.
The cop was still trying to clear his head and either ignored or didn't hear the question.
Wei was still motionless, his eyes darting between Ward, the cop and the dead bodies of his protection behind him.
'I said, what's your name?'

'It's on his badge Mike,' Ward interrupted, and then rolled his eyes.

Lawson shot him a disapproving look.

'Harris,' the cop eventually said.

'Well Harris, my friend here,' Lawson said, pointing flippantly at Ward before continuing, 'Told me that I have to beat you to death. But I don't think that's suitable for you. I mean, let's be honest, I only hit you with about twenty per cent of my strength and if I hit you properly, you'll be unconscious so you won't feel the pain, so I have a better idea.'

'Hold on,' Harris stuttered, 'I can tell you how his whole operation works, where the children are, everything about it.'

'Not interested.'

'Then I can tell you that Yang Li is the one who runs things, not him.'

'I think we've already got that part,' Ward interrupted again.

'No, beating you to death won't work for me, I'm going to suffocate you instead,' Lawson said and then he took one giant stride forward and unleashed a thunderous uppercut which landed full on Harris' throat, crushing his windpipe instantly.

The force of the punch knocked Harris back at least six feet and he landed flush on his back, knocking what little air he had left in his lungs out of his body. He desperately tried to get air into his body but there was no access route for the oxygen to get in, and Lawson stood over him, watching the life drain out of him.

Two minutes later, Harris was dead; his lifeless body spread-eagled as though someone had placed it on the ground with care.

Lawson looked at Ward, 'What is your favourite Chinese food anyway?' he asked.

Ward smiled at him.

Lawson was without doubt the toughest guy that he had ever known, and he was once again impressed with his ability to kill a man with one punch.

'Call it in Mike, get this cleaned up.'

Lawson nodded.

'Let's go you,' he said to Wei, 'Let's go and see your lady.'

Three minutes later they were walking back into the restaurant and Yang Li was still sitting at the same table where they had left her.

She looked up and smiled at them as Wei walked in first, and Ward noticed her frown when she looked at Wei's face and it then turned to concern after Lawson closed the door and she realised that no one else was with them.

Ward pulled out his handgun.

'One move and I'll shoot you.'

She lifted her hands from under the table and placed them, palms down, on the top.

'The Old Man has the clean-up crew on the way and the proper cops will be here in five minutes,' Lawson said as he stepped past Ward, and just for good measure, jabbed Wei hard in the stomach on the way past, a punch that had Wei doubled over on his knees immediately.

Ward studied her.

She looked completely unmoved and not remotely frightened.
So he lifted moved his gun to the side and shot Wei in the face without speaking.
The bullet blew a hole next to his eye socket and his eye ball slithered out slowly.
Li put her hands to her mouth.
'It's not him who is responsible for the misery that you cause to those children, is it?' Ward said softly.
'It was all him. I lived in fear of him; I did what he told me to do.'
Ward smiled.
It was always the same. The real power behind literally all evil had one overriding characteristic. Self-preservation.
'I know every single detail of your operation, from the transport to the sales. I'm going to ask you for two things, if you give me them, I will let you live. But remember, I know everything already,' Ward lied.
Li studied him with a cold, hard stare.
She was sure he was telling the truth and so she nodded. Ward could see she believed him and so he gambled, 'Where is your ledger with all of your information? I want it now.'
Li leant down under the table and pulled out a brown leather book that looked similar to a bible. Ward knew that even in the new technological age, the majority of Asian criminals still preferred the hand written way of controlling their affairs.
She placed it on the table.
'The second thing?' she asked calmly.

There was no second thing, he had all he needed. He always found it important to make people feel terrified before they died but he sensed that whatever he said to her, words were not going to cut it.

So he lifted his gun and shot her in the shoulder.

She let out a loud scream and fell to the floor, her white blouse turning a crimson red where the gaping wound was immediately.

He stepped forward, pushed the table to the side and stood over her.

Now she looked frightened.

She looked up at him and he could see that she was petrified. She saw a seven foot giant standing above her with eyes that were almost goading her.

She started to cry hysterically.

That was all he needed to see.

He raised his gun and squeezed the trigger three times and shot her in the face, her beauty annihilated instantly as the bullets tore away her flesh and bone.

He pulled out his cell phone and typed a text message to Eloisa which simply said, 'It's done' and then turned and walked towards the door, nodding at Lawson on the way past.

'So what is your favourite Chinese food?' Lawson asked once more as he followed him out of the restaurant.

# FIVE

**DUMBO – New York**

Ward walked wearily up the stairs to his apartment. The last few months had been relentless, and as much as he was able to recharge himself physically for the next operation that The Old Man was setting for him, he was starting to feel mentally exhausted. He hadn't had a proper break in the past six months where he was able to relax. He desperately needed a vacation. He opened the door to his apartment and no sooner had he put down his grab bag when his cell phone vibrated in his pocket. He looked at the caller I.D
And saw it was The Old Man. He let it ring out and put the phone back in his pocket. He wasn't in the mood for a new assignment or even a conversation with him.
He opened his fridge and took out a carton of orange juice and ripped it open, and poured half of the contents down his throat, the cold citrus liquid feeling like it was energising him immediately. His phone vibrated again and he didn't even bother to pull it out of his pocket. He knew that it would be Centrepoint once again, just like he knew that it would ring one more time after that. The Old Man always tried ringing three times, one after the other until he gave up.
He walked through to the bedroom and started to undress, and just as he started to remove his jeans, the third ring came.
He ignored it.

**Washington D.C.**

Centrepoint slammed the phone down, probably harder than he normally would. It infuriated him more and more when Ward ignored his calls. He knew that Ward had arrived back at his apartment; his tech guy who monitored his movements had just phoned through to confirm that he was there, and he pictured him looking at the caller display and sliding his phone back into his pocket, before more than likely taking a shower. He was aware that he had pushed him way too hard over the past few months, and he had intended to let him take a couple of weeks to himself, maybe spend some time with the woman in his life, Eloisa Hammond, but there were much more important issues at hand and he had the opportunity to earn some huge kudos with the President himself and he wasn't going to waste it.

While he accepted that he did put too much pressure on Ward, his ability to continuously deliver for him outweighed his leaning to do the right thing and let him have some downtime. He leant back in his chair and likened himself to every boss in the country who has an employee that they can rely on. Every company in the world has people who always go the extra mile for them without reward or recognition, and while he knew that most of those people were thought no more of by their employers, he consoled himself with the fact that he thought more of Ryan Ward than he ever had of any operative that had worked for him. But then he exhaled a long, slow sigh, and told himself that he was being both unfair and unreasonable, and the very fact that he was trying to convince himself that pushing Ward was justified, he knew that he was wrong to do so, and in an instance, he decided to let him have a break for ten days and he would have to call in special forces teams to deal with the issue in the Sudan.

And then with one phone call, everything changed.

His phone ringing startled him for a moment. He looked down at the caller display and saw the White House was calling, he let it ring for ten seconds, just because he could, before picking the phone up,
'Please hold for the Vice President,' a strong female voice said.
He heard a click and then the Vice President, Aaron Wilson, spoke,
'Sorry to bother you McNair, but I'm calling to ask where you are with the problem that we discussed?'
'We aren't anywhere with it at the moment. I don't just wave a magic wand and fix everything. There is a selection criterion to go through, and as I said to you earlier, trying to get operatives to take part in a suicide mission is a pretty complex situation.'
'But this really can't wait. In the interest of national security, it has to be resolved now,' Wilson declared.
Centrepoint could hear the desperation in his voice,
'What aren't you telling me?' he asked.
There was a pause on the line for a few seconds.

'This has come straight from the oval office, and there are certain elements as to why this is so important to the country that I can't discuss, even with you.'

'Then without all of the information, I'm not sure how you expect me to remove Simone from power,' The Old Man said assertively.

There was another pause on the line, this one even longer. Centrepoint knew that Wilson was weighing up what he could and couldn't tell him. Although he was pretty sure that he knew what Wilson was so concerned about anyway.

'What do you know about Simone?' Wilson eventually asked.

'I know that the C.I.A. armed him and helped him to take control of the region so that our multi-national companies could have a free handle on all of the natural resources available. And that he has more than likely gotten greedy, and that is probably the start of a pattern developing that you want nipped in the bud before it escalates out of control. I know that he has committed a number of atrocities and we need to distance ourselves from them as much as we can. After all, a warlord committing crimes with our support would send shockwaves around the world.'

'We never supported him,' Wilson said urgently.

'But we didn't stop him either, did we?'

'It's complicated.'

'And it's not the first time, is it?'

'Look,' Wilson said and then sighed, 'It is no secret that we need your help, and desperately. The President himself knows that you are more trustworthy than anyone he can turn to, and you have a free hand to dispose of Simone and put in his replacement.'

'And how do you know that this Phillipe Bassong character won't do the same thing in eighteen months' time? And do you seriously think that Simone's soldiers will just accept a new leader without question?'

'OK McNair, I get what is going on here. So tell me, what it is that you want?'

The Old Man paused for a brief moment. He knew what he wanted and he knew that he was going to get it. But typical of the snivelling imbecile that he knew Wilson to be, he had to spell it out to him. Only he had to sell it in a way that would make him think that it was his idea,

'I'm just deeply concerned that I go to all this trouble and put my men in grave danger, and whoever you put in overall charge to control the region will mess it up, and you will come running back to me for help once again,' he said, in as much of a resigned tone as he could muster.

Silence on the end of the line yet again.

So he gave Wilson the push he would need,

'I mean, who could you really trust to take control with only the best interests of the country at heart?' he asked. He could almost hear the penny dropping in Wilson's brain,

'You could assume control!' he said, almost excitedly.

'I have enough on my plate, that would take a lot of my time and effort,' Centrepoint replied, smiling as he spoke.

'But you would be perfect for it. I'm going to talk to the President and then I will get back to you,' Wilson said urgently and the line went dead.

He leant back in his chair and smiled to himself. Manipulating Wilson was as easy as taking candy from a child. To say that things had played out exactly as he had anticipated was the understatement of the year.
Ryan Ward's vacation would have to wait.

**DUMBO – New York**

The long shower that Ward had taken had invigorated him, and he was now feeling awake and refreshed. He contemplated calling The Old Man back as he picked up his cell phone, but before he could unlock the screen, it vibrated in his hand and Eloisa's name appeared.
'Hey you,' he answered urgently.
'Are you busy?'
'No, I've just got out of the shower.'
'Are you clothed yet?' she asked softly.
'No, I've literally just stepped out. Why?'
'Because it will save me time,' she said firmly, 'I'm outside the door.'
He hurriedly threw his phone on his bed and walked to the door with anticipation running through his veins. He pulled open the door and before he could even offer her a smile, she slapped him hard around the face and pushed him back into the hallway, and she pulled at his towel firmly until it came loose and she threw it on the floor. It was an action that took him by surprise but excited him at the same time.
She stepped in and slammed the door hard behind her, leant forward with her right arm, wrapping her hand tightly around his hair and pulled him in forcibly

towards her, and their mouths met and they embraced in a deep and passionate kiss which literally left him feeling breathless. Ward pulled at her clothing, fumbling at the buttons of her tight blouse, while she released the grip on his hair, cupped both hands tightly around the back of his head and pulled him in harder to kiss him even deeper.

As their kiss intensified, Eloisa dug her nails deep into his back with such pressure that she instantly drew small droplets of blood as the deep scratches extended further. But Ward was oblivious to this; his whole mind was engrossed in her kiss and the fireworks that seemed to be going off inside of him with more intensity with each passing second.

He pulled open her blouse and started to fondle her pert breasts with much more firmness than he had ever used before.

Eloisa responded to this by running her nails even deeper and further down his back as Ward expertly unzipped her skirt and dropped it to the floor in one smooth, fluent motion.

For a moment, her stunning body mesmerised him, and he took a few seconds to push his head back and appreciate the view. Her long legs melted into the top of her thighs in perfect symmetry, and her firm, flat stomach looked as equally natural as it did defined in a gym. Her breasts, which were now covered partially by her long, dark hair, had a perfect cleavage to them, and her tanned, olive complexion was perfectly complimented by the crisp white underwear that she wore.

She pushed him back against the wall, and then pushed hard on his shoulders so that he slid down until he was sitting on the floor. She stepped over him, pulled her panties to one side, and lowered herself down onto him so that they became one. Ward pulled her towards him and kissed her hard as she started to move on top of him in a rhythm that felt like it was sending electricity through his whole body with each movement. As they frantically moved up and down in perfect sequence, beads of sweat started to roll down their bodies, the glistening of the droplets against her skin exciting him even more, and when they finally climaxed together, her whole body convulsed and she let out a scream that he knew not only the neighbours would hear, but the whole apartment building.

Breathless, Ward said,

'Where did that come from?'

She stared deeply into his eyes while she got her breath back and tried to compose herself, her body still jerking with the occasional spasm, and she eventually said,

'It came from thinking of you and needing you every second that we are apart.'

It was a comment that made him feel like a king. That's what Eloisa always did to him, made him feel like the most important and desired guy in the world.

She climbed off of him and took his hand, pulling him up from his seated position and headed towards the shower. They washed each other and made love slowly under the warm water, this time with much more care and appreciation of each other's bodies and for the first time, Ward felt a stinging on his back as the water sprayed onto his deep, open scratches.

An hour later, they were both fully clothed and sitting at the table in the kitchen drinking the coffee that he had made for them both.

'Tell me how much Wang and Li suffered?' she asked after a long pause.

He explained the events in Boston carefully to her, mentioning how impressed he had been with Lawson and The Optician and finally the fear that had been etched on the faces of Wang and Li just before he killed them.

She studied him carefully for a few seconds after he had finished speaking. He noticed that her smile didn't seem as bright as it had earlier and he knew instantly that there was something on her mind. Before he could ask her what was wrong, she spoke,

'Mike means the world to you, doesn't he?'

He thought it was a strange question but answered all the same,

'Yes he does. It seems that the more time I spend with him, the closer we become. Why do you ask?'

She ignored his question.

'What's wrong?'

'How would you feel if he died?'

'That's an odd question.'

'Just answer it Ryan.'

He thought about it carefully for a good ten seconds before replying,

'When I thought Gilligan had died I felt like I had lost a family member. Lawson and I are even closer so I would feel devastated; it would break me I think. Why?'

'I've never asked you to do anything for me have I?'

'What do you mean?'

'I mean all of the people that you terminate with the information that I give you is for the innocent children isn't it? None of it is directly for me.'

'No, I've always known that. Where are you going with this Eloisa?'

'Do you love me and want to spend the rest of your life with me?'

'Tell me why are you asking me about Mike, and whether I do things for you or not?'

'Just answer the question,' she said firmly.

'You know I do. I have told you that countless times. Why?'

'So if I ask you to do something, not for innocent children, for you or anyone else, just simply for me, would you do it?'

'Yes I would,' Ward replied without any hesitation.

'Then I am going to ask you to do something for me and I want you to promise me you will do it.'

'Ask away,' he replied, smiling at her as he spoke to reassure her.

'Keep away from Sudan and most definitely keep away from Samson Simone.'

# SIX

**DUMBO – New York**

Ward was woken at 07:00 by his cell phone vibrating. He immediately hoped it wouldn't wake Eloisa up, but as he turned to check on her, he saw that she had already left and there was a note on the pillow that said, 'I'll ring later – Take out tonight.' He smiled to himself; he swore that at times she had the ability to move silently with more stealth than some of the best assassins that he had ever met.
He looked at the caller display, it was Centrepoint.
He thought about letting it ring out just for the sake of it, but then instantly told himself that as tempting as that was, being childish was not one of his traits,
'What?' he answered, sounding childish and irritated.
There was a pause for a moment, The Old Man clearly taken back by the bluntness of Ward's greeting,
'Sorry, are you and your good lady in the middle of something?' he asked apologetically.
'She's gone. What do you want?'
'Have you given any more thought about Simone?'
'Apart from the fact that every single person that I speak to tells me that I am to keep well away from Sudan, not really. But I'm guessing you are getting pressure put on you from a lot of the dishonest people you have to deal with on a day to day basis?'
'That's pretty much it in a nutshell.'
'Who specifically is pressurising you?'

The Old Man thought about telling the truth, but then recalled Ward's disdain for the Vice President, and so he lied,
'The President himself, indirectly of course, but he is very, very concerned about the events down there.'
'This other guy you intend on replacing Simone with, you think he's likely to care about women and children, any differently to Simone? After all, a Warlord tends to think he is above reproach and normal rules.'
'I can guarantee that we can keep him under control.'
'How?'
'Because his whole family are here. We moved them here eighteen months ago. This isn't a knee-jerk reaction; it has been in the planning stages for months.'
'Do you actually have an answer for everything?'
'Yes,' Centrepoint replied without any pause at all.
'So if I say no, what will your plan be?'
'You don't need to know that.'
'I think I do, and then I can weigh up the odds of your idea against mine.'
There was a much longer than usual pause on the line, it was something that made Ward feel uncomfortable because he knew something bad was coming.
'Well?' he asked, trying to prompt Centrepoint.
'I'll have no other option but to do something that I don't want to do,' he replied slowly.
'Which is?' Ward enquired.
'Send The Optician in there on his own.'


**Adiela - Sudan**

Samson Simone looked at Yury Glushakov and smiled. Glushakov raised the glass of eighteen year old malt that was holding the expensive liquid and tilted it towards Simone. He felt uneasy because Simone continued to smile at him, like he was holding a forced smile for a camera. Eventually, the uneasiness became uncomfortable and so he spoke,
'Something amuses you Samson?'
'We are now friends Yury. Are we agreed on that?'
'Good friends, and friends for life. Why do you ask?'
The strange smile reappeared on Simone's face,
'Do you want to play a game?'
For a moment, Glushakov felt a shudder of fear, due to the unpredictability that he knew Simone possessed, it was a feeling that quickly physically translated through to his face,
'Don't worry my friend,' Simone said quickly, noticing the panicked look on Glushakov's face, 'You will be in no danger at all.'
Glushakov cautiously nodded.
'And we will record our game and send it to the pathetic man in America who thought he was a warrior when he threatened me on the phone. I'll show him how a real warrior acts,' Simone stated.
'What do you have in mind?'
'Just wait and see.'


### 38 W 31st Street – New York

The cell phone rang for the second time in a minute. He knew it would be Ryan Ward calling, and he momentarily decided to let it ring out again, but changed his mind after the fifth ring,

'Can one of you pass me the phone,' Mike Lawson said to the two naked women in his bed.

'Seriously, right now?' the woman who was sitting astride him asked.

'Right now,' he replied as he pulled his giant frame into an upright position, the small woman's arms still wrapped tightly around his neck, and extended his massive arm forward for the other woman to pass him the phone.

He saw Ward's name on the caller display,

'If there was a world championship for calling me at the most inappropriate moment, you would walk it,' he said curtly as he answered.

''I'm sure she can wait for five minutes.'

'They,' he immediately corrected Ward, 'What is it?'

'Just out of curiosity, when you say, 'They', are you joking or not?'

'What do you want Ryan?'

'You advised me against going after Simone, so did Eloisa, but The Old Man is asking me to get a team together and urgently to go and take him out. People in Washington are panicking, the CIA put him in power in the first place, and there are probably a hundred and one things that he is keeping from us but we have a problem.'

'Which is?'

'He says that if we can't sort the mess out for him that he will be sending The Optician in alone.'

Lawson paused for a moment. In his opinion, that was probably the most sensible thing to do. No one ever sees

The Optician and he was less likely to get caught moving on his own. He really was the best,
'So why is that a problem?' he asked.
'Let me put it another way,' Ward said and then paused for a few seconds. It was a silence that had Lawson pre-empting the next question, something he got hopelessly wrong, as he was sure Ward would say that there would be information that The Optician would not be able to find in the shadows, 'Would you let me go in alone, or Mac?'
'No,' he replied without hesitation.
'Well he is as much a part of our team as anyone. Just because we don't see him, doesn't mean that we don't owe him the same loyalty and protection.'
'I wasn't joking when I said they.'
'From that response, I'll take it that you are in agreement with me?'
'So it seems.'
'Meet me at Nicole-Louise's in two hours,' Ward said firmly and the line went dead.
He dropped the cell phone on the bed and leant back to where he was rested before, the slight woman still with her arms wrapped around his neck,
'You have one more hour ladies, any requests?' he asked.

## Adiela - Sudan

The four young boys were pulled into the room by their hair by four of Simone's men, the high pitched screams and loud sobs that could only come from the mouth of a child unsettling Glushakov immediately.

'They are nothing. Dirt on the sole of my boot, animals picked up from their disease infested village,' Simone said without even glancing at him, 'So don't concern yourself that these rats are human beings,' he added and then laughed loudly.

But they were human beings. They were children who had been born into poverty and had been forced to kill their own fathers three months ago when Simone had raided their village. They had spent their time at the compound working eighteen hours a day, cleaning the soldiers quarters and feeding the dogs the leftovers from the meals, a task that the men enjoyed watching as the hungry children, whose bodies were frail through starvation and malnutrition, looked on enviously as the dogs devoured the scraps placed before them.

Warube Urbano aged nine, Yassir Lupidia aged eight and two seven year olds called Jumma Akech and Samuel Zarambi stood before Simone shaking with fear as the tears ran down their cheeks and the residue from their noses ran into their mouths.

Simone opened a drawer on the grand mahogany desk and pulled out a pistol,

'Elya,' he shouted to the soldier who had pulled Jumma Akech into the room, 'Take out your cell phone and record this game,' a request that was responded to immediately and five seconds later, Elya was holding the cell phone up filming the group as if he was recording a happy event at a family party anywhere in the world.

Glushakov shifted on his feet nervously. As brutal as the Russian SVR were, and they had no qualms about torturing traitors or dissidents to death, children were generally off limits unless they had to be used as a last resort to get a parent or family member to admit to fictitious crimes against the State.

Simone noticed how uncomfortable Glushakov had suddenly become and he shook his head,

'Yury, something bothers you?'

'You don't need to be doing this to entertain me Samson,' he replied, trying to sound as indifferent as he could so he wouldn't appear weak.

'It's not just for your entertainment; it is to send a message to the Americans. I know they won't be very pleased with our new arrangement, so just to make sure they don't get any ideas about trying to move me out of the way, they need to understand that there is a big difference between me and them.'

All Glushakov could manage in response was a nod of his head.

'You four!' Simone shouted at the four terrified boys, 'Sit down at the table,' he demanded.

Warube Urbano and Yassir Lupidia had grown up together in their small village. They were smaller than all of the other boys their own age and were unable to carry out the daily tasks of digging, collecting water and searching for scraps much less effectively than their peers. As soon as Jaffar had set eyes on him, he had decided that they would never become warriors, so he told them that they would be servants to the men, but he knew that they would never be able to do that effectively either, and he also knew that they would not be alive for much longer, so he had told the soldiers to make no effort to train them both, just to beat them every time they failed to complete a task to the men's satisfaction, which it seemed, turned out to be every single day, regardless of how well they completed a task or not. The kudos that went with being Simone's right hand man meant that every order he gave to the soldier's was taken as coming directly from the warlord himself, and so he was never disobeyed, and this gave him a sense of power that he had grown very accustomed to. He believed that he was a warlord in all but title in his own right.

Jumma Akech and Samuel Zarambi were always destined to live very short lives.

Jumma was disabled and was unable to lift his right foot from the ground when he walked, a disability that wasn't noticed by the soldiers when they took him from his village after killing his mother and sister in front of him. When it was brought to the attention of Jaffar that the child would be of no use fighting, he summoned the soldier who had selected him as a future warrior to his barracks, and as his comrades held him; he cut off the soldier's foot at the ankle for making such a stupid mistake.

From that point forward, all of the men had been much more vigilant in their selection of the next generation of Simone's army.

Samuel was born with severe damage to his vocal chords, what feint noises he could originally make were wiped out for good when his parents took him to the local doctor in the village who had attempted to cut into his vocal chords and in the process, damaged them permanently. He had not made a sound in four years.

They all slowly walked over to the table and sat down, Jumma's foot scraping across the floor as his small strides struggled to keep up with the other boys.
Not one of them looked up from the table.
'In this pistol there are four bullets,' Simone began, speaking directly to the soldier recording with the cell phone, rather the four, frail, frightened boys, 'Two of them are blanks, two are live bullets,' he added, raising his voice for effect, and then looking at Glushakov for a reaction.
Glushakov simply stared back, no expression on his face at all, in spite of the sickness he was feeling inside.
Simone turned back to the camera,
'So what we have here is a game of chance. I know that this is a game that appeals to you because you took a chance by joining forces with me. Your mistake was that you went from being grateful that I gave you a chance to seeking control.'
Yassir and Samuel lifted their eyes up from the table and looked at Simone. They both registered the excitement on his face at exactly the same time as he continued.
'Our arrangement is terminated. I have new friends, new people who appreciate the chance that I offer them and they know exactly where they stand,' he declared, as he threw Glushakov another look, an action that resulted in an approving nod being returned.
The boys were now beginning to sob a little louder.
Yassir looked anxiously around the room looking for an escape route, one of the guards noticed the urgency on his face and stepped forward quickly before cuffing him hard around the back of the head and saying, 'Stay still.'
Simone ignored the commotion behind him.

'So we are going to play a little game of chance, to see what happens when you don't value me, and how capable I am of turning the odds in my favour,' he continued, 'And let this be a last warning to you American pigs. We are not savages, we are not intellectually inferior beings, we are warriors, fighting men, who do not understand the meaning of the word defeat. Take note and do not get any ideas about retribution. My new friends are as strong and wealthy as you and they do not have to hide behind your weak rules and way of life. Enjoy the show,' he concluded, aiming a smile at Yuri Glushakov as he did so.

Glushakov smiled back.

But at the same time, he was thinking what a stupid man this African idiot was.

He literally had no idea what was going on, and whose side the SVR were really on and why.

Simone's loyal soldier continued to film as the warlord turned his attention to the four innocent boys who had never done anything wrong other than be born in the wrong place.

When the filming was completed, all that was left was a video that would shock even the most cruel man void of any emotions.

It was also a mistake.

Because it was the video that would convince Ryan Ward that he had no choice but to take on Samson Simone.

And Ryan Ward never lost.

# SEVEN

**Bismarck – North Dakota**

Gary Chandler was wealthy beyond the comprehension of most normal people, something that he checked for confirmation of at least twice every day. This morning alone he had checked the balance of his seven main bank accounts twice, and he was pleased to see that in pure cash alone, he had passed the three hundred million dollar mark for the first time since oil prices had plummeted. He was feeling ecstatic because the market was now turning back in his favour. Like all extremely wealthy men, it was no longer about the money, but the power that went with it. He had created a persona that intimidated all of his employees. He believed that this made him strong, and the fact that no one ever stood up to him, confirmed this belief. Grown men in suits would cower in fear in his office when he would shout at them, something that he made sure happened at least three times a day, and his employees would agree with anything he said, just to avoid getting on the wrong side of him. He wasn't remotely intimidating to look at. He was slightly built, stood just short of six feet and wore steel-rimmed glasses. His greying hair, ridiculously dyed in places to try and salvage the last grains of youth, made him look like he was a failing actor trying to present himself as still the same talent from yesteryear. Without his position of CEO to add power and importance to him, his mannerisms would result in regular beatings if he spoke to people with such contempt and disrespect away from the sanctuary of the plush headquarters that he lorded over. But he was oblivious to that. He was strong, he was powerful and grown men looked at him with fear in their eyes.

He answered the phone that sat on his grand oak desk on the third ring and he had a feeling that his morning was about to get a whole lot better.
'There is an international call for you sir,' his secretary said efficiently down the line.
'Put them through,' he replied abruptly.
There was a click and a pause while the line was connected and he said,
'Hello?'
'Everything is finalised,' the voice on the other end of the line said, 'And as of ten minutes ago, the people in Washington have been notified.'
'When can we make the necessary arrangements? I don't want to be wasting a moment on this, time is precious.'
'When I say you can,' the voice replied sharply.
   The response took Chandler back by surprise, people talking to him in such a manner was something that he was not used to, it was something that had not happened in the past fifteen years. His instinct kicked in and he responded in his usual manner,
'We made a deal, I suggest you think very carefully about speaking to me like that again. So I will ask again, 'When can I make the necessary arrangements?'

'You take that attitude with me again and there won't be any arrangement anymore,' the voice replied and the line went dead.

He sat in his big leather chair, leaning forward with the phone still to his ear as the dead tone rang. He was taken aback by the hostility of the man on the other end of the line.

And all of a sudden, he had a bad feeling that he had made a very, very big mistake.

**Washington D.C.**

Centrepoint looked at the caller display as his phone rang and immediately recognised the White House number. So he left it to ring seven times, an action that made him smile to himself for the first time that day.

'I have the Vice President for you sir,' the efficient lady said again, 'I'll put him through.'

There was a click and then without any greeting, Aaron Wilson said,

'McNair, you have to get your men in there and now.'

'Why?'

'Because Simone has just made it very clear that all access, and safe routes, have been closed to us permanently.'

'It's not as simple as just getting an unofficial team together, I can't force them to do it,' The Old Man replied, trying his best to sound like he was at the end of his tether himself over his inability to meet the Vice President's request.

'My team have just sent you a video. Watch it and you will see why there is such urgency. There are a number of very important people who need access restored immediately.'

'My priority is the safety of my team. You will have to send in DELTA force or Seal's if it is that urgent,' he replied, knowing full well that it would be impossible for the United States to sanction such an operation due to the risk of being caught.

'The British man, what's happening with him?' Wilson asked urgently.

'He's considering it.'

'Can't we do anything to prompt him, money, a threat, anything?'

'You've seen him in action sir,' he said, 'Threatening him would be a very bad idea and money is not his motivation.'

'Then what is?' Wilson asked, sounding more desperate with each passing second.

The Old Man clicked on the email as he smiled to himself at the Vice President's desperation, and a video box appeared, he pressed play,

'The control of Bassong and the region is one hundred per cent mine if I fix this impossible mess for you, agreed?' he asked, putting the emphasis on the word 'Impossible; and raising his voice slightly as he said it, just so Wilson would be eternally grateful for his intervention and hold him in even more high regard than he did already.

'Yes. The agreement has come directly from the oval office and the man in there himself.'

Centrepoint watched the video playing and saw the four pitiful boys sitting at Simone's table,

'Where did you get this video?' he asked.

'It was sent to me by someone very important'
'Who?'
'It doesn't matter. Going back to our British friend, if money isn't his motivation, then what is?'
He watched the scene on his screen play out and shook his head, not in disbelief but in frustration. What did the idiots on Capitol Hill think was going to happen if they got into bed with an animal like Simone, he thought to himself.
'I have his motivation,' he replied, 'Now get off the phone so I can sort your mess out,' he added, and then slammed the phone down on the second most powerful man in the world.


## Park Avenue – New York

'I don't suppose for one minute I can talk you out of this madness?' Tackler asked Ward.
'Hear him out first Tackler,' Nicole-Louise said without even turning around from her workstation.
Nicole-Louise and Tackler knew more about Ward than anyone. They had erased his digital past and pretty much made him impossible to find. He didn't exist anywhere. As well as hiding him from the world, they would create any alter ego that he required for his operations and they could find anything.
They really were the foundation stone on which every successful mission that he carried out was built.
He looked at them as his brother and sister, and he felt closer to them than anyone apart from The Optician.

But no matter how many times he saw them together, and in spite of knowing that they were perfect for each other, he always felt that they didn't look like they belonged with each other. Tackler looked like he had stepped out of a skate park. He was thin, below average height and he always looked unkempt. He always wore long, blue towelled shorts that ran to his knees, revealing less than powerful calf muscles, and a tee-shirt that had a picture from a front page newspaper article that declared 'Sid Vicious is Dead!' Ward was sure that he must have at least fifty of the exact same tee shirts. Nicole-Louise was a good four inches taller than Tackler. She had beautiful, alert blue eyes and long, light brown hair which ran past her shoulder blades. She always dressed casually and she carried off the sweat pants and hoodie look better than any woman that he knew. Tackler was the quieter one of the two and Nicole-Louise was outgoing, strong and confident.
The apartment doorbell rang and Tackler wearily trudged over to it, opening it slowly to see Martin McDermott standing there, with his team neatly in line behind him,
'Hello Tackler,' he said as he walked past him without waiting to be invited in.
'I knew that two hours would mean one,' Ward said as he extended his hand for McDermott to shake as his six loyal foot shoulders followed him in,
'Come in,' Tackler said as the last man walked past him. Martin McDermott looked exactly how someone would expect one of the best Navy Seals that ever served his country would be expected to look. Even though he was now into his early fifties, his arms, exposed by his the short sleeves of his tee-shirt, should a definition that

most gym addicts could only ever dream of achieving. He had grey, short cropped hair and a square, strong jawline. He had a scar that ran down his left cheek where he had been stabbed in the face by a Iraqi soldier while carrying out a rescue mission. He broke the guys neck five seconds after and did not even realise he had been stabbed until an hour after the mission had been successfully completed.

His team were made up of six of the most individually highly skilled and efficient men that Ward had ever seen combined into one team.

And they all looked exactly the same. It would be easily believable that they were all brothers if someone showed a group photo of them together. They all stood about six feet tall, all had cropped hair and all possessed the athletic build that all Special Forces operatives tend to possess.

His son Paul displayed exactly the same traits as his father. He would double-check and then check again every single aspect of an operation. He was desperate to take over the running of the team and both he and his father knew that the day for him to pass the reins over was drawing ever closer.

Lloyd Walsh was the team's explosive expert. He had averted a catastrophic event from taking place in New York recently when he had disarmed a bomb with the kind of calm that Ward had only ever seen displayed by The Optician before.

Danny Wallace was the telecoms expert in the team. He could set up a communications system anywhere on earth and if they were going to move forward with this operation, his role was going to be crucial.

Adam Fuller was the quiet one of the team. Ward had never had an in-depth conversation with Fuller and he was the one guy he didn't really know much about. He told himself that he would put that right soon as he watched Fuller stand at the back of the room, behind the others.

The Fringe was the upbeat guy that every team needs. He was obsessed with eighties music and would play it constantly when the team were on their downtime or waiting for instructions at one of McDermott's warehouses.

And then there was Wired, so called because he most definitely wasn't wired correctly. He had psychotic tendencies and was extremely violent. He literally had no fear and relished the challenge of fighting an armed man when he was unarmed, and then beating him to death. McDermott controlled him well but everyone in the team always felt that he was one incident short of losing control completely.

He terrified Nicole-Louise. She had often commented that he gave her the creeps, something that would have seemed even more frightening if she knew that Wired was secretly in love with her, and he spent countless hours daydreaming about the two of them sharing a life together.

Ward walked around the room and shook hands with them all as Wired smiled at Nicole-Louise and she immediately turned back to face her screen. There was a loud bang on the door and The Fringe walked across to open it,

'Am I late?' a beaming Lawson asked as he walked in.

Tackler rolled his eyes, McDermott and his team all said their greetings and Ward simply nodded at him.

'You look lovely Nicole-Louise,' Lawson said as he walked over to where she was sitting and leant down to kiss her cheek,

'Get lost Mike, your breath smells,' she said without turning around. Everyone in the room laughed.

Ward felt his cell phone vibrate in his pocket and he knew it would be The Old Man,

'Yep?' he enquired as he answered.

'I've just sent a video to Nicole-Louise. You need to watch it before you make your mind up on this one,' he said urgently.

'Another blackmail tool is it?' Ward asked curtly.

'Sorry?'

'You know that we won't leave The Optician to face this alone. That was a low blow and you know it.'

'Fair point. So I'll not put him in there if you say this op is a no go. I can't be any fairer than that. But watch the video and then let me know what you and the others all decide.'

'What others?' he asked, irritated, as always, that Centrepoint knew where he was and with who.

'McDermott, his boys, Lawson, Nicole-Louise and Tackler of course. They are all standing next to you.'

Ward hung up the phone.

'He wants us to look at a video he has just sent you Nicole-Louise,' he said

# EIGHT

Ten sets of eyes peered at Nicole-Louise's screen over her shoulder as she opened up the video.
Samson Simone appeared in full battle fatigue's smiling at the camera. He looked less intimidating than Ward assumed he would be, In the African countries, warlords tended to be physically imposing men. Simone started speaking to the camera while four tearful small boys were made to sit at the table.
Without any comments from anyone in the room, they all knew what was going to happen.
Nicole-Louise got up from her chair and walked out of the room, leaving the video playing.
Tackler stood up to go after her but Ward whispered, 'Leave her on her own, she doesn't need to see this or discuss it,' and Tackler sat back down.
They watched as Simone kept glancing to his right, like he was seeking someone else's approval,
'Who do you think is in the room with him?' McDermott asked.
Ward ignored him.
Simone started to talk louder, and with more aggression in his voice, before he declared,
'And let this be a last warning to you American pigs. We are not savages nor are we intellectually inferior beings. We are warriors, fighting men, who do not understand the meaning of the word defeat. Take note and do not get any ideas about retribution. My new friends are as strong and wealthy as you and they do not have to hide behind your weak rules and way of life. Enjoy the show.'
'It's show time,' Lawson said softly.

They watched as Simone put the pistol on the table, declaring that there were four bullets in the pistol and two of them were blanks.

'You two are way too small to fight in my army so you can show you are worthy of your place in a different way,' Simone said, pointing at two of the boys around the table, 'So Warube and Yassir, who is going to go first?'

'They can't be more than eight years old,' Paul said, with disgust running through his voice.

No one said anything.

The two boys started crying loudly,

'I said who will go first?' Simone demanded.

Instantly, one of the boys scooped up the pistol and put it to his head.

'Stop!' Simone demanded.

Everyone looking at the screen frowned.

'You don't put it to your own head, you put it to Yassir's and pull the trigger,' he said and then laughed a deep laugh and glanced to his right again, 'So put it to his head and pull the trigger.'

The small boy lifted the pistol and the other boy winced, 'Do not cower,' Simone screamed, 'If you move again I will drag you out by your hair and feed you to the dogs alive. Sit on your hands.'

The small boy instantly sat on his hands, closed his eyes and ducked his head into his shoulders.

The other boy lifted the pistol to his friend's temple, his hands shaking so much that the weapon was moving up and down at least two inches.

'Now pull the trigger Warube,' Simone said with almost a look of sexual gratification on his face.

The boy holding the pistol squeezed the trigger and there was an immediate and very loud bang which made Tackler jump.

The other boys head blew apart, like someone hitting a water melon with a sledgehammer. Tackler looked at the floor instantly and put his hand over his mouth.

Everyone else just stared straight ahead.

Simone's loud laugh echoed out of the speakers next to the monitor.

'That's one bullet gone,' he declared, 'Now put the gun to your head and pull the trigger. Your odds have improved dramatically Warube.'

Even though the video was not shot with crystal clarity, it was clear to see the glimmer of hope suddenly appear in the small boys' eyes. In one swift movement, he lifted the gun to his head, closed his eyes, and pulled the trigger.

And promptly blew his tiny head apart, his brain matter and blood covering the table in front of him. His body slumped out of sight to the floor.

'There are no blanks,' Ward whispered.

Simone laughed even louder this time, the camera switched to him again, and he flashed a big smile, like he was on vacation, and then glanced to his right, before the camera returned to the remaining two boys sitting at the table.

'You two were a mistake but today is your lucky day,' Simone said, 'But we will finish the game anyway,' he added before stepping over to the table and bending down to pick the pistol off of the floor that had flown out of Warube's hand as the bullet had entered his brain.

He handed the gun to one of the remaining two boys and said, 'The wrong two have died, you two aren't much use to me, but we will finish the game anyway. Put it against Jumma's head and pull the trigger,' he demanded, not even looking at the small boy as he handed him the gun.
The boy raised the gun, pressed it against his temple and squeezed the trigger.
A loud explosion echoed around the room as the boys head shattered, and a three inch hole appeared instantly before he slumped to the side and fell off the chair.
The boy holding the gun opened his mouth and did a gulping motion, like he was mimicking a scream, but there was no sound.
Simone laughed even louder.
'I must have counted incorrectly Samuel,' he said between his laughs, before glancing to his right yet again, 'But I want to give you a chance to live. Do you want a chance?'
The small boy, with tears running down his cheeks, nodded desperately.
'Then all you have to do is say, I am your servant master, and you can put the gun down and go back to the quarters.'
Lawson looked at Ward,
'Why save him?'
Ward ignored him.
The boy looked up at Simone, with his lips tightly pursed together.
'Well?' Simone asked.
'Just say it!

Tackler screamed loudly enough for Nicole-Louise to hear him in the next room.

The boy started to open his mouth and then made a nodding motion with his head. He seemed to be trying to speak but the words would not come out.

'He can't even speak he's so frightened,' Tackler said and then looked away from the screen.

'I'm waiting,' Simone's voice boomed out, 'I am your servant master,' he repeated slowly and deliberately.

The boy was desperately trying to speak, they could all see that, but no sound was coming out of his mouth at all.

'Just say it,' Tackler screamed.

'He can't speak,' Ward said softly, 'He's a mute.'

'Last chance,' Simone shouted.

The boy stood to his feet and started rocking his upper body backwards and forwards, he looked like he was screaming, but still no sound came out.

And then his whole body jerked back as a bullet smashed hard into his chest and the force of the bullet against his frail, tiny body knocked him back at least three feet and the person holding the camera had to move it very quickly to keep him in the frame. He hit the floor, smashing his head into a metal drawer as he fell. Simone stepped into view, lowered his gun and fired three shots into the poor child's body and then looked at the camera.

'Life means nothing to me. Do not be stupid, do not be brave and do not set foot into my country. There is an army here that will kill you and then feed your bodies to the dogs,' and then he turned and walked away and the camera focussed on the dead boys all scattered around the table.

Tackler closed the video.

'Well, I don't know about you lot,' Lawson said immediately, 'I've never had sex with a Sudanese woman, so I fancy a road trip.'

For once, no one laughed at Lawson's attempt at lightening the mood to bring everyone back into focus.

'Play that last few seconds again,' Ward said to Tackler.

Tackler frowned, 'Seriously?' he asked.

'Yes, there was something there.'

Tackler reopened the video and slid the timer bar at the bottom to five seconds from the end. They all watched again as Simone finished his proclamation and the camera focussed on the dead bodies, before the video ended.

'Have you seen something?' McDermott asked.

Ward ignored him.

It wasn't what he had seen that made him realise that this was far more dangerous than what he had initially thought.

It was what he had heard.

'How long will it take you to get a plan together?' he asked McDermott.

'It's ready. As soon as you started talking about Simone I knew you would go there. We've spent the last week on it. Why do you think we stayed in New York?'

'So you are good to go, now?' he asked with surprise.

'Yes, but as I said, we lead it, and if at any point I say we pull out because the boys or either of you two are in danger, you do what I say,' McDermott said with a stern look on his face and pointing at Ward and Lawson as he spoke.

'You want to run it by me?' Ward asked.

'It's reliant upon you getting this new guy that they want to put in charge giving us the right information once we are there.'

'Phillipe Bassong,' Ward reminded him.

'Whoever it is doesn't matter. What matters is that we can get Simone to a place where we can take him out. We will take care of his men but we need The Optician with us to protect us.'

'He'll be there.'

'Also, something a bit strange happened but I have to put one condition on us taking part,' McDermott said.

'Which is?'

'Nicole-Louise and Tackler are kept here safely.

Ward looked confused, 'I had no intention of bringing them. I would not expose them to that.'

'Good, we're all in then.'

'Can I ask why you mentioned them?'

'It was Wired. He said if they came then he would not go and you know the team can't function properly without him, the sum of all parts and all that.'

'Why would he say that?' Ward asked, still frowning.

'God knows,' McDermott replied, 'But he's in one of his dark zones at the moment, so I just agreed and left him to it. I'm sure that he has his own reasons.'

Ward shrugged,

'Thanks Mac,' he said, 'I can't do this without you.'

'Then you had better get the transport sorted so we can leave.'

'I'll call The Old Man now.'

**Washington D.C.**

Centrepoint smiled to himself as his cell phone vibrated on his desk as he saw Ward's name on the screen. The call was coming thirty minutes earlier than he expected.
'Before you give me a lecture,' he said, before Ward could speak, 'That video was sent to me direct from the oval office.'
'So the obvious question is, who sent it to them and why?'
He knew it was the obvious question. But right now, he didn't have the answer.
'My instinct tells me that it's someone, somewhere in the Senate who has interest that could be affected by the access through to South Africa and throughout Africa being closed down.'
'Then it shouldn't be too hard for you to find out who. Behind every single one of those dishonest scumbags there is a wealthy donor. Just find the one who gets the majority of his sponsorship from people who have links down there,' Ward replied, dismayed that The Old Man hadn't thought of that already.
'That's what I've been looking into but my main concern was getting you on board first,' he replied curtly.
'We're on board. We have a plan.'
'Care to fill me in?'
'No.'
'Why not?'
'Because you won't like it. This is a suicide mission, you know that right, be honest?'
He thought for a few seconds about how dangerous going into Sudan was and then he weighed up the

capabilities of Ward, Lawson and McDermott's team and it made him feel slightly more optimistic,

'I would put it at fifty-fifty. Is that a fair assessment?' he said eventually.

'No,' Ward replied, 'I'd put it at ninety-ten in our favour.'

'How so?'

'Because Mac has come up with an ingenious plan.'

This reassured him a great deal, all of a sudden, he felt in control of the situation for the first time, 'The jet is fuelled and waiting at JFK. When are you leaving?'

'Within the next two hours.'

'Anything else you want me to do?'

Two things,' Ward replied.

'One, you need The Optician there?' he said quickly, pre-empting Ward's request.

'Of course we do but that isn't one of them.'

Now he was confused, he had no idea what Ward would need, and his feeling of control that he felt a few moments earlier started to descend into uneasiness.

'So what are they?'

'Firstly you give me your word that you have complete control over this Phillipe Bassong guy you are putting in charge after we remove Simone and that he does not torture or hurt anyone, especially poor kids. And if he does, you terminate him immediately.'

'You have my word Ryan. We can't risk a mess like this again. I'm furious with the CIA and I will be taking it up with them and making sure heads roll. It won't ever happen again,' he replied with such sincerity, that Ward knew that he was telling the truth and he meant every word of it, 'I've set up the necessary transportation. You will fly to Khartoum and then take a small aircraft to a landing strip in Babanusa, and then a two hour journey across land by jeep to Adiela,' he added to show he was offering all the support he was able to provide at that moment in time.

'Good.'

'And the second thing?' he asked.

'Get Colin Buck to be in New York in forty-eight hours' time,' Ward said bluntly.

'Buck? Why?' he asked, completely confused now.

'Because we are way too smart to pick a fight in Sudan,' Ward replied calmly, 'So I'm bringing the fight to New York.'

# NINE

**Khartoum International Airport - Sudan**

The flight to Sudan was going to take just over seventeen hours from JFK, which included a refuelling stop at London Stansted. That gave everyone on board plenty of time to be fully briefed on the plan and their roles.

As usual, and completely unbeknown to all on board, The Optician had taken his place in the co-pilots seat, and as everyone boarded and glanced at the back of his head, he had smiled to himself as he heard Lawson say, 'Do you think The Optician is there waiting for us already?'
He liked Lawson, he even envied him. He had sat in the same co-pilots seat on numerous flights with Lawson and Ward as passengers, and he had heard the stories of Lawson's sexual prowess from more than one flight attendant who had joined the mile high club with him as they whispered excitedly into their cell phones when they had reached their destination. McDermott being on-board was an unusual thing and it made him cautious. He knew that McDermott had a sixth sense for things, and he would not put it past him to get a feeling that the elusive Optician was on board. And he could not take the chance of McDermott seeing him. But so far, as they flew over Southern Spain, they had all been so engrossed in their planning, something he heard every word of through his headphones, as all of the seats and tables

were bugged as standard, allowing him to hear Ward's plans wherever they went, McDermott seemed focussed on getting the plan understood over anything else. He was very impressed that they were now going through it for the fourth time, word for word, action by action and role by role. In fact, he was so impressed that he felt good about this plan, he even knew the part he would be expected to play, and he was confident that the men on board would all play their part perfectly.

But he always expected the unexpected. That's what made him one of the most revered and feared men on the planet. While they were planning for a straightforward extraction, he was visualising the snipers, the children used as human shields and numbers of men which far exceeded what Ward and the team were expecting.

But right then, he did have one concern. The pilot was not looking very good, and seemed to be displaying a fever judging by the sweat dripping from his temple down the side of his face, and if he suddenly passed out, he would have no idea how to fly the plane. He was reasonably reassured when the pilot told him that he would not be flying them home, as he had already called ahead for a replacement.

'We'll be touching down in Khartoum in two hours; everyone is clear on what they are doing Ryan, so you only have to make sure The Old Man sets up the satellite link for Wallace and we are good to go,' McDermott said as he sat down next to Lawson who was sitting opposite.

'OK, Mac, I'll call him now.'

'What else is there Ryan?' Lawson suddenly asked.

McDermott frowned.
Ward said nothing.
'What do you mean by that?' Mac eventually asked.
'I saw that look he had at Nicole-Louise's when he asked to see the video again. I saw it for the first time when we were all running around hunting Fulken. We're all missing something, what is it?'
'Let's get this sorted and get home safely,' Ward replied. Then we can concentrate on the other issues after that.'

They finally landed in Khartoum and the pilot taxied the jet to the far right of the airport building. True to his word, The Old Man had made sure that their transfer onto a smaller plane would be without interruption or questioning by the local authorities. Ward wondered for a moment how much had to be paid in bribes to the locals. He concluded not a lot when he saw the rickety old plane that they were going to use for the next part of their journey.
'Seriously?' Lawson asked as they disembarked and walked towards the plane, carrying their numerous holdalls full of equipment and weapons 'That won't even take off with our weight.'
'It has to be like that Mike, we have to land on a strip of land in a field for the next part of our journey. The Lear jet won't be able to stop,' McDermott said reassuringly.
'Well I hope those two can fly it properly,' Lawson said as he watched the backs of the replacement pilot and co-pilot walk purposely towards the plane.
Ward smiled to himself.
Lawson had no fear about anything, he knew that without doubt, and he knew that he would be making

light of things to get everyone relaxed as there would be no point in wasting nervous energy for another four hours on the plane until they landed ready for the last part of their journey.

They all boarded, to a man, they all made fun of the plane and laughed loudly. The Optician noted that the replacement pilot looked a lot healthier than the previous one and he would now be able to concentrate solely on what he needed to do.

**Babanusa – Sudan**

The plane took off ten minutes later and to everyone's surprise, it seemed to take off smoothly and effortlessly. They spent the next four hours going over the plan two more times and by the time they landed on a deserted strip of land in Babanusa, not only were they all clear on their individual roles, they knew every single step that each other was expected to take.

McDermott liked to be thorough.

The plane came to a stop and as soon as the doors were opened and they climbed out, they saw the three battered Land Rovers waiting for them, all lined up in a neat line. Strangely, to the left and forty feet further back, there was a gleaming red Kawasaki KMX 125cc off road motorbike waiting.

'Is the bike for us?' Wallace asked.

'No, The Old Man was clear that we took the three Land Rovers and that was all. It must belong to the spotter that they have waiting for us to collect them I guess,' Lawson said, a statement that seemed to satisfy everyone's curiosity fully.

The pilot stepped out of the plane and walked across to Ward and handed him a satellite phone,
'You are to call me on this when you are ten minutes away so I can get the engines running,' he said, 'It's already pre-programed, speed dial one.'
Ward took the phone from him and nodded.
They all helped unload the equipment from the plane and packed everything into the three Land Rovers.
Paul, Wired and Fringe climbed into one Land Rover, while Fuller, Walsh and Wallace climbed into the other parked at the back.
'You have to admire how resourceful The Old Man is,' Lawson said as he climbed into the Land Rover with Ward and McDermott, 'I mean he's got all the transport arranged without a hitch, comms set up with the pilot and intel on where our target will be. Not bad for an old man.'
Both Ward and McDermott ignored him.
'Yes Mike, not bad at all,' he muttered to himself as McDermott pulled away and they began the one and a half hour journey to Adiela.

His resourcefulness knew no limit. The Optician always moved behind Ward on a Kawasaki Superbike but out here, with the desert and rough terrain, that would be impractical. Centrepoint had said he would provide transport for him, and he had insisted that it would be a Kawasaki KMX 125cc as he knew the capabilities of the machine and that it would be ideal for this operation. He was pleased to see he had got it exactly right as usual as he slung his rifle bag over his shoulder and started the engine. Checking the GPS linked to Ward's phone so he would never be more than three minutes behind them, and five minutes ahead when he was needed. As he looked down at the map linked to the tracker, he saw Ward's name appear on his caller display. He flicked the switch on the Bluetooth device in his ear.

'Are you in Sudan yet?' Ward asked.

'I've been here twelve hours,' he lied, 'How was your journey?'

'It was effortless. You know where you need to be?'

'Yes. The Old Man has told me where Simone will be and when. I'll be there by the time you are ready for the extraction.'

'Remember, we need him alive.'

'That's your job. I'll get myself set up and take care of anyone who gets in your way, and Ryan?'

'Yes my friend?'

'This isn't home, remember that. The rules are different and whatever happens, don't get caught.'

The line went dead.

**Adiela - Sudan**

The two hour drive to Adiela was mainly along a dirt track of a road across barren land and stretches of desert which gave very little cover. Fortunately, apart from the odd battered truck, they passed very little traffic. The people that they did see were carrying excessive weights in their arms, and the majority of them were children. Ward noticed that as they approached in their vehicles, they would look at the floor, reluctant to make any eye contact with the vehicles inhabitants, in case they were Simone's men no doubt. They reached the outskirts of

Adiela and pulled off of the main road and drove a few hundred yards down a side track until they were out of sight and under the cover of the trees.

Adiela was no more than an average sized place in comparison to American towns and cities. It had a population just short of three hundred and forty five thousand inhabitants according to the last census that was carried out in 2008. Like any other government figures produced, their accuracy had to be doubted. Samson Simone lived in splendour in a compound a few miles outside of Adiela, but today Phillipe Bassong had told The Old Man that he would be taking Simone to an appointment with some South African businessmen who wanted to offer a proposal to him about mining some of the remaining unclaimed minerals that their geologists had discovered. The meeting was to be held on the side of the town where they were now parked, the opposite side of town to Samson Simone's compound, and more importantly, at least twenty five minutes between them and the majority of his army. The meeting was going to take place in a motel which was the only place that offered alcohol freely in the town, and they had been informed that there would only be a maximum of six armed men with him.

Wallace, Walsh and Fuller climbed out of their Land Rover and unloaded all of the communications equipment, while everyone else carried out a weapons check in silence.

Ten minutes later, with everyone now wearing an earpiece which fed directly to each other and Wallace, Paul said,
'We have two hours until he arrives. I'll take the others to carry out the recon, and you three stay here and do whatever it is that you three normally do.'
'We do the thinking,' Lawson quipped.
'No Mike, they do the thinking,' Paul replied, and they all climbed into two of the Land Rovers and pulled away, leaving just Wallace to carry out the final checks to his comms equipment which was set up on the floor behind a large bush.
'You can't hold him back much longer Mac, you know that, right? He's more than ready to take over,' Ward said softly.
'I know. It's just getting used to the idea that my time is over. Can you imagine me sending them off to places and sitting on my ass?'
'We all have a shelf life. You've earned the rest, like really earned it. You should take up a hobby, something to distract you.'
'Killing people distracts me,' McDermott said with a smile.
'Have either of you ever had sex with a Sudanese woman?' Lawson interrupted.
They both shook their heads and rolled their eyes at the same time.
The Optician had found the perfect vantage point to see everyone who came and went into the bar from the top of a three story building, slightly to the left of the entrance. After he had settled himself into position, he began to watch, to feel and smell. It was his way of

getting lost in a place, and his heightened senses picked up everything that was going on around him. So good was he at becoming part of what he was looking at that he spotted both Wired and Fringe creeping around the back of buildings carrying out their recon work. He knew the others would be there and within three minutes, he had also spotted Paul, Fuller and Walsh, even though everyone else on the street was totally oblivious to their movements. There were three market stalls to the right of the entrance where vendors were selling fruit, fabric and items of pottery and the street was becoming busy as it approached late afternoon.

All of a sudden, his Zen like calm was broken by the rumbling of vehicles in the distance. A few moments later, five open top Land Rovers pulled to a stop outside of the bar, and most of the passengers stepped out of the vehicles and headed into the bar, leaving only the drivers in the Land Rovers, and three sentries standing guard outside. A few moments later, a dirty looking Mercedes pulled up and two men in suits stepped out accompanied by two guys who looked very much like ex-Special Forces soldiers, most likely South African he concluded. He picked up his cell and called Ward.

'Hey,' Ward answered.

'We have a problem.'

'What?'

'Simone decided to turn up early, he's here now and so are the guys he is meeting with.'

'We are four minutes away, it won't be a problem.'

'That isn't the problem,' The Optician replied.

'What is?'

'There aren't six guys with them, there are at least twenty, and they are all heavily armed.'

'We can manage.'

'There are also some ex-Special Forces guys with some suits, they look like they are South Africans.'

'Don't do anything until we get there,' Ward said urgently and the line went dead.

Ward looked at McDermott and Lawson,

'He's there early, he has at least twenty guys with him and a couple of South African mercenaries. Get on to Paul and tell him we are en route. Wallace, are you all good to go?' he asked.

'All good,' Wallace said briskly.

'Let's go,' McDermott said as the three of them jogged towards their Land Rover.

# TEN

**Bismarck – North Dakota**

Gary Chandler was now very worried indeed. Not only had his contact on the phone spoken to him with such hostility, he now had a clear feeling that the caller knew something that he didn't. He dialled the number in Washington urgently and was dismayed to be put straight through to the voicemail service. In his desperation to find out what it was that he might not know, he did something that he had never done before.
'Lauren,' he said as he picked up his phone and called through to his receptionist, 'Can you get Karl Phillips on the line for me urgently.'
'Karl Phillips, from Endco sir?' she asked, sounding as though she was sure she had misheard him.
'Yes. And quickly,' he replied and slammed the phone down.
Two minutes later, his phone rang,
'I have Mr Phillips on the line for you sir,' Lauren said and then there was a loud click while the call was connected.
'Gary Chandler, this is a surprise,' Phillips said.
Chandler hated Phillips. He hated the fact that he was so media savvy and the media seemed to love him. He hated the fact that he took corporate risks and gambles, that he himself had run away from, and even worse, that his risks always seemed to reap huge rewards. He resented the fact that Phillips was held in such high

regard by their peers, and how even his employees seemed to love him. But most of all, he hated the fact that Phillips was richer and considered more influential than he was.

'Thanks for getting back to me Karl, I just had a couple of questions if you could be so kind as to spare me five minutes of your time?'

'Always eager to help one of my main competitors,' Phillips replied, 'After all, that's good business practice,' he added, and laughed a long and genuine laugh.

Chandler really did hate this man. He was mocking him and he wasn't even hiding it.

He feigned a laugh himself,

'It's not relating to any of our practices, just a question about one specific thing,' he said.

'OK, hit me with it.'

'Do you know what is happening down in Sudan, I seem to have hit a lot of snags down there, and no one seems to know anything? I know you share some of the same routes as us and I just wondered if you knew what was happening?'

'I hear the rumours but no more than that. You know that we have an award winning ethics and community care programme that we are very proud of here, so we have never got involved with the intricacies and politics of the region, as some of our competitors have allegedly done.'

'I've heard those allegations too,' Chandler said through gritted teeth before composing himself quickly, 'But I can assure you that we are not one of them. So what are these rumours?' He asked, trying his best to sound curious rather than worried.

'Some of our less than ethical competitors had an arrangement with the CIA to assist the local warlord in seizing power from the previous regime, and now he won't play fair. Of course, they are only rumours, I can't imagine any CEO would knowingly get involved in that murky business, after all, imagine what it would do to a company if that got out, not to mention the jail time that he might be liable to do?' Phillips said, sounding more condescending by the second.

'Are you still using the route?'

'My dear Gary,' Phillips said, 'We carried out an analysis and risk assessment of the situation twelve months ago and concluded that alternative arrangements should be sought. Whatever mess certain individuals have created down there, fortunately, it won't affect us.'

'You still need access?' Chandler said, forgetting for a moment that he was talking to one of his main competitors.

'Anything else I can help you with?' Phillips asked, indicating that he wanted the call terminated.

'No, I'll keep my ear to the ground and as a return favour, I'll let you know if you hear anything.'

'No need,' Phillips replied, 'but it was good to talk to you.'

The line then went dead.

I hate that man, Chandler thought to himself, he knows more than he is letting on, and he was definitely trying to goad him into thinking he was going in a different direction. But everyone needs access through Sedan. And soon he would be the only one who had it.

**430 South Capitol Street SE - Washington D.C.**

The Democratic National Committee is the formal governing body for the United States Democratic Party. The committee's role is to coordinate strategy to support Democratic Party candidates throughout the country for local, state, and national office. Research would suggest that while the committee can offer support for party candidates, it does not have direct authority over any of its elected officials.

Since 2002, after the committee was fined for fundraising violations, it has, on paper, run the committee in line with all guidelines set before them. But paper can lie.

The deputy chair of the committee was fully aware of the political fallout if news of their shady involvements in certain events ever became public knowledge.

Former North Dakota Democratic chairman Dorian Schulz had held the position of deputy chair of the Democratic party for the past six years, and this was the first time that he had been faced with a crisis of this magnitude.

And he wasn't coping with it very well.

He dialled the private cell phone number which was stored in his contacts list under 'VP'.

Aaron Wilson answered on the second ring.

'Tell me you have some good news for me Aaron?' Schulz said.

'Actually I do. The problem should be resolved within the next few days.'

'McNair came through?'

'Yes he did. He has got his best men on it too, and so I have full confidence that in three days' time, you will have good news for your friends.'

'They are more yours and the President's friends Aaron, it was their money that got you both into office. You would do well to remember that.'

'How could I possibly forget,' Wilson replied with a sigh, 'You have reminded me every time we have spoken over the last ten days.'

'These people can't take chances, I suggest you pop into the oval office and tell the President that we need updates and urgently.'

'He's busy with the European contingent.'

'Then I suggest you talk to McNair and get me an immediate situation report.'

## Washington D.C.

Centrepoint rolled his eyes as he saw the White House number appear on his caller display yet again. For a brief moment, he toyed with the idea of not answering just to irritate the idiot Wilson for the sake of it, but then he thought that he might have something else directly from the President and so he picked the phone up slowly.

He was surprised not to hear the voice of the White House telephonist as Wilson spoke before he said anything,

'How are things looking McNair?'

'You do know that getting to Sudan isn't just a question of jumping on the Metro and going two stops to Capitol South and arriving at your destination? It takes twenty-four hours in travel alone to get to where they are going.'

'I was just asking,' Wilson said apologetically, while remaining conscious of the fact that he did not want to irritate McNair any more than necessary. As much as he didn't like grovelling to him, he had enough dirt on him to destroy him and this whole administration.

'But there are a couple of points that I need you to clarify for me sir,' he said, still aware that however incompetent and perverse Wilson was, he was still the Vice President of the United States of America.

'If I can answer them, I will.'

'To keep my team safe, and to avoid any surprises that they might encounter, I need to know who is putting the pressure on you and the President to get Simone removed from power?'

'I can't answer that I'm afraid.'

'You just have.'

'I haven't.'

The Old Man shook his head, a common occurrence whenever he spoke to the Vice President.

'Only two sets of people could put that amount of pressure on you both that you are running scared,' he said, knowing that Wilson's next reaction would indicate which one of the two it would be.

'We aren't scared.' Wilson replied.

'Then you've just confirmed that the Democratic National Committee want this resolved. So, looking at the importance of the route, and the companies that need access to it for their own profit and development, my guess is that Dorian Schulz is putting pressure on you.'

There was silence on the line, longer than three seconds, something which confirmed to him immediately that he was correct.

'I'm going to search and find out in the next few hours anyway sir, so you can save me the time and I can spend that time making sure that everything goes to plan in Sudan,' he added before Wilson could even respond.
'How do you know everything McNair?' Wilson asked with a clear air of resignation in his voice.
'It's my job to know sir,'
'I want Schulz kept out of this. There can be no link to him on any of this.'
'So do I, and much more than you realise.'
'Why? Is he important to you?'
'No not at all.'
'So why are you so concerned about keeping him out of it?'
'Isn't it obvious?'
'No. What is it?'
'Because if my man, the British guy, gets wind that Schulz is behind this, he will go after him. And you know he will get him, and you also know, through your own personal experience, I can't stop him.'
There was a long silence on the phone again, and then Wilson said what only a despicable and cowardly politician like him would say,
'Just don't mention anything to your man about me McNair, is that clear?'
'I'll update you when I have news Sir,' he said, and he hung up the phone.

## Adiela – Sudan

By the time everyone had taken their positions, ten minutes had passed since The Optician had called.

Paul, Wired and Walsh had taken up position at the rear of the building. Fortunately, there were two side doors on either side of the bar that led out into wide alleyways, and Fringe and Fuller had taken up an elevated position on both sides, so that anyone walking out of either door would be a sitting duck. The Optician patiently watched the front of the building and lined up the guys in the vehicles and the three sentries in his crosshairs with a slow sweeping motion that ran from right to left. In terms of securing a building it was a perfect set up.
In terms of getting Simone extracted and away from his protection, it was a living nightmare.
This was not a plan that they were carrying out on home soil, where they could blend in, rely on The Old Man for support, or even intimidate the occupants in the bar. It was in the middle of one of the most dangerous places on earth. Any of the men being spotted would result in the locals becoming involved and that would soon escalate into them throwing stones at them or firing their archaic weapons, and Simone would be alerted immediately to their presence and no doubt his army would be summoned instantly, leaving them hopelessly outnumbered.
Facing certain death.
Ward, Lawson and McDermott were now positioned to the left at the front of the building, hidden behind some old and very rusty rectangle water tanks that stood over eight feet high. There was enough of a gap between them all for all three of them to have a perfect view of the entrance to the bar.

Unbeknown to them, they were also positioned thirty feet directly below The Optician, a fact that made their mystical colleague on the roof above smile to himself. Ward took out his cell phone and hit the speed dial.

'Hey,' The Optician answered in a whisper, conscious of the fact that if he spoke too loudly, they would probably hear him down below.

'Are you set up?' Ward asked.

'Yes, I'm facing the front, directly opposite, you?'

'We're slightly to the left, can you see us?'

'No, I have a wall obscuring my view,' The Optician lied.

'Paul and the boys have the rear and sides secured but we are going to need a subtle and clear route into the front of the building. Can you take out the guys in the vehicles and the three guys standing guard?'

'With my eyes open or closed?'

Ward smiled to himself, he knew that The Optician wasn't joking, 'Give us three minutes from now and as soon as you take the first shot, we will move.'

'Affirmative,' and then the line went dead.

'OK Paul,' McDermott said into his receiver, 'As soon as The Optician takes his first shot, we are moving in the front. You five take the back and sides as planned. Are you all ready?'

A chorus of 'Ready' came back into their ears.

Ward looked at McDermott and nodded.

McDermott gripped his silenced machine gun tighter.

Ward looked at Lawson and nodded.

'There just has to be one Sudanese woman in there,' Lawson said, and eight ruthless, efficient killers, about to embark on one of the most deadly missions that they would ever be involved with, all smiled to themselves as they heard Lawson's words echo into their ears.

# ELEVEN

The Optician looked through his scope one more time. He knew that his first shot would be the signal for the team on the floor to move forward.//
There were eight targets for him, the three men standing guard outside the bar preventing anyone from entering, not that any of the locals would even consider wondering inside knowing Simone was in there, and the five drivers of each vehicle, all sitting at the wheel, waiting patiently. One of the drivers was smoking a cigarette, it was hanging from his lips and he toyed with the idea for a moment of shooting the cigarette out of the guy's mouth, for a spot of target practice, but then took into account the seriousness of where they were and the consequences for the men down below if anything went wrong, and so he decided against it.

He hadn't always hid away in the shadows. There was a time when The Old Man first recruited him when he had been given his own operations, but as the importance of The Deniables grew, and a different kind of operative was recruited, where more analysis and interaction was required, he was moved into the position of protector and path clearer that he held now.

He thought back to his very first mission on his own. The Old Man had discovered that a pharmaceutical company were spreading a virus to enhance their profits and he had been tasked with fixing the problem. He hadn't enjoyed all of the interaction that was required on a one to one basis, and he started doubting his own abilities. He was then asked to assist an operative called

Gill Whymark on a mission where Whymark required protection from the shadows, and he soon discovered that he felt much more comfortable eliminating people rather than talking to them. He had been doing it ever since and now the only thing that mattered to him was keeping Ryan Ward safe, hence his decision not to entertain himself by shooting out the cigarette.

He calculated that he could take out the eight guys in ten seconds. The three guys standing outside the door were no more than three feet apart and they could be eliminated in two seconds. And they had to be put down first to prevent them running inside and warning Simone what was happening. The five guys sitting in the vehicles were spaced out a good twenty feet apart, and so that would take another eight seconds. If he was shooting from front to back he could do it two seconds quicker, but the problem with that sequence of shots would mean that the drivers sitting behind would see the kills taking place, and would more than likely duck down behind the dashboards and out of sight, so he had to shoot back to front.

He made his decision and looked at his watch. Fifteen more seconds and the three minutes was up.

He breathed in deeply and exhaled slowly before setting up the crosshairs in the centre of the guy's head who was standing to the right of the entrance.

He counted down in his head from ten, and then commenced an extraordinary sequence of shooting that enhanced his legend even more in the minds of the watching Ward, Lawson and McDermott.

When he reached zero in his head, he squeezed the trigger.

Shot number one. The 7.62mm bullet glided through the air and hit the guy standing to the right of the door in the centre of his forehead. Such was the accuracy of the shot that an autopsy on the guy would have revealed it hit only a quarter of a millimetre out of dead centre. The bullet hit so true, that there was virtually no blood or noise, and he had swung his scope slightly to the left just as the guys knees started to give way as the signal from his brain had been turned off permanently.

Shot number two. He had got the shot off just as the guy standing on the left of the door caught a glimpse of movement to his right as his colleagues legs started to give way and was starting to turn his head slightly. He had anticipated that this would happen and so he had lined up the head shot slightly to the left so that when the guy's head turned the bullet would hit in the centre of his forehead. The guy didn't turn quite as much as he had calculated and the bullet smashed into his forehead a bit too much to the left for his liking, and the spray of red mist exploding from his brain leapt forward, and bone and brain matter sprayed out to the left.

Shot number three. Before the third guy standing in the middle had any chance to react, he squeezed the trigger again. He had already started to sweep his rifle far to the left to line up the guy sitting in the vehicle at the rear of the convoy. Had he have kept his scope fixed on the third guy, he would have seen his mouth start to open just as the bullet smashed into his forehead before there was enough time to make a sound. It smashed through the hard bone in his forehead as easily as hammering a nail into sand, and the force of the impact knocked his whole upper torso back violently and he smashed the back of his head hard against the wall of the building with a sickening crunch.

The third guy was dead two hundredths of a second short of the two seconds that he had anticipated that it would take.

The human brain is a curious thing. If it hears a loud bang, it instantly reacts by telling your body to move, and a person will duck, move their hands up to protect their head or, in the case of an armed man, point their weapon towards the threat. When you don't hear anything, the brain relies on the eyes to give the signal to protect yourself. This was one of the most important lessons that he had learned when he first picked up a gun. Because his rifles were always fitted with a modified suppressor, his shots were literally silent, which meant there was no chance of an instant reaction. The five guys in the vehicles heard nothing but saw clearly what was happening, but the process time for their brain to give their bodies a signal to move was too slow.
It always was.

Shot number four. The guy sitting in the rear vehicle was oblivious to what was happening in front of him because he was looking at the vendors on the street and trying to work out where he recognised the guy selling the pottery from. He looked very familiar to him but he knew for sure that he was not from the same village that he had grown up in. Just as he finally realised how he recognised him, a 7.62mm bullet smashed into the right side of his head and hit with such ferocity that it blew a two inch hole in his skull immediately as the bullet lodged firmly into his brain, and the force of the impact knocked him sideways so that his head landed firmly onto the passenger seat. He was dead before he had time to get out of the vehicle and approach the vendor to remind him how much he had enjoyed raping his wife six months ago.

Shot number five was the cigarette guy. It was still hanging from his lips, a light plume of smoke escaping from his mouth every few seconds, and his brain was starting to register that something was happening because his right hand was moving up towards his mouth to remove his cigarette. It was a movement that for a split second had The Optician wondering if he was removing it from his mouth so he could see more clearly what his brain was trying to tell him was happening, or if he was trying to protect his nicotine filled stick. Either way, it didn't matter. It was the last fix he was ever going to get as the bullet smashed hard into the right side of his head, hitting him expertly on the temple, and lodging itself firmly into his brain. Surprisingly, the impact didn't knock him sideways, instead, his head fell back and his arms dropped to his side.

Shot number six, was the best shot. As he had anticipated, the three guys at the front had started to register what was happening and so in a split second, a period of time that most people can't think in, he changed tactics as he could see movement in the vehicle at the front out of the corner as his eye and so he bypassed the guy in the middle and next vehicles and swept his rifle all the way to the front, just as the driver was just starting to climb out. He swung the rifle around and dropped it eighteen inches, all by instinct, and squeezed the trigger as soon as the guy appeared in his crosshairs and the bullet smashed into his chest and hit the dead centre of his heart and it exploded inside of him, like a balloon being over-filled with water, just as his right foot was placed flat on the floor, and he toppled forward and landed face down in the dirt and gravel.

Shot number seven. Sweeping back instantly, he saw the guy in the next vehicle reaching down to grab a weapon in the split second that he was squeezing the trigger, and he lightly flicked his wrist down a slight fraction just as the firing mechanism kicked in to account for the target being smaller than he had originally calculated, and such was his incredible ability to almost feel like he was the bullet, he had judged the movement to perfection and it smashed hard into the top of the guy's head, about three inches above his ear lobe, and it blew the top of his head clean off. Parts of his brain splattered against the vehicle windscreen and he slumped forward, smashing his face against the gearstick in the process.

Shot number eight. Due to the need to adjust his original order of the kills, the last shot was now much more complicated than he had originally anticipated, and he quickly cursed himself for potentially failing to conclude the kills in the original ten seconds that he had allowed. To someone who wasn't a perfectionist, the concept of considering his actions a failure if he went over his allocated time would be pretty much impossible to comprehend. But he likened himself to an Olympic sprinter where every fraction of a second counted, and right then, he felt like he was an athlete failing in a major race. The guy in the vehicle was now climbing across the seat and reaching for a bulky looking machine gun. The guys' buttocks and legs were all that were clearly visible. But he knew exactly what to do.

The human body reacts in a very specific way to pain. If someone is punched on the right arm, their left hand immediately comes up to cover the struck area. If something goes into a person's eye, their hands come up immediately to the eyes. One part of the body will always instinctively adjust to protect the other. To The Optician, the bodies of bad guys were simple objects that worked to a specific mechanism.

He lowered his rifle all the way down to the floor of the vehicle and squeezed the trigger. The bullet tore through the air and smashed squarely on the guys' right ankle and he immediatcly shot upwards and back to the right and clasped his hand around the entrance wound. Mechanics, simple mechanics.

He now had a clear shot of the guys' head and he took the shot with absolute certainty, knowing that it would hit him on his right temple and blow his head clean apart. As a cloud of blood dispersed all over the vehicles interior, he lowered his rifle.

He was more than disappointed with his performance on this one; he felt that he had let himself and the guys below him down. He knew that he had taken longer than ten seconds.

He knew that it only took about half a second more but a failure was a failure in his eyes.

He told himself that he would practice some more when he had some downtime.

He then started to dismantle his rifle, ready to jump back onto his Kawasaki and head back to the plane to take up his position in the co-pilots seat once again.

'Jesus,' Lawson said as the three of them looked on in awe at the stunning sequence of shooting that had taken place in front of them, 'He is the most lethal killing machine that has ever existed,' he added, and Ward and McDermott nodded their agreement without needing to add anything else to Lawson's proclamation.

'Go, go, go,' McDermott said into his microphone, and the three of them came out from the cover of the water tanks and strode across the street with their silenced machine guns, locked, loaded and ready to unleash hell.

# TWELVE

At the rear of the building, on McDermott's command, Paul approached the back door and tried the handle. The door opened.
He ushered Wired and Walsh over and he counted to three, using his fingers to indicate each number, and he pulled the door open sharply while Walsh moved in from the left, his machine gun pointing into the doorway and Wired stepped in.
Paul and Walsh followed in through the tight hallway and they stepped through an opening into a small kitchen.
There were four people inside, two women and two men, the men were washing up and the women preparing food. They all turned around and looked at the three men, all dressed in black and pointing machine guns and they stayed surprisingly calm. They stopped what they were doing immediately, and Paul noticed one of the women turn off two gas stoves.
The four of them stood still, just staring at them with their hands down by their sides.
Then he understood. They were probably so used to Simone's men rolling up into their lives and threatening them and hurting their children that they knew being passive and non-threatening would be their best chance of staying alive.
'Is there anyone else in here?' Walsh asked the woman nearest to him.
She shook her head.

'We don't want to hurt any of you, do you understand that?' Paul said to one of the men who had a look of fear on his face that he had seen many times before.
The man nodded.
'But we can't let you leave, is there a cupboard anywhere?'
The man pointed to a door on the right.
'Go in there and wait for all of the noise to stop and then five minutes after that, start screaming. That way you can say we locked you in there. Do you understand?' he asked.
All four of them nodded and without prompting, they headed over to the door, opened it and walked in, closing it quietly behind them, Paul clasped the padlock hanging on the hasp immediately.
They stepped through the kitchen slowly, in a neat line, one stride at a time. When they reached a large opening they could hear lots of male voices and even some laughter. They stopped three feet short of the opening, still out of sight from whoever was in the adjoining room and Paul spoke into his microphone,
'We're in, three feet inside the kitchen. It's down to your signal now gentlemen.'
'Understood,' McDermott's voice came back.

They stepped over the three dead sentries and stopped just outside the door.
'I'll take centre, you take right Ryan, and you have the left hand side of the room Mike,' McDermott instructed.
'Remember, we have to take Simone alive, this will be a waste of time if we don't,' Ward reminded them.
They both nodded.

McDermott gripped the door handle and pulled it open slowly. As soon as there was an eighteen inch gap they could all see the backs of at least eight men in front of them. McDermott extended the door fully open and they stepped in.

It was a poorly lit place and Ward was surprised to see that it looked quite welcoming inside. A long bar ran alongside the right hand side of the room and it reminded him of the old-fashioned pubs that they had back home in England. All that was missing was a burning log fire and he could quite easily have been somewhere in the Home Counties on a winters night.

And then carnage unfolded.

One guy turned around and saw them step through the door and reached for his handgun.

Lawson was the first to squeeze his trigger as the guy was standing on his side, and he fired a short burst which ripped a baseball sized hole in the guy's stomach instantly. He then swung around to the furthest point on his side and swept a burst of gunfire back to the right, slamming the bullets into their backs, killing two more guys instantly.

As soon as Lawson had let of a shot, Ward opened fire. The two guys on his side scrambled for their handguns in their waistbands but before they reached them, he blew gaping holes into their stomachs, their guts and intestines starting to spill out even before they had hit the floor. Beyond them, he saw three guys standing who appeared to be unarmed.

They should have armed themselves, he thought to himself, as he put a short burst into their chests, knocking them back off of their feet and clattering into the tables and chairs that filled the room on their way down.

McDermott paid no attention to what his two friends were doing either side of him as he opened fire. First he hit the two guys standing in front of him in the centre of the back and then he aimed his machine gun at the table in front of them and put down four more guys in a three second burst of gunfire that obliterated their chests and sprayed blood everywhere.

As soon as they had heard the first burst of gunfire, Paul, Walsh and Wired stepped through the opening that led from the kitchen and into the bar.

The remaining men in the room were standing up to face Ward, Lawson and McDermott, and just as they had planned, over, and over again, all of the men were preoccupied with the men at the front of the bar and that gave easy picking s for the team stepping in through the kitchen.

Paul fired off a burst of gunfire and put down three men, all taking bullets that tore through their backs and punctured their hearts and lungs and they were all dead before they hit the floor.

Walsh made eye contact with the two South African bodyguards and shook his head as they went for their guns. They stopped immediately and lowered their hands.

Wired got excited, as he tended to do, and unleashed a five second burst of gunfire, putting down four men; the last guy he shot was sitting directly next to Simone at a long table. It was an action that earned a disapproving look from Paul, and so he stopped firing immediately, while Walsh shot the two men who were in front of him in the chest from no more than three feet away, and got his machine gun and arms covered in the guy's blood for his efforts.

Ten seconds.

Twenty three men dead.

All that was left was Simone, the two South African businessmen and their bodyguards.

'Secure the front and back entrances now,' McDermott said into his microphone.

'Understood,' Fringe and Fuller replied in tandem as they moved from their positions at the side of the building to their new posts.

'Where's all the Sudanese women?' Lawson asked, a line that had every man holding a machine gun in the room laughing.

Ward walked over to the table and stared at Simone and the two South African businessmen for a few moments and then he turned his attention to the bodyguards.

'What were you two in?' he asked.

'We were Recces,' one of the guys replied in his thick South African accent.

Ward knew about Recces. They were officially known as the South African Special Forces Brigade. And they were good.

Very good.

He knew that they specialised in combat reconnaissance better than anyone and that they had completed some of the most daring parachute jumps into battle ever made.

McDermott stepped forward and pulled out some cable ties from his jacket and pulled Simone onto his feet by his hair. He let out a scream.

He pulled the cable ties tightly to Simone's wrists and shoved him towards Paul,

'Take him to the depart point and collect Wallace on the way back, and take Wired with you,' he said.

Paul nodded and pulled Simone through the opening and into the kitchen

The only people left alive were the four South Africans. Ward approached the two businessmen who were sitting in stunned silence, glancing at their protection, desperately waiting for them to do something.

He looked at them and shook his head,

'There can only be one reason you are dealing with scum like Simone,' he said softly, 'And that is that you want to use the terror and fear that he has over the region to make more money for you. Am I correct?'

'No,' the older looking guy of the two said, 'It was only to….'

Before he could finish his sentence, Ward raised his gun and fired a short burst into the guys face. It literally blew his head apart. The other guy at the table jumped up and stood back, knocking his chair over in the process.

'So I'll ask you,' he said turning to the businessman who was now looking at his bodyguards, desperately willing them to earn the money that he was paying them.

'They won't help you. Do you know why?' he asked.

The guy said nothing, he just shook his head.

'Because they aren't dumb.'

'They look dumb,' Lawson quipped.

'So I'll ask you,' Ward continued, ignoring Lawson's comment, 'What did you want Simone to do for you?'
'We are making new arrangements with him for drilling equipment to be brought into South Africa without interruption,' the guy said with a tremor in his voice.
That was the answer that he wanted.
The rest he had already worked out.
He lifted his machine gun and shot the guy in the face. His head blew apart as if he had just shot a giant watermelon.
'We have to go,' McDermott said to him.
He turned and looked at the two South African body guards,
'We work to a code, you know that?' he asked.
They both nodded.
'And we have a mixture of Seal's and SAS here with us. If you were in our shoes right now, what would you do?'
'We would stick to the code. You won, we lost. We aren't the enemy, you know that. We have worked with both of your units in the past. We would walk out the door and advise you to get the hell out of here,' the taller of the two guys replied.
'I believe you Ward said, 'Get in your car and leave now.'
They both nodded their gratitude and walked towards the front door.
'Wait!' Ward said quickly, 'One question?'
They both stopped and turned towards him.
'Have you heard of The Optician?' he asked.
The taller guy smiled, 'Of course we have, but we also know he is just a legend made up to demonstrate how elite the Americans are.'

'Well,' he said as he passed them, with Lawson and McDermott following, 'I'd suggest that you leave by the back door, just in case he's real.'

**Babanusa – Sudan**

During the planning phase of the operation, McDermott had anticipated that Simone's men would be searching for them and that getting back to where the aircraft was waiting for them in Babanusa would be the most dangerous part of the journey. He had briefed everyone on the contingency plan if they encountered resistance and Paul had taken a different route to them back to the landing strip, as had Fuller in the other Land Rover.
He was surprised that not only had they not come face to face with any of Simone's men, the roads seemed as empty as they were on the way in too.
'I think I overestimated how much the people are loyal to Simone I think,' he said to Lawson.
'Fear doesn't always guarantee loyalty Mac, you know that.'
Ward put the satellite phone that the pilot had given him to his ear, and after a pause, he said,
'Ten minutes out.'
McDermott studied him for a few moments.
'What?' Ward asked when he saw him looking at him.
'You're doing it again, aren't you?'
'Meaning?'
'There is something else going on and we are all totally oblivious to it apart from you. I'm right, aren't I?'
'I told you he had that look when we were at Tackler's,' Lawson interrupted, 'I'm used to it. I'm just waiting for

him to hit us with whatever it is, so I can sit there and mumble to myself about being dumb and not seeing it sooner. Don't fight it Mac, just accept it as part of working with him. I did a long time ago.'

Ward shook his head and looked out of the window across the barren desert.

But they were right.

He knew there was something completely different going on than just clearing up another mess that the CIA had created.

He knew that when he got back to New York, he could start to piece it all together, piece by piece.

They eventually reached the landing strip and they were relieved to see that the engines were running and the other two Land Rovers were already there and they could see the faces of the rest of the team on board, looking through the small windows. They left their vehicle ten feet away from the tail of the aircraft and unloaded the bags of equipment from the back.

Ward noticed as he headed towards the plane that the motorbike had moved and was now lying on the floor. Perhaps the spotter had to go and grab some food he thought to himself.

They boarded, glancing towards the pilot and co-pilot, Ward nodded to the pilot they were good to go and he put his thumb up in understanding.

Two minutes later, they were high up in the air and on their way back to Khartoum.

They would be safely back in New York in twenty four hours' time.

And then the war was really going to start.

# THIRTEEN

**Washington D.C.**

'What the hell is happening McNair?' Wilson screamed down the line as The Old Man picked up his phone. He was just about to leave the office when it rang and he saw the White House number on the caller display yet again, and as much as he really couldn't be bothered to listen to the snivelling idiot of a Vice President, he concluded that he would need his help to achieve his objectives.
Or the bigger picture as he always referred to them. Giving him overall control of the region was important for a number of reasons to him and as much as he disliked the fact, it was going to be Wilson who gave it to him.
'What do you mean, what is happening?' he asked curtly.
'I've just had yet another call from someone who wants updates on your progress and once again I have had to tell him I don't know. I'm supposed to be reassuring him that I have everything under control.'
'With the greatest respect sir, you are not in control of anything. Right now, even I have no control. We are at the mercy of our British friend, but if you want to call him and speak to him in that tone of voice, I'll give you his number and you are welcome to do so.'
'I'm sorry McNair,' Wilson replied with no sincerity whatsoever, 'But I really need to know where we are with this.'

'You sound nervous sir. Are you sure that it is just a simple question of your sponsors demanding what they paid for and nothing else?'

It was a question that clearly made Wilson uncomfortable, as intended, because there was a slight splutter on the line, followed by a pause, and then Wilson eventually said,

'The elections are fourteen months away. It is imperative that we win a second term and the polls are indicating a very close race. Like it or not McNair, it will once again come down to who has the most money and influence to convince the people which way to vote.'

'Shouldn't policies come into it?'

'Don't be naive McNair. Policies have never come into it. Buying the networks and air time is what wins an election. It's not about the people for God's sake.'

He despised Wilson.

In fact, he despised all politicians because he knew that virtually every single one of them was corrupt, weak and greedy. He didn't even believe that most of them started out wanting to change the world with good intentions because he had seen even the new kids on the block start out on their political careers with the shady money men in the background, giving them the opportunity in the first place.

'As soon as I hear anything I will let you know,' he said.

'You want my private cell number?'

'Don't worry sir, I already have it.'

'How do you have it?' Wilson asked nervously.

Centrepoint hung up the phone.

**Stanstead Airport – London**

They stopped over in London to refuel the Lear jet and McDermott opened his eyes. He had told his team to get some rest on the flight, and everyone, including Lawson, had taken his advice on board.

Beyond the doors that separated the main fuselage from the cockpit, even The Optician had managed to get four hours sleep which was unusual for him, but there is not much to be looking out for when you are on a seventeen hour flight.

McDermott pulled himself up in his chair and looked down the aisle to where Ward was sitting, and was surprised to see that he was not in his seat. Spinning around anxiously, he was relieved to see Ward sitting next to Simone, who they had handcuffed securely to the seats at the back of the plane when they had boarded in Khartoum.

He climbed out of his seat and slowly paced up the aisle until he reached Ward.

He looked down at Simone and saw that his face was covered in blood and all of the fingers in his left hand had been contorted out of shape, clearly broken.

Ward looked up at him and nodded,

'Go back to sleep Mac,' he said calmly, 'Me and this guy are now ready to have a conversation about a number of things, isn't that right?' he added, poking Simone in the ribs.

'Yes, I promise I'll tell you all I know,' Simone said desperately.

McDermott shook his head,

'Some warlord you turned out to be,' he said as he turned and headed back towards his seat.

A moment later, the cockpit doors opened and the pilot gave Ward the thumbs up to indicate that they were ready for take-off back to New York.

Ten minutes later, they were high above the clouds speeding towards home.

'Now,' Ward said as he took Simone's badly broken fingers in his right hand and squeezed hard, 'My first question.'

## Adiela – Sudan

Yury Glushakov was dreading having to make the call but he couldn't put it off any longer. Moscow did not suffer fools lightly. And it especially did not tolerate insubordination in the form of lateness.

His Commander, a General by the name of Viktor Zhirkov, was a ruthless and unforgiving man. In essence, he was the Russian version of Centrepoint. He had the control and power to make any decision in the best interests of Mother Russia and he had a close relationship with the President himself. They had served together for a number of years in the KGB and while the American politicians always shied away from any involvement with The Old Man, the president made it very clear to everyone that Viktor Zhirkov was one of his most trusted men.

He had a direct communication line to the very top of The Kremlin in every sense.

He dialled the number cautiously, holding his satellite phone reluctantly in his hand, somehow thinking that dialling the number slower would make the response to the news he had to relay easier to take for Zhirkov.

He lifted the phone to his ear as the ring tones began. After four rings, he was starting to feel hopeful that Zhirkov would not answer, until his hope was shattered into a thousand pieces when a voice said abruptly,
'You were meant to update me three hours ago Yury.'
He paused before responding,
'Please forgive me sir, I had to make sure that I was clear of everyone, and you know the chaos that is everywhere down here.'
Zhirkov sighed down the line. It was a weary sigh, as though he had been awake all night and he was feeling both irritable and impatient.
'The Americans have been notified that all access routes have now been closed. Our spies have told me that a video was sent. I'm assuming that was under your influence Yury, so well done. It has certainly had the desired effect; I have been told that the video has bounced around the place all the way to the White House.'
'Thank you sir,' was all he could reply.
'In terms of the timetable, and proof, we need you to isolate and correlate all of the data as soon as possible. Once it is in our possession, we have achieved our goal.'
He wanted to tell him that a major obstacle had been put in their way, but then he realised that the events of the day would not prevent him from obtaining what they were ultimately looking for, so for the first time during the conversation, he felt that he had a starting point to soften the blow,
'I will have all of the data that we need by the end of the week, I can guarantee that sir,' he said, more in hope than confidence.

'Good Yury. The President will be very pleased. Your next posting will be to a place of your choice. This is a crucial operation for us, one of the most important that we have had in years, and it has to be completed in every sense. You know the benefit to Mother Russia, and she is proud to call you a son,' Zhirkov said firmly.

He was sure that the operation would ultimately be successful, because he knew that he could steal everything he needed. But he also knew that failure to reveal all of the details of the operation would lead to a thorough investigation afterwards, and a high likelihood of him spending the rest of his life in Siberia.

So he took a deep breath and said,

'Sir, we have a problem.'

### JFK Airport – New York

They landed at JFK just after 03:00am. The Optician watched as Ward and Lawson disembarked the plane and stepped into a Ford Taurus and drove off speedily towards the airport exit. He waited patiently as McDermott and his team unloaded all of their equipment from the plane and placed it into the two black Range Rovers that were still in the same place that they had left them before they had headed to Sudan. He had heard Ward instruct McDermott to take Simone back to his warehouse, or vehicle repair shop, as it appeared to the outside world, but not to speak to him at all and secure him to a chair with a hood on his head to disorientate him, before they would question him first thing in the morning. He smiled as Simone was pulled from the jet, across the tarmac and shoved into the back of one of the

Range Rover's, with Fuller giving Simone a hard kick to push him into the middle of the rear seat for good measure.

He had to admit, their plan was pure genius. The Old Man probably wouldn't be too impressed that Ward brought Simone to New York, but he had no doubt in his mind at all that Ward knew something that everyone else was missing, and that is why he needed him here. He had heard Ward insisting that Simone was taken alive no matter what, and when McDermott had questioned him and asked why, he had ignored him.

He had been protecting Ward for long enough now to know that when he ignored a question, he did it because he didn't want to influence anyone else's thinking, and that he was trying to get everything into the right order in his head first before laying it out for everyone else to see.

But whatever it was Ward had going around in his head, he knew one thing.

Ryan Ward would be right.

'Seriously, who goes all the way to Sudan and doesn't get to sleep with one local woman?' Lawson asked as they headed towards Ward's apartment.

New York is called the city that doesn't sleep, but in truth, it does. At 03:30am, the roads were completely empty.

Most sane people were asleep.

'I would have thought that you had someone waiting for you at home Mike,' Ward replied.

'Who says I haven't?'

Ward ignored him.

They drove another half a mile and Lawson then said, 'I don't suppose you are ready to share what you think this is really about yet?'
He shook his head.
'That's concerning,' Lawson said with a frown on his face, 'You didn't ignore me and yet you didn't speak. What does that mean?'
'It means this is much, much bigger than we were led to believe and that there can only be one possible explanation for why this has happened.'
'Now I'm really concerned.'
Ward ignored him.
They drove the rest of the way in silence and reached Ward's apartment in DUMBO. Lawson pulled over to the sidewalk right outside.
'Pick me up at eight in the morning Mike, we will need to see Nicole-Louise and Tackler first thing,' he said as he climbed out and closed the door without waiting for a response.
Lawson watched him walk into his building. There wasn't the usual spring in Ward's step that he normally saw when he dropped him at his apartment, and this concerned him slightly, but he decided that a few hours' sleep would probably put Ward in the right frame of mind to discuss things a little more in-depth.

Thirty minutes later, Ward stepped out of the shower and quickly dried himself down before throwing on some jeans. He wanted a few hours' sleep but knew that he had better call The Old Man first, so he picked up his cell phone and pressed speed dial'

'I assume that you have woken me up with good news,' Centrepoint answered, sounding remarkably alert for someone who had just had their sleep interrupted.
'Some good, some bad,' Ward replied.
There was a pause on the line for a few moments before The Old Man said,
'Can I tell the White House that Simone is dead?'
'Not yet. But he will be soon. But that is the least of our problems.'
'Meaning?'
'What exactly did they tell you we had to do and why?'
'You know what. Why are you asking me questions that you already know the answer to?'
'Just humour me and run it by me again?'
'The CIA had put Simone in power to enable safe passage through the region and into Africa.'
'Safe passage for who?'
'The big mining, mineral and oil companies. Why?'
'What politicians are involved?'
'Directly, none I don't think, but indirectly, a lot of them, because they get their campaign funding from a lot of these big companies and they will pull their big bucks if they don't get what they are paying for.'
'You said it came directly from The White House?' Ward asked.
'Yes I did. But the President and VP were not involved in the actions of Simone, neither were the CEO's of the big companies. Why so many cryptic questions?' The Old Man asked, starting to feel very uneasy that Ward was starting to question a simple assassination operation.
'And your replacement will reinstate the routes and everything goes back to the way it was?'

'Yes. Why so many questions. And why is Simone still alive?'

'Because I need him in New York.'

'All you had to do was eliminate him,' Centrepoint said, frustration now creeping into his voice.

'He's alive because I have a very bad feeling about this.'

'A bad feeling about what? In what way?' The Old Man asked urgently.

'We are being played, all of us, from the White House down.'

'Then take Simone out of the equation, like you should have done in Sudan. You don't need him here.'

'We really do,' Ward replied sarcastically.

'Why?'

'Because I'm pretty sure that Simone is being played too,' he said as he hung up the phone.

# FOURTEEN

**Park Avenue – New York**

'Explain that to me again?' Tackler said as Ward told him that McDermott had Simone safely secured in his warehouse.
Ward ran through the plan, the execution of the mission and what he needed him to do next.
Lawson seemed distracted this morning. Unusually, he had arrived at Ward's apartment forty minutes early to take him to Tackler's apartment and even Nicole-Louise had noticed that he wasn't his usual self.
'What's wrong with him?' she asked Ward.
'No idea,' Ward replied, 'He's probably sulking because I only gave him a three hour window to share some female company.'
She smiled and then said,
'You do know that is all a charade, don't you?'
'Of course, he's one of the best killers on the planet, certainly the toughest, he acts dumb at times but he's smart, very smart. I just let him go with it. It's good for morale.'
'God Ryan, for someone so smart you are dumber than anyone.'
Ward frowned,
'What does that mean?' he asked.
'I didn't mean about the way he acts, I meant about his constant obsession with women.'
'I don't follow.'
'Have you ever asked him why he is the way he is?'

'No need. Women literally throw themselves at him, you've seen that yourself. Most men would probably be the same if they looked like him.'
'You wouldn't.'
'I don't look like him.'
'God you are stupid.'
Ward was taken aback by her tone.
'Am I missing something here?'
'Mike is like that for a reason. He's searching for something. He goes from one woman to another to compensate for losing something,' she replied, shaking her head as she spoke.
Ward was completely confused.
'Seriously Nicole-Louise, I have no idea what you are talking about,' he said, turning his hands so his palms were face up as he spoke, and then shrugging.
'Some friend you are,' she said as she turned her back on him and headed towards her workstation.
He looked at Tackler,
'What was that all about?'
Tackler just shrugged and then said,
'So, when do you want me to do this?'
'I need to make a few calls first, you track the number and then tell me when you have us connected and I'll speak to him.'
'I'm still confused as to why you think it's a good idea to have this fight on the streets of New York?'
Ward smiled and simply said,
'I'm going outside to make the calls.'

**The Kremlin – Moscow**

General Viktor Zhirkov walked with purpose and urgency towards the President's office. There were very few people who were allowed to enter the office without making an appointment, or going through one of the four female KGB operatives that sat at their desks, or beyond the six heavily armed soldiers twenty feet from the door, doubling as his personal security. He nodded at them as he strode past and knocked three times on the door.
'Come,' the voice shouted from inside.
He walked in.
The president was sitting at his desk, head down and writing, so Zhirkov stood six feet from the desk, with his hands down by his side, waiting for the President's attention.
He looked around. He always revelled in the sense of history and power that he felt whenever he was inside the office, much as an American would in the Oval Office.
Behind the desk where the President sat, the walls were covered in thick, dark oak panels, highly polished and not a crack in the varnish anywhere.
Behind him, two flags hung down, symbolic of the new and old Russia, and the giant Persian rug on which he stood did not have one thread hanging from it. Before he could picture the likes of the immensely wise Joseph Stalin and the weak willed Mikhail Gorbachev engaged in discussions with other powerful men, the President spoke.
'How are you Viktor?'
'I am very well sir, thank you.'
'And Anna and the boys?' he asked, and smiled.
'The whole family is very well thank you sir.'

They had been close friends a very long time. They had served together in the KGB, eliminated those who had threatened the national security of the country side by side, and as the President had turned his attention towards politics and the good of the country, he had brought Zhirkov up through the ranks with him.
The only difference was that while the President had amassed a personal fortune that was in line with most of the Russian oligarchs, Zhirkov was simply comfortable.
'How can I help you Viktor?'
'The situation in Sudan has changed a little sir.'
'In what way?'
He paused; he didn't want to make the President angry. He had seen how he reacted to failure in the past, and he knew that their friendship would not get in the way of his displeasure.
There was a time when he had stood guard while the future President elect had tortured rebels in Chechnya, who had dared to stand up to the might of the Red Machine, and he had shuddered as the prisoners had endured the most shocking treatment before telling him everything that he wanted to hear.
'Your reluctance to speak is worrying me Viktor,' The President said, immediately erasing the vision of the torture that he had witnessed from his mind.
'Forgive me Sir,' Zhirkov replied, 'I have received a call from Comrade Glushakov and it's not good news.'
'Tell me clearly what this news is?' The President asked sternly, before putting his elbows on his desk and clenching his right fist to support his chin.

Zhirkov explained in the exact same detail that Yury Glushakov had passed onto him all that had happened. The President leant back in his chair and sighed,
'And we can trust the word of these South African mercenaries, can we?' he asked.
'Comrade Glushakov swears by what they have told him. He has told me that the Sudanese are preparing for war.'
'And this British man, what is he, MI6?'
'One would assume SAS.'
'The others that they spoke about, they were Navy Seal's?'
'Apparently that is what they said.'
The President leant back in his chair and exhaled.
For a moment, Zhirkov could swear he could see a hint of resignation in his face. He was sure it was resignation that he was going to have to destroy an old friend for failing Mother Russia.
But then he smiled.
'This couldn't be any more perfect Viktor.'
'I don't understand sir?' Zhirkov said with as much surprise visible on his face as was evident in his voice.
'A dual UK and US operation in Sudan, with both reigning governments authorising it, what could be better? There will be records, data, flight plans, and personnel records.'
He understood immediately the importance of this.
'Then do you want me to tell Comrade Glushakov to get what information that he can and come back to Moscow?' Zhirkov asked.
'No,' the President said firmly, 'I want him to offer the Sudanese our assistance in getting him back.'

Zhirkov stamped his feet, stood to attention, saluted and turned his back to leave the office. When he reached the door and turned the handle he stopped. He turned back towards the President and said,
'There was one other thing Sir. Something that I think will make you smile.'
'What is it Viktor?'
'The British man tried suggesting the man they call The Optician was working with them.'
The President burst out into a long, loud laugh that lasted a good five seconds, before eventually managing to speak,
'A fictitious character dreamt up by the Americans to frighten the new recruits and intimidate us Viktor,' The President said, smiling broadly, 'Everyone knows that The Optician is not real.'

### Park Avenue – New York

His first call was to Colin Buck. He had not spoken to Buck since he had said goodbye to him in California a few weeks ago. They had been attempting to bring down a sex trafficking empire that was run by a Russian National called Andrea Yeschenko. Buck had been stationed in Russia, undercover for a long time, but had to make a swift return to The States when his real identity was leaked to the Russian mafia. Buck had been put on the team by The Old Man and Ward had instantly liked him. His expertise of the Russian way of doing things had been invaluable.

McDermott and the team had teased Buck relentlessly and had dismissed him to the car to sleep because his snoring had been keeping them awake in their downtime. When Ward had first met him, he was immediately reminded of his old dentist in England, and the two of them had shared a running joke about the need to look after their teeth.

'Hello?' Buck answered.

'I did not expect to be contacting you so soon Colin. How are you?'

'I'm good. But I didn't have a choice. The Old Man demanded that I make my way to New York immediately and wait for you to contact me. I was curious though, he has no idea what you want my help with. Is it one of those times that you keep secret from us again?'

Ward ignored the question,

'Where are you now?'

'I'm in Times Square.'

'We will pick you up in an hour.'

The next call he made was to someone that he did not really want to get involved, but he had no choice. He needed someone who knew every bad guy in New York and where their loyalties lay.

On the fifth ring, a deep voice said,

'I thought you had forgotten I was alive.'

'How are you Sean?'

Sean Gilligan had come as close to death as it was possible to come without dying. He was a giant of a man and to see him lying in a pool of his own blood had shaken Ward to the core. The two of them had been in

New York at the apartment of some suspected terrorists when a sniper had fired a shot at them both. Gilligan had taken the bullet. Initially, Ward had assumed he had died and to avoid questions by the local police department he had made a quick escape, using the loss of his friend as the driving force to complete a complex mission. The Old Man had informed him that Gilligan had made a recovery in a New York hospital shortly after, and Ward had visited him at home to tell Gilligan that he had two young boys to think of and he should concentrate on a less hazardous career.

But he needed Gilligan.

'I'm good. Sitting behind a desk is the most boring thing in the world and is more likely to kill me than working with you. Why did you tell The Old Man to keep me out of harm's way?'

'Because you are useless at helping me for a start,' Ward replied, and Gilligan's loud laugh boomed down the line.

'And yet here you are calling me? I know you aren't checking after my well-being, you and sentiment don't mix, so what is it?'

Ward smiled to himself. He admired Gilligan's honesty. He was New York born and bred and of African-American and Irish heritage.

He said it how it was.

'I need you in the field with me Sean. A war is coming to New York.'

'Tell me more?'

The final call that he made was to Centrepoint. He knew that he wasn't happy with the choices that he had made so far, but that was par for the course on most missions, so he did what he always did and just spoke as though nothing was wrong,

'I think I've worked this all out,' he said as The Old Man answered the phone,

'What did you mean that Simone is being played too?' Centrepoint replied, picking up their conversation from where Ward had left it.

'That isn't important right now. It's trying to flush out the person who is playing him first that is critical.'

'Any ideas who?'

'I have a very good idea why but not who.'

'Explain it to me.'

'No.'

'Why not?'

'Because Simone is going to tell me.'

'I thought you said that he didn't know he was being played? You aren't making any sense Ryan.'

A lot of this wasn't making any sense to Ward, but he could see how it was all fitting neatly together.

The Old Man knew that Ward often saw things that no one else could see, including him, but for once, he literally had no idea what it was he could see,

'It was a simple assassination Ryan. Kill and replace, that was it. What have you found to make you so sure that it is more than that?'

'I'm going to find that out now.'

'By talking to Simone and then eliminating him?'

'No.'

'Sorry?'

'It's a little more complicated than that.'

'How?'

'It just is.'

'No more games Ryan. I want to know right now what you are going to do with Samson Simone.'
'When he gets here I will kill him.'
'Gets where?'
'Here, in New York.'
'But he's here; you said McDermott has him secured?' The Old Man said, confusion running through his voice.
'We don't have him.'
'So who do you have?'
'We have his son, the younger Simone, and I'm going to call his dad to come over and get him,' Ward replied and the line went dead.

# FIFTEEN

**Adiela – Sudan**

'I've been authorised to give you any support that you need,' Yury Glushakov said firmly to Samson Simone, who was pacing up and down in his command centre, 'I will kill them and their families, and anyone who has ever known them. Bring me the people from the hotel kitchen,' Simone spat.
One of his guards immediately opened the large doors and left the room.
'Do you know what they want with him?' Glushakov asked.
'Patrick is my son, my heir and the most important person to me. I want you to find him for me Yury.'

**University Ave, Bronx – New York**
McDermott's garage was set back in a row of six units on a small industrial park half a mile away from the Yankee stadium.
It only seemed like yesterday that Ward was walking into it for the first time. In fact, it was eight weeks ago. Such was the relentless nature of the life he life he lived that he had been to California, Florida and Washington D.C. in the subsequent weeks but it all just seemed a haze to him. McDermott had an identical lock up in every State in America.
And they were identical.
The main building had roller shutter doors that were big enough to fit a bus or large truck through them. They

were originally a shiny grey colour, but years of grime had turned them into a lighter shade of black. There was a sign that was fitted above the doors that said 'L & B Auto Repairs', with a phone number and website address below.
The website was fully functional and the number would be answered by Lloyd Walsh giving the impression he was an employee of 'L & B Auto Repairs'.
But the callers were always told they were fully booked and unable to take any new customers.
Inside there were two top of the pile Range Rovers with the window's blacked out.
To the left there was a small reception area. Ward walked through it and into the main warehouse.
Inside and to the right, there was a work bench that stretched at least thirty feet along the side wall with every conceivable firearm that the Seals liked to use, laid out in a neat line.
At the far wall directly in front of them were countless items of communication equipment.
As usual, everything in McDermott's world was organised.
To the left of the interior was a communal area which had a kitchen sink with very sparse coffee making materials on a table next to it, a refrigerator to the right, a TV that wasn't on and a radio that was playing tunes that were definitely from the 1980's. There was a small table with six chairs around it and an old beaten armchair placed in the far right corner of the table.
The seats were all taken by McDermott and his team. To a man, they all looked up and nodded at him.

'Our guest is a little disorientated,' McDermott said, nodding towards a guy cable tied to a chair ten feet away from them, with a hood placed over his head, as Lawson pulled up a chair and had the team laughing within five seconds of sitting down.

Patrick Simone was 24 years old. He was his father's only son and was as feared throughout Sudan as much, if not more than his father. He was much smarter, that was for sure. Whereas his father relied purely on brute force and intimidation, Patrick was a child of the new world where internet access opened up so many new doors and provided an opportunity to spread the word of his evil acts without any of them ever actually being carried out. He had instructed two of the more computer literate soldiers from his father's army to spend week after week spreading stories of his brutality over the internet. One such story he instructed them to tell was of how he made a woman cut out the eyes of her children and eat them just so she could save their lives. After all, having two blind children was better than having two dead children. The truth was, Patrick Simone was a coward. He had only ever killed one man, and that was from ten feet away with a handgun while he was tied to a pole.
Even then it had taken him four shots because he kept his eyes shut and also kept flinching every time the gun fired.
Ward nodded back to McDermott and he rose to his feet and followed him over to where Simone was seated. McDermott slowly removed the hood and Simone blinked as the bright, fluorescent light of the warehouse

replaced the darkness that had been his prison for the past eight hours.

Ward studied him with no emotion on his face at all. Simone's eyes met his and widened as he recognised the man who had led a team of men into his own backyard and taken him prisoner in an almost effortless manner. He was fully aware that any man who could carry out such a daring raid would not be afraid of anyone.

Ward eventually spoke,

'So, do you think that forcing a woman to cut out the eyes of her children and eat them makes me afraid of you?'

Simone went to speak but before he could make a sound, Ward continued,

'The thing is, I've seen it all. The last person I met who had a liking for removing people's eyes had his own removed by these very hands,' he said, raising both hands slightly so that Simone could see the tools of his trade.

He noticed a look in Simone's eyes that showed he was on the brink of believing him,

'His name was Pablo Cardona,' he said quickly. He could see that Simone believed him completely now. Putting a specific name to a specific act always had that effect on a person.

Patrick studied him nervously. He could see that Ward was telling the truth.

Playing at being a fearless warrior and coming face to face with one were two very different things.

Back home in Sudan, he felt powerful and untouchable, and the truth was, literally no one would dare question him. Even without the lies that he had instructed be sown

about his ferocity, such was the fear that his father inspired throughout the region, that the very mention of his surname, sent shivers running down the spine of everyone who came into contact with him.
Eye contact was something that no one made with Patrick Simone through fear of it being interpreted as a challenge to his authority.
But right at that moment, he was looking up at a man whose deep, dark eyes were burning right through him. They were eyes that gave nothing away, showed no emotion, yet filled him with such fear that he instinctively looked down at the floor.
As soon as Patrick's eyes averted away from him, he could see him clearly for what he was,
'But none of that is true, is it?'
Patrick Simone said nothing, which immediately indicated to Ward that he was correct in his assumption that far from being a warlord in the making in his own right, he was clinging onto the coattails of his father's evil dictatorship to build his own legend without actually doing anything.
Right then he had an idea,
'You do realise what the Russians are doing I take it?' he asked casually.
Patrick glanced up, the look of fear replaced by an inquisitive frown. It was a look that told him immediately that he knew that the Russians were involved but he had no idea to what extent.
'The South African guys you were making a deal with, what did they want?' Ward asked, thinking back to the extraction of Patrick in Adiela.

'Just confirmation of a specific access route. They were paying just for one straightforward point of access,'
'Do you normally make these arrangements?'
'Sometimes.'
'What's the name of the Russian guy advising your father?' Ward asked firmly, altering his tone of voice to indicate that he already knew the answer and was testing Patrick to see if he would play ball.
McDermott, glanced at Ward as he asked the question and frowned himself.
'Yury,' Patrick replied instantly.
'Yury what?'
'I don't know.'
'Why don't you know?'
'Because my father has not involved me in discussions.'
'Because he knows what a cowardly piece of shit you really are?'
Patrick Simone looked back at the floor.
Which was as good as agreeing with Ward.
He smiled to himself.
McDermott caught his eye and nodded to the left of the building and walked away. He followed casually,
'What is this about the Russians?' McDermott asked.
'I'm still trying to piece everything together.'
'I thought this was a simple replacement op? Simone out, this Bassong guy in?'
'So did I. And so did The Old Man. But certain things didn't add up.'
'Like what?'
Ward studied him.
'What didn't add up?' McDermott repeated.
'Everything is too neat.'

'What does that mean?'
Ward ignored him.
'Picking a fight with Simone was dumb but now trying to pick one with the Russians is just reckless,' McDermott said and shook his head.
'We aren't picking a fight with them,' Ward replied softly.
'So what's happening then?'
'They are picking a fight with us.'
Before McDermott could respond, Ward turned and walked back towards Patrick Simone.
'Do you know why we have taken you?' he asked Patrick, whose eyes had followed Ward back to him every step of the way,
'Because you want to exchange me for something?' Patrick replied, more in hope than complete belief.
'You don't hold any value to me, just so you know,' Ward replied flippantly.
'My father will come looking for me.'
'I'm counting on it.'

**Times Square – New York**

Forty minutes later, Lawson was pulling over to the sidewalk in Times Square, just a few feet up from Maxie's restaurant and deli. As soon as they stepped out of the car, Gilligan's loud, deep laugh boomed out towards them, and he approached Ward and offered his giant hand for him to shake.
'This is Mike Lawson,' Ward said.
'Aint you a pretty boy?' Gilligan said and shook Lawson's hand warmly, 'And aint you big too?' he

added, as for the first time in his life, someone's hands dwarfed his own.

'He's ex-SAS Sean and helped me eliminate the douche who put a bullet in you, so don't be fooled,' Ward said sternly.

'God, you look like that old boxer, what's his name, Marvin Hagler?' Lawson quipped.

'It's not just me then,' Ward said quickly.

'So, what's so urgent that you need to wheel an old desk jockey back into the field?' Gilligan asked.

'You know everyone on the street. All the different gangs, nationalities, religious fractions, criminals and everything, right?'

'You know that for sure, who are you looking for?'

'Sudanese.'

'Specifically, Sudanese what?'

'Men who would be loyal to a warlord from the region.'

Gilligan laughed,

'What?' Ward enquired.

'If they were loyal, they wouldn't be here. The only master the Sudanese guys I can think of have is the old greenback,' Gilligan replied, still laughing to himself.

'Just remember I can shoot you in broad daylight and get away with it Sean,' Ward said with such seriousness that Gilligan immediately stopped laughing, 'So do you have anyone in mind?' he asked.

'There is only one group of guys that fit that bill. They have a few small scams going on but nothing major, the usual people smuggling rackets and prostitution antics but that's it.'

'You know where they are?'

'I know that they meet early evenings in La Savane over on W 116th Street.'

'What's that, a bar?'

'No, it's an African restaurant.'

Before Ward could ask another question, Lawson's voice echoed out behind him,

'Jesus Buck, you looked like crap.'

'That's the consequence of sleeping with your wife,' Buck replied wearily.

Ward extended his hand for Colin Buck to shake,

'He's right though Colin, you really do look like crap.'

'Well some idiot tells me I am needed in New York and knowing this idiot as I do, I assume that he requires my expertise on certain nationals here, so I spent last night and this morning catching up with some old contacts. Unfortunately, drinking vodka is non-negotiable when old friends meet.'

'This is Gilligan, this is Buck,' Ward said to them both and waited for them to shake hands.

'Are you related to Marvin Hagler?' Buck asked innocently.

Ward and Lawson laughed, Gilligan rolled his eyes. Buck simply looked confused.

'I've heard nothing that would be of interest to you yet,' Buck said to Ward, 'So do you want to tell us what this is about?'

'Sudanese and Russians. What's the likelihood of an alliance between them?'

'Not very high. There is nothing that they could offer them. Why?'

Ward shrugged.

'So, just for my own clarity,' he continued, 'The Sudanese have no loyalty to any leaders in their homeland and the Russians are unlikely to ever get into bed with the Sudanese?'
Both Buck and Gilligan nodded their heads in agreement.
Ward went quiet for a moment.
They both looked at Lawson.
'Don't look at me. I gave up trying to guess what he was thinking a long time ago,' he said and shrugged his shoulders.
The three of them stood motionless on the sidewalk, waiting for Ward to speak.
It was thirty seconds before he said anything,
'OK. I've got it.'
'Well that makes me feel a lot better,' Gilligan said.
'No, I mean I have got how we approach this.'
The three of them still stared at him, waiting for him to elaborate on whatever it was they had to approach to be revealed.
'We can't concentrate on both at the same time, particularly when one opponent is in the dark, like the Sudanese are,' He said to himself rather than the group.
Buck looked at Gilligan.
Gilligan looked at Lawson.
Lawson just shrugged.
'OK. I've got it, let's go,' he said and headed back to the car.
Lawson extended a few giant strides to catch up with Ward and said,
'Seriously Ryan, you aren't making any sense. Help me out here?'

'Take us back to Macs,' Ward said urgently, 'I am now ready to make the call to start this.'

# SIXTEEN

### University Ave, Bronx – New York

'I hope you've got a hotel Buck because you won't be sleeping in here with us,' Fuller said as soon as he set eyes on Buck walking in behind Ward and Lawson, not forgetting the last time that they had worked with him in Los Angeles, where his abnormally loud snoring had kept the whole team awake until he had been banished to the car outside.
'Your wife doesn't complain,' Buck replied.
'You look well for a dead guy,' McDermott said to Gilligan.
'You lot still look as scary as ever,' Gilligan said to no one in particular.
The obligatory handshakes took place and then Buck pointed at Patrick Simone and said,
'Who's that?'
'This gentlemen,' Lawson said as he strode across to where Patrick was sitting, 'Is the terrifying Patrick Simone. One of the feared Sudanese warlords,' he added dramatically, before unleashing a sharp jab to the side of Patrick's face, just because he could.
Patrick let out a scream. A jab from Lawson was equivalent to a fully loaded punch that most average guys deliver. Ward was conscious of this fact and said,
'That's enough Mike.'
Lawson just shrugged.
Ward stepped over to Patrick and looked down at him and shook his head,

'What I don't get is how your father is so stupid?'
The glare in Patricks eyes told him that he had clearly never heard anyone speak using the slightest detrimental term in relation to his father, and that no one had definitely ever dared refer to him as stupid.
Ward continued to stare down at him, waiting for a response. After a good forty seconds, Patrick finally spoke,
'Why is he stupid?' he asked quietly.
'Because he is going to be dead within forty eight hours.'
The proclamation seemed to alarm Patrick to such an extent that he pulled at the cable ties attached to the arms of the chair.
'And what's your plan?' Ward asked with a smile,
'Break free and what? Fight me? You'll be dead before you are standing upright.'
Patrick instantly stopped struggling.
'There is a solution. You want your father to come and rescue you, and I need to talk to him. So as we both need to talk to him, perhaps you could give him a call and tell him to come and see us?' Ward asked in as reasonable tone that he could muster.
Patrick looked confused.
He was convinced that these people wanted more than just to talk to his father, but he had no idea what they really wanted.
'So you can set a trap for him and kill him. I would not do that to my father.'
'Twenty four hours ago, I wanted to kill him, but now I'm not so sure. I've established that he has been used as much as everyone else in this matter, so I might now be

willing to exchange you for some certain information from him, and then we can all carry on with our lives as before,' Ward lied.

He had no intention of letting Simone live. Not after seeing the game of Russian roulette that he had exposed those poor children to.

But he needed an opening to gain trust and start a decent dialogue with Patrick, and he was happy to say anything that he had to, to give the impression that he was more of a friend than a foe.

'What do you mean, used?'

'He got greedy, that's actually fine, it's human nature, it happens. I have no problem with that.'

'So what do you have a problem with?'

'That he is so stupid.'

'How?'

'He let himself be used for the benefit of others?'

'The Russian man you asked about, Yury?'

'Not just the Russians.'

'Who else?'

'The Americans too.'

'I don't understand any of that.'

'You're in good company, I don't understand any of it either,' Lawson said over Ward's shoulder.

'Why have Americans used him?' Patrick asked, curiosity now overwhelming his sense of fear.

Ward shook his head,

'That's a conversation that I need to have with your father.'

'How?' Lawson asked from behind him.

Ward ignored him.

'Your best chance of keeping your father alive is to let me speak to him. Right now there is a drone being prepared to hit his house and obliterate him. I'm pretty much your best friend in the world right now,' he lied once more.

He could almost see the cogs turning in Patrick's brain. It was a look that he had seen from the many coward's that he had stood toe to toe with over the years.

He anticipated that Patrick would say exactly what he hoped he would say after eight seconds and started counting silently in his head.

It took four seconds.

Patrick was an even bigger coward than he thought.

'I have a number that I can contact him on. Very few people know it, we can talk to him now.'

### Bismarck – North Dakota

Gary Chandler knew that he had gotten involved in something that he shouldn't of, simply because his sixth sense was telling him. Every business decision that he had made over the past twenty five years had turned out to be spectacularly correct, and he always had a feeling of complete conviction in every decision that he reached. He had not had that feeling once from the very first day that the proposition was put to him, and with each passing day, he knew that he had made a terrible mistake. But he was now trapped, in spite of the promises that were made to him, which would be honoured politically; he wished that he could just walk away.

His phone rang and he wearily picked it up,
'There is a call for you from Illinois sir,' his secretary said.
This was the call that he hated taking. This was the call from the very top of the tree, the call from the person who had made the suggestion in the first place, and this person was way too powerful to suddenly say that he had changed his mind,
'Put them through,' he said wearily.
There was a click and a brisk voice said, 'Hello?'
'I'm here, how are you?'
'The situation in Sudan has taken an unexpected turn, we will have to delay going public for a few days.'
Chandler felt the relief wash all over him,
'Nothing too serious I hope?' he asked, willing the answer to be that the whole situation had become so messy that the most practical solution would be to abort the whole ludicrous plan.
'Nothing that can't be fixed in a few days at most. You just wait for Schultz to contact you and leave us to worry about the complexities of the whole thing.'
'But everything is fully under control, yes?' he asked.
'Just wait for my call.'
The line went dead.
He leant back into his plush leather chair and cupped his hands over his face,
'What have I done?' he said loudly to himself as he rubbed his face hard, 'What have I done?'

**University Ave, Bronx – New York**

Patrick Simone recited the number from memory loudly and clearly,

'Zero, one, one, two, four, nine, seven, six, one, nine, eight, seven.'

Ward pressed the numbers slowly and deliberately into his cell phone so as not to make a mistake. He put the phone to his ear and waited, after a few seconds, the international ringing tone, of long, uninterrupted rings, echoed in his ear.

'Yes?' a voice answered

'Simone?'

'No. Who is this?'

'Who is this?' Ward asked.

'Hamid.'

He looked down at Patrick,

'Who is Hamid?'

'He is my fathers most trusted soldier,' Patrick replied.

Ward smiled to himself,

'You have one minute to get Simone on the phone or I am going to slit Patrick's throat wide open,' Ward said as menacingly as he could, 'And if I'm not talking to him in one minute, I will tell him that you delayed the call and you cost Patrick his life.'

He could hear the instant scurrying of feet.

If this Hamid guy was his most trusted soldier, he knew that he would not want to fail Simone. Thirty seconds later, he heard some muffled voices before a deep, gruff voice barked down the phone,

'Who are you?'

He knew that this was Samson Simone.

'I'm the guy who walked into your backyard and took what I wanted. Your pathetic excuse of a son. I must say, I'm disappointed how easy it was, and even more disappointed in how pathetic he and all of your men are. Not really an army are you? You are more like a group of uneducated and untrained hunters than warriors,' Ward said calmly, knowing full well the rage that those insults would create in Simone. The one thing you should never do to an African man was insult their masculinity. They were proud people.

'I am going to rip you apart, limb by limb and then feed you to my dogs. And after that, I will find your mother, sister and family and do the same to them,' Simone screamed down the line.

Ward smiled to himself.

'We'll put up much more of a fight than the women and children you kill, so bring it on, you will be crying like a coward within a minute, just like your pathetic little son is crying now.'

'I want to talk to him,' Simone demanded.

'Sure,' Ward replied instantly, 'But first I want something from you.'

'What?'

'The guy in the room with you, the Russian guy, put him on the phone.'

There was a pause and then silence, when Simone was covering the handset with his hand Ward assumed.

He now knew that he had worked this out perfectly and that he had the reason why all of this was happening, even if he did not yet know the key players involved. After a long minute, Simone came back on the line, 'There is no Russian here,' he said abruptly.

'Listen to this,' Ward said, and he leant down towards Patrick, clasped two of the fingers that were protruding from the end of the chair in his hand, and bent them back sharply.
Patrick let out a sickening scream that lasted for over five seconds. Ward was impressed how long the scream lasted, it would make the next part easier as he put the phone to his ear,
'That was my knife going into his cheek,' he lied, 'The next time I am going to cut his eye out and make him eat it. After all, that's what he likes doing to children. So I will ask again, put the Russian on the line.'
There was a pause.
He smiled to himself once more, he knew that the next voice he heard would be Russian.
'Yes?' a voice eventually said after twenty seconds.
'What are you, KGB?' Ward asked.
'No, I am just a Russian businessman.'
'Well that was an impressively quick response, so I'm guessing that you must be SVR. Let's be honest, we both know what is happening here.'
'No, I don't know what you think I am, but I really am just a businessman.'
'Well you've just confirmed you are SVR idiot,' he said laughing, 'A businessman would have been very concerned and frightened that I would accuse him of being SVR but you just shrugged it off. Your cover is blown Yury.'
He knew that mentioning his name would lead him to believe that they knew much more than they actually did, it worked, the three second pause was enough for him to realise that panic was setting in, so he continued,

'My guess is that the general's at the Kremlin won't be happy with you at all. Siberia would be the best case scenario for you right now, unless…..' Ward deliberately tailed off. If Yury prompted him to continue, then he would know for sure he was SVR.
'Unless what?'
He was definitely SVR.
'Unless you can fix this.'
Silence on the end of the line and so Ward continued,
'I want Simone, you want the route. It's a simple exchange. You bring him to me and maybe we can avoid any more bloodshed?'
'That seems reasonable,' Glushakov replied immediately. A response that told Ward that he was right in what he believed was really happening.
He could hear muffled voices in the background, a clear indication that Yury was in discussion with Simone and then Ward said,
'I'm in New York. I'll give you twenty four hours to get here and then I'll call again,' and he hung up the phone. He looked down at Patrick who seemed energised and more hopeful by the side of the conversation that he had heard. Ward noticed the hope in his eyes and smiled at him,
'Don't get too excited,' he said as the smile disappeared from his face, 'I'm still going to kill you, but I'm going to make your father watch me torture you before I do.'

**The Kremlin – Moscow**

Just ten minutes later, Viktor Zhirkov was knocking on the door of the President's office once again.

'Come.'

He walked in and closed the door slowly.

'Your body language is indicating that you have some concerns Viktor?' the president said as he dropped his pen onto the stack of papers in front of him and leant back into his chair.

'I've heard from my operative in Sudan sir, and they have located the warlords' son but there is a problem. He is in America.'

'And they have invited your agent to come and get him? In exchange for the warlord?'

Zhirkov looked at the president, was there anything he couldn't fathom out, he asked himself.

'Yes sir.'

'You think that they have an understanding of what your objective was Viktor?'

'No I don't sir. I think they are desperate to clean up the mess that their CIA created down there and they want Simone, the warlord, terminated and they want to do it by their own hand. I think it is fair to assume they have already decided who is going to replace him.'

'Perhaps they will get The Optician to eliminate the warlord,' the president said and laughed loudly.

'And then get the bogey man to chase us away from the region,' Viktor added and laughed loudly himself, before stopping abruptly when he realised by the look on the presidents face that he was the only one allowed to make jokes in his office.

There was an awkward silence for a few moments,

'So what do you propose?' the president eventually asked.

'There will be men in New York willing to help us. We have a few cells that we have funded with our money to get a stranglehold on the drug business. There would be no come back on us and the Americans would have no idea that there has been any involvement from our office.'

'Our office?'

'Your office sir,' Viktor corrected himself immediately.

The president pondered the proposal for a few seconds and then said,

'And you have faith in the ability of your operative that he can carry this out without any of it coming back to me?'

'Yes I do sir.'

'And if he fails?'

'Then he has shamed Mother Russia and will be dealt with accordingly.'

'That's the thing with failure Viktor. No matter how much loyalty you have towards a person, failure is failure. There has to be a price to pay.'

Viktor immediatcly realised that the threat was being aimed towards him and it sent a shudder through his body.

'I won't fail you sir,' he said with as much belief that he could muster.

'I hope not dear friend,' the president replied, 'I truly hope not.'

# SEVENTEEN

**La Savane Restaurant – 239 W116th Street New York**

It was now 5:00pm as Lawson pulled the car to a stop thirty yards up from the restaurant. They had dropped Buck off on the other side of Harlem as he had arranged to meet a contact from the Russian mob who ran a couple of crack houses and brothels there. Buck had already reassured Ward that he was pretty sure he knew the Russians that were most likely to help the mysterious Yury from the SVR.
La Savane didn't look much like a restaurant, certainly nothing like the grand restaurants that were scattered all around New York, where it seemed to Ward that the grander the entrance, the more likely people were to eat there, regardless of the food quality.
To him, from the outside, it looked like an inviting book store or the tea rooms that were commonplace in England. It had two panes of glass, only separated by a thick dark oak frame that ran down the middle, and a door to the right. There were two large pots outside in front of the window with tall, palm looking, green plants growing from them. It was just possible to see a few tables inside the restaurant from outside.
'So this is where they all hang out? Seems a bit quiet,' Ward said to Gilligan who was sitting in the back of the car without even turning around.
'There's a room in the back where the boys hand out. Their main man is a guy called Akram Agab. He was only on our radar initially because we thought he might

have had links to a terrorist organisation, but he is as clean as a whistle in that aspect,' Gilligan replied.

'Just so I'm clear, we are going to pay these boys a visit, warn them off prior to Simone landing in New York, and then we are done for the day because I have two friends waiting for me at home and a lot of pent up energy to release,' Lawson suddenly interrupted.

Ward ignored him.

'How do you put up with all that sexual tension swirling around inside of him all the time?' Gilligan asked.

Ward ignored Gilligan too.

He was too busy watching the three men who were walking out of the restaurant, moving ten yards closer to them and lighting cigarettes.

'Is one of them Akram Agab?' he asked Gilligan.

Gilligan craned his neck around the passenger seat, narrowed his eyes and stared long and hard, taking a few moments to adjust to the bright lights out on the street, 'No. He's a big guy, around six four. They are all too small.'

Ward opened the door and stepped onto the sidewalk. Lawson and Gilligan instinctively followed suit and joined him. He started to walk towards the three guys with purpose, not taking his stare away from them as he got closer. One of the guys noticed the three men walking towards them urgently and nudged the guy next to him, before saying something that they couldn't hear as they were still at least thirty feet away. All three guys turned to face them and stepped across the sidewalk and took up a defensive position, their weight evenly distributed on their feet so they were ready for any

confrontation and acts of aggression that might come their way.
In Ward's experience, only people with something to hide were always ready for a fight.
And these guys looked like fighters. All clearly African, due to their dark skin, and built with the solid bone structure that gave the impression that they could all pass as boxers.
The one who had initially spotted them had a thick neck and arms that bulged under the sleeves of his tee-shirt. As her got closer, he noticed that all three of them had their fists clenched.
He smiled to himself. He had no doubt that Lawson could have all three of them on the floor unconscious within five seconds without him or Gilligan raising a hand.
But unconscious guys can't speak.
And beating one of them would not result in the others talking either, that would only enrage them further and then they would most definitely fight back.
So he figured he would apply reason to the situation.
His reasoning.
The reasoning that always got him what he wanted.
The one form of reasoning that three guys who weren't afraid to have a fist fight with anyone would understand.
As he got ten feet away, and he was still striding forward with great authority in his steps, her put his hand behind his back, pulled the silenced Glock that was tucked into the back of his waistband out, swung it around to the front in one swift movement and squeezed the trigger.
The bullet smashed into the dead centre of the kneecap of the guy standing in the middle and his legs gave away

under his weight and he let out a deep, throaty scream that echoed down the street.

'Jesus Ryan, was that necessary?' Gilligan asked.

Lawson smiled.

The two other guys stood rooted to the spot while their friend writhed around the floor, still moaning.

Ward reached the group and with his Glock still raised midriff-high said,

'What do you think of Sansom Simone?'

The two guys looked at each other nervously, suddenly totally oblivious to their friends pain laying on the sidewalk.

'Well?'

The guy standing to the left went to say something but then changed his mind immediately. Ward spotted this and aimed his Glock at the guys knee,

'Last chance. What do you think of Simone?'

'We live in America now, we don't think anything of him.' The guy replied.

A fighter.

A guy who wouldn't give anything away, even when faced with a gun pointing at him.

A warrior.

So Ward squeezed the trigger and shot him in the left knee cap. His scream was at least thirty decibels higher than his friends as he clutched his knee with both hands, before falling to the floor and screaming, in between desperate pants of breath where the pain was kicking into every pour of his body.

That left one guy standing.

The last guy always talked.

'We have a loyalty to him only because he gave us the money to come to America and he arranged our transport,' he said quickly.

'But you are six and a half thousand miles from Sudan. I'm not having it that would buy his loyalty, not now. What else is there?'

'This guy is bleeding bad Ryan, I'd better call a paramedic,' Gilligan said behind him.

He ignored him.

Yet again.

'He sends us women, to provide them with a better life.'

'Prostitution?'

The guy didn't respond.

'Why does everything always revolve around trafficking and sex?' Ward said to no one in particular.

'That reminds me, hurry up will you, I have some friends waiting,' Lawson quipped.

Ward rolled his eyes.

'Is Akram Agab in there?'

The guy nodded.

By now there were a few people gathering across the street and Gilligan was getting nervous,

'There's people watching Ryan,' he said quietly.

'Take care of it then. Call whoever you have to call,' Ward said without even looking around, keeping his eyes fixed solely on the last guy standing.

'Take me to Akram Agab.'

Ward and Lawson followed the guy into the restaurant while Gilligan took care of matters on the street. Inside the place was poorly lit and dark. Presumably to create a particular type of eating experience, perhaps the guests

liked pretending that they were on a safari, he thought to himself. There were three rows of tables that stretched the length of the room and the majority of them were empty. The last guy standing led them between three rows of tables towards the back of the restaurant and through two large doors which hung from a thick, solid door frame. As the guy led them through into the rear room, the atmosphere immediately changed from a place of culinary delight into a more sinister environment. Inside there were eight, long oak tables with seating enough for eight people around each one, and all of them bar one were full. Even Ward knew, however ruthless and efficient he was when it came to killing, picking a fight with sixty guys would be suicide.
'Seems you miscalculated just how many guys he would have here,' Lawson said and smiled, 'Thirty each?'
Ward ignored him.
He was too busy focussing on the furthest table in the room. It was placed out of sync with the others and only three people sat at the table. One of them was a big guy, almost Lawson's size.
The hierarchy always insisted there was an order to everything. No matter where you went in the world, the bad guys always somehow positioned themselves above, and separate, from their foot soldiers.
It was just how it was.
Even without the description that Gilligan had given him, Ward knew that the big guy was Agab.
Simply because Agab wanted everyone who came into the room to know he was above all others.
The last guy standing headed towards the table as every set of eyes in the room fixed onto Ward and Lawson and

when they got ten feet away, Ward stopped and let the guy reach the table and speak to Agab.

A frown instantly broke out on the face of Agab and the two other guys sitting with him moved their hands under the table in a less than discreet manner and clasped whatever weapons that they had hidden.

Something was shouted in their direction in a language that Ward didn't understand, and then Agab beckoned them towards him.

Like a king summoning his subjects, which instantly irritated Ward, so just to antagonise him, he turned around and started slowly looking around the room, smiling at all of the other men who were, by now, staring at both of them with curiosity.

He turned back around to face Agab,

'Please, come and sit,' the last guy standing said.

They walked over to the table and stood, choosing not to sit by instinct rather than deliberately.

Seated guys were never good fighters.

Ward didn't wait for Agab to speak.

It was his choice to come here and so it would be on his terms,

'I don't like certain people, or rather certain types of people,' he said.

'Black people, Muslims or just Sudanese?' Agab said and laughed.

Ward ignored him.

'I don't even mind criminals as long as they have standards. I know one of the biggest criminals in London and he has certain things that are off limits,' he said, thinking of his contact in London, Charlie 'Dunno' Dunman.

'I thought you sounded English.'
Ward ignored him again and continued,
'The thing is, you traffic women for sex and make their lives miserable. That's what I don't like. It bothers me'
'So why do you think I care what bothers you. Look around? You're pretty outnumbered.'
He had such an arrogance about him that Ward had to resist the urge for a moment to pull his Glock and shoot him in the face right there and then,
'Because two things are going to happen. Firstly, I'm going to give you a chance of closing down your trafficking operation, the rest you can keep, whatever it is. You will accept my offer and be thankful for it.'
Agab burst out into raucous laughter, the other guys on the table joined in and Ward could hear loud laughs starting behind him.
Agab raised his hand to silence the room.
He now had a stern look on his face.
'And why would I do that? You have rules, you can't just threaten people. I love the land of the free,' he exclaimed and everyone laughed again.
He despised what the liberals and politically correct politicians had made the country become. How everyone who came and settled in The States viewed them as weak and stupidly tolerant. He admired the majority of immigrants who settled, integrated, and worked hard, but the criminal element exploited their weakness beyond belief.
It was only the bad people who did that.
He really did despise the crooks and the system.
He despised it so much in fact that a vacant look appeared on his face while he stared at Agab.

Lawson immediately recognised the look, and shifted uneasily on his feet, his right hand clasping his own handgun in his jacket pocket, ready to draw it.

He knew what was coming.

He knew that Ward despised certain people and what they stood for, and he knew that Agab sat well and truly in the middle of that group.

Without another word, Ward pulled his Glock out of his waistband in one lightning quick movement, and shot the guy sitting next to Agab twice in the centre of the face. The bullets hit just above his nose and his face shattered and his whole body jerked back violently. The blood and bone sprayed in all directions, covering Agab instantly, 'The second thing,' he said without sounding remotely phased, 'Is that Sansom Simone will be coming to New York very shortly. He will demand your help. You will decline the offer and be grateful that I am letting you keep the remainder of your little business after you have given up violating those poor women. I have no rules and there is a hundred of me. No tolerance, nothing, just my decision. Also, when he does contact you, I want you to call me immediately. Mike, give him a card,' he said to Lawson, knowing full well that Lawson carried cards with just his number on to hand out to the many women who swooned whenever they saw him and asked for his number.

Lawson dug into his jacket pocket and pulled out a handful of cards and tossed them on the table.

The whole room was quiet.

Much to Lawson's surprise, no one had risen to their feet or drawn a weapon.

All of a sudden he realised what, and exactly why, Ward had done what he had done.

'As I said, this is your one chance. Do not fail me,' Ward said and turned away and walked calmly out of the room with everyone's eyes, to a man, following him, but no one speaking.

Outside, Gilligan was talking to a paramedic who was dealing with the two injured guys when he spotted them.
'We done here?' he asked.
Ward nodded.
'I know exactly what you have just done and why,' Lawson said to Ward.
'What was that Mike?'
'You showed them the one thing that they are afraid of.'
Ward raised his eyebrows, an indication for Lawson to continue.
'You showed them our type of Warlord.'

# EIGHTEEN

**Park Avenue – New York**

The phone rang in the apartment and Nicole-Louise said to Tackler,
'You get it; you can give him the news.'
Tackler was used to having a bad feeling about things, anxiety was in his nature, but ever since a recent incident in California where he and Nicole-Louise had been kidnapped, he felt more on edge than ever. The fact that he was starting to understand the scale of what was unravelling before them made him even more anxious than usual.
He picked up the phone slowly and pressed answer,
'Hello,' he said wearily.
'What's wrong with you?' Ward asked, sounding a little more buoyant than usual and less matter of fact. He had noticed a slight change in Ward since their last mission, like he spoke to him more as an equal than down to him, and he thrived on this, but he worried for Ward. It seemed he literally had no limit to what he would do, and who he would upset, to get to the truth.
'You and your insistence to take on the world is getting to me Ryan,' he replied.
'So what do you have for me?'
'I hacked into the flight plans for both Sudan and South Sudan and drew a blank. There is nothing scheduled coming our way.'
'So then you did what?'

'I thought about what you had said and started looking at the Russian companies who have access to Khartoum and I got quite a comprehensive list.'
'Then?' Ward asked, and for a moment, he could have sworn that he heard him sigh, but chose to ignore it and continue,
'Then I looked at direct routes including a refuelling stop and found nothing. No one is heading for New York from Sudan.'
'You are missing something Tackler, he has to be on his way, if he's not already here.'
'He'll be here in three hours.'
'Short version please?'
'Not this time Ryan. You need to hear the long version to see what you have got yourself mixed up in this time.'
There was a pause on the end of the line and Ward eventually said,
'How bad is it?'
'Probably exactly what you thought knowing you, but it's pretty unsettling for us mere mortals.'
'So how is he getting here?'
'I then thought I was looking at it the wrong way so I looked at Flight plans that had Russian companies flying anywhere into Europe from Sudan and after I had hacked into all their records, and I found one flight that was only authorised four hours before it took off. And it was going to Amsterdam but no further.'
Everything suddenly fell into place for Ward,
'But the same company had another flight booked straight to New York, so Simone jumped from one plane to the other?'

'That is exactly what happened. Just five registered passengers'
'And it lands in three hours? Where?'
'White Plains Airport in Westchester County.'
'So about twenty five miles away from us?'
'Yes. It lands in just under three hours from now.'
'Good work Tackler.'
'Ryan, there's something else.'
'What?'
'Don't you want to know who owns the plane?'
'Who does?'
'Jefkept. The biggest state owned Oil Company in Russia.'

**Harlem – New York**

As Lawson pulled the car over at the pre-arranged collection point for Buck, they all spotted him deep in conversation with a group of six guys. It seemed to be a very animated discussion, with lots of hand waving and gesturing taking place.
'Where did you find that guy?' Gilligan asked as they waited for him to finish his conversation, 'He seems a little off base.'
'He's a good man Sean,' Ward replied, 'The Old Man sent him to us when we needed help with some Russians. He's the best we have when it comes to what the Russians do.'
The mention of Centrepoint's name suddenly made Ward realise that he had better brief him on where they were with the operation.

'I've got to make a quick call,' he said as he opened the car door and stepped out.

'He certainly likes keeping his cards close to his chest,' Gilligan said to Lawson.

'We've known him long enough to trust his judgement. He'll tell us everything we need to know when the time comes.'

'That's what worries me,' Gilligan replied, 'Last time that happened, when it came to the moment of revelation, I got shot!'

Lawson laughed.

'Do you have any single friends?' he then asked Gilligan seriously.

**Washington D.C.**

'Finally,' Centrepoint mumbled to himself as his phone rang and Ward's number flashed on the caller display. 'I've been waiting for you to call for hours,' he said curtly as he answered.

'Sorry,' Ward muttered, sounding distracted.

It was a response that took The Old Man by surprise. Ward had never once apologised to him over his inability to keep in touch, and he immediately knew that something was troubling his most effective assassin.

'What have you done Ryan?' he asked.

'I have a question. Did you authorise Gill Whymark to put Simone in place? I know he was involved in the supply of weapons,' Ward asked, thinking back to a chain of evidence that he had uncovered when investigating mass shootings no more than a week ago.

'Yes I did,' he replied without hesitation, 'Just like I am authorising you to replace him, but you seem to be making a very big meal out of a simple task.'
'Did he have any help from the Russians?'
'Of course he didn't. What is this Russian angle all about?'
It was starting to make him feel uneasy that Ward seemed to be heading off in a totally different direction to his original instruction.
'Are they the ones playing us?' he asked.
'I am sure they are but I can't make it fit yet.'
'Why?'
'For a start with their own supply of natural energy they don't need to step into Africa, so what would they gain?'
'Just causing major inconvenience to our companies down there would be a huge coup for them. It's how they work, you know that.'
'Not this time, I'm sure there is more.'
'Such as?'
'I'll let you know when I find it,' Ward replied and the line went dead.

### Bismarck – North Dakota

Gary Chandler was completely on edge. But that was nothing compared to the pressure that Dorian Schultz had invited onto himself when he accepted the offer that was put to him.
Twice in the past six years an election had been held to select a new chairperson for the Democratic Party and both times he had been overlooked. It staggered and angered him that a poor politician like Aaron Wilson

could end up being the Vice president while he couldn't even get elected to run his own party. He had come to the realisation eighteen months ago that he wasn't held in very high regard by his colleagues. The accusation that he was a sexist and out of touch politician, had all but ended his political dreams, and he had grown to hate the politically correct direction that politics had taken in The States with a vengeance. As much as he knew that politics was now about saying the right thing, rather than actually believing it, he just couldn't conform to the idea that offering no opinion was better than having an opinion that upset the liberal media. So he had convinced himself that he had earned the right to be suitably rewarded for the years that he had dedicated to politics, and the fact that he could severely damage his party for the contempt that they now held for him, gave him all the justification that he needed to see this through.
But now the pressure was getting to him and people were starting to notice.
He had control over Wilson, he knew that, but he didn't find that very reassuring because the rumour mill in Washington was in full flow now with stories of the elusive McNair having control over the Vice President on the basis that a number of secret bills were passed that gave McNair almost complete unaccountability, and when the content of these bills was requested, people had been informed that in the interest of national security, only a small handful of people would have access to them. He had tried bullying Wilson into telling him what they are, but for once, even he stood firm, so Schultz knew for sure that it had to be big news.
Yet they still kept him out of the loop.

So, he told himself once more as he picked up his phone and dialled the number he wanted, they've put all of this on themselves for trying to put him out to pasture.

Gary Chandler jumped as his phone rang. He picked it up immediately and his secretary said,
'There is a call for you from Washington sir.'
'Put them through,' he replied, almost on auto pilot.
Here we go, he thought to himself, as he felt nauseous almost instantly.
The phone clicked and Schultz's hostile tone said,
'Are you there Chandler,' before he even had the chance to offer a greeting.
'Yes,' was all he could muster in response.
'OK,' Schultz said firmly, 'I think that you are going to have to start doing some groundwork for your big announcement.'
'Everything is now resolved?'
'No. There is still a small issue with this idiot Warlord, but I've been informed that he will be replaced within the next twenty four hours, so now would be a good time to start planning what you are going to say to the world.'
Chandler had been putting off even preparing the announcement. For some strange reason that even he couldn't figure out, he had slipped into a state of thinking that if he never prepared for it, then it would not happen. And that went in the opposite direction of every business decision that he had ever made. For him, preparation was crucial and it had served him exceptionally well over the years.
'I'll get to it right away,' he said wearily.

'I'm surprised that you haven't prepared it already,' Schultz said, 'After all, this time tomorrow your name is going to be known all over the world,' he added with a snigger.

'And my guarantee of exclusive access in the region?' Chandler asked, ignoring Schultz's attempt to unsettle him further with his boast of impending fame, 'It's written down and set in stone I presume?'

'Yes it is.'

'Then once you've faced the world's media, you can go back to making even more money, so don't sound so glum about the whole thing.'

'I just want a guarantee that as you said, within twenty four hours, Simone will be gone?'

'I guarantee it,' Schultz replied, 'Now, you have a statement to prepare, so get to it,' he added and the line went dead.

Dorian Shultz's prediction that Simone would be replaced within twenty four hours was a little off. Because at the exact moment he was hanging up on Chandler, a coup was taking place.

### University Ave, Bronx – New York

Ward, Lawson, Gilligan and Buck walked into McDermott's warehouse through the reception area and were surprised to see that only McDermott was there, sitting in his old armchair staring intensely at Patrick Simone, who was still secured tightly to his chair. Simone glanced at Ward and then looked straight down at the floor as soon as their eyes met.

'Where is everyone?' he asked.

'The boys have gone to the diner two blocks away to get some food, maybe you three want to join them?' McDermott said, nodding at Lawson, Gilligan and Buck.

Ward immediately knew that was a signal for everyone to leave him and Mac alone, and so he echoed what had just been said,

'That's a good idea. I think things are going to move pretty fast in the next few hours, so it would be best to get some hot food now, while we have a window of calm.'

Lawson laughed and said,

'Or you could just say get lost you three because Mac obviously wants to talk to me on his own.'

'You are so full of cynicism Mike,' Ward replied, 'It's unhealthy.'

'Get lost you three; I want to talk to Ryan alone,' McDermott said.

'How rude,' Lawson said and then turned and headed back towards the reception area, with Gilligan and Buck in hot pursuit.

Ward walked across to McDermott and sat down at the table next to the armchair,

'What's wrong?' he asked.

McDermott shifted uncomfortably in his seat.

'That's the first time I've ever seen you look awkward. You're worrying me Mac, what is it?'

'I've made a decision Ryan.'

'Regarding?'

McDermott shifted his position again.

Ward now felt very concerned.

'In one month from now, I'm done,' McDermott said after a long pause of almost five seconds.
This was a conversation that Ward didn't want to have. He knew that he could normally talk anyone into doing anything, but here he was, faced with one of the few people that he trusted in his world, the greatest warrior that he had ever known, telling him he was finished. He felt instantly deflated,
'Can I ask why?'
'You can't tell me this is a surprise? It's been coming for a long time now. I've been sitting here for the last forty five minutes alone and it hit me that the time is right now. You should understand that more than anyone, you have always had moments of clarity when you know what the right thing to do is on every operation that we have worked together.'
As much as he didn't like it, he did understand,
'But why?' Ward asked again.
'Two reasons. First Paul has earned the right to take over, all I'm doing now is holding him back.'
Ward nodded. He could understand and more importantly, he knew that Paul would prove to be as equally capable a leader that his father had been,
'What's the second one?'
'You aren't going to question that?' McDermott asked, raising an eyebrow as he spoke.
'I know better than to get between a father and his son. I hold Paul and all the others actually, in the same regard that I hold you in. I know how capable he is, I have no worries on that count.'
McDermott nodded.
'The second reason?' he asked again.

'I'm getting old Ryan. Our game is no place for a guy into his fifties to be running around out in the field.'
'That's rubbish Mac. You are still fitter than virtually everyone I know.'
'You don't understand. I'm tired too. I'm tired of the death and constant living on edge that I have to do. I don't know how to switch off. I just want to do normal things like go fishing, and stare at the water and think of nothing, like a normal person.'
'You hate fishing!'
'You know what I mean,' McDermott said with a look of annoyance on his face which reminded Ward what a big deal this was for him,
'Maybe see how you feel in a couple of months?' Ward asked.
'I've made my mind up Ryan. I can't do it anymore. I've had thirty years of it. Could you even see yourself doing this in ten years' time?'
Ward thought back to the conversations that he had recently had with Eloisa about living this life of deceit and death for another twelve months and then going away to the Mediterranean to live a normal life and raise a normal family. He understood perfectly.
'No,' he said as he sighed and got to his feet, 'I think you have given more than enough and you more than anyone in the world has earned the rest,' he added, as he leant in and patted McDermott firmly on the shoulder. McDermott smiled his appreciation.
'How does Paul feel about it?' Ward asked.
'He doesn't know yet.'
The answer took him by surprise.
'Why?'

'Because I don't want him to lose focus.'
'When are you planning on telling him?'
'In exactly one month's time when I walk away and tell him that I'm going fishing.'
Ward laughed. It was typical McDermott. No fuss, no drama, just facing the task in hand with simplicity. He really was the most remarkable man that Ward had ever known.
'I'm going to miss you.'
'I'm sure I'll be providing a support role behind the scenes, so it's not like I'm disappearing for good.'
That gave Ward all the comfort that he needed for now, 'Well as I have you for the next month, stop with your tiredness line and get your act together. There is a big problem coming and it's landing about now.'

# NINETEEN

**White Plains Airport – Westchester County**

Russia has one of the largest petroleum industries in the world. It has the largest reserves of natural gas and the second largest coal reserves, as well as being one of the largest producers of oil on the planet. It produces around thirteen percent of the world's oil and exports a similar figure. The U.S. Geological Survey estimates that there is still a mind numbing twenty two billion barrels that remain undiscovered throughout Russia.
Pretty much all of the pipelines were run by the state owned Jefkept.
This simply meant that they were controlled by the Kremlin, which also meant that Samson Simone had some serious support behind him as the Jefkept company jet touched down in Westchester County.
Viktor Zhirkov had made the necessary arrangements with one of the SVR sleeper cells to inform them that Yury Glushakov would be arriving in New York and he would be making contact with the most brutal Russian criminals available. These men had already been informed that their assistance would be required, and that their assistance was not a choice. Failure to provide the necessary support would result in the Kremlin rounding up every member of the criminal organisations extended family in Russia and eliminating them.
The Russian crime lords that were absurdly allowed to operate on American soil, due to the weakness of the liberal politicians of the West, were scared of no one.

But they were terrified of those who ran the Kremlin. Glushakov had been told that he would be met at the airport by some foot soldiers, and transported to a safe house in Brooklyn, where he would meet a man called Igor Vasin.

Vasin had built up a pretty efficient and ruthless operation which was predominantly made up of convicts and petty thieves from the émigré community. The reality was that none of these men were genuine cases that wanted to settle in The States for political reasons; they were simply men that had been selected, or approved, by the top men who ran these organisations. The Russian criminal organisations were extremely well organised, and much more so than the original Mafia families.

Each organisation was run by a figure known as a Vor v Zakone, which translated to 'thief-in-law', and he controlled operations both at home, in , and overseas. The head of Vasin's organisation was called Yanik Korataev and his lieutenants had selected all of the criminal element that had descended on Long Island, Westchester County and New Jersey. There was somewhere in the region of fifty thousand of these men living in Brooklyn around the Brighton Beach area, which had become known as 'Little Odessa' due to its Russian and Eastern European communities.

Viktor Zhirkov had contacted Yanik Korataev in Moscow and told him that he had to provide Glushakov with a fifty strong army of his best men to assist in the rescue of a very important person, and that failure to do so, would result in the full weight of the president's office falling on his empire and crushing it.

He promptly passed on the same threat to Vasin.
A threat direct from the Kremlin was akin to a death sentence if their demands were not met.
Yury Glushakov stepped down from the plane with Samson Simone following no more than three steps behind him and stretched his arms high and wide when he reached the bottom. A thick set looking guy approached him and said,
'We have to take you to meet someone of great importance.'
Glushakov smiled at the man, noticing that he was trying his best to look as menacing as he could, forgetting that while it was easy to play on the fear of the American's that he came into contact with, trying to intimidate a man with direct links to the Kremlin was both pointless and foolish,
'No one is of greater importance than me you fool,' he said as his smile turned into a threatening glare, 'You and your family back home would do very well to remember that.'

### 3068 Brighton 6th Street – New York

Glushakov and Simone arrived at the safe house on Brighton 6th Street just an hour and twenty minutes after the wheels of the jet had touched down on American soil. The thick set guy who had collected them from the airport had not said a word throughout the entire journey, until he pulled the car to a stop and said,
'Mr Vasin is expecting you sir,' the threat that Glushakov had delivered at the airport enough to make the guy terrified of him.

He stepped out of the car without responding and Simone followed suit. He stood in front of the house for a minute and carried out a quick assessment as to exactly how safe this house was.

The house was unremarkable; in fact, the only thing that made it stand out was that on the plot next door sat an identical house. Both houses were only separated by a long alleyway that ran between them. There was a set of steps that ran up to the front door, which were adjacent to a large porch, and on the first floor there were just two small windows about three feet apart. He glanced down the alleyway and he could see that the house stretched back a long way. It was at least six times longer down the side as it was at the front. He noticed there was an excessive number of windows that ran along the side of the houses, but soon realised that was simply so that Vasin could always keep an eye on what was happening next door. He knew immediately that one of the houses would be where Vasin would live and the other would be where punishment would be administered to anyone who crossed him.

He looked to his left and saw two spotters at the end of the road, casually leaning on a fence smoking cigarettes, and a quick glance to his right reassured him that Vasin had his house in order when he saw another three men at the other end of the street.

He was happy with the location. It was now down to Vasin to earn his approval.

'We don't have time to waste,' Simone barked behind him and interrupted his assessment, 'I want to find my son and quickly.'

Glushakov nodded and walked through the gate hanging on the wrought iron fence that the airport guy had kindly opened for him. He headed up the path, and as he started to climb the steps, the front door was opened by an intimidating guy who stood at least six foot five and had arms the size of tree trunks, emphasised even more by the tight tee shirt that he wore,
'My name is Taras,' he said abruptly.
The guy was huge.
His frame literally filled up the whole doorway and he didn't seem to be in any rush to move out of the way. Glushakov continued moving forward and stopped no more than eighteen inches away from his chest.
Taras lived in a world where the tougher you looked the more effective you were. The whole point of being an enforcer was that you could intimidate most people just by speaking a short sentence or narrowing your eyes. Since he had moved to America and started working for Vasin, he had been generally surprised to find how easy it was to frighten Americans that crossed their paths by his simple size alone. In the backstreets of Moscow he had quickly learned to hit first and then talk, but here in America, and often to his disappointment, he more often than not never resorted to hitting anyone. A scowl would often do the trick.
He had arrived in America five years ago. He was invited to act as the standard muscle for a small time criminal way down the food chain from Vasin. His job was to simply collect monies owed to his boss from the local Russian community, small cash loans which were given by his boss and then charged at a ridiculous and often unpayable interest rate. He enjoyed the violent

nature of this work, the Russian men he came into contact with were loath to show any fear to anyone, no matter how big they were, and most of his visits would end with him beating whoever he had visited, regardless if they had paid up or not. He had quickly built up a reputation on the streets, and he was approached by a gang boss higher up the ladder from his existing paymaster and advised to accept the job offer that was being put before him. Part of accepting the new employment was to demonstrate his loyalty to his new boss by beating to death his former employer.

'Move out of the way,' Glushakov said equally as abruptly as the welcome that Taras had given him, a command that surprised the giant of a man for a few short seconds, until he had a sudden vision of his mother and sister back home in Russia and he promptly turned and walked into the house with Glushakov and Simone closely following behind him. The inside of the house was poorly lit, an environment that made Glushakov smile to himself, for he knew without doubt, that this was deliberately done to add a sense of fear to anyone who would be summoned there. Taras led them to two large oak doors with gold handles in the middle and opened them wide in a dramatic motion, as much to ensure that he could get his giant frame through them, as to convince the visitors that they were stepping into the lion's den.

Igor Vasin was sat at a desk which strangely sat in the dead centre of the room. Even more bizarrely, there were three leather sofas positioned behind him where five men sat. A strange set up Glushakov thought to himself. He would never be stupid enough to have people, particularly criminals, sitting behind him where he could not see them approaching. Vasin was an unremarkable looking man. He didn't look intimidating, but he didn't look soft either. He had short brown hair which was combed to the side, he wore black pants and a white shirt, and he had no visible markings that would indicate he lived in the murky world that he did. Taras reached the desk and stopped and turned the two men, standing loyally next to Vasin to his right.

'You are clear on what I require from you?' Glushakov asked, without any introduction.

'Yes,' Vasin replied without hesitation.

'Your men are now under my command until I have finished with them, is that clear?'

'They have already been briefed,' Vasin said as he reached into one of the draws in his desk and pulled out a burner phone and placed it in front of him, 'In the phone there are five numbers, mine. Taras, your driver Vadmin and two trusted men, Yegor and Robert, we will respond to any request that you have. There are fifty men available and I have already started asking questions as to where this person you are looking for could be,' he added, eyeing Simone up and down suspiciously as he spoke.

'It's really simple,' Simone interrupted, 'These people took my son and they will pay for it. I will cut them to pieces, very slowly, so I can hear them begging, so you need to make it very clear to everyone that they are to be taken alive when you find them. Their death is my pleasure. Do you understand?' he asked.

Vasin looked Simone up and down with contempt without answering.
'Do you understand?' Glushakov demanded.
'Yes I do.'

**University Ave, Bronx – New York**

Ward's phone vibrated in his pocket, he pulled it out and saw Tackler's name on the screen and pressed answer, 'Hello Tackler,' he said.
'Hello Ryan, the plane landed a couple of hours ago and we've been doing some more digging and we can't seem to get an answer as to why the Russians would be assisting Simone, it's like we've hit a wall.'
Ward knew why, at least he was pretty confident he knew why, but he was having trouble linking the right people to the right actions in his mind, so he was letting everyone run with it like he normally did,
'Is there any reason why the Russians need access to the Sudanese region?' he asked.
'Not with their natural resources,' Tackler replied, 'it would be a big expense for very little gain.'
'So maybe you need to figure out who could gain from it?'
'What do you think we are trying to do Ryan?'
'I have a question,' Ward said, deliberately ignoring the agitation in Tackler's voice, 'And I want you to put yourself in my shoes for a moment.'
'Easy, I'll just run out and kill six or seven people and then come back to you.'
Ward ignored him again and continued, 'You're easily as smart as I am Tackler, so if you had to follow one line

of probability over what is happening here, what would you do?'

The boost to his ego worked.

'Well, the first thing I would do is go back to the beginning.'

'You mean about Whymark putting Simone in place?'

'No. We know that the CIA and The Old Man did that for the benefit of the American companies and the politicians so, in spite of them claiming that it was done to bring stability to the region; we know exactly why that happened. I mean the beginning of your involvement. You're called in when the most complex and sensitive problems need taking care of. So if I were you, I would look to find who needs you to fix it the most.'

'Or who needs me to fix it the least?'

'I don't understand what you mean?' Tackler said.

'Let's just say that someone doesn't want us to fix this one? Let's say for a moment that it's not about Simone, access or natural resources. What could it possibly be about?'

Tackler was quiet for a good few seconds and eventually said, 'But why wouldn't they want it fixed? Simone is evil, the CIA are linked to him which would not go down well on the international stage, and the opportunity to make even more obscene amounts of money would end if you don't fix it. There is no possible reason why they wouldn't want it fixed.'

'So in summary, you think it comes down to money and the oil companies and the politicians who are in their pockets?'

'Yes I do.'

'Then I want you to do something really simple for me. Find out the biggest companies who have the most to gain by being able to move freely in the area, link them to the relevant politicians and if you're theory is correct, we will find the answers in there somewhere.'

Tackler was quiet yet again. Ward waited for the next question, which eventually came after Tackler had exhaled a long sigh down the line,

'You think I'm wrong, don't you?'

No,' Ward replied instantly, 'I think you're right. I'm thinking exactly the same. I just think that you are completely wrong as to why it is happening.'

'You realise that you say that to me during every mission that we carry out?'

'I do.'

'So why do you always goad me into asking the question?'

'It's simple,' Ward said softly, 'You and Nicole-Louise are the smartest people I have ever known, and if someone can make you think something that they want you to think, they can fool anyone.'

'But they never fool you, do they?'

Ward hung up the phone.

# TWENTY

**Adiela - Sudan**

The mercenaries had arrived twenty four hours earlier. They were made up of ex-DELTA Force and Marines who had performed a number of tasks for the US government throughout Africa over the last five years. Hired hands always gave the government complete deniability. Seventy five assassins led by a former DELTA Force Captain called Mark Robinson. He had a formidable reputation and had been further enhanced by the fact that he had once carried out a mission in his DELTA Force days accompanied by a legendary sniper known as The Optician.

Robinson indirectly worked for a company called Short Solutions, which fronted as a security company, but in truth had a very healthy annual turnover which was solely generated by payments made from secret CIA slush funds.
His brief had been simple.
Upon arrival in Adiela, he would be met by soldiers loyal to Phillipe Bassong and he would assist them in eliminating anyone loyal to Samson Simone, installing Bassong in a position of power. This would involve small teams of his mercenaries, between four and six men, accompanying Bassong's men into the local towns and villages and spreading the word rapidly and with a brutality that would cause panic. In every town or village there were men known as 'Jelema Lalajo's' which

roughly translated to 'People Watchers'. These men were Simone's eyes and ears. In the villages there would normally be one man who carried out this role, in the towns up to five.
They were the ones who would need to be eliminated and Bassong's own men installed in their place. Once Simone was blind and he had lost the loyalty and fear of his soldiers, he was finished. His task was being made somewhat easier by the fact that he had been almost guaranteed by the people in Washington that Simone would never be returning.

He had met Bassong after being driven to a house just outside of Adiela and led through grand doors onto a giant patio that looked out across immaculate grounds where Phillipe Bassong was waiting for him, dressed in full combat fatigues and leisurely leaning back into a swing chair. Bassong caught a glimpse of Robinson and rose to his feet,
'Welcome to Sudan' he boomed, extending his hand to Robinson, who took it and shook it firmly.
'I was thinking what we could do was….'
'You don't think,' Robinson interrupted, something that caught Bassong off guard, 'I don't like you. I'm a soldier and soldiers have loyalty, something you know nothing about. So you will leave the thinking to me, and do as I say, or I will choose someone else to take your place. Is that clear?' he asked, holding a steely glare into Bassong's eyes.
Bassong could do nothing but nod and this irked Robinson even more, the guy was a traitor as well as a coward he thought to himself.

'You have the list of towns and villages that we need to visit?' he asked.

Bassong snapped his fingers and a small man ran over to him and handed him a crisp piece of paper, he then passed it on to Robinson who studied it for a good three minutes without even speaking, something that unnerved Bassong even more as he felt that he was being questioned. He wasn't now feeling the power he had been feeling before Robinson arrived.

'OK,' Robinson eventually said, 'It looks like the strongest and largest town is this one he said,' pointing to a name that he couldn't pronounce but had a list of eight 'Lalajo's' next to it.

Bassong nodded.

'Then we will go there together with fifty of your men and twenty of mine. We will round up the names on this list and make it clear that you are now in charge. For the rest, you will provide ten of your men and I will give four of mine to ensure that you are sending out the correct message. How long before you will be ready to move?' he asked without once taking his eyes away from the piece of paper in his hand.

'Four hours.'

'Good. Get water and whatever else my men want so they are ready, and get them somewhere to prepare,' he demanded.

'You two,' Bassong shouted at two men standing in the doorway to the house, 'Get the captain whatever he wants for him and his men and get it now or I will cut your hands off.'

Robinson shook his head and turned and walked into the house.

## El Daein – Sudan

Six hours later, and after a two hour journey across dusty and mountainous terrain, Robinson was in the lead car heading into a town called El Daein. It initially looked more modern than he thought it would as they headed towards the centre but it soon became obvious that this was no different from Adiela to him. They pulled up outside a gas station and Bassong stepped out of the car behind him and approached his vehicle, he slowly and deliberately took time in lowering the window so Bassong would have to wait.
'My men will have the Lalajo's here within the next ten minutes. And I have instructed them to summon the mayor and all of the towns people too,' he said through the gap in the window, feeling back in control once again.
'Have everyone assembled over there,' Robinson replied as he pointed towards a large dusty patch of land which had two soccer goals about sixty yards apart.
Bassong barked out some orders to his men in Sudanese, the only words that Robinson could make out being 'death' and 'children'.

Fifteen minutes later, there was a crowd of well over four hundred people assembled on the square. For the first time, Robinson felt suitably impressed by Bassong and the speed with which he had managed to get such a large group together.
But he still didn't like him.

He watched as Bassong's men separated the crowd into four different groups. Women, children, men and a group of eight men who he knew would be the Lalajo's. His own men had split into a neat formation. Two of them stood at each end of the pitch, and three along each side, leaving the other ten mercenaries to position themselves in groups of two among the crowd.
It looked random to the untrained eye.
But nothing trained killers did was ever random.
Bassong walked over towards him and Robinson stepped out of the vehicle. Before Bassong could speak, he said, 'Let's deal with the Lalajo's first and talk in English, I want to be completely clear that they understand that everything is changing.'
Bassong simply nodded and headed towards the group with urgency while Robinson followed behind, slowing down so that Bassong got further away from him with each stride. This was not a random movement either. He knew that if Bassong waited for him to reach the group before speaking, then he would be confirming to him that he understood comprehensively that he, and more specifically, The United States, were the ones really in control.
Bassong reached the group and looked back over his shoulder.
And then waited for Robinson to catch up.
When he finally stopped to the left of Bassong, ten seconds had passed.
Bassong began his declaration of intent, something he had been practising over and over for the past week, 'It is time for change people,' he shouted, his voice booming as he turned three hundred and sixty degrees so

that everyone in the square would be able to get a glimpse of his face, 'I am the change. There is no more Samson Simone,' he continued and then spat on the floor as he said his name, an action which was the ultimate insult to a Sudanese male.

Some of the women gasped while the men immediately looked at the floor. The Lalajo's looked at Bassong with disbelief.

'I have killed him with my bare hands,' he lied, 'I am now the only master that you all have. You will all kneel and pledge your loyalty to me.'

Almost in an instant, everyone fell to the floor.

Apart from two people.

One was a woman well into her eighties, the challenge of kneeling down seemingly too much for her, and the other was a young boy who was holding a wooden crutch in each hand.

Bassong immediately caught sight of them.

'Deal with the disobedient animals,' he screamed to no one in particular.

One of his men standing next to the children lifted his machine gun immediately and unleashed a short automatic burst of gunfire into the young boys' stomach. His intestines spilled out almost immediately and the children on either side of him were covered in thick blood. The whole group screamed.

At the same time, one of his men standing next to the group of women to the left of the children, pulled out his handgun from its holster and fired two quick shots into the old woman's head. The crack of the gunfire echoed around the square even after she had slumped to a distorted shape on the floor.

'Now to deal with you traitors,' Bassong shouted even louder as he stepped forward towards the line of Lalajo's, completely ignoring the unnecessary death of an old woman and child, 'You cannot be trusted to be as vigilant for me as you were for the weak coward Simone, so I will give you a simple choice of death with honour or death for your whole families,' he added, slowly waving his arm towards the two groups of women and children for added effect and to impress Robinson at the same time.

But Robinson wasn't watching.

He was too busy making eye contact with his men on the pitch.

He gently shook his head, and to a man, they all nodded once gently to confirm that they understood.

'Those of you that want to die with honour and save your families, stand up now,' Bassong demanded.

All eight of them stood up, slowly and reluctantly, but they all stood up.

'At least you have honour,' he said dismissively, and he pulled out his handgun from his side holster and stepped to the left of the line, pushed his gun against the man's forehead standing furthest away and pulled the trigger.

One of the Lalajo's turned to run and was cut down by a burst of automatic fire from one of Bassong's men.

Bassong looked at his dead body lying in the dry dirt in disgust,

'Where are this man's family?' he shouted to the group of women.

No one looked up from the floor.

'I will ask one more time, show me his family or I will kill all of the children right now,' he screamed.

In an instant, at least ten women pointed at a woman kneeling three rows back, sobbing gently.
'Come here now!'
The woman slowly got to her feet and stepped over the two women in front of her, glaring at one of those who had given her up as she did so.
'Get your children now,' Bassong demanded. The woman paused for a moment,
'We had no children,' she said through her sobs.
'Bassong slapped her hard on her face and she fell to the floor,
'You,' he shouted to a woman kneeling at the front of the group, 'You have ten seconds to bring her children to me or all of the children die.'
The woman looked at the others around her and Robinson noticed at least six others prompting her to give them up to save their own children.
She stood up, moved to the group on the side and pointed at two young girls, neither of them could have been more than ten.
Robinson knew what was going to happen and he didn't like it, but this had to be done to an exact specification. All of his men were looking at him, waiting for the nod. He gently and reluctantly shook his head.
One of the men stepped forward and pulled the young girls out into the opening between the groups and threw them on the floor by Bassong's feet.
Without any hesitation, he pointed his gun at them both and fired three shots into each of them.
Silence fell over the square.
Robinson's men all looked at him; he could tell that they were becoming agitated.

He gently shook his head.
'This is what happens if you don't die with honour,' Bassong shouted out, turning to face the group of Lalajo's again, 'Does anyone else want to run?'
The men all stood still.
He then proceeded to walk along the line putting a bullet into the forehead of every man as the women and children screamed.
Thirty seconds later, there were eight dead bodies in a neat line at his feet.
'Now,' he declared as he strode over to the group of men, I need ten new Lalajo's, any volunteers?'
The whole group of men raised their hands, 'Good,' he said feeling very satisfied that he had shown that he was even more merciless than Simone, 'My men will organise you.'
He turned to face Robinson and before he could speak, he noticed something odd.
Robinson nodded his head.
And immediately the square was filled with the noise of automatic gunfire. Bassong fell to the floor and put his hands over his head like the coward that he was and Robinson just stood motionless, not moving a muscle.
After fifteen seconds, the noise stopped and an eerie silence descended over the square.
'Stand up,' Robinson shouted to Bassong.
Bassong looked up and got to his feet slowly, he could see the dead bodies of his men everywhere he looked. He was trying to count them as he looked around, right, left, in front, and behind.
'We've just killed twenty five of them, 'Robinson said casually,' We will let the others live.'

Confusion consumed Bassong. Robinson noticed this, 'We are allowing this man to rule you,' he shouted out to the civilians who were all still knelt on the floor, 'But make no mistake, we are the real masters, and whatever fear you have for them, you should be much more afraid of us. If we have to come back here again, you will all die. And there will be lots more of us next time.'
No one spoke.
'Just so you're clear,' he said to Bassong as he finally reached an upright position, 'You are there master, but we are yours, and if you ever get greedy like Simone and try and push us out, you will wish that you had never been born. This isn't a partnership, this is us doing you a favour so don't ever forget that. Understood?'
Bassong nodded immediately.
Robinson hated him, he hated all cowards.
'Good,' he said casually, now can we leave this crap hole,' he added as he turned and strode purposefully towards his vehicle.

Inside the vehicle, he pulled out his satellite phone and dialled the number he had for Washington D.C. and waited for the call to connect.
Eventually it rang.
'Hello' the voice said curtly.
'The mission has been completed to your exact specification Sir,' Robinson said without waiting for any questions, 'Bassong now has control of all of the men and they have sworn their allegiance to him. A few of the men are picking off the few loyal soldiers that are left, but within twenty four hours they will be eliminated. You now have control of the region.'

'Stay there for a week and make sure that the transition of power is completed without any hitches, is that clear?'
'Understood,' Robinson replied, just before he heard the line go dead.

In Washington Centrepoint leant back into his chair and smiled to himself. He now had control of the region through Bassong, and with that control came an ability to choose who went there, and the idiot Vice President Wilson had even begged him to do it. Once again, everything had been handed to him on a plate through the greed of the politicians and money men, and now he was within touching distance of being the force in Washington that he had always planned on being.
Finally, he thought to himself, I can do things my way.

He now just needed Ryan Ward to piece everything together and identify who was behind things to get the complete picture, and with it the complete control.
And he was positive that Ward, his most prized asset and most revered operative would get to the bottom of it.
He always did.

# TWENTY ONE

**430 South Capitol Street SE - Washington D.C.**

Dorian Schultz was no longer a Democrat. That had been confirmed by the phone call that he had just received. He had just spoken to the head of the National Committee who had told him that yet another complaint of harassment had been lodged regarding his behaviour, and unfortunately, this would be the last time that they would be able to brush it under the carpet. The whole world of politics had become ludicrous to him. Being a senior Democrat used to represent power and social standing. He was becoming more and more disillusioned at the influence that the liberal element had on politics and the media now. He hated them for their self-righteous views. And he hated the power they now wielded. Liberalism really was everywhere. He knew, deep down, that even the people he represented hated them, but he was powerless to stand up to them. It seemed to him that everyone had rights apart from the middle class Americans that made his country great. The ethnic minorities, the non-heterosexuals, the refugee's and the religious zealots all had people falling over themselves to protect them, and he knew that people were now too scared to say anything that might offend anyone within those groups. The country was becoming weak and everyone was laughing at them.
And the empowerment of women and their constant complaining about him was the worst part of it. The women who used to come to Washington with ambition

understood that this was just the way it was, and if they wanted to get on, there would be certain expectations on them from senior politicians.
Even former president Bill Clinton played this game.

The latest woman to have the nerve to think she had reason to complain was a young intern by the name of Sasha Holland. A pretty young thing from Houston who had been working at the Democratic headquarters on an internship, and he knew she had taken a shine to him in spite of the fact he was nearly forty years older than her. Her smiling and willingness to impress him was her way of saying she was attracted to him. What else could it be? He had arranged for her to work late, and when they had finished, he had said that as a reward that he would take her out for a nice dinner. She accepted and he had done this countless times. He knew that if she could be seen out and about with him that it would do her career no harm at all. He had plied her with drinks and at the end of the evening, suggested that they share a cab back home. Once in the cab, he had leant over to kiss her and he touched her leg and she had completely overreacted and become upset. This was typical of the young women who came to Washington, they always led people on. She then had the nerve to make a complaint, something he had just told the secretary to the chairman on the phone was complete fabrication and without foundation, and she was just yet another young woman trying to work her way up in politics by lying.

Without even realising it, Dorian Schultz was everything that was wrong with people and politicians in the twenty-first century. He literally saw nothing wrong with his actions. He was a despicable human being in every way. But in his archaic mind, he was the victim.

So now, everything that happened from this point forward would be for himself.

Any doubts he had about what he was doing had been comprehensively wiped out by the phone call that he had just received. Now he was well and truly going to put pressure on Gary Chandler.

## Bismarck – North Dakota

Gary Chandler had been expecting the call from Schultz and yet he didn't want it to come. The moment he had confirmation that the access route was all his, he knew that Schultz would be issuing the one clear instruction that he had insisted was the only non-negotiable part of their deal. Chandler had agreed, and now he was wishing that he wasn't so driven by greed. He almost envied the normal men who worked his oilfields and rigs because they never had this kind of problem to worry about.
His phone rang.
'There is a call for you from Washington D.C. sir' his secretary said.
'OK' was all he could muster in response as he heard the click of the connection, which today, seemed much louder than normal.
'Hello, Chandler?' Shultz's voice boomed down the line. Even with that simple question, Gary Chandler could tell that Dorian Schultz seemed extremely agitated.

'Hello Mr Schultz,' he passively replied.
'The time has come for you to earn your money,' Shultz declared, 'You need to let the Democratic Chairman know that you will no longer fund the party due to the rumours that you have heard coming out of Sudan. Then as soon as the Washington Post contacts you, and they will, you can explain that such an upstanding and transparent company as yourself cannot be involved with a political party that sponsors people who carry out what amounts to genocide in the region.'
Chandler felt a sick feeling in the pit of his stomach. He didn't want to ask Schultz what he meant by 'Genocide' and he certainly didn't want to be complicit in anything so serious. He somehow had always known that the CIA used warlords to maintain control in the region and their methods might have been a little extreme, but he had never given any thought at all to the victims. He was too busy running a billion dollar company.
His thoughts were broken by an even more agitated sounding Schultz,
'Are you there Chandler?'
'Yes, sorry,' he mumbled, 'So does that mean that I now have access to the region and we can start moving our equipment? He asked.
'Not yet, I need to get confirmation from my source in Washington. As soon as he gives me the go ahead, you'll know. It will take twenty four hours for the post to get wind of your decision.'
'And the initial guarantee that only my company will have access still stands?' Chandler asked, returning to the greedy corporate shark that he was in an instant.

'If you do exactly what you signed up for and stick to it, regardless of the pressure that gets put on you by the VP or even the President, then as agreed, I will ensure that your competitors have to go a very long way around to get anywhere.'

'OK. I'm on board and will make the call after we have finished this conversation.'

'It's finished,' Schultz said curtly and the line went dead.

Gary Chandler placed the handset back and with his elbows resting firmly on his desk, planted his face into his hands. This whole sequence of events was escalating out of control, he could feel it. He was fully aware that he was just a simple pawn in a grand game of chess, and he was starting to become more and more convinced that somewhere down the line, this was all going to come back to haunt him. It wasn't Schultz or even the possibility of the President putting pressure on him that was bothering him. For the first time, he realised that there was a much bigger play going on that he was totally oblivious to. And even more worryingly, that he wasn't a part of.

**Washington D.C.**

Just forty minutes after Gary Chandler had made the call to the Democratic headquarters, the phone on Centrepoint's desk was ringing and the White House number illuminated on the caller display. Just because he could, and he knew it would infuriate Vice President Wilson once again, he let it ring out, and told himself that it would ring again in two minutes. Thirty seconds later, it rang again.

'Hello?'

'McNair, what on earth is happening?' Wilson almost screamed down the line.

'Who is this?' Centrepoint asked, trying his best to make Wilson feel insignificant once more.

'It's me, Vice President Wilson. What on earth is happening in Africa for God's sake?'

'I don't know what you are asking?'

'How has word of your operation got out to our contributors?'

The Old Man paused for a moment; he literally had no idea what Wilson was talking about.

'Well?' the Vice President demanded.

'Tell me exactly what you know?'

'One of our main contributors, Gary Chandler has withdrawn his funding for the party based on apparent rumours coming out of Sudan.'

'Chandler?' Centrepoint replied, 'The boss of Sovec Oil?'

'Yes.'

The Old Man knew of Chandler. He knew every single contributor to both parties and he had an extensive log of subsequent deals and favours that were given to them for the large sums that they invested in getting people elected. He knew that if it ever came to light then what little faith was left in democracy in the States would evaporate in an instant. There was no honour in politics. Everything was done for financial gain. The bosses of all major companies in America, whether that was in the oil, tech, weapon or construction business, all had at least three or four politicians in their pocket that enabled them to make more and more profit, often unopposed and always without fair competition.

What didn't make sense to him was why Chandler would suddenly stop funding the party when the main benefactor of what they were doing with deposing Simone would be Sovec Oil.

He suddenly remembered that Ward had said that maybe they were all being played, and an unusual haze seemed to cloud his mind and he couldn't see a clear picture like he normally could.

'What rumours had he heard?' he eventually asked.

'He told the chairman that his men down there had heard of our support for Simone and acts of genocide being committed to our knowledge. Can you believe that? Genocide! That would bring this whole administration to its knees.'

'What are you doing to keep it under wraps?'

'I'm going to have to call him, and if that fails, I'm going to have to get the president to call him. So where exactly are we with Simone?'

'He's been taken care off. We have installed Bassong in his place and my men are just ensuring a smooth transition of power. The region is now fully under our control, and I can assure you that Bassong will be compliant in every way,' he said firmly, thinking back to his conversation earlier that day with Captain Mark Robinson who had called him from the square in El Daein.

'So if I offer Chandler immediate safe passage, can that be guaranteed?' Wilson asked, sounding a little less agitated now.

'Yes it can. You have my own personal guarantee on that.'

'Then I'll call him with that now and hope I can change his mind. Don't go anywhere McNair, I might need you.'

'With respect Wilson,' Centrepoint said curtly, clearly affording the Vice President no respect, 'I've done exactly what I agreed to do for you, even though it was an impossible task, so if you have problems with your contributors that is a party matter and nothing that concerns me. Goodnight,' he said abruptly and slammed the phone down.

He immediately hit speed dial for Ward, not expecting him to answer, surprisingly, he did,

'Hello?' Ward said.

'Where are you?'

'Babysitting, why?'

'Something else is going on here, what is it?'

'You tell me, you're the boss.'

'I'm not in the mood for our usual sparring match Ryan, just give me what you think?'

'I don't know to be sure yet, I have my suspicions but can't even speculate on that being right until I have dealt with Simone.'

'Unusually, I can't make sense of this,' Centrepoint said wearily, 'This was meant to be pretty straightforward, you sorted out Simone, I sorted out putting Bassong into control, and Wilson would leave me to look after the area ensuring that an element of calm got restored. Now one of the main contributors to the party has withdrawn his support because he has heard rumours of genocide. What doesn't add up is that this contributor stood to benefit more than anyone else from access to the area.

Some feedback that you have a few ideas what is happening would be much appreciated.'

Ward could hear a tired tone in The Old Man's voice that he hadn't heard for a long time.

'Who's the contributor?'

'Gary Chandler, he is the CEO of Sovec Oil.'

Ward absorbed the information that Centrepoint had just given him for a few seconds without speaking.

'Thoughts?' Centrepoint asked.

He thought about Simone arriving in The States on a plane owned by the huge Russian oil company Jefkept, and then he thought about the boss of one of America's major oil producers withdrawing his funding and suddenly growing a conscience, when every company who accessed the region had known what was really happening for the last thirty years, and eventually, when he was sure that he now knew who was playing who, he did the one thing that he always did when he wanted to work without The Old Man's interference.

He lied.

'It's definitely about oil,' he said.

'Well get to the bottom of it and quickly Ryan, this has moved right up to the oval office.'

Ward hung up the phone.

# TWENTY TWO

**University Ave, Bronx – New York**

Ward looked at Gilligan, 'Have you got any more information for me regarding where these Sudanese men are?' he asked.
'I'm pretty sure that Simone will be fully aware that you are looking for him right now. These guys are generally low end crooks who just dabble in a bit of protection and prostitution. I can't really see the benefit of hunting them.' Gilligan replied.
'You're going soft Marvin,' Ward replied and laughed.
'Actually,' Lawson interrupted, 'For once I do see the point.'
'Is he having a religious moment?' McDermott quipped.
'It makes perfect sense,' Lawson continued, 'One big hit will bring Simone out to where we want him. There is no point in us running around New York trying to find him when we can bring him to us.'
'It's not him that I'm trying to bring out,' Ward replied, 'He's just an inconvenience that I want out of the way.'
Patrick Simone was looking around at each of the men nervously. Ward noticed this and strode across to him, 'That's right,' he began as he leant down towards Simone, 'You are completely unimportant to me and everyone else. I'm only wasting my time on your father now because he deserves to be punished for the cowardly things that he has done.'
'He was protecting the people, bringing order and control to the towns and villages, just because our way is

different, it doesn't mean we don't operate to a democracy.'
Ward shook his head, 'I watched a video of him making young children play Russian roulette. That isn't a democracy. I'm going to kill him and I'm going to make you watch before I kill you.'
'I doubt very much he will be alone,' Simone replied defiantly.
'I'm banking on it.'
He felt his phone vibrate in his pocket and saw Nicole-Louise's name so he answered immediately,
'Hey Nicole-Louise, all good?'
'As usual I'm busy working things out for you while you pretend that you are the brains of the outfit.' She replied.
He was unsure if she was joking or serious but by her tone, he knew that she had something of value to tell him.
'What have you got?'
'Tackler told me what you had said about who would want us to fix it the least and so we worked back from that point.'
He recalled the conversation that he had with Tackler earlier, 'And?'
'Well the first thing we did was look at the oil companies as you asked, we drew up a list of companies who would have the most to gain, which ones had enough power to be putting pressure on The Old Man and why him controlling the region was so important.'
'And you found?' Ward interrupted, then wished he hadn't when Nicole-Louise said curtly,
'For once just be quiet and listen, because you need to understand the whole thing.'

'Sorry.'

'We found the following. A company called Sovec Oil will probably stand to gain the most through the access routes as they have lots of different mining interests close to the border.'

'I know about Gary Chandler,' Ward said quickly, then wished that he hadn't because he knew how much jumping ahead antagonised her.

'So what else do you know as you are so smart?' she asked.

He thought about it for a few seconds and then remembered how desperate the Vice President had been to get Simone overthrown and said, 'Wilson is behind it? He wants Chandler to continue to fund the party in return for exclusive access.'

He was sure that she was going to say he was correct. The only problem with that was that it blew the theory that he had silently been working through in his mind out of the water.

'Wrong!' Nicole-Louise said triumphantly.

A frown crept across his face.

'Now you want me to continue without pausing I guess?' His frown turned into a smile.

'Yes please Nicole-Louise,' he said softly.

' Sooooo,' she began, extending the word for added effect, 'We thought about what you said and we took everything that seemed obvious and discarded it. We just assumed we were meant to look at the obvious, and so we then looked at who had the least to gain.'

'Which is who?'

'The same people who have the most to gain.'

'I know I often talk in cryptic messages but I don't get your point?' he said.

'OK,' she began, 'We realised Chandler was clearly funding the Democrats for his own gain, as you know, that's commonplace in our politics anyway, and not even illegal, so we did what we always do and hacked into his phone records and found calls that he had been receiving from Washington.'

'From Wilson?'

'No, not that animal,' she said abruptly. Nicole-Louise disliked Wilson as much as Ward did. She had discovered video evidence of him abusing children when they were hunting down a sex trafficker a couple of months ago, 'He has received no less than eleven calls this week alone from Dorian Schultz.'

'Who's he?'

'He's the Democratic party vice chairman.'

'So he's Wilson's mouthpiece I guess?' Ward asked.

'No.'

'No?'

'That's what I said. He is an ancient politician, on his way out. We've broke into the party's records and there are countless complaints of sexual harassment and bullying being levelled against him. There is even one under review as we speak.'

'So what has he got to gain?' Ward asked.

'The same as it always is.'

'Money?'

'Yes. He has had three deposits placed into an off-shore account in the Cayman's in the name of his wife, each one for two million dollars.'

'From who?'

'We don't know yet.'
'Can you….'
'Tackler is on it.' She interrupted firmly, 'We're not stupid. He'll find it.'
'Sorry. So Chandler and Schultz are somehow working together, yet Chandler is threatening to pull out his funding for the party. Which wouldn't make any sense, unless….'
'Unless what?'
'Keep digging Nicole-Louise. You're halfway there.' He said, 'You need to find the rest of the puzzle to confirm what I'm thinking.'
'Which is?'
'Summarise what we have so far again, just humour me?' he asked.
Nicole-Louise sighed, but she was used to Ward working like this and admired his technique, he would give her no clues as to what he was thinking, instead he would wait for her and Tackler to come to him with the proof that he needed,
'In real simple terms for you Ryan, The Democratic party have the most to gain by continued funding from their donors and the least to gain if word of their involvement becoming public.'
And with that one sentence, Ward knew that his initial gut feeling had been exactly right.
He had one battle to fight in the shape of Simone and one war in the shape of the real enemy.
'You really are both geniuses,' he said and ended the call.

While he had been on the phone, Gilligan had been making a call to a detective who owed him a few favours. The guy worked in the little known NYPD anti-terrorism department. He had informed him that the highest concentrations of Sudanese criminals were today gathering in a restaurant called Kurtuma which was just off of 113th Street. He knew this because his branch of the NYPD kept tabs on the Sudanese at all times, ignoring any crimes they were committing as long as they weren't religiously or racially motivated. He told Gilligan that they had all been summoned to the restaurant and that he believed that they were just there to discuss and agree what neighbourhoods each man could work.
But Gilligan knew different.
'Now you've finished, I think I might know where Simone is going to be,' Gilligan said.
Ward raised an eyebrow.
'There's a place near to 113th Street that all the Sudanese men are meeting at right now. If we're quick, we might get lucky.'
'Is everyone ready to go Mac?' Ward asked McDermott, and then he immediately realised it was a stupid question because the moment he had said it, the whole team were moving towards the Range Rovers.
'Let's go then,' Gilligan said to Ward, Buck and Lawson.
'I'm working on something else,' Buck said, 'I'll meet you back here later.'
'OK' Ward said.
Lawson led the way to their car while Gilligan gave McDermott that exact location,

'Thirty minutes,' he heard Paul say.
'What's Buck working on?' Lawson asked.
'He's working on the real problem Mike. This is going to get very, very serious.'

## Kurtuma - 113th Street New York

They were parked on the street around the corner from the restaurant exactly thirty minutes later. Fringe and Wired had just stepped through the door of Kurtuma as the others watched from their vehicles. McDermott had instructed them to walk in, book a table for tonight, carry out a quick head count and report back.
They had done better than that.
As Ward watched them climb back into the Range Rover, Lawson said,
'This isn't about Sudan or Simone, is it?'
Before Ward could answer, his phone vibrated. He saw McDermott's name on the caller display and answered immediately,
'Is everything OK Mac?' he asked
'I'm going to send you something. Wired and Fringe did well, Fringe pretended to be texting someone and got a picture of everyone in there, I'll send it and await your instructions,' McDermott said before the line went dead.
A few seconds later, his phone vibrated again and he opened the text message that contained a picture. He studied it in silence for a good ten seconds and then used his thumb and forefinger to enlarge the picture on his screen. He counted eighteen men in total. After studying the picture carefully for another ten seconds, he passed

the phone to Lawson who did the same without speaking and took almost exactly the same amount of time studying it before passing it to Gilligan who after just five seconds of looking at the picture said,

'Two of those punks were in the first place we went to.'

'He's dynamite, isn't he?' Lawson said.

Ward laughed.

'What now?' Gilligan asked, 'Am I missing something.'

Ward and Lawson had both seen it. He knew that McDermott had seen it, and by now every single one of his team would have seen it.

In the picture were eighteen men.

Five men were Sudanese criminals sat around a table.

Five men were Sudanese muscle standing behind their bosses.

Six men were serious Russian gangsters; their tattoo's and battle scarred faces giving away their ethnicity.

One man looked out of place, his smart suit not fitting in with the group, but his steely eyes indicating that he was the most dangerous man in the room.

One man stood at the head of the table and even from the rushed picture it was clear to see that he was shouting at the men sat around the table.

His name was Samson Simone.

His phone vibrated again and Gilligan passed it back to him,

'How do you want to play this?' McDermott asked.

'We need Simone alive and preferably a couple of the Russians, the guy in the suit definitely. He should be able to give us the answers that we need.'

'Give me a few minutes; I'll get back to you with a plan.'

Ward hung up the phone.

'You're not going to go in there shooting the place up I hope,' Gilligan said, 'It's light and there are people everywhere.'

'Does he always get like this?' Lawson asked.

'It's OK for you pretty boy, you're thousands of miles away from home.'

'And I wish I wasn't,' Lawson said loudly, 'I'm missing my boys Rupret and Barnacle like crazy being here, so don't talk to me about sacrifice.'

'I'm sorry man, I didn't realise,' Gilligan said and leant over towards the driver's seat and patted Lawson on the shoulder.

Ward had to turn to look out of the window to stop Gilligan seeing the huge grin that had spread across his face.

Ward was relieved to feel his phone vibrate in his hand; he could see that Lawson was itching to tease Gilligan even more.

'Go ahead Mac,' he said as he answered.

'Walsh, Paul, Wallace and Fringe will go in through the back entrance and secure the rear of the table. That leaves me, you, Lawson, Gilligan, Fuller and Wired to come in through the front door. The Russians will definitely be armed and will shoot without hesitation, we have to assume the Sudanese guys are too so we go in and we shoot to kill, keeping Simone and the guy in the suit alive. Agreed?'

It was exactly what Ward had pre-empted McDermott would say and exactly the way that he wanted it to be. He turned around and looked at Gilligan,

'You need to stay here in the car and call for a clean-up crew as soon as we enter the restaurant,' he said.

'No way,' Gilligan protested, 'You aren't going to do that to me every time bullets start flying around. I'm over what happened, I'm good to go.'

'Well I'm not over it yet,' he said as he opened the car door, 'So do as I ask and make the call.'

Lawson joined Ward outside and they watched as Walsh, Paul, Wallace and Fringe scurried down a side alley and McDermott and the others walked over to them, holding their machine guns as discreetly as they could down by their sides.

'Let's go,' Ward said when they reached them, and they turned the corner and walked slowly towards the front entrance. When they got ten feet away, Ward and Lawson drew their handguns and Wired strode past them and put his hand on the door handle and pulled it open, just as Paul and the others had walked in through the rear door.

All eyes of the men inside immediately turned and looked towards the door as it opened, just as Paul, Walsh and Fringe unleashed a volley of automatic gunfire that cut through the five Sudanese muscle men and four of the Russians, while Walsh stood with his back to them watching the rear. Blood sprayed everywhere, and all of the tables were knocked over with the impact of legs and bodies hitting them, and the sound of glass smashing almost drowned out the noise of the gunfire. As they approached the table, both Ward and Lawson fired two shots each into the chests of two of the Sudanese guys sitting where the table had been a split second earlier,

and they both shot back into their chairs as the force of the bullets knocked them off, and at the same time, Fuller and Wired took out the other three Sudanese men Fuller's burst of fire had come just in time as one of the men had raised his handgun and was about to pull the trigger, while McDermott took out one of the two remaining Russian Gangsters.
It seemed to take an age for the echo of the gunfire and furniture breaking to stop.
'Where is the guy in the suit?' Ward asked urgently.
'He didn't come out the back,' Paul said, 'Check the bathrooms,' he barked to Fringe and Wallace, and the others watched while they both entered the bathrooms and returned ten seconds later and both said, almost in unison, 'Clear!'
'Where is he?' Ward asked the last surviving Russian gangster.
The guy Just shrugged.
'Let's just kill him,' Lawson said and raised his gun.
'Stop!' Ward said quickly.
Lawson looked at him quizzically.
'You have a cell phone?' Ward asked the Russian.
He nodded.
'Get it out,' he demanded.
The guy reached into his pocket and pulled out a cell phone.
'Now take this number,' he said and continued to recite his number as the guy punched it into his phone.
'Got it?'
The guy nodded.
'When we've gone, go back to your friend in the suit and tell him to give me a call in two hours. Is that clear?'

The guy nodded again.

'We need to go now,' McDermott said urgently.

Ward turned and looked at Samson Simone who was still sitting in his chair, hands placed on his knees, and smiled,

'You and I are going for a family reunion,' he said as Lawson stepped in and with one giant yank of his right hand pulled Simone to his feet.

# TWENTY THREE

**University Ave, Bronx – New York**

An hour and ten minutes after leaving the warehouse they were driving back in through the rollers shutter doors. For once, McDermott allowed Lawson the privilege of driving his car inside the warehouse, something both he and Ward assumed was down to the fact that McDermott would not risk anyone seeing Simone for the political value he held.
Gilligan had to stay behind at the restaurant to deal with the clean-up crew, and so on the journey back, Ward had sat in the back of the car pointing his gun at Simone even though they had tied his hands behind his back with cable ties.
As usual, Simone had tried on numerous occasions to get some kind of dialogue going, but Ward had simply ignored him. This unnerved Simone even more and fifteen minutes into the journey he had spoken for the last time and had not uttered a word since.
Lawson pulled the car to a stop, eased his giant frame out of the car, and opened the back door and took a handful of Samson Simone's hair in his hand, yanked him violently out of the car, and frog marched him over to the chair which had been placed next to his son.
'Patrick, have they hurt you?' Simone asked his son. Because of the tape that had been placed around his mouth, Patrick mumbled something inaudible, and

Lawson slapped him hard around the back of his head indicating that he was to be quiet.

While Lawson started to cable tie Simone to the chair, Ward approached him.

Simone looked up at him and Ward could see the rage burning in his eyes, which was something that he wanted to see, because an angry man tends to think with emotion when answering questions, not calculation,

'Tell me about Gill Whymark?' Ward said.

The mention of Whymark's name made Lawson look up and McDermott adjust his position so that he could hear Simone's response.

They were both aware that Whymark had become an obsession with Ward, and it seemed to them all that Whymark was involved in one way or another in everything that they had gone through in the last few months.

Simone glared at Ward but didn't speak.

So he asked again,

'Tell me about Gill Whymark?'

'I'll tell you nothing. My friends will be coming for me, I will not die today, but you will.'

Ward pulled his handgun out, pointed it at Patrick and said, 'For the last time, tell me about Gill Whymark?'

Simone immediately started talking,

'He helped us a long time ago with guns.'

'And?'

'He was our link to Washington.'

'To the CIA?'

'To the businessmen as well.'

This response surprised Ward. He could understand how the CIA would use Whymark to arrange the transportation of weapons, but not to arrange access directly with the companies that wanted it. That would be left to the politicians and Washington power brokers. The more Ward thought about Simone's reply, the more he was becoming convinced that not only had Whymark gone rogue, he was actually trying to build a crime dynasty with all the contacts that he had made over the years.

'Your friends,' he continued, 'The Russians, what do they want from you?'

'What you all want, safe passage.'

'Are they paying for it with money and support?'

Simone did not respond.

Ward shrugged and then stepped forward and sent a short sharp jab onto the bridge of Patrick's nose. As his fist connected, the breaking of the bone echoed around the warehouse,

'He won't be able to breathe through his nose now, so if you don't want him to suffocate, answer my question and I'll remove the tape from his mouth,' he said calmly. Simone struggled against the cable ties but soon realised it was a pointless exercise and the sound of Patrick gargling got him talking immediately,

'Please, remove the tape and I'll tell you everything.'

Ward ignored his request and repeated the question,

'Are they paying for it with money and support?'

'Yes they are,' Simone said quickly, 'Now please let him breathe.'

Ward stepped forward and yanked the tape hard from Patrick's mouth. The gasps where he was drawing in air to fill up his lungs were deep and short.

'I think he's having an orgasm,' Lawson, now standing upright, said from behind the chair.

Ward smiled and then continued,

'Yury, your friend, he is SVR?'

'He says not but I think he is.'

'He says not? So who does he say he is?'

'He says he represents a Russian conglomerate.'

Ward thought about this response. In essence, Yury was telling the truth, the Kremlin had its fingers in every pie going.

'And they need you in power why? Did you not ask yourself that question?'

'The same reason that you did,' Simone replied.

'You're missing my point. Why did they just not do what we did and remove you from power themselves? Look how easy it was for us. We wanted a change, so we instigated it. They could have done the same but chose not to. So why do you think they want you kept alive?'

'Because they know that no one can bring control to the region like I can.'

A moment of clarity swept over Ward. He had just realised why the Russians needed Simone to be kept alive.

'Last question,' he said, 'How much of your communication with Whymark is on record?'

Simone looked confused,

'What do you mean?'

'It doesn't matter,' he said as he turned away from Simone and walked back towards McDermott, 'I have two people who can answer that question for me.'

He watched as Paul and the rest of the team walked silently over to the table and chairs and sat down and continued doing what they were doing before, a couple of them reading, Fringe listening to music through his headphones and Paul started to clean his gun.
McDermott saw the smile on his face,
'What are you looking so pleased about?' he asked.
'Look at them,' Ward replied, looking towards the table, 'Sitting back down as though nothing has happened. You must be so proud of the way you shaped them?'
'We have no time for sentiment Ryan, what are we going to do about them?' McDermott replied pointing at the two Simone's.
'After we have got what we need from them and we have shown them the error of their ways, kill them of course.'
'I have to say this. I was against this operation from the start, I thought you were crazy going into Sudan and attempting this, but you've somehow managed to pull it all together,' McDermott said, and patted Ward gently on the shoulder.
'Jesus Mac, I know you are winding down but please don't start going all soft on me,' Ward replied without once taking his eyes off of the Simone's.
'Did I just say that?'
Ward smiled,
'You've managed to pull it together Mac; the boys did all of the work.'
'And The Optician,' McDermott added, fixing his own stare on the Simone's himself now.
The mention of The Optician reminded him that he should check in with him,

'I'm going to make a call,' he said as he headed towards the reception area for some privacy.

He closed the door and hit speed dial.

Three rings later, The Optician answered,

'Yep?'

'Where are you?' Ward asked.

'I'm close. Why?'

'So you know we have Simone?'

'Yes, I watched Lawson bundle him into your car.'

'Did you ever watch Whymark when he got involved with Simone?'

'No. It wasn't unusual for The Old Man to instruct me to watch someone else at that time. Why?'

'He's gone rogue, we know that, but do you think that he could ever become a traitor and get into bed with the Russians?'

'I think he is capable of anything now after his involvement in all of the things you've uncovered. Why are you asking about him?'

'It's just a theory I have.'

'As I keep telling you Ryan, as far as Whymark is concerned, be very careful. You aren't as good as he is yet.'

Ward noticed that The Optician seemed to be talking in a very matter of fact tone of voice. It wasn't like him, and he knew instinctively that something was wrong with him. So he pushed, not hard, just enough to see if he could offer an ear,

'Whatever you dealt with in Boston, if you want to talk about it, you know that you can trust me with any secret and I will never share it?'

There was a pause on the end of the line, which was an indication to him that he had permission to push a little harder. A pause generally meant that someone wanted to say something but didn't know how,
'I'm your family,' he continued, 'What's your problem is my problem.'
There was an even longer pause; it lasted a good five seconds,
'I went to see my dad,' The Optician eventually said.
He knew the resentment and anger that he held for his father and how he blamed him, and rightly so, in Ward's eyes, for the traumatic childhood that the best assassin on the planet had endured. He then had a bad feeling in the pit of his stomach,
'And you killed him?' he asked softly.
'I had intended to, but I looked at how pathetic and alone he was and realised that his own regret was killing him anyway. He's dying. He's all alone, living in squalor and he only has a few months left to live at best.'
'But you vented your anger at him?'
'No. I actually celebrated myself, my family and my friends to him. I actually realised that I'm not alone anymore. I have my blood family and my extended family with all of you; I could see the envy in his eyes along with the fear that he was going to die all alone.'
'Finally!' Ward declared, 'You get it!'
'So it appears.'
'So why the matter of fact tone?'
'Because your obsession with Whymark is going to get you killed if you are not careful.'
'I'm always careful, plus I have you to protect me.'
'I'm serious.'

'So am I.'

'I'll be careful.'

'Let me know where you want me to move next,' The Optician replied and the line went dead.

Ward thought about the last few months and operations aside, thought of the emotional journey that The Optician had been through, and how most normal people would struggle to cope with the enormity and impact of the things that he had faced, and he realised that his own downbeat moments about wanted to lead a normal life with Eloisa paled into insignificance by comparison. He decided at that moment to be more appreciative of what he had in the here and now.

His thoughts were interrupted by his phone vibrating and when he glanced at the caller display, it listed that it was an unknown number calling him.

He was sure it was the Russian, but just to establish how important Simone was to them, he didn't answer, he decided if they called back within the next ten minutes that they needed Simone back desperately.

He had a more important call to make anyway.

## Park Avenue – New York

Nicole-Louise and Tackler had made good progress. They had just been discussing their own theories on what the evidence they had found was telling them when her phone rang. She saw Ward's name on the caller display and said to Tackler,

'Do you want to take that, because you just know that he is going to have a million questions?'

'I'll give you the honour,' he replied, and promptly turned his back on here and started tapping on his keyboard again, 'He is frightened of you and gives you a less hard time than he does me,' he said to his screen rather than to her.
She answered the phone,
'Are you frightened of me?' she asked without greeting.
'Everyone is,' Ward replied.
'Seriously? Why?'
'Yes seriously. Because you, like the other two women in my life are the only people who put me in my place, know what I'm thinking and feeling, even when I can't put it into words myself, and you're smarter than me,' he answered without any hesitation.
'Ridiculous,' she replied.
'A point you have just proved. Now can we talk work?'
'What do you need?'
'How have you got on by tracing the money and calls made by Schultz?'
'We've made good progress, we were just discussing it.'
'Have you found anything of any importance?'
'We have found a couple of numbers that frequently called him, and we are currently tracing them, and then when we find out who they belong to we will trace, trace and trace again.'
'And what about the money?'
'It will be the same with that. When we find where it came from, we'll trace it back. We'll find it in the end, you know that.'
'Yes I do. I've just had a call on my cell phone, it showed as an unknown number, any chance you could trace it?'

'Do you know who it belongs to?' she asked.
'Yes, it belongs to a Russian guy, probably SVR.'
'Then I can tell you know that there is no way that you will be able to trace it. They are probably even further ahead than us in terms of technology used to shield things.'
'So I guess that makes your job harder?'
'No.'
'What do you mean?' he asked, sounding surprised.
'It's obvious Ryan. Anything we find that is relating to the Russians, we will find only because they want us to find it.'
He was quiet for a few seconds; Nicole-Louise could almost hear the cogs in his brain turning,
'If I send you a picture, can you hack into the facial recognition data base in the CIA to see if you can put a name to it?'
'We don't need to hack. The Old Man has granted us access to all CIA files, all to do with the new powers that you have risked life and limb to give him. It kinda makes our job a little less exciting but does save time. Send it now.'
'OK. Chase Schultz, then his money man, then let me know where that came from, and I would appreciate it if you could text me the name of the guy in the picture I send wearing the suit. His is using the name Yury, it's probably not his real name, but it might help.'
'Do you want to hear our theory?'
'No,' and the line went dead.
'It is so infuriating when he does that,' she said over her shoulder to Tackler.
'Did you say something?' he said.

She rolled her eyes and sighed, these boys are useless she thought to herself, no wonder they are all frightened of me.

# TWENTY FOUR

**The Kremlin – Moscow**

Viktor Zhirkov strode less purposefully this time towards the President's office. He nodded at the four female KGB officers again as he passed them and knocked quietly on the door.
'Enter,' the President's voice said immediately.
He walked through the doors, closed it, took the eight steps forward, stood to attention and saluted.
The President nodded,
'You have some news for me Viktor?'
'Comrade Glushakov has been in contact Sir.'
The president stopped writing on the paper in front of him, dropped his pen and then placed his elbows on the desk and cross-locked his fingers into his hands,
'What news did he give you?'
'He told me that the MI6 agent now has Simone and his son and that he and his team killed a number of our comrades.'
'How many of them?'
'Five. He let one of them live.'
'Why?'
'So that he could go back to Comrade Glushakov and tell him that they had Simone.'
'Do we have any evidence of this?'
'No Sir. But he gave a contact number for Glushakov to contact him.'
'And has he?'

'I gave him permission to try before I came to tell you the news in person.'

The President started to rub his chin, deep in thought. Zhirkov knew that now was the time to be quiet and not interrupt him while he was thinking. Eventually, he said, 'Our friend in Washington, they have been briefed about this?'

'Not yet. I was waiting for your instruction.'

'Good. For now, let's keep it away from them. Can Glushakov fix this and discreetly try and find out what the MI6 agent knows? It does concern me that the British are involved. You know how skilled they are at working things out.'

'I'm confident that the Americans would not willingly share too much information with them. I think as far as they are concerned, this is just about Simone. The Americans have replaced him with someone else now and have control of the region again, so I am sure that as far as they are concerned, the matter has reached a satisfactory conclusion.'

'Don't underestimate them Viktor. Let's assume that they know everything, that way we can protect ourselves.'

'What is your instruction Sir?' Zhirkov asked.

'We need Comrade Glushakov to prove they have him alive, tell him that immediately. Once we have that, you know what to do.'

'Yes Sir!'

'Go now,' the President said, using the back of his hand to wave Zhirkov out of the office.

**University Ave, Bronx – New York**

It was now getting late and Ward had already decided that there was nothing that anyone could do until the morning, and so he had just finished a call to Buck asking for an update.

Buck had established through his contacts that there was someone very important in New York, sent directly from the Kremlin no less, and that there was going to be a big shootout somewhere. But so far, a lot of the information that Buck had received had been second hand and was a bit hazy. He told Ward that there was going to be a meeting tomorrow morning somewhere and while he didn't know where yet, he would know by the morning. Ward told him to be careful and before Buck could respond with one of his 'Mom' quips, he hung up the phone.

'Will we be ready to go first thing in the morning at a moment's notice?' he asked McDermott and then realised it was a dumb question to ask as McDermott was always ready.

'Where to?' was all he replied.

'I'm not sure yet. Buck is going to provide us with an address in the morning. I'm just figuring that if they are planning on hunting us, hitting them first and sending out a message will put them on the back foot.'

'Yes we'll be ready and I agree, it's the right way to play this.'

'Mike,' Ward shouted across to Lawson, 'Go home and get some rest and meet back here by seven in the morning.'

'Go home and rest? I think not!' Lawson shouted back and ran across to his car and jumped into it, started it and reversed it towards the roller shutter doors within about five seconds.

The guys around the table all laughed.

He realised that was the second dumb thing he had said in the space of a few seconds, Lawson would not be resting, he was sure of that.

'I'll send the boys out for food and to unwind and I'll stay and watch these two,' McDermott said, pointing at the Simone's, 'You should go home and get some rest Ryan; everything is more than likely going to start tomorrow.'

Ward nodded and put his hand up to stop Lawson leaving, 'Take me home first Mike,' he said.

**DUMBO – New York**

Ward felt much better after having a shower and changing his clothes. He noticed there had been another missed call from the unknown number and two from Centrepoint. He thought it would be best to call him to give him an update.

He hit speed dial.

'Was that mess you left Gilligan to sort out necessary?' The Old Man said immediately.

'It was if you want this resolved.'

'Where are we?'

The truth was, he wasn't exactly sure where they were. Until he had spoken to the Russian guy and Nicole-Louise and Tackler had worked their usual magic, everything he had concluded was all guesswork.

'We know that Schultz has been receiving payment from someone and that he was the one putting pressure on Chandler. We know that the Russians are assisting Simone, but we can't see any gain for them in doing so, and for some reason they want him back, we have a lead, but until Nicole-Louise and Tackler give me formal identification on a Russian guy, it's only speculation. I'm assuming that you now have your own warlord running the region, so as far as the original objective goes, if we kill Simone and his son and you dispose of the bodies, it's been a resounding success.'

'Maybe this time, there is nothing overly sinister going on?'

'What do you mean?'

'Perhaps it is as simple as the Russians wanted access to make things more awkward for our companies to operate down there? They want Simone back because they know they can control him, and with regards to Shultz and Chandler, maybe the money came from Chandler as a sweetener to Schultz and now he is getting cold feet and is trying to distance himself from it because he's got wind of the coup that we instigated down there?'

In all fairness, Ward thought to himself, it made as much sense, probably more so, than the theory that he had running around in his own mind. And the fact that The Old Man seemed comfortable enough with that scenario to mention it made him feel it would be the most likely answer out of the two, after all, he was the most cautious man that he knew, his whole life had been about protecting the country and the deceitful, greedy politicians, and if that outcome was sitting fine with him, it would more than likely be correct.

And then Centrepoint said one thing that made him realise that it would be a mistake to think that things could be so straightforward,

'And you know how Wilson panics,' he said.

Wilson, the vile Vice President who Ward had discovered was not the stand-up guy he portrayed to the world. The mention of his name reminded him that he had been involved in something that The Old Man knew nothing about and was genuinely surprised to discover when he had revealed it to him. He knew how stupid Wilson was from personal experience and he knew that if Wilson thought one thing, the opposite was probably happening.

'Agreed?' The Old Man asked, interrupting his thoughts.

'Perhaps you're right.'

'I can tell by your tone that you don't think so. I know you too well Ryan. So I'll let you run with whatever theory you have at the moment for a couple of days. If you don't find anything after that, we'll conclude that it was straightforward and you can eliminate Simone and his son. Agreed?'

'Agreed.' He replied and hung up the phone.

For once, he did agree with all that Centrepoint had just said to him.

Well nearly all of it.

There was one part that he didn't agree with, and it was crucial that he didn't agree.

He was not going to kill Samson and Patrick Simone.

He tried calling Eloisa but it went straight to voicemail. He felt frustrated that even though he was at home he still couldn't get to see her, but he consoled himself with the fact that when she finished work, there was a high chance that she would come straight to his apartment to surprise him. He knew how she worked.

## 38 W 31$^{st}$ Street – New York

On the drive back from dropping Ward off, Lawson had decided that today would be the day. It was actually a simple comment by Ward that had convinced him that he could no longer hide from the fact that he felt alone, and needed more than just emotionless sex in his life. He had asked Ward if he was seeing Eloisa later and he had replied, 'I hope so, I just want to feel normal.'
He had not felt normal since she had broken his heart twelve years ago. He was fully aware that most women that he came into contact with found him attractive and that the countless women he had slept with would give anything to have a relationship with him, but it was what he wanted that no one, not even Ward, understood.
He was tired.
Tired both of the women that threw themselves at him and of the façade that he constantly kept up that he was happy and obsessed with sex, because neither of those things cured the heartbreak that he constantly felt or were representative of the real him.
He wanted to be normal.
He wanted Lucy Corrigan.
He had never stopped wanting her.
They had been together for three years and he was sure that he was going to spend the rest of his life with her. She made him feel alive and content. She was everything and more that he wanted. The day that she walked out on

him was the darkest day of his life and something that he had never recovered from.

They shared a house in Hereford, three miles from the SAS barracks where he was stationed, and when he wasn't working a mission, he would rush home every night to her and her face would light up when he walked through the door. They would cook, decorate, go shopping, and do everything together. And they always knew what the other was thinking.

Or so he thought.

He came home one evening and she was waiting for him on the sofa, with two suitcases packed and waiting by the front door. She had told him that she couldn't see a future with him because he was too accommodating, too nice, too reliable and too predictable, and that she was starting to feel bored and almost trapped, and she needed more excitement in her life. She pointed out that while he was running around the world on secret missions with the SAS, she was carrying on with the mundane, normal things that life brings, and when he was home, he never seemed to bring any excitement to the party.

Hearing her say the words ripped his heart in two. He begged for another chance, said he would leave the SAS immediately and explained how after doing the life threatening things that he had to do in his job, all he wanted was simplicity and calm when he came home between missions.

She told him that she could never live with him leaving on her account. She would not be responsible for him walking away from the one thing that she knew he loved equally as much as he loved her. She had walked out of the door, leaving the giant of a man that he was in tears on the sofa, she had said that maybe one day, if it was meant to be, they would find each other again.

He had secretly kept tabs on her over the past six years through the tools available to him through MI6, and he knew that she had been in a relationship for five years with a guy who worked in finance in the city of London, but they had broken up two years ago and her phone records had only shown three regular numbers being constantly used since then, and he had established that they belonged to her parents, sister and her friend called Annabel, whom he had met on a number of occasions as she had been her best friend since her school days.

He had almost called her so many times over the years, but as much as he wanted to hear her voice and talk to her, he was afraid of knowing that she had never given him a thought and that he had become a distant memory to her.

So he had filled the constant emptiness that he felt with sexual encounters that meant nothing to him, and as much as he joked about it to others, it often left him feeling ashamed of himself and that he was creating a bigger void than he had before.

Normality was all that he had secretly craved for the past twelve years.

Today he had to know.

With his heart beating fast in his chest, and an overwhelming feeling of sickness in the pit of his stomach, he scrolled down through the numbers in his phone until he came to her name, and then without

hesitation, he pressed the call button and lifted the phone to his ear.
He heard a click and then the international ringing tone in his ear.
One ring.
Two Rings.
Three rings.
'Hello?' a soft voice said.
He almost hung up.
'Lucy?'
'Yes. Who is this?'
He wanted to end the call there and then. He decided that today should not be the day after all. He didn't want to know that she had moved on and that her life had become all she wanted, full of excitement and the fun that she had craved so much all of those years ago. He started to panic. He suddenly realised that his life was probably more hectic now working with Ward than it had ever been in the SAS or MI6 and he cursed himself for not thinking it through properly.
'It's Mike. Mike Lawson.'
There was silence on the end of the line for a few seconds. He was sure that so many people had walked into her life in the last twelve years that she would even struggle to remember him.
'Mike?' she said, emotion running through her voice.
'Yes.'
'You have got no idea how many times I have prayed that you would find me again over the past twelve years.'

Lawson didn't sleep all night. Not for the reasons that Ward and McDermott and the team would expect him not to sleep though.

He didn't sleep all night because he spent eight hours straight talking to Lucy Corrigan on the phone.

# TWENTY FIVE

**DUMBO – New York**

Ward had just finished speaking to Eloisa on the phone, and while he was disappointed that she had not turned up to visit him last night, her explanation that she had been at work until gone midnight preparing information on some very bad people for him, and her promise that she would definitely be with him by seven that evening, he was feeling in good spirits and positive about the day ahead. By not visiting him last night, she had given him a lot of time to think about Simone and the Russians and he knew exactly what he was going to do.
There had been four more missed calls from the unknown number but he had decided that he would wait for the call to come in the morning before answering, just to see how it fitted in with his theory.
He saw Lawson turn the corner and pull into the kerb. He opened the door and before he had sat into the seat, he noticed the huge grin on Lawson's face.
'I don't want to know,' he said.
'I'm not going to tell,' Lawson replied.
'Whoever she is, I'm impressed that she taught you the meaning of discretion.'
'My dear Ryan, you have much to learn about me.'
Ward decided that he didn't want to pursue the conversation any further because he was sure it would

end up with a revelation of sex with multiple women at the same time,

'I've been thinking about this thing with Simone all night, what do you think about it? What do you think is the driving force behind it?' he asked.

'I think it is too straightforward just to be about Simone being deposed and someone else being put in his place. From the snippets that you allow us mere mortals to hear, I think there is political involvement, but not for money. I also think that killing Simone would be a big mistake. I think that's what certain people want to happen.'

'Pull the car over.'

Lawson pulled the car to a stop.

'Who are you? What have you done with Mike Lawson?' Ward asked, looking as serious as he possibly could.

'Hilarious!'

'Seriously Mike, how did you reach that conclusion?'

'Why else would the Russians be bringing Simone to you if they didn't have an ulterior motive?'

'Go on?'

'They'd allegedly made a new deal with him to control the region, the last thing they would want to do is give him to you on a plate. They would wrap him in cotton wool. Probably use their own guys who are already here to find you, but no, they gift wrap him for us? I'm not buying it.'

'That's exactly what I think. And you know there is money changing hands?'

'Not specifically with who, you haven't shared that.'

Ward spent the next few minutes explaining his theory to Lawson and was surprised to see how energised he seemed, and even more surprised that Lawson didn't feel the need to be humorous and interrupt him once.
'That's exactly the conclusion I would have come to and the only possible reason,' Lawson said when he had finished explaining it all.
Ward knew that Lawson was incredibly smart, in fact his main frustration with him was that he constantly dumbed himself down and made light of things.
But today, something was different; he could see it and also sense it. The giant of a man sitting next to him, a man he trusted with his life, had changed, almost overnight and he couldn't figure out why.
'Anything you want to talk to me about?' he asked.
'No, I'm good,' he replied, 'Let's get going and see if Buck kept true to his word,' he added as he pulled the car away from the kerb.

### University Ave, Bronx – New York

Buck had kept his word and discovered where the Russians were going to be meeting. He had made his way to the warehouse at six that morning, armed with coffee and bagels for everyone. He had walked in to find McDermott and the team drinking coffee and eating bagels.
The two Simone's were still tied firmly to the chairs and he noticed that there were takeout boxes and empty water bottles on the floor below their feet. He didn't see any point to making their stay remotely comfortable and if he was in charge, he would be torturing them just for

the fun of it, but even though he had only worked with Ward a short time, he knew he had a reason for everything that he did and if he had instructed McDermott to make sure they were fed and watered, he would have had a good reason.

'Nice gesture Buck but we couldn't wait,' Walsh said from the table.

'They aren't for you,' he replied quickly, 'Your mom gave them to me to feed the waiting que when I left her bed ten minutes ago,' he added, a comment which everyone found funny apart from Walsh, which made it even funnier.

'I will kill him one day,' he mumbled under his breath.

Buck spent the next thirty minutes running through the information he had for the meeting that was to take place that morning, with both McDermott and Gilligan, who had turned up shortly after Buck, carrying ten coffee's which the men all gladly took, much to Buck's disgust, and by the time Ward and Lawson arrived at the warehouse, they were ready to run over the plan with everyone.

'The Russians had been summoned to a house in Annadale I have been reliably informed,' Buck began, everyone's eyes fixed firmly on him, 'It was called by a man called Igor Vasin. Now Vasin isn't a huge player in the eyes of the Russians but he is one of the main guys in New York. But generally, he isn't too much to worry about.'

'So this is a straightforward hit?' Paul asked.

'No,' Buck replied.

Ward raised an eyebrow,

'So hit us with the bad news?' he said.

'While Vasin isn't really a big fish, he is under the control of a guy called Yanik Korataev. He is a major player.'

'Here in new York or across the country?' Ward asked, thinking back to the last Russian that he had recently come into contact with, a guy called Andrea Yeschenko. Yeschenko ran an operation that stretched all over the States.

'Neither. In Russia.'

'Explain that?'

Buck explained to everyone how the organisations are run by the Vor v Zakone's and that they stayed in Russia controlling their operations. The fact that he told them that it is actually The Kremlin who allows these people to operate under their control, confirmed a few things to Ward. but he didn't comment on them. Surprisingly, Lawson looked at him and gave him a knowing nod.

'I came across some of Korataev's men when I was stationed in Moscow. They were some of the guys who had taken up the contract that had been put on my head, and they were communicating directly with the Moscow police. If it wasn't for The Old Man, I would be dead but he somehow managed to get me out of there alive. So I know that if he is involved, it will go right to the top of the Kremlin.'

Ward looked at Lawson again and the same knowing nod was exchanged.

'So they appoint and control the bad guys?' Wired asked.

'Yes.' Buck replied.

'Just like we did Simone and now Bassong,' Paul said, 'It's just how it is.'

Ward felt his phone vibrate in his pocket and he pulled it out and saw the words unknown number flashing, so he put it back into his pocket. He was sure that he would be seeing whoever was calling very shortly.

'So this place where they are meeting, what is it?' he asked Buck, 'A bar, house, empty building, what?'

'It's a house,' McDermott interrupted, 'I have the rough outline of my plan for hitting it already drawn up in my head, it's just a matter of going through it with you,' he said to Ward.

Ward nodded his agreement, even though he already knew that McDermott's plan would be both thorough and faultless.

He felt his phone vibrate again and he was going to ignore it as he was sure it was the unknown caller again, but he pulled it out anyway and saw Nicole-Louise's name flashing.

'Hey Nicole-Louise, do you have some news for me?' he asked.

'Don't I always?' she replied.

He smiled to himself, 'Shoot?'

'The guy in the picture is called Yury Glushakov and he is definitely SVR. He works for a guy, a general called Viktor Zhirkov, that's pretty much all the CIA have on file. Actually, it was MI6 because we had to……'

'Where are you with the money trail?' he interrupted.

'Seriously, your manners! We are making progress. If Tackler didn't have to waste hours and hours trying to find a guy in a picture we might be there already. And a little appreciation wouldn't go amiss!'

'Sorry, I'm just in a rush,' he replied, feeling suitably told off.

'I'll let you know when we have something,' she said and ended the call.

He cursed himself for being so short with her. He told himself that he would make it up to her later, not that she would let him forget about it anyway.

'Buck, what do you know about a General by the name of Viktor Zhirkov?' he asked, pulling Buck's attention away from the map that he was studying with McDermott.

'Zhirkov?'

Ward nodded.

'That's bad.'

'Why?'

'Whoever gave you that information didn't tell you?'

'Tell me what?'

'They should have told you the one thing I know for sure, if Zhirkov is involved, it's coming right down from the President's office.'

Ward and Lawson exchanged knowing nods once again.

## 155 Preston Avenue – Annadale, New York

The house on Preston Avenue looked very presentable. It was tucked neatly back in a quiet suburban area. It had a red brick front with a porch leading to the door ,and the side wall was cladded with white timber all the way down with a garage on the side. It was a split level building, something that was only visible from the side, and it was surrounded by a white picket fence. It looked well cared for, which was unusual for the Russian criminals, they generally let their properties run into a state of disrepair.

McDermott had gone through the plan four times with everyone, and Ward had called The Optician three hours ago to ask him to get in place and let them know how many people were likely to be there.

Ward had decided that the team were to hit the place as hard as they possibly could, much to Gilligan's displeasure, as he knew that he was going to be put on clean-up duties once again. Ward's thinking being that he wanted to send the strongest possible message back to The Kremlin that whatever they had planned, the Americans were onto it.

The only concession he insisted upon was that Yury Glushakov, assuming he was there, had to be kept alive, no matter what. He knew that if they lost Glushakov, then the solution to this whole mess that he had worked out could not be implemented.

McDermott had divided everyone into two teams as usual, one to enter through the front, one for the back. The Optician would deal with anyone outside of the house with his usual efficiency, and Gilligan would cover the clean-up by arranging for them to park out of sight and call them in when they were needed, all from the safety of the car.

They had parked the Range Rovers fifty yards either side of the house so that both sides could be seen clearly. Everything looked calm and quiet.

Almost too quiet.

Ward pulled out his phone and called The Optician.

'How many men?' he asked.

'None.' The Optician replied.
'You haven't seen anyone?'
'Not one person in the last two and a half hours. Which means one of two things.'
'Which are?'
'You have the wrong place is the obvious one.'
'Or?'
'They know you are coming.'
Ward hung up the phone and frowned.
'Problem?' McDermott asked.
'The Optician says that there has been no movement in the house since he arrived here.'
'They know we are coming,' McDermott said.
'I don't think so.'
'Why?'
'You know as well as I do that if there was one person in that house, The Optician would know by now how many and in what rooms they are. Agreed?'
McDermott nodded.
'Buck is the most reliable guy I know when it comes to the Russians; he wouldn't have got it wrong because….'
He tailed off.
'My thoughts exactly,' Lawson said from the rear seat, 'Shall we just go and knock on the door?' he asked.
Ward opened the car door and stepped out with Lawson following.
'Paul,' McDermott said into his microphone, 'Mobilise the boys now,' he added as he jumped out of the car with Wired and Fuller following. Around the side of the house, Paul and the others were already approaching the back door by the time Ward climbed the steps of the porch. He pulled out his gun as he reached the top of the

steps and Lawson strode past him and lifted his foot and with every ounce of his powerful body, slammed the sole of his right foot six inches away from the door handle and the door flew open, the force so great that the top hinge of the doorframe was ripped from the wood and the door tilted at a forty degree angle.

They stepped inside and the place was completely quiet. Ward heard the back door shatter and by the time that the last pieces of glass had hit the floor, he knew that Paul and the others would have secured the back two rooms.

He led the way up the hallway and turned slowly into the first room, which had the door half open, and he casually pushed it fully open with his left hand and led with his gun pointed in his right. He stepped in no more than three feet with Lawson right behind him and stopped.

'That's different,' McDermott said from behind them and stopped to join the others in staring at what was in front of them.

Lined up neatly on the sofa were three men. They had all had their throats cut and bled to death. It was a bloody mess everywhere.

The first guy had his eyes cut out.

The second guy had his ears cut off.

The third guy had his tongue cut off.

See no evil, hear no evil, and speak no evil.

It was a message to them from the Russians. They had fed Buck the wrong information which meant that Yury Glushakov was smarter than Ward had given him credit for being. And it also meant that they knew who Buck was.

On the lap of the guy in the middle with no ears was a note written in large capital letters that said.
'I WANT SIMONE BACK ALIVE.'
Paul and the others joined them in the room and they had to shift to the side to let everyone step inside. Everyone looked at the bodies for a few moments.
'On the plus side,' Lawson said to Ward, eventually breaking the silence, 'That's just proved beyond doubt that your theory is right.'

# TWENTY SIX

**Republican National Committee – 310 First Street, SE, Washington DC 20003**

Samantha Ivey, former chair of the Illinois Republican Party, had an unusually rapid rise to become the chair of the party's national committee. There were some who had questioned both her suitability and her appointment, not to mention her methods, in that she made no secret of the fact she was happy to walk over anyone to get to where she wanted to get to. But the senior committee felt that ruthlessness was something that they needed in abundance to attack the liberal democratic president in the polls, and they had decided that being ruthless was something that Samantha Ivey could do as easily as she could breathe. The most impressive thing about her was her ability to see a shortcut that would benefit the party and seize it without hesitation.

She was currently feeling very pleased with herself. She had orchestrated a chain of events that would propel the Republican candidate into the White House.

Harold Clark Howard was their big hope, and she was confident that her carefully laid plans would give him the presidency.

Howard was a tough talking businessman who had become a billionaire through property investment and funding oil exploration. He was the opposite of the liberal president. As far as he was concerned, the

American people came first and the rest could go to hell. He had no interest in world order, just in putting money and security the way of the middle class Americans. He believed that too much emphasis had been put on Middle East events, and not enough on the people who mattered. He felt the Chinese were trying to take over the world and the real enemies were not the Russians but China with their cheap imports and labour.

He had preached this on the campaign trail and he was gathering a lot of momentum, in spite of the Democrats calling him a racist and bigot. The slurs were wearing thin and having no impact anymore because the people in the street were buying into what he was saying. There was panic in the media and academic world that what they considered laughable, when Howard had first appeared on the scene telling the world that he was running for president, had now become a possibility that their worst nightmare would come true.

Samantha Ivey was in the process of ensuring that that possibility became a reality, and the irony was, the Democrats were doing all the work for her.

She picked up the phone on her desk and without calling through to her secretary to connect the call for her, dialled the number herself.

A few seconds later the ringing tone echoed down the line.

'Hello?' the voice said.

'Good morning General Zhirkov,' she said brightly, 'It's time to pitch the last ball.'

**University Ave, Bronx – New York**

Back at the warehouse there was an air of disappointment. McDermott's team had geared themselves up for a battle that never materialised, and Buck was extremely concerned that his contacts, men that had always been so reliable, had turned against him, and that made him feel vulnerable. He knew that the only thing that could make a Russian man turn was the Kremlin, and he was fully aware that he would still be on their hit list and he was even more concerned with the fact that they would be doubling their efforts to find him. Once the Kremlin had decided that they wanted you dead, the threat remains, no matter how many years it might take them.

The only person in good spirits was Gilligan who had not been required to sort out another discreet extraction of a pile of dead bodies.

The two Simone's were still secured side by side and Patrick had his head tilted forward, the tiredness now becoming too much to fight, and so he was drifting in and out of sleep, and his father was still staring at everyone in the room with hatred burning from his eyes. Everyone walked around the warehouse ignoring him; something that they all knew would infuriate him even more and was being done on purpose.

The warlord who had been so revered in Sudan was nothing to these men.

Lawson had stepped outside to make a call which had made Ward curious, but he was too engrossed in trying to plan his next move to bother to ask Lawson what was going on in his life to warrant the sudden and obvious change in his demeanour.

He knew what he wanted to happen, and why it was imperative that it happened, but that part of it was out of his control.

'Why make such a grand gesture that they want Simone back?' McDermott asked him as he casually walked over to him, 'I mean, I get that they want to demonstrate that they are bad guys who are not to be messed with, but you've tried moving dead bodies before and positioning them in an upright position, particularly positions that are so specific, would have taken ages, you know that.'

Ward nodded,

'I was thinking the same thing. It's clearly a message. See no evil, hear no evil, and speak no evil. So let's break it down.

'OK. The see part first. You think that could be a reference to the fact that we put people like him in place,' McDermott replied pointing in the direction of Simone, 'And then we turn a blind eye and condemn him like the rest of the international community? Like we choose to see only the evil we want to see?'

Ward shook his head,

'Buck, over here,' he shouted across the floor.

Buck came over, 'You realise that my cover has now been completely blown?' he asked.

'Yes, so maybe you should step back from this one for now?'

Buck looked at him in disgust.

'I'm not running,' he said curtly, 'Anyway, if I step back then I will have to do something that I don't want to do.'

Both Ward and McDermott raised their eyebrows,

'Go and service both of your moms, and I'd rather face the full might of the Kremlin thanks,' he added without a hint of a smile.

Ward smiled, McDermott rolled his eyes, and then Buck pulled a face like he was sucking on the most bitter slice of lemon imaginable.

'So what do you want to know?'

'The way the bodies were positioned, Mac thinks the see no evil part could be a reference from the Russians that we ignore the evil that we choose not to see, like it doesn't exist. What do you think?'

'The Russian's aren't into poetic statements. It will be much simpler.'

They both looked at Buck, waiting for the revelation, but he just stared back at them.

'Well?' McDermott asked.

'It means that you won't see them coming. That they will come for you at their will and you won't know. The Russian mafia use it a lot in Moscow. They normally cut out the eyes of wives and children to send the message.'

That made perfect sense to Ward. He was finding more and more bad people that he encountered were cutting people's eyes out, it was a sickening and highly intimidating act to most normal people.

'The hear no evil part means the same thing, that you won't hear them coming?' Ward asked.

'It could, or it could mean something else.'

Once again, they both waited for Buck to explain what he meant but he just stared straight back at them. Ward realised that he was inviting them to come up with an alternative without prompting.

'It could mean that we have heard things that we shouldn't have heard and we would do best to forget we heard it?' McDermott asked.

Buck nodded.

'So the speak no evil part means we are not to mention it?'

'No,' Buck said, 'It means that you are not to believe anything that people have told you about them, no doubt referencing anything he might have said to you,' he added, pointing towards the Simone's as flippantly as McDermott had earlier.

Ward smiled. The message meant that they were to wish that they had never seen Simone with the Russians, forget that they had heard any information regarding them that Simone might have passed onto them and they were most definitely not to communicate any Kremlin involvement to anyone,

'Well,' he said when McDermott noticed the smile on his face, 'I don't know about you two, but I would have just left a note saying that myself.'

'Same here,' Buck replied.

'Here's what we will do. Mac, you sit down with Buck and try and establish where the people helping Glushakov are likely to be holed up and then plan an all-out attack. Let's send them a message of our own. But we need to do it quickly, how soon can it be arranged?'

'Do you know where they are?' McDermott asked Buck.

'I know one of three places, let me make a couple of calls and if I still have any of my contacts who haven't got wind of the Kremlin's involvement, I'll have a target for you in ten minutes.'

'I'll leave that with you two then,' Ward said.

He knew that he would be receiving a call from the unknown number sooner rather than later, but he decided right then that he would ignore it once again.

If this was going to work out right, he had to frustrate and antagonise the Russians so that they took their eye of the ball. He would wait until after Buck and McDermott had come up with a plan and they had carried it out before speaking to them.

He noticed Lawson walk back in, grinning from ear to ear. He waited until he had walked over to him before speaking,

'What's going on with you?' he asked.

'I've been thinking about why the Russians positioned those bodies the way they did,' Lawson replied, 'I don't think they were trying to taunt us by saying we ignore things, I think they were warning us away from their involvement.'

'I don't know what's going on with you but….'

'I also think you need to ignore the next call that you get from them, you need to get them agitated so that they focus more on you than their end game, and the last thing I strongly suggest that you do is try and get Buck to establish where this Glushakov guy is hiding out and then we hit it with all we have to show them we have contempt for them. That should be enough to unsettle them and get them to come to us.'

'That's it! Outside, now!' Ward said as he walked out of the main warehouse and into the reception area. Lawson followed behind and closed the door.

'It took three of us fifteen minutes to come to the same conclusion. I want to know right know how you have gone from loyal, and generally unfunny foot soldier, to commander and chief analyser overnight?'

Lawson smiled at him.

'I'm serious Mike. You are one of my closest friends in the world and I want to know what's happened. I've always known how smart you are and I've told you over and over that you would be the best if you took things more seriously. Now you are, I'm not sure if I like it,' he said with a smile, 'But I need to know what's going on, as your friend.'

'You preferred the old me?'

'Well, it made me feel better about being me, so in some ways yes.'

'You can have him back if you want?'

'No, this is good. So tell me, what's happened.'

Lawson spent the next five minutes explaining about Lucy and his previous relationship with her. How he had felt completely alone since the day that she left him, and he was constantly jumping from one sexual partner to another so he would not need to form any attachment to anyone, and therefore he could never be hurt again. Ward listened carefully and didn't interrupt once.

Lawson then went on to explain how it was a comment that he had made yesterday about normality that had convinced him to make the call to her last night, and how she had spent hours telling him that she regretted leaving him almost instantly and had tried so desperately to find him again but he had vanished into thin air. His work with the SAS, and then MI6, had taken him underground, and apart from a couple of relationships that were never going to work out, because they were poor substitutes for him, she had pined for him constantly from the day she left.

'So, I found my normality again.'

Ward looked at him and smiled. He was surprised to find that he felt pride for Lawson. He knew the turmoil that he sometimes felt when he was away from Eloisa and he couldn't comprehend how hard it must have been for Lawson to miss someone so much for such a long period of time.

'You never mentioned her before. I thought you viewed women as objects of fun and it always irritated me to be honest, I felt it was disrespectful, but now it makes sense.'

'It's what I needed to do. Every man knows if he is honest with himself that women are the strongest and most important of the two sexes by a mile.'

Ward thought about this. He thought about Eloisa, his mom and Nicole-Louise and he knew that they were much stronger than him and that he respected them all more than he respected anyone else in the world. He recalled Nicole-Louise saying that he was blind or stupid if he didn't' understand why Lawson was the way he was. There was no limit to the effect or impact that a woman could have on a man he concluded.

'When do I get to meet her?' he asked.

'Well I seem to recall that you were keeping your good lady well away from me when I asked about meeting her.'

'That's different.'

'Why?'

'Because I didn't want to have to shoot you in the face when you started flirting with her,' he replied completely seriously.

Lawson smiled.

'But as I am not as insecure as you and don't have a stunningly handsome colleague to make me feel inadequate lurking in the background, she's flying over next week, so how about a foursome?'

'You're talking a date, nothing else?' Ward said and smiled again.

'Those days are past me dear Ryan.'

'Finally, you have a life that is problem free on the woman front. And you'll be a better man for it.'

'Well not completely problem free,' he replied.

'Why?'

'Because when I get home tonight I am going to have to tell the three naked women who will be waiting for me in my apartment that they will have to leave and give me my keys back.'

# TWENTY SEVEN

**3068 Brighton 6th Street – New York**

Buck had discovered exactly Where Glushakov had made base in New York. He had been told by his contact, a petty Russian thief who was the younger brother of one of his main contacts in Los Angeles, that the big boss, a man called Igor Vasin, had been told that he had some very important visitors coming and that all he had been told by some men who frequented Vasin's house was that one of them was a big black guy from Africa. The fact that Vasin had been told to accommodate his guests told Buck all he needed to know.
Only the Kremlin could put that pressure on people thousands of miles away.
When he had asked his contact about Vasin, he had told him that he was the most evil of evil men, and he would think nothing of killing people to make an example of them. His preferred method of killing was to slit the throats of people who crossed him and watch them bleed out. The Russian community generally knew that if someone was found with their throat cut, and left on display to bleed out, then it was almost a certainty that Vasin had ordered it to be done.
The contact had also told Buck that while everyone was afraid of Vasin, they were all completely terrified of his enforcer, a guy called Taras. Even taking into account

the fact that legends tend to get exaggerated more and more each time they are passed on, Buck had concluded that Taras must be a huge guy who was very handy with his fists. He doubted the contacts claim that Taras was nearly seven foot tall, but he believed him when he said that Taras frequently beat people to death and had once beat someone so severely that their neck snapped and tore the muscles and the victims head had almost completely been separated from the body.

He had communicated all of this to McDermott, and they had planned accordingly, before filling in Ward and Lawson once the plan had been finalised.

The Optician had been sent to the house to carry out the recon and had called in to tell Ward that there were at least fifteen guys in the house, if they took care of the inside of the property, he would pick of anyone trying to escape, a fact that made Gilligan groan loudly,

'I swear that this is the last time, next time I'm coming in with you,' he had protested, 'He can do the cleaning,' he added pointing at Lawson.

As usual, the plan had been to divide the team into two parts, front and back, Paul leading the rear, Ward and McDermott from the front.

'The Optician will take out anyone who comes out the front, everyone else is fair game, shoot to kill, with the exception of Glushakov, and you've all studied his picture. Is everyone clear who he is?' McDermott had said before they left the warehouse, a question that was meant with a resounding 'Clear' from everyone in the room.

They had parked the Range Rovers about fifty yards up from the house, one at either end of the street. Ward was surprised to see that there were no spotters along the street. Buck explained that the Russians were so arrogant, and so sure that the NYPD would steer clear of them that they didn't need them. Vasin would not want to pay someone to stand on the street when he could be using that manpower collecting debts or extorting money from people.

The house stood out to Ward, purely because on the plot next door sat an identical house. A long alleyway that ran between them was all that separated them. There was a set of steps that ran into a porch for the front door, with only two small windows about three feet apart on the first floor. There was a long alleyway which ran between the two houses which was only about three feet wide, and it seemed to be about six times as long at the side as it was at the front, just like the last house they had visited where they discovered the evil triplets.

'Why are there so many windows along the side of the house when there is no sunlight there?' Lawson asked.

'So one house can watch the rest obviously,' Ward replied, almost feeling pleased that Lawson was back to asking dumb questions again.

'Let's go Mac,' he said, picking the right moment when the street was almost deserted.

'Go,' McDermott said into his microphone, and two teams of assassins stepped out of each Range Rover at the same time in perfect tandem.

Ward led the way, with Lawson next to him, matching him stride for stride, with McDermott, Buck, Wired, and Fringe in a neat line following two paces behind. Paul and the others were in the same order heading towards the rear of the house.

Gilligan was parked in his car on the other side of the street, the clean-up crew parked just forty yards around the corner, three big vans at the ready.

They reached the steps and climbed up to the front door. Without speaking or instruction, Lawson leant forward and knocked hard, three times.

Then they waited.

At the rear of the house, Walsh had tried the back door and found it to be unlocked and so they stepped into a short, unlit hallway which had a door ahead of them to the left where he could hear voices coming from. It would be the kitchen; it always was the first room to come across when you came in through the rear of a house. He ushered Paul, Wallace and Fuller inside and Paul stepped to the front and stopped a foot away from the door frame, pushing his body hard up against the wall. He could hear at least four different voices coming from inside. He raised four fingers to the others to indicate that there were at least four people in the kitchen. He knew that the house was much longer than an average house and he wasn't entirely convinced that he would be able to hear the silenced gunshots coming from the front of the house and so he decided to count to ten in his head before moving.

The others slid up next to him, their bodies hard against the wall, waiting for instruction.

Then they waited.

The front door was opened after a good twenty second wait, by a topless guy holding a large kitchen knife in his hand, something he did as standard to intimidate anyone coming into the house Ward assumed.

But it didn't intimidate him.

Before he could speak and register that he was looking at six men all pointing guns at him, three of them silenced machine guns, Ward raised his hand and shot the guy in the centre of the face with two short bursts of fire. The blood sprayed forward all over his outstretched hand as the skin tore away from the flesh, the flesh tore away from the bone, and the bone splintered. He fell backwards in an almost rigid fashion onto the floor. There was a gaping hole in the left side of his face at least four inches wide, and the blood was starting to run out all over the dirty floor. He stepped over the body and made his way into the house. There was an open stairway in front of him, he headed towards it slowly while Buck and Fringe went to the left to deal with the rooms on that side, and McDermott and Wired headed to the right. He started to climb the stairs with Lawson walking backwards checking the rear. Care, caution and quiet, the three most important things required when entering a house full of armed Russians.

And then the silence was broken by a blast of muffled machine gun fire, which lasted a good five seconds, coming from the far end of the house.

Paul had stepped across the open door to the kitchen to the far side, allowing Wallace to gain access through the nearside, and they had both been surprised to see there was eight men in there, all sitting around a large table eating. They both opened fire at the same time and sprayed the group with bullets, Paul wiping out the right hand side of the table, Wallace the left. By the time they stopped firing, the kitchen looked like a bomb had exploded, and such was the volume of blood that had sprayed around the room from the bullets, it was hard to see the tiles on the floor under the blood. All of the men around the table had taken at least three direct hits to the head and chest each.

'Reload,' he said to Wallace, as Walsh and Fuller stepped in with guns scanning the dead bodies in case, in the highly unlikely event, that Paul and Wallace had not delivered kill shots.

None of them moved.

'Eight down' Paul said into his microphone after he had changed his magazine, a count that was heard by everyone through their comms.

As soon as he heard the fire, Ward and Lawson quickened their pace up the stairs. Another burst of fire from down below echoed out and McDermott's voice echoed in his ear, 'Two down,' promptly followed by another short burst and Buck saying, ''One down here.' As he reached the top of the stairs, a quick calculation told Ward that The Optician's assessment that there were fifteen men in the house, meant that if he was right, the last three in the house would be Vasin, Taras and Glushakov.

He looked at Lawson and raised his hand, indicating for him to stop, 'Mac,' he whispered into his microphone, 'Clear the downstairs and then you, Buck and the boys join us on the stairs. Paul and three others can secure downstairs.'

There were three different replies of 'Affirmative, understood and OK,' the unprofessional response clearly coming from Buck, and within sixty seconds, there were six people standing at the top of the stairs, pointing their guns, covering every direction so they would not be surprised.

Ward pulled out his phone and called The Optician, 'Has anyone left the house?' he said as soon as the ring tome stopped in his ear.

'No. I'm getting rather bored, this is the second time. Are you sure you actually need me?'

Ward hung up the phone,

'They are in the house. The Optician said he counted fifteen men, he won't be wrong, we all know that, so I'm assuming that Glushakov is up here in one of the rooms with Vasin and Taras. Remember, kill the other two but we need Glushakov alive.'

Everyone nodded.

There were four doors on either side of the long corridor, and one door at the end, all of them closed. The floor was covered in a dirty burgundy carpet and the walls were a dirty off white colour.

McDermott assumed control, 'Wired, you take that door nearest on the left, Buck you watch his back, Fringe, we'll take the right, you two head towards the door at the end, because I'm pretty sure that they will be hiding in there,' he said looking at Ward and Lawson.

Ward nodded and started to walk purposefully towards the door at the end with Lawson by his side, as the others cleared the rooms behind them, Lawson walking backwards with his gun raised protecting the rear once more.

He reached the door and noticed that it wasn't closed but was slightly ajar, he looked at Lawson, who promptly nodded.

He pushed his body hard against the wall to the left and gave the door a shove, the door opened fully. He quickly peered around the side and the room initially looked empty. He did another check and the room was clear but there was another door in the far left corner of the room and that was closed. It had to be a bathroom.

He stepped through the doorway and Lawson followed him in. The room was clearly being used, the folded clothes on a chair and toiletries on the sideboard confirming that to him, they both headed towards the bathroom door, and Ward put his ear against it when he reached it, and he couldn't hear anything. He looked at Lawson and shook his head, so Lawson stepped in front of him, turned the door handle and walked in with his gun raised.

It was empty.

He was just about to get everyone to double check that they had not killed Glushakov when he heard Mac's voice say, 'You'd better come here Ryan.'

He turned and walked out and saw McDermott standing in the doorway of one of the rooms on his left. As soon as he looked inside he smiled to himself. Lawson peered inside and said to him, 'Are we missing something?'

'No. We're not.'

'It looks like we are to me,' McDermott said.

'No, it's meant to make us think we are. I know what to do now.'

'What.'

'The opposite of what the Russians want us to do.'

Inside the room and lined up neatly on a sofa were three men. They had all had their throats cut and bled to death.

The first guy had his eyes cut out.

The second guy had his ears cut off.

The third guy had his tongue cut off.

On the lap of the guy in the middle with no ears was a note written in large capital letters that said.
'I WANT SIMONE BACK ALIVE.'

See no evil, hear no evil, and speak no evil.

# TWENTY EIGHT

**Park Avenue – New York**

'There isn't one piece of this information that wasn't meant to be found eventually,' Tackler said to Nicole-Louise, 'But I can't seem to make sense of it all because it seems to me that one part of it contradicts the other.'
'I agree,' she replied, 'And I'm finding it impossible to find where the money originated from. I mean if you cross reference the money trail against the phone records, it's easy to follow, even though I can't see where it first started from. It's like we were meant to find everything but whoever is behind this, they want us to have to work extra hard to find the source.'
Nicole-Louise was probably the best financial hacker on the planet. She could find anything eventually, and while she felt overwhelmingly frustrated at that moment that someone was getting the better of her, she let out a sigh and leant back into her chair. She knew that she would find it eventually, she always did, but she hated telling Ward that she was struggling to find some information. Tackler noticed her pull her hands away front her keyboard and stare at the screen in front of her, and he knew her well enough to know that was an indication to not speak to her and to leave her alone with her thoughts for however long she needed to be.
She hated letting Ward down.

Her relationship with him was as important to her as her life with Tackler. She looked at him as her younger brother who constantly needed looking after, even though Ward was a good few years older than her. She seemed to be the only one of the team who could deal sternly with him and he accepted it. She had seen him dismiss and ignore McDermott, Lawson and The Old Man on numerous occasions, but he had never once done it to her. She found it ironic that Ward was probably the most fearless man she had ever known, and yet she knew that she had the power and ability to put him firmly in his place just by looking at him in a contemptuous manner.

She and Tackler were problem solvers, the best, but right now, she felt like Ward had given her a thousand piece jigsaw puzzle to complete with a hundred pieces missing,

'You can call Ryan and give him everything that we have, he'll be waiting on it,' she eventually said to Tackler.

'Thanks!'

'I've got work to do,' she replied, and leant forward and started typing on her keyboard again.

Tackler picked up the phone and hit speed dial for Ward, four rings later, it was answered,

'Hello Tackler, I was just about to call you,' Ward said.

'Probably a mistruth, but I'm here anyway.'

'That's a fair point. Where are you with things?'

'This is going to take a bit of explaining, do you have five minutes?' he asked, hoping Ward would say he didn't so that they would have more time to find what they wanted to find.

'I always have five minutes for you. Hit me with it?'
'Damn!' he silently mouthed to himself
'From the beginning,' Ward said before he could utter a word, 'I don't want to misunderstand anything.'
Tackler breathed in deeply and began,
'Do you know who Samantha Ivey is?'
'No.'
'She's the Republican party chair.'
'OK,' Ward replied. It surprised him that Ward sounded so flippant. He was convinced that he was giving him some ground-breaking news.
'Well, she was the one who paid the money to Schultz.'
'You are referring to the six million dollars, the three payments of two million dollars each that you found?'
'Yes. The Republican Chair paid the deputy chair of the Democrats six million dollars over a four week period.'
'And you've linked that to specific events in Sudan, such as the rumours about Simone selling out, our involvement over there and the successful coup being carried out?'
'Shit!' Tackler mouthed to himself. They had both been so wrapped up in trying to find the source of the money that neither of them had thought to do that, 'Exactly, Nicole-Louise is working on that right now,' he lied.
'No need to waste your time, it will do, and it doesn't actually matter if it doesn't, because that is definitely what it is for, so tell her not to bother,' Ward replied, much to his delight.
Tackler continued, 'So Schultz then gets involved with Chandler, there are very extensive phone records of the calls they have shared. I assume this was to do with

giving Chandler's company complete and exclusive access to the region?'
'That's what it was meant to look like.'
'So what else could it be?'
'Carry on,' Ward said.
'Our friend Vice President Wilson then makes a number of calls to Chandler, and that brings us to where we are now. The worrying thing is, all of that information was too easy to find. It was almost as though someone made no attempt to hide it. Can I ask you a question?'
'Of course you can.'
'Is Simone still alive? I know the Russians want him back and you have that Glushakov guy hunting him, but you've not mentioned him or them for the past day.'
'They are both still alive.'
'I'm surprised you would want to keep an animal like that alive.'
'Everything is for a reason Tackler. Trust me on this one, as soon as he can be killed, he will.'
'I can't see any reason for you keeping him alive. If you want my opinion…….'
'Stop right there,' Ward said sharply.
'I was just saying.'
'I know you too well. You are trying to change the subject for a reason.'
'Damn!' Tackler mouthed to himself for the second time.
'The one part you haven't yet resolved is the part most crucial to everything. I want you both working on it and find proof of it no matter what. It is more important than anything. You work forwards, I'll work backwards.'
'What do you mean backwards?'

'I think it's time to pay Chandler a visit. Send me his details as soon as I end the call.'
'I will. But just so I'm clear, which part do you think I was deliberately avoiding not mentioning?'
'Nothing is more vital than finding out where the money that was paid to Ivey originated from in the first place?' Ward said and the line went dead.
What Tackler couldn't see as he hung up the phone was Ward standing in McDermott's warehouse, putting his phone back into his pocket, with the most satisfying grin spread across his face.

**University Ave, Bronx – New York**

'Why are you looking so pleased with yourself?' Lawson asked.
'I've just spoken to Tackler and he has found a hell of a lot of information, as you predicted, but we now have to start doing our bit.' Ward replied, before detailing everything that Tackler had told him. His phone vibrated in his pocket and he pulled it out and read the text from Tackler,
'I want you to go to North Dakota to get what you can from Chandler.'
'Just like that?' Lawson replied in mock surprise,
'You're giving me responsibility and a free hand?'
'I like this new you, you'll do the right thing. There is no point in both of us spending eight hours getting there and back, I have plenty to do here. Get it sorted with The Old Man.'
'Do I get The Optician?'
'Seriously?'

'Why not? This new me is smarter than you, equally as capable, and definitely more handsome, so the next logical step would be for me to take over as the Deniable in chief, so I may as well get used to having a babysitter every time I have to do something remotely dangerous.'

'I think I preferred the old Lawson,' Ward replied and walked across to the Simone's as Lawson made the call to Centrepoint.

Samson looked tired and beaten.

'You know that you have been played and none of this was ever about your country and your precious access, don't you?'

'They need me; they will be coming for me.'

'You're right, they do need you, much more than you realise. But here's the thing,' Ward said calmly, 'As much as I want to kill you, I can't.'

Simone's eyes lit up. He turned his head sideways to look at his son, whose face looked equally as delighted to hear the news.

'You've actually got no idea how frustrating I find that,' Ward continued, 'I want to kill you more than anything. You have terrorised women and children for way too long. You're a coward; the worst type actually, because you hide behind soldiers and get them to do your dirty work. I saw your video of you making those poor kids play Russian roulette. Did that make you feel like a warlord? Did it make you feel al powerful?'

McDermott and Paul saw Ward talking and strolled over to listen,

'What do you two think?' he asked, looking at them both as they stood either side of him, 'You're real soldiers, do you think this guy is all powerful?'

'He must be,' Paul said, 'He kills women and children and he sells out to the big bad Russians. I'd go as far to say that he is terrifying.'
Ward smiled, 'Mac, you're opinion?'
'I'm almost too frightened to speak, especially after watching that video of him with that mute kid. He's the meanest warrior I have ever come across.'
'But we can't kill him anyway, he's too valuable,' Ward said.
'The best thing you can do is let us both go and I give you my word I will leave America and never come back. It would probably be in your best interests to do that, and then I will forgive you your insult of coming into my country,' Simone said calmly, the first time that he had spoken in anything but an aggressive or frightened manner since they had trussed him up in the warehouse.
'Do you think we can trust him?' Paul asked.
'He seems honourable enough,' McDermott added.
The excitement that his ordeal might be coming to an end was etched all over Simone's face; even his son forced a pathetic smile.
'You can trust me,' Simone said eagerly, 'After all; you have nothing to gain by keeping me here. As you said yourself, you can't kill me.'
'True,' Ward replied, 'But I most certainly can hurt him while you watch,' he added and pulled his Glock out of his waistband, pointed it at Patrick Simone from no more than three feet away, fired two bullets into his leg. The noise of the gunshots echoed around the warehouse, Wired jumped to his feet and pointed his gun which had been lying on the table in front of him, Walsh did the same and Wallace hit the floor. Fringe had his

headphones on, listening to music, his feet up on the table and his eyes closed tight and didn't flinch, and Fuller started laughing at everyone's reaction.

Buck, who was looking at a map laid out on one of the workbenches did not even turn around.

Two bullets from three feet away make one hell of a mess to someone's leg. The blood started running onto the floor, but fortunately, they had missed any main arteries, so as intended, Patrick wouldn't die but it would hurt a great deal..

Simone let out a deep and wild scream and started trying to rock his chair violently, but the chair had been so well secured to the floor by eye bolts that he was never going to tip it over.

'Look at the mess on the floor,' McDermott said, the three of them studying it for a few seconds, deliberately ignoring Simone, even though it was difficult with the Banshee like screams bouncing off of the warehouse walls.

'Last one to say 'Not me', has to clean it up,' Paul shouted to the table,

'Not me,' Said Wired, Fuller, Walsh and Wallace in one voice.

'Not me,' Buck said without even turning around, 'I have enough to do cleaning up the mess your mom leaves in my bed thanks,' he added.

Everyone laughed except for Mac and Paul.

Patrick was rocking on the chair, sobbing and screaming, and so Paul stepped forward and hit him hard in the face, three times, his fist breaking his nose the moment the first punch landed. The fourth punch was the one that rendered him unconscious.

'I would have done that in one,' Lawson shouted from behind them, just having finished his call to The Old Man, 'Now if you girls have stopped playing, I need to get to the airport, I'll ring when I get there.' And he turned and walked towards the reception area.
'Someone better tell Fringe,' Wired shouted across. Wallace nudged Fringe's leg and he opened his eyes. He removed his headphones and looked over at the bloody mess on the floor.
'We have just finished playing the 'Not me' game,' Wallace said, 'you lost.'
'You have got to be kidding me!'
Ward felt his phone vibrate in his pocket and pulled it out.
The words 'unknown number' were flashing on the display. He had intended to answer this time but had now decided to unsettle the caller a little bit more.
'Have you decided if there are any places worth hitting where we can play a game with your Russian friends Buck?' Ward shouted across to him.
'There are three places. One is a shop owned by a small time hood in Newark. He will be able to tell us what we want to know; as he is the biggest snitch in New York my contact has told me. The second one is a house on Brighton Beach where the tough guys meet to divide their share of the pie, and I've been reliably informed that they sit in the garden all day drinking vodka, so your friend with the scope can deal with that one, and the third one is a place in Queens. But the last one can wait,' Buck replied.
'Why wait?' McDermott asked.

'Because I guarantee you that after we have done the first two hits that is where Glushakov will go.'

'Happy?' McDermott asked Ward.

'Yes. I trust anything that Buck says about the Russians.'

'OK, we'll start making plans.'

'And I had better call The Old Man now and tell him what is happening,' Ward said and headed towards the reception area.

# TWENTY NINE

**Washington D.C.**

'What instructions have you given Lawson?' Centrepoint asked as he answered the call.
'I haven't given him any, I've left dealing with Chandler at his discretion,' Ward replied.
While Ward knew how he would deal with Chandler, simply for the fact that he clearly had no conscience in using an access route that he would know was created for him by the monster Simone, he wasn't sure how Lawson would respond to the pressure that he knew The Old Man would have put on him not to eliminate the CEO of one of the major oil companies. Lawson had to tread carefully, he was still relatively new in Centrepoint's eyes and Ward knew that he would be measuring every decision Lawson made against his own strict criteria. The problem was that Lawson had seen how he was with The Old Man and if he thought that he could act the same way, he would be very mistaken and he would be sent back to England with his tail between his legs before he knew it.
'You don't leave anything to chance Ryan. But for your information, I have told him to do whatever he deems necessary.'
The response took Ward by surprise,
'Well that's unlike you. What's changed?'
'The bigger picture has changed.'

Here we go again, Ward thought to himself, the big picture once more,
'Specifically?' he asked.
'Chandler has notified the Republican Chair that he intends to stop his sponsorship of the party due to their involvement in putting Simone in place in the region. That has caused mass panic with Wilson and the president and so the pressure has been put on me.'
'So if Lawson eliminates Chandler before he can formally do that, the money keeps coming?'
'In a nutshell, yes.'
'You know everything that is happening?'
'From our point of view, pretty much.'
'What are we going to do about the Russians?'
The Old Man paused for a moment, that gave Ward the opportunity to jump in,
'You know I can't do this without you,' he said.
'Have Nicole-Louise and Tackler found the money source?'
'You're asking me? I know you bug their phone and see on your screens what they are looking at, so you tell me?' Ward replied.
'No they haven't.'
'So do you think that you know exactly what is happening?'
'I think I'm the only person in Washington who does, but let's say that you run it by me to confirm?'
'No, you run it past me?'
'We are on dangerous ground Ryan. We both know that the SVR could only have been sent here directly from the president's office. Agreed?'
'Agreed.'

'So you know that we can't get involved directly, by we, I mean Washington?'

'I understand that. But you also know that I have to finish this to change the dynamics of it back in our favour, so I'm surprised that you are speaking in cryptic messages to me about it.'

'Which could only be for one reason,' The Old Man replied abruptly.

There could only be one reason Ward thought to himself, such was the severity of this plan working out that all hell would break loose. Which meant the NSA would be monitoring every word that he said, and there was not one political player, including Centrepoint or even the president, who would issues instructions on this one. He almost felt sorry for him. He knew that he wanted to help and protect him, but he would be under such immense pressure right now to make this all go away, from both sides of the house, that he was in a lose-lose situation, so the best thing he could say was nothing,

'OK. I understand. But it is my way, no advice, interference or instruction. Are we agreed on that?' he asked.

'You will do what you think is for the good of the country, as always,' Centrepoint replied so formally, that Ward knew it was simply for the benefit of the listening ears.

'Just one thing, if this goes as far as I think it will go, can you guarantee me that any diplomatic mess will be sorted out by our top man?' Ward asked.

'He is in the picture.'

'I prefer you when you lecture me,' Ward said and hung up the phone.

Centrepoint leant back into his chair and sighed. He Had been careful not to implicate anyone else in the matter apart from Chandler simply for his own safety. He was caught between a rock and a hard place. On one side, the President wanted him to deal with it and make it go away, and on the other side, the more than likely future president wanted it dealt with to not go away. He wished that he could have told Ward exactly what was happening in the corridors of power in Washington, but he couldn't because until Ryan Ward had decided what he was going to do, the whole of the American political establishment would have to wait and see.

**University Ave, Bronx – New York**

While The Old Man was waiting on Ward to deliver something firm, he was waiting on Nicole-Louise and Tackler. He was going to call them but then told himself that they would call as soon as they had something to tell him and pestering them was the last thing that they would need right now.

He walked back into the warehouse and saw a hive of activity. McDermott was leaning over a map issuing instructions to Paul and the others and Buck and Gilligan were leaning on a smaller map looking like they were talking about the Mets latest defeat rather than planning a hit.

He smiled to himself. He might be the conductor, but he had the best orchestra playing for him in the world.

He felt his phone vibrate in his pocket and was hoping it was either Nicole-Louise or Tackler as he pulled it out, instead, he saw the words 'Unknown Number.'
Now was the time to talk,
'I can talk to you now Yury,' he said as he answered. There was no response initially and so he added, 'Look, we're both highly skilled, highly smart operatives, so let's not play games and act like adults, shall we?'
'Perhaps.'
'OK, me first,' Ward said, 'Your name is Yury Glushakov. You are an SVR operative and you work under the direct orders of General Viktor Zhirkov, who is probably your President's closest friend in the halls of The Kremlin, so I know who you are, and exactly what you want.'
'You have an advantage over me,' Glushakov replied, 'Could you tell me why MI6 are involved in American matters?'
Ward smiled to himself. Glushakov had just confirmed that he had no idea who he really was, which meant that he had no idea who Lawson, McDermott and Gilligan were either. Buck was a known entity to them, but he had been anyway, and he knew that he would work out a way to stay out of their grip. However, as he was still waiting on Nicole-Louise and Tackler to come through with the information that he needed, he couldn't give too much away, so he played along,
'We have interests down there that we keep away from the Americans, so we need to protect ourselves first and foremost. I'm sure you understand that?' he lied.
'I need Simone back.'

He smiled to himself. Glushakov was as reluctant to say anything as much as he was, so he changed tact,
'The bodies you lined up, the three wise monkeys, we can't work that part out. Can you give me a little clue?'
'You need to look more carefully at the bodies.'
Ward smiled to himself. They had established that the whole point of the Russians trying to imply the bodies meant something was to distract them, to make them think it had some hidden, deeper meaning, and they had almost fallen for it, but Glushakov had just given it away by making such a giving statement.
'We've got our people on it,' he replied, 'We will get to the bottom of it,' he added for effect.
'I want Simone back.'
'How did you know that we would be coming for you? The way you vanished impressed me a great deal. So tell me how?'
Glushakov laughed, it wasn't a false laugh either, he could hear the genuine amusement in it.
'Please my friend, give me some credit,' he replied and then paused for another laugh.'
'You send two men into a restaurant who may as well have had 'I used to be a US Navy Seal' written on their foreheads, and one of them pretends to be writing a text when his hand movement shows him clearly to be taking a picture of me, and you expect someone with my skill set not to notice? You should have done it yourself, at least you British tend to look non descriptive.'
Ward smiled to himself, you haven't met Lawson, he thought to himself. He also made a mental note to pass on the comments to McDermott, and smiled again when

he pictured him lecturing both Wired and Fringe on making a mistake.

'You wear a suit well,' he said.

'I want Simone back.'

'Why don't you tell me where you are and we can meet up and discuss it like adults?'

'You are keeping him alive for a reason, what is it?' Glushakov asked.

'You have something very important that the British government need,' he lied, 'Perhaps we can make a deal, come to an arrangement?'

'What is it?'

'You know what it is, you give me that, I'll give you Simone.'

'I have no idea what you are talking about,' Glushakov replied.

Neither do I, Ward thought to himself, but now it's your turn to chase a dead end,

'You really don't know, do you?' he said.

Silence on the end of the line.

'Then you have been kept in the dark for a reason, so I suggest that you give General Zhirkov a call, get it sent to you, so we can meet up and exchange, and then we can all go home happy and the Americans are none the wiser,' Ward said firmly and ended the call.

### The Kremlin – Moscow

Just twenty minutes after Ward had hung up on Glushakov, General Viktor Zhirkov was standing in front of the President's desk once again,

'I have spoken to Comrade Glushakov and he has made contact with the MI6 agent. He says that they still have Simone alive but that we have something that the British government want back. Apart from the three year old list of their operatives, we don't have anything to my knowledge, unless there is something that you know on the matter Sir?' he asked cautiously, making sure that there wasn't the smallest hint of accusation to his tone.

'The list we had is now worthless Viktor, we both know that. Their operatives would have been completely changed by now,' the president replied, leaning back into his chair and looking deep in thought for a moment.

'I can't imagine what it can be then. The few defectors that we know about who had settled in Britain that we have repatriated would be of no use to them, and the ones that are left there have nothing of any value to concern us. So what else can it be?' Zhirkov asked, now looking equally as deep in thought.

'An MI6 operative working with the Americans, who take something that is of no concern or value to them in the shape of Simone, and now they want something that they claim we have and won't say what it is? They are leaving the European Union thank God, so that intended super state will now implode, so my initial feeling is that perhaps they want Simone for themselves, because they can then threaten Bassong with his return and then they can have the access for themselves and British companies. That seems like the only logical reason for their involvement to me. But we have nothing of theirs. The American's have control of the region and they have Simone, and I can't see them so openly betraying the

American's. So there can be only one conclusion,' the President eventually said.
'Which is Sir?'
'They aren't British.'

They were interrupted by a knock on the door. This was something that surprised them both because clear instructions had always been given that the President was never to be interrupted when he was in a meeting with someone.
'Come,' the President shouted in an annoyed tone.
A very nervous and very flustered young General walked in and saluted.
'What do you want?' the President demanded.
'I am so sorry to dare to interrupt you Sir but I have something of grave importance to tell you that could not wait.'
The President nodded, indicating that he would hear it.
'Five minutes ago our system was compromised.'
The President shot upright,
'What system?' he demanded.
'Our financial tracking system.'
'Was anything taken?'
'Yes Sir, nine files.'
'Do you know who took it?'
'No Sir, the trail has stopped dead in Egypt. Whoever it was has disappeared.'
'Our system should be impenetrable. I want General Holskof here immediately,' he shouted at the top of his voice, his face visibly turning red and standing up as he screamed.

As the young general turned to scurry out, the president shouted,

'What was taken General?'

'Some payment records Sir.'

'Of what?'

'Payments made to individuals.'

'To whom?' he demanded.

'They were all Russians living in Europe apart from one Sir.'

'The name of the non-Russian?'

'Samantha Ivey.'

The President thumped the desk hard and swung his right hand, knocking off his desk lamp onto the floor. He leant both hands on the desk and then sighed deeply. Zhirkov looked terrified. He stood still like a schoolboy standing in front of his fearsome headmaster.

The President eventually looked up at Zhirkov and said, 'Viktor, my friend, you have failed me. I will give you one chance to put it right.'

# THIRTY

**78 Wakeman Avenue – Newark, New Jersey.**

Gilligan and Buck had taken the journey from the warehouse over to Newark. They were still arguing as they pulled into Wakeman Avenue, because Gilligan had insisted on taking the I-95 freeway and going on the Newark-New Jersey turnpike, insisting to Buck that it was the quickest route. Buck had said that he thought going via I-95 and 1-280W would have been quicker, but Gilligan had just scoffed at him. It had taken almost forty five minutes due to the volume of traffic
'You can say what you like Gilligan, but I'm from out of town and even I know that hitting the turnpike at this time of day was a bad move,' Buck said for the fifth time in five minutes.
'For someone who is only here because he knows a little bit about the Russians, you've got a lot to say on the matter,' Gilligan replied dismissively, for the fifth time in five minutes.
'Oh, I get it now. The new boy is not allowed to have an opinion?'
'Your place has to be earned.'
'Well, from where I sit, all I've seen you do is drive a car and call in the cleaners. How long did it take you to earn that lofty position?'
Buck knew how to push people's buttons, he was a master at it, and he had hit Gilligan dead centre with that comment,
'You think that's all I have ever done?' Gilligan asked. Buck instantly knew he had stepped over a line,

'No, I didn't mean that. I know what happened. When I first met the others in Los Angeles I heard your story,' he said apologetically.

Gilligan didn't say anything.

'And I have to say, you're probably a better man than me. I think if I would have almost died, I would call it a day. I know that Ryan holds you in very high regard and that says an awful lot about you.'

'It was an easy choice to make,' Gilligan said, sounding reasonably appeased, 'He saved my life, I owe him. He's just keeping me at arm's length from danger until he's sure I'm over what happened.'

'Are you?'

'Yes I am. I have always thought that the number of people he killed was way too excessive, but I've worked with him long enough to know that he only ever kills people who deserve it. He's a good guy, just a little too trigger happy at times.'

Buck nodded. He had been impressed with Ward from the first day that he had met him, and even though he had spent a long, long time moving throughout the Russian mafia in Moscow, he had never come across anyone as violent as Ward. Yet what had always impressed him the most was the decency that Ward possessed and his respect for normal everyday people. He had heard him say time and time again that it was his duty to stand up for the little guy on the street. He admired him greatly for that sentiment.

'So what's your story?' Gilligan asked, 'You seem to be the joker in the pack, there's much more to you than that I assume. Plus your 'Mom' jokes are wearing a bit thin.

Do you only have one gag line? Are you a mommy's boy who can't stand to be away from her?'

'It's a defence mechanism,' Buck replied quickly.

'What do you mean?'

'My mom was the most important person in my life. She got into money trouble with some loan sharks in L.A. because of a gambling problem, and they broke into her house one night, took her and tore her arms and legs from her. They literally, pulled them off with some kind of machine. Then they dumped the body parts in five different States to send out a message. It took six years to find all the parts and put her back together again. So I mention 'Mom' every day because it keeps her memory alive for me,' he replied and looked down at his lap.

'I'm sorry man. I didn't mean to upset you. I mean, I had no way of knowing that,' Gilligan replied, now feeling completely stupid, 'When did this happen?' he asked.

'Well,' Buck said, looking up from his lap, 'It didn't. But it could of. And you would feel like a complete jackass for saying anything about her. So learn from your lesson driver,' he said, and waved his hand forward in front of him, an instruction for Gilligan to continue driving.

'You are one sick man,' Gilligan said.

Buck smiled, 'Which your mom says is her favourite thing about me.'

They never spoke again until they reached their destination. Gilligan would occasionally tut and shake his head, and then throw Buck a contemptuous look, something that Buck found extremely funny.

'OK, pull in here. That's the shop there,' Buck said, pointing to a small shop front with a sign saying 'Groceries' above it.

'Are we likely to encounter any bad people inside?' Gilligan asked.

'Let's find out,' Buck replied and opened the car door and climbed out before Gilligan had even had time to apply the handbrake. He climbed out himself and scurried after him, discreetly pulling out his gun from his waistband and holding it firmly down against his leg to hide it. Buck strode forward, pushed open the door and strode up to the counter. There was a middle aged woman serving, and only two other elderly women browsing the shelves. He said something to the woman behind the counter in Russian that Gilligan had no chance of understanding, and the woman immediately left her place at the counter and headed towards a door on the left at the end of one of the isles. Buck followed and once again, Gilligan scurried after him. They walked through the door into a small room and there was a middle aged man sitting at a desk with a mountain of invoices to his left and a worn looking calculator sitting on the desk in front of him.

'Evgeni told you that I was coming?' he asked the man.

'Yes, I have asked around and I think I have found what you need,' the man replied, eying up Gilligan suspiciously, something that Buck noticed.

'He's with me,' he said quickly, 'And he's not in a good place right now, he's just had some bad news about his mom, so if I were you, I would make sure that what you tell me is one hundred percent correct.'

The man gave Gilligan a nervous look. He wanted to punch Buck in the face right then, but in response, he did the only thing that he could think of, he looked back at the man and growled. It was an act that had Buck raising an eyebrow and he had to use all of his self-control not to burst out laughing.

'It is correct,' the man said.

'So now I want to know what you know about the guy the Kremlin sent and what the whole point of him being here is?' Buck asked.

The man started talking immediately. His cousin had told him that Buck was a CIA agent and he would kill a Russian as soon as look at him, so he had to make sure that he found the information that he needed and to make sure it is accurate, or there would be repercussions that he could not protect him from.

'Moscow has sent their man here for one simple reason,' he said.

'We know that,' Buck replied, and pulled out his handgun and pointed it at the man, 'He's here to take someone back. You aren't telling me anything I don't know, so you are wasting my time.'

'That's not the reason.'

Buck and Gilligan both raised an eyebrow at the same time.

The man just sat there, waiting for the prompt.

'Well?' Gilligan interrupted.

'He's here to make sure that you kill the person in question.'

**University Ave, Bronx – New York**

Ward knew full well that right now, he was completely isolated from The Old Man and that even when he had the information that he needed, he would still have to weigh up the best way to deal with it. He had broken it down into three parts in his mind. How to deal with Simone, how to deal with those responsible, and how to make sure that the Kremlin kept quiet.

He felt his phone vibrate in his pocket and pulled it out quickly.

Nicole-Louise's name was flashing on the caller display.

'Hello,' he answered quickly.

'Well you sound pleased to hear from me,' she said sarcastically.

'Do you have anything for me?'

'I have everything for you.'

A big smile spread across his face. He knew that they would find it, he even knew that what he was asking them to do would be really difficult, but he always knew that they would find it.

Nicole-Louise was going to give him the final piece he needed to resolve this whole matter in a fashion that would protect the country. He wanted to give her the biggest hug right then. As he couldn't, he decided that he would let her tell him what she had found and how she had found it in her own time, without any prompting for once.

'OK. What have you got?' he asked.

'We have the complete picture,' she said without a hint of arrogance in her voice, 'Shall I tell you how we got it, or shall I jump to the bottom line, like you normally insist I do?'

He felt a calm wash over him. For once it was nice talking to her without having to rush her. Gilligan and Buck were in Newark, Lawson was in North Dakota. and McDermott and the team were going over the plans for the eventual attack on the house in Queens where they were reliably informed by Buck that Glushakov would eventually be, so he had time on his hands.

'No, I want to be clear on this. Tell me what you have, working backwards from Wilson.'

'We have the evidence for everything, the why is still unclear, but my guess is that you already know, you just want proof to tie it all together for you.'

'I just need the last piece of evidence. The why became clear to me after talking it through with Lawson.'

'Wow! Mike actually solved something?' she asked and laughed down the line.

'He certainly helped. He's a new man.'

'Mike will never be a new man.'

'I'm serious Nicole-Louise. He shared something with me. Something that he has never told anyone which made a lot of sense about why he was the way he was,' he replied.

'Was, as in the past tense?'

'You know I would never share a private conversation I have had with anyone else, so let's just say that I have a feeling that from now, we will see a totally different Mike.'

'Interesting,' she replied.

'It is. And let's just say that when you said to me a while ago that he is the way he is for a reason, you were right,' he replied, starting to feel that he had already said too much about Lawson's love life.

'Oh my God! He got in touch with Lucy?' She screamed down the phone.
He wasn't expecting that,
'He told you about her?' he asked, almost sounding disappointed.
'Well, only after I had told him about it and asked who she was. It was obvious to any female. Seriously, do you ever take the time to look at any of us closely?'
He thought he did.
'Obviously I don't,' he replied.
'Just think about it in future,' she said softly, 'Now, shall I begin?'
'Yes please.'
'Wilson wanted The Old Man to resolve the problem with Simone, which he did, and the reason he wanted it done was because Chandler wanted the sole access route for his company. He threatened that without it, he was going to withdraw his ample funding to the Democratic Party. Schultz was dealing with the matter on behalf of the party, and we then discovered that he was receiving payment from the Republican Party in the shape of Samantha Ivey, six million dollars in total, three payments of two million pounds. But you already knew this and so the only question was where the six million came from in the first place. Agreed?'
'I know where it came from, I just need proof.'
'Which you know have. The Russians take great pride in the fact that they are very good at flooding our systems with fake news and mistruths, but even more pride in the fact that their data systems are pretty much like Fort Knox. But that didn't stop me and Tackler. We hacked directly into the Kremlin financial system,' she said with

such pride in her voice that he instantly forgave her for implying he had no interest in the lives of the people that he considered to be his closest friends.

'You have that proof, completely authentic and definite?' he asked.

'We have more than that. We even have the name of the person who authorised it.'

'Hopefully you are going to tell me it was a General Viktor Zhirkov?'

'How on earth do you know that?'

'It was just a lucky guess.'

'What I don't understand is why go to all of this trouble with Simone in the first place , and why is Schultz trying to deprive his own party of funding that they are desperate for, and why the Russians would pay a Republican to pay a Democrat. Can you answer that without any cryptic sentences?'

'If you ever took the time to look at me closely, you'd already know how I work these things out,' he replied and hung up the phone.

# THIRTY ONE

### 1325 E Broadway Avenue – Bismarck, North Dakota

Lawson was feeling on top of the world as he completed the short drive from Bismarck Airport to the head office of Foundation Resources, Gary Chandler's company. He had managed to fit in another two hours on the phone to Lucy, and he felt almost as though the last twelve years had never happened.

The offices were situated in the middle of a run of the mill industrial park, and they were both new and plush by comparison to the majority of the other buildings that he had passed. It wasn't overly welcoming. It was a large square building with lots of windows to let light into the offices and the reception entrance was just a large double door with a brass plaque on the left with 'Foundation Resources' written on it.

He walked through the doors towards the reception desk which was manned by a middle aged lady, who adjusted herself upright into her chair and moved her hair behind her left ear when she caught a glimpse of his handsome face. While he now had no interest in any other woman in the world other than Lucy Corrigan, he wasn't stupid enough to stop using his greatest weapon which was his charm and the fact that he was so handsome.

'Hello,' he said to the lady, as he smiled and gazed deeply into her eyes.

She blushed instantly, 'Hello Sir, how may I help you?'

'I need to see Mr Chandler.'

'Do you have an appointment?'

'I don't but it's really important,' he said as sincerely as he possibly could.

'I'm sorry Sir; Mr Chandler will not see anyone without an appointment.'

'I think he will want to see me.'

She looked at him quizzically. She was now in two minds. She could insist that he would have to make an appointment and come back, or she could listen to what he had to say.

He made the decision for her.

'Can you just tell him that I am an assistant to Mr Schultz and I have something to give him that will clear the whole Sudanese mess up as though it never happened, I'll wait over there while you call through,' he said, pointing to the comfy looking leather sofa opposite the desk and walking across to sit down.

He could see the woman's reflection in one of the windows, and he could see her pause for a few moments before finally picking up the phone and talking to someone. He sat on the sofa looking nonchalantly around; a purposeful act designed to convince the woman that he knew that Chandler would want to see him, even though he was now regretting not saying that there has been a problem with Chandler's involvement in Sudan instead.

After a couple of minutes, he heard the phone on the desk ring and the woman spoke into it briefly and then put the phone down,

'Second floor, turn left and follow the hall to the large doors at the end,' she said to him, pointing to an elevator.

He stood up, smiled at her and headed towards the elevator. When he reached the second floor and stepped out into the hallway, he was surprised to find that it wasn't an open plan office as he expected but a long hall with doors to offices every ten feet. There were no windows to be able to see inside, but he figured that there was so much light that came into the building through the giant windows outside that it would not be needed.

He reached the doors and walked in without knocking.
'You can go out and then knock and wait to be invited in,' a man sitting behind a desk said.
Lawson looked at him. He could tell that he was not a well-built man and the steel-rimmed glasses he wore made him look untrustworthy and shifty. His hair was dyed a strange black colour in places which looked more like someone had used a permanent marker to colour it in rather than dye it evenly. He smiled.
'Leave and knock,' he repeated.
Lawson closed the door.
A rage seemed to spread across the man's face, something that made him look like he was having an attack of some sort.
Lawson smiled and approached the desk,
'I'm going to ask you some questions. You are going to answer them. Do you know why?' he asked.
Chandler had never before had anyone in his office who would dare to confront him let alone threaten him, he wasn't going to start letting it happen now,
'Don't you dare come into my office and speak to me in that tone of voice. Who do you think you are?' he demanded.

Lawson walked over to the desk, and pushed his huge thighs hard up against it. Then with lightning speed, he shot his right hand forward and flicked Chandler hard on the nose.

A normal sized man flicking another man on the nose would maybe feel like a slap. With the immense strength that Lawson possessed, it was like jabbing someone with your fist.

Chandler's head shot back and he screamed, before bringing both hands up to his nose and covering his face and screaming.

'What's wrong with you?' Lawson said, 'I flicked you for God's sake!'

'You've broken my nose,' Chandler whimpered.

Lawson rolled his eyes,

'Who told you to withdraw your funding to the Democratic Party?'

Chandler looked up at him, understanding the question but having no idea who this giant of man standing over him was.

Lawson walked slowly and deliberately around the desk and put his massive hand on Chandler's shoulder,

'I really am one of the bad guys,' He started, 'I'm one of the people who went into Sudan and took Simone. I'm also one of the people that they call in when the politicians do things they shouldn't and they want it cleaned up. So to say you are completely out of your depth here is the understatement of the year.'

Chandler looked terrified,

'It was Schultz,' he said immediately.

A typical coward's response Lawson thought.

'How much money are you worth?' he asked.

'Sorry?'
'You heard me, how much money are you worth, to the nearest million?'
'I don't know two fifty or something.'
'Million?'
'Yes.'
'When I get back to where I came from, I'm going to get my friends to steal it,' Lawson said, suddenly realising that he was starting to sound exactly like Ward.
'I've told you that Schultz told me to withdraw my funding,' Chandler protested.
'How did that come about, tell me the discussion that took place?'
'He contacted me, told me that they were having trouble with access own in Sudan….'
'When?' Lawson interrupted.
'Six months ago.'
Lawson knew that was a long time before anyone was aware that Simone was going to jump to the other side, something that confirmed the theory that he and Ward had discussed from the start,
'Continue,' he said.
'I told him that access was paramount to the success of our operations down there and he said that he had a solution that would be beneficial to us both.'
'Go on.'
'He said that Simone was about to shut down all access routes for American companies through there, but if I did something for him, then the government would put someone in place of Simone who would allow exclusive access to my company only.'
'And that something was to stop funding for his party?'

'Yes.'
'You didn't find that strange?'
'Of course I did. I couldn't see any logic to it at all.'
'But you did it anyway.'
'Yes I did, but only after he threatened me a few days ago.'
'Threatened you how?'
'He said that they now had control of the region and if I didn't call the Party Chair and inform them I was withdrawing my support then access would be closed to me. My company needs that; it will cost us millions to transport everything around Sudan.'
'What do you know about Samson Simone and the Russians?'
'What do you mean the Russians? I don't understand the question?'
Lawson could see that he had no idea what he was talking about, so he skipped it,
'What do you know about Simone?' he asked.
He knew that Chandler was now faced with a huge dilemma. If he answered the question truthfully, he would have to say that he was fully aware that Simone tortured and killed thousands of innocent people, mainly women, old men and children throughout the region, if he lied, he would be distancing himself from the actions of a vicious warlord.
He lied.
'I don't know anything about what he does really. I just know that he has a relationship with our government. How he established that relationship, I have no idea.'
Lawson shot his hand from Chandler's shoulder and flicked him hard on the side of the face.

He screamed out again.

'Lie to me again and the next one will be a punch,' Lawson said, 'Last time, I want to know what you know about Simone?'

'I know that he rules the region with a fist of iron,' Chandler replied through a whimper.

'Was it worth it?'

'No.'

'I mean was it worth it for a few more million dollars?' Lawson asked.

Chandler shook his head.

For the first time in his life, Lawson understood why Ward always felt the need to go into a long speech before he killed someone. He wanted Chandler to understand why he was going to die. He hadn't intended to kill him when he arrived in Bismarck, but he finally understood Ryan Ward completely at that moment. He wasn't going to kill Chandler because he was a greedy, selfish man who felt money defined him, he was going to kill him because if it wasn't for faceless people like him, there would be no need for people like Samson Simone, and therefore no need for the death and agony that all of those thousands of innocent people had been made to suffer in Sudan.

But he needed to understand why he was going to die.

'By the time I get back to New York, you will be penniless and dead. Also, I'm going to get a story leaked and authenticated through the media that you personally funded Simone's reign of terror and your greed got you killed because Simone came for you. Everything will be wrapped up nicely so the government are completely clean.'

'Please, I beg you, I was put under immense pressure, what was I going to do? There are thousands of people who work for my company and I have an obligation and responsibility to them to keep them employed. Much more so than I have loyalty to the Africans. My people all have families and bills to pay. I'll do anything you ask, just please don't hurt me.'
Lawson smiled at Chandler,
'Thanks,' he said as he raised his other hand that had been hanging down by his side to reveal his phone had recorded the whole conversation, 'I just needed you to clarify what we already knew.'
He pressed stop on the screen and slid the phone back into his pocket.
'Please, don't hurt me,' Chandler said and started crying.
It felt different not having Ward standing next to him. He normally would have said something totally inappropriate at that moment had he of been there with Ward, but he was actually discovering just how empowering and gratifying it could be to decide if the bad guys lived or died.
He had decided.
He unleashed an uppercut which came from his right hand side and carried the full force of his power the eight inches to Chandler's head and connected flush with his temple. The force of the punch was so great that the pressure running through Chandler's body snapped off the arm to his chair as he feel and landed three feet from where he had been sitting.
He stepped over the broken chair and felt for a pulse. There wasn't one, Chandler was dead.

It was not the first time that he had killed someone with one punch, he had done it on numerous occasions, but this one was definitely the most satisfying he thought to himself.
He walked out of the office and closed the door.
By the time he reached the reception area he had completely composed himself.
'Was everything alright Sir?' the same lady manning the desk asked him.
'It went very well thanks,' he replied, 'He asked me to tell you on the way out that his calls need to be held for the next hour, and under no circumstances is he to be bothered. Probably best you don't bother him, you know how scary he can be,' he said with a smile.
'Don't I just,' she replied.
Just ten minutes later, he was stepping back onto the jet for the return flight to New York.
He called Ward.
'How come Nicole-Louise knew about your lady before I did?' Ward asked immediately.
'Simply because she asked.'
'I told you on many occasions that you needed to settle down and stop trying to sleep with every member of the female race,' Ward replied.
'Exactly,' Lawson said.
'Exactly what?'
'You lectured, she asked. There is a not so subtle difference.'
'Are you all ganging up on me for any reason?'
Lawson laughed,
'I thought you liked the new me?'
'I've changed my mind; I'm starting to feel challenged.'

Lawson laughed again.
'Is it all resolved?' Ward asked.
'Yes.'
'Chandler?'
'He's dead and I have a full confession recorded.'
'There's no need for that, your word would have been enough.'
'Perhaps I'm just being thorough.'
Now it was Ward's turn to laugh down the line,
'I'm not sure I like this Lucy woman, you've now turned into me and Mac in a flash!'
He smiled to himself.
'Are you on your way back?' Ward asked.
'Yes I am. And before I get there, it would be nice if you got Nicole-Louise and Tackler to steal all of Chandler's money and distribute it where you think it would do some good. See you soon.'
'Who put you in charge?'
'The one and only Lucy Corrigan,' he replied and hung up the phone, desperate to make a call to London.

# THIRTY TWO

**University Ave, Bronx – New York**

Ward knew that the best thing that they could do now was wait for Glushakov to make contact again before making the final move.
He had decided to go home and freshen up, but before leaving the warehouse, he thought he would call Eloisa, even though he wasn't expecting her to answer.
He was even browsing over the map that McDermott had been painstakingly studying of the house in Queens when her end started to ring, such was his conviction that it would go to voicemail.
'Hello you,' her soft voice said into his ear, catching him off guard for a few seconds,
'I wasn't expecting you to answer. It must be my lucky day.'
She giggled down the line.
'Will I be seeing you tonight?' he asked.
'Where are you now?'
'I'm just going back to the apartment to freshen up. You didn't answer my question; will I be seeing you tonight?'
'No.'
He instantly felt deflated. It was rare that he worked in New York on a mission and he felt that he was seeing less of her lately than he usually did.
'Busy at work I presume?' he asked, fully aware that he sounded sarcastic as he said it.
'Ryan, you are so sweet.'
He didn't feel sweet.
She giggled again,

'You won't be seeing me tonight, shall I explain why?'
'There is no need to justify it,' he replied.
'You won't be seeing me tonight because I can't wait that long, so be at yours in an hour, I want you. It's your lucky day,' she said and the line went dead.

He asked Paul to run him back home, the smile on his face telling Paul that he too happy just to be going home to freshen up. And he had also been meaning to talk to Paul regarding the conversation that he had with McDermott about him retiring. He was fully aware that nothing had been said to Paul about it, but he wanted to know what his own thoughts were about the team.
'I told your dad something a few months ago,' Ward said as they inched through the late morning traffic.
'To hang his gun up and retire I hope?' Paul asked and Ward laughed,
'No. I told him that you were desperate to take over. Which I guess is the same thing?'
'What did he say to that?'
'He said he knew. Do you think that you are ready to take over? Don't forget, if you take over, you'll be losing probably your best soldier. You can't lead, plan and organise as well as be the prized fighter. It's just something else to consider.'
'You manage to do all of that Ryan. Why can't I?'
Ward knew instantly that he had a point. He knew that Paul was definitely as capable as he was, and he had to admit to himself that the young McDermott was probably a more efficient killer; as Ward himself preferred the up close and personal approach, whereas Paul seemed to apply a more methodical approach to

killing people. He also knew that Paul was very smart, the key component required if he was to lead the team effectively.

'I have no doubt that you can Paul. Now, between you and me, I think whenever the day comes for your dad to step aside, I think you'll bring a new, up to date and energetic angle to the team. Just do me one favour?' Ward asked.

'Of course, Ryan, what is it?'

'For God's sake don't tell him I said that, because along with The Optician, he's the only other person in the whole world who frightens the crap out of me!'

**DUMBO – New York**

He walked into his apartment and for one moment he thought that Eloisa was inside already when he caught a glimpse of the mug on the kitchen worktop but then he remembered that he had left it there in his haste to get out into the street to meet Lawson earlier that morning. He looked at his watch and decided that he would have a quick shower as she wouldn't be arriving for another fifteen minutes. He stripped and jumped into the shower and a few minutes later, out of the corner of his eye, he saw movement through the glass partition between the shower and the rest of the bathroom. He spun around and saw her standing there smiling at him.

She was wearing a smart suit, a dark blue colour, with a white blouse underneath. No doubt another excessively expensive purchase from one of the designer shops where she got all of her clothes he thought to himself, but she wore it with a style that made her look sexy, strong and in control, yet sweet and beautiful all at the same time. It was most definitely money well spent wherever she had got it from. He felt almost instantly aroused. She had that effect on him; just standing a few feet away from her excited him.

She took off her jacket slowly, let it fall to the floor and kicked her shoes off. Then she walked into the shower, fully clothed, slid under the shower head and put her lips softly against his, and just held them there for a few seconds while the warmth of the water consumed her from head to toe.

He went to speak and she grabbed a handful of his hair and yanked his head back,

'Sssshhh,' she whispered as she put her finger to his lips. She then removed her finger, pressed her lips softly against his again, and then let her tongue slide slowly into his mouth, almost melting into his own tongue instantaneously.

He pulled at her blouse as their kiss became more intense, but she yanked his hands away by grabbing his wrists, and then pushed her tongue even further into his mouth. The water had soaked her clothes completely, and they were now sticking to her body, as she pulled away from their kiss and fell to her knees and started to pleasure him. He lifted his arms above his head and slammed his back hard against the shower tiles as he felt the ecstasy that only she could make him feel start to rip through his body. She got him right to the point of orgasm and then stopped, sliding her body up against his as she came back up to kiss him deeply again. He pulled at her blouse and this time, she let him remove it, and he

then hurriedly undid her skirt and let it drop to the shower floor, where she stepped out of it urgently. Their kissing became harder and deeper, and he used his hand to pleasure her within two minutes as their bodies slid together under the warm water. She was breathing heavily as he spun her around and forced himself into her urgently, her hands flat against the shower wall, supporting her weight. He placed his hands hard against her hips and began to thrust deeper and harder, she started to scream with pleasure with each thrust and the deeper he seemed to go, the louder she got. The movements got quicker and the thrusts more aggressive and within three minutes, they were reaching the point of climax in perfect tandem. Her whole body shook as she orgasmed, and such was the degree of pleasure flowing through her body that she forgot to keep her weight supported by the wall, moved her hand and slipped on the water into a pile on the floor.
They both burst out laughing and Ward slumped down to join her, kissing her softly as he knelt beside her and he looked into her sparkling green eyes,
'I told you that I took the spare clothes that you leave here to the homeless shelter last week, didn't I?' he asked with a smile.
'You didn't,' she said seriously and feigned surprise, 'But I think I might have forgotten to tell you that you've been paying for my dry cleaning bill for the last year, so I guess we are even,' she added.
'Let's get cleaned up,' he replied, and gently pulled her to her feet.
An hour later they were sitting next to each other in the kitchen, both fully dressed and sipping coffee.

'Have you resolved the issue that you were working on?' she asked.

'I have an understanding of it, but resolution is probably a few days off and will involve people way above my pay grade.'

'So what will you do?'

'I'll finish it and deal with them.'

'Don't you ever get worried that you are stepping too far out of line? You get involved with people like Simone and these are international criminals you are dealing with Ryan, there are councils and courts to deal with them.'

'And how is that working out?' he asked.

'Fair point,' she replied and nodded at the same time.

'I'll deal with it, confront whoever needs to be confronted and then leave it to The Old Man to sort out. That's his job,' he said after a pause of a few seconds thinking about the ramifications of what he was going to do.

'Is everything alright with you?' she asked.

'Of course it is, I'm sitting here with you, why wouldn't it be?'

'I meant in general. You've had a crazy few months. I worry you will burn yourself out.'

She was right, he had lived a relentless and intense few months, he had pretty much been running around The whole of The States on top of trips to England, Ireland and Africa, and while he felt highly engaged and focused at the moment, there was one constant thing that kept nagging at him,

'Gill Whymark, I mentioned him to you before,' he said.

'You have briefly. What about him?'

'It seems everything I've been involved with lately he was behind. He was the CIA operative who armed Simone, so he's appeared again.'
'Maybe you are overthinking this one?'
'How? It's a fact. He was the handler for a terrorist who planned on setting of a bomb in New York, he was involved with Yeschenko and Cardona and he's appeared again.'
'He went rogue, yes?'
'Yes he did.'
'And he was under the control of your boss when this happened?'
'Yes.'
'So he's left one hell of a mess to clean up. A mess that if it isn't resolved and became public knowledge, would lead to some highly embarrassing questions being asked on Capitol Hill. Agreed?'
'And in Westminster.'
'So of course he is going to keep resurfacing. It's his mess that you are trying to fix to stop your boss from being hung out to dry. Isn't that obvious?'
Now that she said it out loud, it did seem obvious to him.
'And there is one simple way to understand that completely,' she said.
'Which is?'
'If you wrote a list of all the things that you have done recently and someone looked into the big political events that had happened in the past six months, they would definitely be saying that Ryan Ward has been involved in everything and keeps resurfacing. See?'
He did see. He hadn't once looked at it like that. For all his high intelligence and analytical capability, he was

often unable to simplify things. The nature of what he did meant that it was habit to look beyond the obvious and find an ulterior motive. Sometimes simplicity was exactly what was needed.

'You're right,' he said, 'He's gone bad, of course someone would have to fix it. Just like you ask me to fix the bad things that you bring to me. You have a huge list at work of the people that you want hunted and the same would apply. If someone knew what had happened to all of the bad people that you send my way, my name would appear constantly. It would look like I was trying to take over their operations.'

She smiled at him,

'Overthinking is not cool!' she said loudly and punched his arm gently.

'Since when have I not been cool?' he asked with a stern look on his face, 'And also, if someone did look into the bad people that have died lately, your name would keep resurfacing too, so you are as bad as me,' he said quickly, almost to reiterate her own point to her, like it was something that he had said initially.

She smiled and rolled her eyes.

'What?' he asked.

'I give you the answer and then you try and give my own answer back to me. Who does that?'

'Pretty much every boss in the world,' he replied and laughed at his own joke.

'Talking about bosses,' she said, 'I have someone else that I would like you to take care of.'

'You have the information with you?'

She leaned down into her large handbag and pulled out a much bigger than usual brown envelope and handed it to him.

'Who is it?' he asked, making no attempt to open the envelope and laying it down next to his empty coffee cup.

'Who are they? There is a man called Neil Rourke, he needs taking care of first.'

'What does he do?'

'He owns an air freight business.'

'What else does he do?'

'That's it.'

'I'm confused,' he replied, 'Normally you bring me people who have a legitimate business on the front to hide their secret murky operations. But this guy just runs an air freight business?'

'He does. He runs planes out of Washington, LA and Europe. But he knowingly takes money from the animals that transport children, pornography involving children, and all sorts of other distasteful and disgusting things that he floods into the country. He covers for them by fixing paperwork and ensuring whatever they want moved, gets moved without question.'

'Then he deserves to die,' Ward said, sounding like a guy who was just passing judgement rather than actually going to do it, 'I'll get Nicole-Louise and Tackler on it.'

'No need, you don't need to do anything but eliminate him, and quickly.'

'We always take the money, you know that, we can't have anyone profiting from a sick trade like that.'

'There are a number of employees who have families and so on. There is a good guy who is vice president of the company and it was him who brought it to our attention in the first place. The company will be in safe hands, and once it is run properly, they will be providing free flights for the delivery of international aid as a way of putting things right.'

Ward nodded. It made perfect sense.

'I'll send someone to take care of it,' he said, thinking it would be a lot quicker to get The Optician to take him out.

'No Ryan.'

'No?'

'No. This guy is the worst kind. He is profiting from it and trying to pretend that he's doing nothing wrong just because he isn't directly involved. I want you to do it personally and look into his eyes and tell him why.' She said, staring deeply into his eyes as she spoke.

'OK. I will,' he said.

She leant forward and kissed him on the cheek.

'Good. And make sure you terrify him,' she said and smiled.

'And the other one?' he asked.

'They are catholic priests.'

'I get the picture without you needing to explain,' he said casually.

She smiled at him, a soft, appreciative smile.

He smiled back,

'You are in the wrong job,' he said, 'You should come and work with me.'

'No Ryan,' she said and picked up her bag to leave, 'I'm in the right job,' she added and then kissed him softly on the lips and walked out of the door.

# THIRTY THREE

**University Ave, Bronx – New York**

Ward was standing in front of the two Simone's just two hours after he had been in the shower with Eloisa. He thought for a moment how bizarre his life was that he can step from sitting opposite such a thing of beauty to standing opposite two evil men in such a short period of time. Samson Simone seemed to have lost all of his hostility and aggression and was slumped in the chair looking almost resigned to his fate, and Patrick was asleep. Paul had strapped his leg, not out of compassion, but because Ward insisted he was kept alive. He smiled at them both, shook his head and turned his back on them. He pulled out his cell phone and was about to call Nicole-Louise and Tackler when the display flashed and the words 'Unknown Number' appeared. He hurried into the reception area and closed the door before pressing answer.
'Nice to hear from you again Yury,' he said.
'I think we have wasted enough time, don't you?' Glushakov asked.
'I do. I'm getting bored now. I just want a bit of clarification from you. It could wait, if it has to, when we are face to face and I will get it out of you by shooting you in each of your limbs until you speak, but in the spirit of an understanding that we are both busy men, I figured we could save time.;
'You sound like a busy man?'
'I have a boss of a freight company to find,' he replied flippantly.

'Freight company?'
'I know everything. And I know exactly what you need, and as I said, I am happy to give it to you. Where did you get with the thing that I asked you to get for me?'
There was silence on the line for a few seconds,
'There isn't anything is there?' Glushakov eventually asked.
'The Kremlin won't give it to you will they? You've asked them and they are denying any knowledge of it, even to you. You have a big problem. You'll have to give me something if you want me to give you Simone back. What have you got to offer me?'
'What do you want?'
'I have this friend,' Ward began, 'He's gone from being mister carefree and single to husband of the year overnight and I'm worried for him, some advice on how to cope with it would be good?'
Glushakov laughed.
'It is refreshing to find an opponent who has the time for humour, I like you English men, you are a very humorous nation.'
'I'm not English you idiot,' he replied, knowing full well that Glushakov was desperate to confirm that Ward was working for MI6, it was a cheap trick that he almost felt insulted that Glushakov had played on him, 'And more to the point, I'm not joking about my friend. I'm actually finding it unsettling.'
Silence on the line again.
He decided he was getting bored with confusing Glushakov, but he needed to wait for him to ask for Simone back and say where and when. So he didn't speak, he just waited.

Then the situation became somewhat comical. Ten seconds passed and Glushakov had not spoken.
Twenty seconds passed.
Glushakov still didn't speak.
Ward started smiling to himself.
Eventually, after a good thirty seconds, Glushakov finally spoke,
'I have something that can be of great value to you,' he said.
'Which is?'
'I can give you the names of all of the undercover agents that we have in New York.'
'I'm not American so why should I care?'
'London then?'
'You're clutching at straws. It's almost embarrassing,' Ward said and sighed, 'You SVR guys are meant to be very tough and very smart. You might well be tough, we'll find that out soon, but you aren't very smart. If it was me, I would have just said that I have what you want, then given you your five minutes of glory while you told me that you had made it up and that this mysterious 'Thing' never existed in the first place.'
'So what can I give you?'
'Just simple answers.'
'I can do that.'
'OK. Do you know any of the following people are?'
'I'm listening.'
'Gary Chandler?'
'No?'
'Dorian Schultz?'
'No.'
'Samantha Ivey?'

'No.'
Ward knew that he was telling the truth.
'I need to speak to your boss,' he said.
Silence again.
'Viktor Zhirkov,' he said, for clarification.
'He won't talk to you.'
'Yes he will. Tell him to tell the President that it was me who stole the information from the Kremlin's servers. He has exactly one hour from now to call me,' he said and hung up the phone.

He walked back into the warehouse just as Buck and Gilligan had returned. He walked over to them.
'How are you feeling Sean?' he asked Gilligan.
'Bored and I don't know why you have to keep putting me with this idiot. I told you I feel great and I want some proper action, you know, head busting and stuff.'
Buck mumbled something in Russian while he looked away in the opposite direction.
They both ignored him.
'What did the guy you visited say?'
'He said the Russians were here to make sure that we killed Simone. It doesn't make sense. If it's anything to do with him, I'm not surprised it makes no sense,' he said pointing at Buck.
'It makes perfect sense to me,' Ward replied.
'How?' Gilligan asked.
'Where would Glushakov most likely ask us to meet?' he asked Buck, completely ignoring Gilligan's question.
'In Queens, it could be one of two places.'
'Which one would be more likely?'
'I don't know without looking at it.'

'Don't send me out with him again,' Gilligan protested, 'It's actually painful.'
'That's what your mom says;' Buck replied and he turned and headed out of the warehouse once again, with Gilligan in pursuit muttering under his breath.

**The Kremlin - Moscow**

'Firstly, you told me that your man was more than capable Viktor,' The President said as he stood up from his chair and leant forward, the rage he was feeling inside turning his cheeks a crimson red, 'And now this MI6 agent wants to talk to you, asking for you by name?' he screamed.
'That is correct Sir,' Viktor Zhirkov replied, standing to full attention with his arms rigid down his side.
'That means that they are accusing me as well because they know that you were one of my most trusted aides,' The President spat at him.
Zhirkov noted the word 'Were' immediately and he felt an icy shock run through his body.
'Is there any chance that any of this can be linked to me personally?'
'No. You will have complete deniability as always, I have already prepared a statement about…'
'Stop!' The President shouted.
Zhirkov stopped talking immediately.
'We still don't know who this British man is working for? I want to know who he is and I want him killed. He is ruining everything.'
'I can send……'

'Stop!' The President screamed again and this time slammed his fists down on the desk, 'You no longer make any choices or decisions. I want to know what he says. You will call him.'

'Yes Sir!' Zhirkov replied and stamped his feet together and saluted, 'I will prepare you a transcript....'

'Stop! I have told you, do not think. I want to hear what he says and to make sure you do not make matters any worse than they already are. I want you to get the call put through to my office so I can hear it on speaker. I want that called made now!'

## University Ave, Bronx – New York

Fifty nine minutes after he had ended his call to Yury Glushakov, Ward's phone vibrated in his pocket, he pulled it out and saw 'Unknown Number' on the caller display. He now knew that he could play this one of two ways. It simply depended if it was Viktor Zhirkov on the end of the line or not.

'Hello' he said casually as he answered.

'You want to speak to me?'

'Your name?'

'General Viktor Zhirkov.'

For once he didn't smile at the fact that things had gone exactly as he thought they would. The very fact he knew that it was Zhirkov on the end of the line told him how high this had gone.

'Can I call you Vic?' he asked cheerily, knowing that Generals literally had no sense of humour the world over.

'What do you want?'
'Answers.'
'Answers in relation to what?'
'Well ideally, I'd like answers about my friend and how he has changed character overnight, but I'm guessing that you Kremlin boys don't get out much, and so I doubt you'd be able to help much, so I'll settle for the obvious one. You never needed Simone's access routes and you certainly don't need him back for that reason, so why the urgency to recover him?'
'Is he dead?'
'My friend who has changed character? Well I guess the old him is: but it's like he's been reborn. Why? Have you suffered something similar?'
'Simone?'
Ward couldn't help but smile now. Then a sudden realisation washed over him and he realised why Zhirkov was being so rigid in his answers.
He stopped smiling.
'It would be easier for your boss to talk to me.'
'You will talk to me.'
'I want to talk to him.'
'I do not know where he is.'
'I do,' he replied, 'He's in the room with you.'
There was silence for no more than a second but it may as well have been for a minute, because Ward knew in that split second, Zhirkov was looking at his President. He also knew the reputation of the President and how Russian men hated being insulted about their masculinity. So he pushed the right buttons.
'Mind you, if you're at a table with him you might have to lift him up and sit him on it so he can reach the phone.

He's only a little man I believe? What is he, eighteen inches tall?'
Silence for even longer this time.
'He's probably going to kill you for making a mess of this Vic; you do know that, don't you? I'd kill you if I were him. Then again, he's probably much more forgiving and softer than I am.'
'What do you want?' Zhirkov asked again, the uneasiness in his voice virtually screaming out that The President was definitely in the room with him.
Ward knew and even understood why The President would not make the mistake of speaking out loud, he couldn't risk the chance of any involvement that he might have had in Simone and the subsequent events being recorded.
So he changed angle.
'I'll make a deal with you. You make sure your boy meets me, alone, with sufficient transport and I'll give him the Simone's back in return for one thing.'
'I'm listening,' Zhirkov replied.
'I need all of the names of your live operatives in Chicago, and I need them urgently,' he lied and hung up the phone.

He immediately dialled Centrepoint.
'Where have you been?' he said curtly as he answered.
'We have a big, big problem.'
'How big are we talking?' The Old Man Replied.
'As big as it can get. I know exactly what has happened and even why, and also why they want us to personally give them Simone back.'
'Explain it to me then?'

'I can't yet.'

'If it's as big as you say Ryan, this isn't a moment for games, I need to know now.'

'I'm not saying that I won't, I'm saying that I can't. I have one more thing to do and then I will be able to give you every single answer that you need. Please, trust me on this like you have never trusted me before. If I don't do it this way, you will run the risk of your precious political system collapsing, so for once, I'm thinking of the bigger picture.'

The urgency in his voice was something that The Old Man was not used to hearing. So he knew that whatever was happening was much more serious than usual. But he also knew that Ward only called him when he wanted something and he needed to know what that was,

'So what do you want from me?'

'How well do you know The President?'

'I don't know him at all. No President has ever, or would ever deal directly with me; there would be no deniability for them. Wilson only talks to me because he knows that we have him over a barrel. He definitely knows who I am, but why do you ask?'

'Because you are going to have to be the one who relays everything that I am going to tell you later this evening and pre warn him that two senior politicians, one from each party, are going to be dead by tomorrow evening.'

# THIRTY FOUR

**Park Avenue – New York**

'How do you think Ryan knew that this was never about Simone?' Tackler asked Nicole-Louise.
'Because we find all of the information for him to prove it of course,' she replied.
'No, I mean when he arrived back in New York, before we found all of the other information for him?'
'Lucky guess?'
'I'm being serious. We're smart, he's always telling us that we are the smartest people he knows, but to me removing Simone from control seemed pretty straightforward, yet he sensed something else was happening.'
She leant back in her chair. It was a good question she thought to herself. Time and time again he always seemed to be thinking ahead of everyone else,
'I think I know. I think he never trusts anything he sees. I think he approaches everything he does with about three different scenarios, the obvious, the unlikely and the ridiculous. It's invariably never the first one. That's life in general I guess,' she said and nodded her head in self-agreement.
'Well we have everything laid out in a neat line for him now, I still can't fit Simone into the last piece of the puzzle but I'm sure we will find out any day soon. What are you working on anyway?' he asked casually.
'Nothing you would be interested in.'
'I'll get on with dispersing Chandler's money for the starving in Sudan then,' he replied bluntly.

'Don't be like that; it's just research on someone.'
'Who?'
'Just a woman.'
'What's her name?'
'Lucy Corrigan.'

## University Ave, Bronx – New York

Lawson arrived back at the warehouse and walked in with purpose. McDermott noticed his stride and said to Ward,
'God help us, he's even walking like a man with purpose. I think I preferred the old Mike.'
'I've been thinking about this,' Lawson said without even a hint of his usual greeting smile, 'We must not kill Simone under any circumstances.'
'I know Mike,' Ward replied.
'You do. How?'
'Because I was focussed and smart a long time before you, that's how.'
McDermott burst out laughing.
'What's so funny?' Lawson asked him.
'Let's face it Mike, it's great that you've found a woman to love, but you've literally turned into this mean, moody and determined animal overnight. You can be in love and still smile. No one likes a mean and moody persona on a person,' McDermott said calmly so he wouldn't antagonise Lawson.
'Exactly,' Ward interrupted, 'So lighten up.'
Lawson and McDermott both looked at him without speaking.

'What?' he asked them.
'You really can't see the irony in you agreeing with that, can you?' Lawson asked.
Before he could answer, his phone vibrated in his pocket.
Unknown number.
He pressed answer and put the phone to his ear but didn't speak.
'Hello?' Yury Glushakov said.
'You have what I need?'
'What is so important in Chicago?' Glushakov asked. The truth was, Ward had no idea why Chicago was the first city that came into his head when he had spoken to Viktor Zhirkov, and he knew that any list of names that was passed onto him would be complete fabrication but he needed to play along for authenticity reasons,
'That doesn't concern you. Do you have the list?'
'Yes I do.'
'Then let's meet and do the exchange. But I warn you now, do not try and come at me mob handed. If I can walk into Sudan and take what I want, I can certainly do that here. I want you to be really clear on that. My people are everywhere, I will know if you try and get people together for a fight but that is a really bad idea for two reasons. Firstly, I'll disappear and you'll never see Simone again and secondly, I'll be talking to your boss because he has something else I need which is way above your pay grade. Is that clear?'
'Yes it is.'
'Where do you want to do this?'

'There is an apartment on sixty ninth drive in Queens, number one hundred and fifteen, apartment twenty three. Be there in an hour.'

'I'll be there in two,' he replied and hung up the phone. He looked at McDermott,

'You have forty five minutes to come up with a plan for the exchange. But we have to keep the guy from the picture that the boys took alive. If he dies, this whole thing falls apart,' he said.

'Give me the address.'

## 115 69th Dr - Forest Hills – New York

An hour and a half later, they were driving past a large apartment block in Forest Hills for the third time. There were seven floors to the building, it was built out of red brick and looked neither new or run down. The area they were in had a large Russian community and the likelihood that the property was owned by a Russian landlord and let out to Russian occupants was very high. There was only one entrance door at the front and that was below a large fire escape that cascaded down from the top floor.

Paul, Walsh and Fringe were already at the back of the building preparing an overview, and simply by the fact the building looked equally as well lived in as it did cared for, Ward was confident that it would be full of genuine tenants and not Russian mobsters.

In the back of their Range Rover, and guarded by Lawson, sat the two Simone's, trussed up and unable to move.

Gilligan and Buck had met them there and were currently inside the building checking out the layout, and Buck was still feeling annoyed that the address was not one of the two places that he was sure the meeting was going to take place, a fact compounded by the fact that Gilligan was taking great pleasure in reminding him constantly that he knew nothing about East Coast Russians.

Wired, Wallace and Fuller were sat in the Range Rover parked directly behind them, awaiting instructions.

'What's your initial feeling of this Mac?' Ward asked McDermott.

'I don't like it,' McDermott replied.

'Too quiet?'

'Not only that. If it's full of Russian gangsters, great, I fancy our chances in a shoot-out, but of it isn't, there's a high chance of innocent people getting hurt.'

'So what do you suggest?'

'Hit the apartment hard.'

'I don't think that will work. He'll be expecting that, I would.'

'So what do you propose?'

'I know what I would do.'

'Go on.'

'I would fully man the apartments either side. He can't take the chance of losing these idiots in the back,' he said, pointing over his shoulder to the rear of the car.

'Don't call Mike an idiot, he's just in love,' McDermott said.

'I never realised how unfunny you lot where until I stopped being your entertainment,' Lawson said, sounding slightly offended.

'So I think we should take our chances and hit the apartments either side with all we've got, if they're empty, great, if not, and they are full of Russians, even better, if they are innocent people in there, just make sure the boys don't shoot them. Is that easy enough for you?' Ward asked.
'Good idea Ryan,' Lawson said from behind them.
'Actually, it was The Optician's. Are you happy with that Mac?'
McDermott nodded, even though he did feel some trepidation, knowing The Optician was watching them always made them all feel much safer. Entering a room where you knew there could be innocent civilians inside was always a dangerous manoeuvre. Your natural instinct is to put less pressure on the trigger, just in case, and your reflexes slow by a split second while your brain computes whether a target is hostile or friendly.
Buck and Gilligan came wandering out of the building and headed towards their car.
Ward lowered the window,
'It all looks calm in there. On the floor above and below, they are definitely civilians,' Buck said.
'You know that for sure?' Ward asked.
'Yes. I knocked on the door and said I was from the department of sanitation and was looking into a drain leakage and they all invited me in to check the water from their taps. Fortunately, I'm fluent in Russian with no hint of an accent. Can you speak Russian Gilmore?' he asked Gilligan, deliberately getting his name wrong.
'You know I can't,' Gilligan replied.
'Your mom can.'

'OK Mac,' Ward said, putting an end to the childish exchanges before Gilligan could respond, 'It's your show. You and the boys go ahead and call down when you've cleared the adjoining rooms.'

McDermott stepped out of the car, and headed towards the building, talking into his microphone as he strode forward, completely unaware that he was being lined up in the dead centre of the crosshairs in the scope of the second best sniper on the planet.

The Old Man had linked The Optician into all calls received by Ward for the past forty eight hours; such was his anxiety about the extent of how high this episode with Simone was going, and he was positioned on the flat roof of a building opposite which was of roughly the same height as the third floor of the building Ward was heading to. He had a good angle on the second floor apartments and he was set up well over an hour before he saw the Range Rovers pull up. Ward had called him and asked him if he was at the property, and if so, what could he see, and he had told him that the curtains were drawn for the apartment in question, but the two either side were also closed, which seemed unusual as the rest of the apartment had theirs open. As he settled himself into his zone, he saw a slight movement in a window above the second floor and as he put his focus on it, he saw the window being opened slightly and the curtains were pulled back just enough to reveal a face.

It was a face he knew.

It belonged to a notorious sniper called Fyodor Gazinsky. He was a Russian national who was known for selling his talent to anyone who could afford to pay for it. No one was off limits to Gazinsky; he had eliminated women, children and anyone who he could receive a high fee for. His work for the Russian government was notorious. As with all Russian criminals, they are generally controlled by the Kremlin and his work for them was done free of charge. The fact that his family and extended family was kept safe in Russia was considered payment enough.

He was widely considered the best sniper in the world. But this was only because most of those who had heard of The Optician didn't really believe that he existed. But he did exist.

And right then he had Gazinsky lined up in his sights, and he was currently in two minds whether to toy with him or kill him, until he saw McDermott start to move towards the entrance to the building and Gazinsky's barrel move slightly in the line of McDermott's direction and so he decided to fire.

In the split second that he calculated Gazinsky's height, crouching position and reach, McDermott had only moved forward one more step.

The Optician squeezed his trigger and watched as the 7.62mm bullet smashed through the glass of the window and hit Gazinsky directly on the side of his temple and embedded in his brain. As he fell backwards, his barrel caught the curtain and The Optician caught a glimpse of Gazinsky's obliterated head as he fell.

I wonder who the second best sniper in the world is now he thought to himself.

He called Ward.

'Hey,' Ward answered.

'I've just taken out their sniper, a guy called Gazinsky.

Use his name when you do what you have to do, they will know that you have the place surrounded,' he said casually and he hung up the phone.

Ward smiled to himself.
'What's wrong with you?' Lawson asked from behind him.
'Have you heard of Gazinsky?'
'He's a Russian sniper, meant to be one of the best,' Lawson replied, 'Why?'
'I've heard of him too. The Optician has just taken him out, he probably couldn't decide whether to toy with him or kill him, but either way, he's just killed him.'
Lawson laughed,
'I wonder who the second best sniper in the world is now?' he asked.
'Whoever it is, he'll be a long way behind in second place compared to our friend.'
'Agreed,' Lawson replied, 'I have something to ask you?' he said.
'Shoot?'
'If you have some urgent adventure coming up tomorrow or the day after, you'll have to do it without me OK?'
He thought about the envelope that Eloisa had given it and realised that he hadn't even opened it. But it was a straightforward assassination, and he was happy doing that alone,
'Of course, that's OK, they are always an option. Any chance we get to meet the famous Lucy Corrigan during her visit?'
'None at all,' Lawson replied and then he poked Samson Simone in the ribs just for looking at him.

'Let's go Mike,' Ward said, 'And bring those two pieces of crap with you.'

# THIRTY FIVE

**115 69th Dr - Forest Hills – New York**

Paul, Walsh and Fringe had come in through the back of the building and climbed the stairs to the first floor apartments. They had stepped into the hallway and been delighted to see that there were only three doors on each side of the hallway, numbered neatly in order. Paul had instructed that Walsh shoot the lock of the door out and move to the left while he stepped into the room with his gun raised and Fringe would stand back to back with Paul in case anyone came out from the apartment opposite. It was a standard manoeuvre that they had carried out a hundred times between them. McDermott appeared at the far end of the hallway with Wired, Fuller and Wallace two paces behind. They took up exactly the same position outside the door, the only difference being that McDermott would have Fuller stepping into the apartment with him with their guns raised. Just as they had taken up their positions, Ward appeared at the end of the hallway with Lawson, both with their handguns drawn, and the two Simone's.
McDermott looked at Ward and he nodded an indication that they were ready. McDermott raised three fingers and with everyone's eyes fixed firmly on him started the countdown. Three, two, one………

**Apartment 24**

The sound of Walsh's automatic fire rang down the hallway as he blew the lock out and stepped urgently to the side, like a synchronised swimmer, Paul swept past him and took one stride into the room. Inside, there were three men and two women, sitting on a long sofa and two armchairs, none of them holding the handguns that were on the table in front of them. One of the men went for his handgun, and Paul swung around to the left and fired off a short burst of gunfire that hit the man full in the face and his head shot back and he fell to a heap on the floor. The flesh that the bullets had ripped off had sprayed over the people on the sofa, and the blood was teaming out of his open head wound. His body was jerking on the floor as his nervous system was getting confused with the half completed messages that his obliterated brain was trying to send. One of the women started shouting something in Russian, Walsh pointed his gun at her and she stopped immediately,

'Get Buck in here now,' he said without turning around. For a moment he was trying to compute why they seemed so under prepared, it didn't seem right. Fringe stepped past the doorway and was relieved to see Buck and Gilligan coming through the stairwell door,

'In here Buck,' he said urgently, pointing to the open door.

'She's saying something in Russian,' Paul said as Buck stepped into the room. Buck started speaking Russian very quickly, Paul knew a few words of Russian but such was the speed of Buck's words coming out of his mouth, he literally couldn't hear where one word was finishing and another was starting.

The dialogue went on for about thirty seconds, Buck would occasionally scream at the woman and point his handgun at her, and she would pause for no more than a second. By now, Paul, Walsh and Fringe were all pointing their guns at the four of the Russians.

'Ask them why none of them look worried?' Paul said to Buck, who almost instantaneously and without seeming to insert a break into his words asked what Paul assumed was the question. One of the men started saying something and Buck started to look concerned, and then he moved a few steps to the left.

'What are you doing?' Paul asked him.

'We have a real serious problem,' he replied.

'Well?'

'There is a guy called Fyodor Gazinsky. He is a legend like our friend The Optician, but this guy kills anyone, and he is feared throughout Moscow. He's not as mysterious as our friend but all the Russians used to say he was the best sniper in the world and I believe them,' he said as he moved even further to the left, out of line of the window.

'And they are saying that he has us all lined up now in his sights and if we go for them once more, he will take us out.'

'Paul to Mac,' Paul said into his microphone.

'Here.'

'Is The Optician here on site?'

'Affirmative.'

'Understood.'

He looked at Buck and shook his head, 'Seriously, your mom would be ashamed of you,' he said with a smile and then he simply said 'Fire,'

Paul, Walsh and Fringe unleashed a volley of fire from their machine guns that ripped into the four people in front of them. The noise in the apartment was deafening, even though the machine guns had silencers fitted, and they kept firing until their magazines were empty and then almost as one, changed magazines effortlessly in a matter of seconds.

'Now let's guard the hallway,' Paul said and they stepped out of the room while Buck slid along the wall keeping as low down as he possibly could.

## Apartment 22

In almost perfect harmony, and at exactly the same time, as Walsh was shooting out the lock on apartment twenty four, Wallace was doing the same thing, with exactly the same burst of gunfire to the apartment two doors down.

The door flew open and McDermott stepped in with Wired by his side and their guns pointing forward. There were four men in there, standing up, legs slightly apart in a position where they were ready to lunge. They were not holding firearms.

They were holding three foot long machetes, which were slightly curved and pointed at the end. Their faces dropped when they saw the sheer scale of the firepower that was facing them.

One of the men screamed and lunged forward and both Wired and McDermott fired off a short burst each which hit the guy in the stomach and chest, ripping them both open much more brutally than any sword could ever do. His body fell forward and his machete fell from his hand and landed at Wired's feet. Wallace stepped into the room while Fuller guarded the hallway.

Wired bent down and picked up the machete.

McDermott noticed the deranged look that suddenly

seemed to consume his face. It was a look that McDermott knew too well.

Wallace noticed Wired's change in demeanour and muttered, 'Uh oh.'

Wired put his machine gun on the floor and held the machete up in front of him and ran his finger down along the blade, he then looked at McDermott.

The three guys could see exactly what was going to happen and one of them dropped his machete, the look on Wired's face frightening him to such an extent that he moved behind the other two men.

Wired continued to stare at McDermott, willing for permission to attack, and McDermott knew it was pointless even trying to stop him as Wired had already made his mind up that he was going to have a machete fight. So McDermott did the only thing that he could do. He nodded to Wired.

With bulging eyes, Wired stepped forward towards the two men who were holding machetes and started swinging it in front of him. Unlike their cowardly compatriot, the two guys seemed up for the fight and raised their own weapons.

McDermott had never seen Wired have a sword fight. He had seen him kill many men with a knife, but never with what was effectively a small sword, so he was curious as to how this would play out.

Wired sprang forward and rather than swing with his arm, jabbed hard in a straight line and forced the blade through the guys guard and the tip of the blade cut right into his windpipe about two inches. The Russian dropped his machete as Wired pulled his arm back, and he fell to the floor with both hands clamped firmly around his neck. In one swift and strong movement, he put all of his strength into his right shoulder and with lightning speed, spun the blade forward and the edge of the blade cut deep into the other guy's neck and severed his main artery immediately. Blood started pumping out of him at an alarming rate, and covered an alarming distance. The third man in the room, who had surrendered the machete that Wired was holding, started speaking in Russian, even though he knew that no one was going to understand it. Wired lifted the machete up above his head with both hands and slammed the blade down hard on top of the Russians guy's head and he let out a scream as the blade sunk three inches into his skull and sliced into his brain.

By now, Wired was completely covered in blood and all three guys had about two minutes left to live before the lights went out on them.

And then the one thing that McDermott didn't want to happen, happened, because Wired screamed and started hacking at the bodies on the floor. Not once or twice but constantly. Ten strikes on one body before moving to the next, then onto the next, then back to the first.

'You two had better stop him,' McDermott said to Wallace and Fuller, who had now stepped into the room to see what was happening,

'No chance boss,' Wallace replied, 'You don't pay either of us enough to try and stop him when he is like that.'

**Apartment 23**

While the mayhem was going on in the apartment next door, Ward simply walked up to the door of the apartment and knocked on it four times.
Lawson smiled to himself. It was the most effective form of entry that he had ever seen anyone use in the field, yet Ward was the only person he had ever seen do it.
Yury Glushakov opened the door almost immediately. The gunfire and the screams from next door, where Wired was by now being wrestled to the floor by McDermott, Wallace and Fuller, an indication to him that any resistance would be futile. He simply turned and walked back into the room, leaving the door ajar.
Ward stepped in and Lawson ushered the two Simone's in after him.
Glushakov walked to the back of the room and stood to the left of the large window. There was a small coffee table between them, keeping them about five feet apart, and Ward had to stand to the right of it to be able to talk to him face on, almost right in front of the window. It was the perfect position for a sniper to shoot him through the window.
'You haven't really impressed me with the calibre of men that you have been using,' he said flippantly.
'I had to use what was available. If you came to Moscow, I'm pretty sure you would have the same frustration.' Glushakov replied.
It was a valid point Ward felt, but also a stupid one, 'I wouldn't be stupid enough to go anywhere without bringing the right people with me,' he replied, before walking forward to the window and stopping in front of it as he feigned a big stretching movement. Scanning

around the room as he did so, looking for something that he really needed to be there.

'Get this done with Yury,' Samson Simone said. Lawson clamped his hand around Simone's neck and squeezed hard, Simone's whole body cramped over, 'Speak when I say you can,' he said.

'You have my list?' Ward asked.

Glushakov stepped to the side and picked up a white envelope and handed it to him. He made a big gesture of opening it slowly and staring into Glushakov's eyes as he tore it open. He pulled the piece of paper out and scanned down the list. There were at least forty names on there. But he knew that they were all worthless. If any of them were authentic, they would be people that the Russians wanted eliminated anyway.

'Now I can take those two back,' Glushakov said, pointing at the Simone's.

Ward knew exactly what Glushakov wanted him to do, in fact, needed him to do, but he needed the opposite to happen.

The final piece of the jigsaw.

'I thought we could have a little talk first,' he said calmly, 'There are a few things I need cleared up.'

'I'm not sure what I can help you with. I'm like you. I'm given orders, I follow them through. I knew nothing about your list until it was sent to me. But if I can fill in the spaces with what I know, I'll try.'

Ward was impressed with how calm Glushakov was being. He was also very convincing. He knew that he was lying, but his SVR training had clearly been so thorough that he was sure that Glushakov could convince anyone of anything.

So it was time to throw him off his game.

'You were in the room when he made those kids play Russian roulette. Did you enjoy that?' he asked, turning slightly and pointing at Samson Simone.

Glushakov looked surprised for the first time. He knew that the video had been sent to the powerful American politicians, and he was unsure how this British man, who seemed interested only in Russian spies in Chicago, could possibly know this.

'I was. As a bystander, I took no part in it.'

'But you didn't try and stop it either.'

Glushakov shrugged,

'As unfortunate as it is, there are always innocent casualties with events like this. We are both just pawns, you must know that?'

He didn't reply. He was scanning around the room, looking for the most likely place that he would find what he was looking for. He noticed that the screaming from next door had stopped, so whatever McDermott was doing had clearly finished.

'But no, I didn't approve of it, if that's what you want to know?' Glushakov added, trying to prompt Ward back into the conversation.

'Before I go any further, I want to tell you something,' Ward said.

Still scanning the room.

'Go ahead.'

'Have you heard of The Optician?'

Glushakov started to look a little uneasy, not because he believed The Optician really existed, but because he was concerned that this man standing opposite him knew that he had the best sniper the Russians possessed locked onto him,

'I've heard of the rumours,' he answered honestly, 'It was a story the American's created to show they had a man as deadly as one of ours.'

Still scanning the room.

'He is actually a real person. He is as evasive and mysterious as you have probably heard, but I assure you that he is real.'

'Why are you telling me this?' Glushakov asked.

'Because before we came in here, he took out Gazinsky. Actually, I think he took him out with his eyes closed. He does that sometimes I think, just to make his work more challenging.'

For the first time, Glushakov didn't look composed, 'That surprises me. We were always told that he didn't exist.'

'He's very real. So as we are being open and honest, I need us to be able to share something. You have a job to do, I have a job to do, so let's at least try and make our jobs easier. Agreed?'

Before Glushakov could answer, he finally saw what he was looking for, nestled behind a plant on top of a tall bookcase.

And in an instant, he knew exactly how he was going to get Glushakov to give him exactly what he wanted.

# THIRTY SIX

**115 69th Dr - Forest Hills – New York**

The one thing that Ward really admired about the Russian SVR was their sense of loyalty. He knew that he would never be able to get Yury Glushakov to turn on Mother Russia, so in that split second when he had found what he was looking for, he knew that to get what he wanted; he would have to make Glushakov feel he was protecting his country.
'Here's the thing,' he said, 'I just needed you to see that these two were alive. You're not having them. I need you to go back to your boss and tell him that not only are they going to be kept alive, they are going to make statements to the world about how the Kremlin have sponsored them to commit genocide and it was all done just because they decided it would destabilise the region and the world.'
Glushakov kept his composure, but Ward could see him calculating his next move in his mind before he spoke,
'I'm not entirely convinced that the world would believe anything that they say,' Glushakov replied.
'Yury, do something about this,' Samson Simone shouted.
Lawson sent a sharp uppercut which landed just under Simone's chin and his legs gave way immediately,' I told you not to speak,' he said as Simone just about retained consciousness.
'You know they are both cowards,' Ward continued, 'They will say anything to protect themselves. Your name, your boss's name, pretty much anything we tell

them to say. So everything has gone completely wrong for you. We're going to leave, and you can break the news to your General, although I have a feeling that he won't be very pleased.'

'People won't believe it.'

'Does it really matter? Isn't this just about fake news anyway?'

He had held back making the implication that this whole episode was about fake news, because Glushakov's reaction right now would confirm beyond any doubt at all that he had everything right.

'Yes it is,' he replied.

Ward smiled.

He knew Glushakov was lying.

He knew that it was not about fake news.

He knew that he was as loyal to Mother Russia as he had thought.

He knew that the gamble he was going to take right then would work.

'Have you ever been to Chicago?' he asked as he pulled out the list again and started to scan it, placing his Glock on the coffee table between them as he spoke, 'Is it always as windy as they say?'

Glushakov lunged forward picked up the gun in one rapid movement and almost in one completely fluent motion, fired a shot into the chest of Patrick Simone and in a split second, lowered the gun slightly and fired off a shot that hit the kneeling Samson Simone in the heart. They both died instantly.

He then swung his arm back up, pointed the gun directly at Ward's chest, and pulled the trigger.

The gun clicked.

No bang, no bullet, just a click.
'I'm so glad he is as good a shot as you predicted,' Lawson said and then pointed his own gun at Glushakov. It took a moment for him to realise what had happened, his nervous glance towards the bookcase telling Ward he had worked it out exactly right.
'My gun please,' he said, stretching his arm out and holding his palm face up.
Glushakov handed him back the gun, without any attempt to fire again.
Ward took it from him and dropped out the magazine and pulled the spare one from his back pocket and loaded it,
'You knew I would do that and only had two bullets in the gun,' Glushakov said and smiled, almost in appreciation for the fact that Ward had played him so well.
'And I also knew that you never use Glock's so you would not know by the weight of the gun that it was virtually empty.'
'Well played, so what now?'
'I'm going to kill you and take your phone. If you hand me the phone now, I'll be merciful and shoot you quickly in the heart. If you don't, I'll shoot you bit by bit so I can enjoy watching you suffer,' he replied flippantly.
Glushakov put his hand into his pocket and handed over his cell phone.
'Thank you.'
'There is nothing in Chicago, is there?' Glushakov asked.

'No,' Ward replied and he lowered his gun and fired a shot into Glushakov's thigh. He fell to the floor and started screaming. Ward then stepped forward and fired a shot into the other thigh, the screaming intensified, his hands clutched at the wounds, trying to stem the flow of blood, and so Ward fired a bullet into his left shoulder and the impact forced Glushakov to slide to one side
He stepped forward and stood over the whimpering Glushakov and said,
'You stood in a room and watched Simone make innocent kids kill each other and I can't let you die quickly for that reason alone. Is it hurting? I hope so.'
There were tears of in Glushakov's eyes, induced by the pain that was coursing through his body, but he could still this man standing over him clearly. He looked like a giant, and he had no emotion on his face at all.
Ward looked down at him and could see the fear in his eyes.
That was enough.
He lowered his gun, pointed it at Glushakov's face and pulled the trigger four times, one second apart.
He had no face left after that.
He walked across to the bookcase, reached up and picked up the camera with the USB attached and put it into his jacket pocket,
'That went rather well,' he said to Lawson.
They walked outside into the hallway and he saw Buck standing outside the apartment next door looking in through the doorway. His mouth was open and he was looking stunned. They walked up to him and turned and looked inside.

There was blood everywhere. It looked as though a firefighter had walked into the room and turned on his high pressure hose. The walls and furniture were covered in blood. Wired was on the floor and he looked like he had been dipped in blood, he seemed to be covered from head to toe in crimson. On top of him sat McDermott, Fuller and Wallace.

Ward could hear Gilligan screaming into his phone that the person on the end of the line wasn't listening properly, there is blood everywhere, he was saying over and over, he then glanced up at him and shook his head.

'Is he alright Mac?' Ward asked, pointing at Wired.

'A few more minutes and he will be.'

'Well you need to be quick because Gilligan is calling in enough cleaners to sanitise the Empire State and they will be here shortly.'

'That's different,' Lawson said, 'are we done here?'

Ward nodded,

'Can I take your car and meet you back at the warehouse Mac?'

McDermott didn't say anything, he was too preoccupied with holding his knee into Wired's back, waiting for his episode to pass, so he just reached into his pocket, took out the keys and tossed them at Ward.

'Are you coming with us?' he asked Buck as he turned to walk away.

'No chance. I'm not going to miss a second of this.it has to be the strangest thing I have ever seen in my life,' Buck replied.

Both Ward and Lawson laughed.

'Now you need to lay it all out for The Old Man I suppose?' Lawson asked.

'Not yet Mike, I have one other person to talk to first.'
'Who?'
'The Russian President.'

**University Ave, Bronx – New York**

Ward had found the number for Moscow and specifically for General Viktor Zhirkov, by simple deduction, because it was the only number in Glushakov's cell phone that wasn't a New York number. It had too many digits, and while he could see that it wasn't a Moscow landline number, he knew it had to be Zhirkov using a number that was being bounced all around the world so couldn't be traced.
He pressed call and a woman answered in Russian and said something that he couldn't understand, so he simply said,
'Tell Zhirkov that Glushakov is dead and I have everything,' and hung up.
He knew they would ring back very soon.
He looked around for Lawson and couldn't see him, no doubt he was making a quick call to Lucy, he thought to himself. He had to admit, he was very curious about her. He found himself feeling desperate to meet the woman who Lawson had pined for all of these years, and he was also still feeling a little disappointed that Nicole-Louise knew all about her and he didn't.
He thought about calling Eloisa but decided it could wait because he doubted very much she would answer anyway, even though it was late now, he had no doubt

that she would still be at work, saving the young innocents.

His thoughts were interrupted a few minutes later when Glushakov's cell phone rang.

'Hello, international rescue,' he answered.

'We held up our end of the bargain. You are making a grave mistake double crossing us,' Zhirkov said.

He could tell by his voice that he wasn't sounding assertive, in fact, it was full of apprehension.

He knew why.

'I'm not talking to you. Put the midget on the line,' he said.

'That will not happen.'

'You do know that this has gone so far south that he is going to make an example of you, probably kill you and your family because I literally have everything. So put him on the line. I'll give you my word as an Englishman that I will not record or use the conversation that I have with him in any way, shape or form.'

Silence.

So he gave him a push,

'And I will also tell you that I have much worse stuff on American leaders than I do you two, and that will never see the light of day either, so let's see if we can resolve this between the two of us. But I won't talk to you. I assume that he is listening so I apologise for the personal attacks about his height. I was just trying to goad him into reacting. I will respect him.'

He could hear faint whispers down the line and finally a voice said,

'What do you want to say?'

He didn't really know how the President of Russia sounded but he knew that Zhirkov was the top General and the only person he would step aside for would have to be the President so he took it as it had to be him.

'I have everything to prove beyond doubt what your plan was and why. If it became public, we both know that you would get hit with sanctions that would cripple you. But that doesn't really affect you sitting in your grand palace, just the people in the towns and villages, so I can't really see much point in me doing that,' he said, sounding factual rather than threatening on purpose.

'Why don't you tell me what you think you have?'

'Not think. I do have. Here it is briefly. This was never about oil or access; it was about the upcoming presidential elections. You want the Republican candidate Harold Howard to be elected because he is more sympathetic towards your nation, he sees China as the real enemy and so do you.'

'Continue with your theory,' the President said.

'So to do that, you enlisted the help of the Republican Chair, Samantha Ivey, who in turn blackmailed Dorian Schultz, a Democrat, to turn on his own party, Schultz then bribed Gary Chandler with promises of access, who in turn withdrew his support for the Democrats and was meant to go public. I have the proof, because I got into your Kremlin accounts, you really need to tighten up your cyber security by the way, and the part you don't know is that I have Glushakov on tape, confessing to all of it and then killing Samson Simone and his son. You have to admit, I'm pretty good.'

There was a long pause and the President then said, 'So what do you want?'

'To avoid an international incident, you need to call the American President and inform him that you have discovered a plot by a rogue General to destabilise your relationship, and that you will deal with it. You can inform him of Schultz and Ivey by name and also that Howard was aware of what was happening. They will be able to deal with all of that internally in Washington. You will apologise profusely and as a show of good faith, tell him that you will refrain from any involvement in American affairs that have no direct impact on your own country. I think that's fair.'

'And the people involved, what is stopping them from speaking?'

'Chandler is dead; Schultz and Ivey will be dead by tomorrow. That leaves just me and you. Because Glushakov is dead, I assume that Zhirkov will soon be dead, and as I'm not going to tell anyone, and I'm pretty sure that you aren't going to mention it to anyone, after all, you lost to me, I think that will bring the matter to a satisfactory ending. Don't you?'

'I do. But now I have some questions.'

'I thought you might.'

'Will you destroy the tape as a show of trust to me?'

'No. But I will keep it safe, along with another tape that I have which would do much more damage to America than your misdemeanour ever could, so you don't need to worry about that. I give you my word.'

'As an Englishman?'

'As an Englishman.'

'So you are MI6?'

'No. Neither am I CIA. Let's leave that there.'

'You seem honourable. I will trust you. I am sure that you are aware of the consequences of going back on your word to me?'

'I am. Do we have an agreement?'

'Yes we do. I will call your President within the next hour.'

'He is not my President.'

'You fascinate me. I don't suppose you want to come and work with us do you?'

Ward laughed and the President joined in. Ward could see him for what he was; he was probably much more similar to him than he would like to admit,

'I'm fine thanks, I have my own team,' the mention of the word 'Team' suddenly reminded him of something,

'There is one last thing that I want to tell you, I suppose I should tell you,' he said quickly before the call could be terminated.

'I'm listening.'

'Have you heard of The Optician?'

After a slight pause, the President said, 'Yes?'

'Well, he is real, very real. In fact he is so real that he killed your main man, Gazinsky, with his eyes shut. It's just that I found it amusing that Glushakov said that you all believed that he was a fictional character. So now you know who looks after me. I have resources behind me that you could never match as a standard. So no threats, we'll end the call with a mutual understanding and respect, after all, you were me once, so you know how lonely my life can be. Acceptable?'

'Yes it is. I will find out who you are. I'm curious more than vengeful, so do not worry.'

'I never worry,' Ward replied and ended the call.

# THIRTY SEVEN
**Washington D.C.**

'And he said that he would call the President and apologise?' Centrepoint asked on the phone as he leant back into his plush leather chair, with an overwhelmingly satisfied grin on his face, as Ward repeated the conversation that he had just finished with Moscow almost word for word. He could still not comprehend that Ward had spoken directly to the Russian president, 'I hope you didn't goad him Ryan. This is a massive win, probably your biggest win ever; it really would be in everyone's interest if you left him licking his wounds without any inclination to take it further.'

'I don't think it comes close to my biggest win. I'd say that protecting innocent people from a terrorist, shutting down a sex trafficking ring, stopping a super drug from hitting the streets and destroying millions of lives and preventing mass shootings from taking place in schools across America is much more important,' Ward replied, sounding very defensive, 'I mean really, what has happened here? Once again those immoral politicians and money men get greedy for money and power and we interrupted their plan. We've removed Simone from control but what does that mean? This new guy you have in place will probably end up going exactly the same way and in twelve months' time we will probably be exactly where we started from again.'

The Old Man thought Ward had a valid point. Even he found himself becoming increasingly more tired with the cycle of deceit and corruption that swirled around

Washington, but it was his job to keep some semblance of order,

'I can guarantee that there will be no repeat of events in Sudan,' he replied.

'How?'

'Because I have control of Bassong and will keep the appropriate people in place there to ensure that order is maintained and that no more atrocities will be committed. That is important to me.'

'You know that I have to finish this?' Ward said in a tone that was telling him, rather than asking for permission.

'I do. It is going to create a massive headache for me, but the extent of how far that both Schultz and Ivey were prepared to go for their own gain, leaves us with no other option, I see that. It's just how and when. They are two of the senior people in each of the two parties and their sudden disappearance is going to raise one hell of a lot of questions.'

'As you have always said, it is your job to look at the bigger picture. I'm coming to Washington to eliminate them both. How you sell that to the world is up to you. I'm sure your friend Ashurst-Stevens will help you out. Or even the VP. I mean, they both owe you big time,' Ward said flippantly, referring to the two despicable men who had recently crossed his path.

He ignored the comment. He felt that Ward had earned the right to get away with saying anything for now, because he had fathomed out something that neither he, nor anyone in Washington, had the faintest idea was happening.

'Have you spoken to the President yet?' Ward asked.

'I'm waiting for a call. Wilson has been calling me constantly but I keep ignoring it.'

'I'd suggest that you explain it to him and not leave it to the scumbag to relay the information, he'll get everything wrong, you know that,' Ward said, referring to the Vice President of the United States of America.

'I will, leave that to me. I suppose you are coming to Washington right now?'

'We all are, but there is no point in coming now, it's late, we'll leave early in the morning.'

'All of you? All of you are coming here to take out two people?'

'We will all be needed. I'm pretty sure that both of them will know by now that everything has blown up in their face. I suspect that they are running around right now trying to find someone else to blame and cover their own pitiful asses.'

He knew that Ward was right again. He had been so wrapped up in the extent of what had happened that he had not really given a thought to either of them,

'I will find out where they are and get the information to you. I'll make a call and have the jet cleared to fly up here. But please remember Ryan, this is Washington, and everything that you do requires discretion.'

'There is always one thing that really irritates me with all this Russian involvement, and the things that your friend's like Ashurst-Stevens get up to with this fake news angle of the new world,' Ward said, completely changing subject.

'Which is what?'

'Why do the liberals in Washington and the media assume that people are so stupid that they only believe what they read? It's like they think they are the only people intelligent enough to analyse information and make an informed decision. I mean, what harm would it really do if people knew what actually happened out here?'

'There would be no faith in politics or pretty much anything else left.'

'I think you underestimate how clever the normal, everyday people who work hard and raise families actually are,' Ward replied, sarcasm ringing through his words, 'Perhaps one day I'll write some books and share our stories,' he added.

'I don't think anyone would really believe them even if you did,' The Old Man replied and smiled to himself.

'Get me the information that I need and we can finish this tomorrow,' Ward said and the line went dead.

He slowly put the phone down and leant forward, resting his elbows on the desk and his chin on his cupped hands. He had left three messages with the White House that he needed to talk to the President urgently and he had yet to receive a call back. He was weighing up if it was wiser to pre-brief him on the impending call that was coming from Moscow, or to pre-warn him that there was no option available other than to eliminate two prominent party members to make the whole thing go away for good. Before he could decide on the most suitable approach, his phone rang. He glanced down at the caller display and saw the words, 'White House.'

He slowly picked up the phone and put it to his ear.

'Hello, Mr McNair?' a man said.

'Yes?'

'I have the President on the line for you. One moment please.'

He heard a click and then a voice said,

'Mr McNair, we speak at last.'

'Good evening Mr President,' he replied.

'I'm aware that this is very unconventional. None of my predecessors have been inclined to have any direct dialogue with you, but I think I know what this is about, so I think we need to talk.'

He's spoken to the Russian President, he thought to himself.

'You've had a version of events from Moscow I take it Sir?' he asked.

'I've just had a very interesting conversation with my Russian counterpart, yes?'

'Was he apologetic?'

'Yes he was, and very much so, which leads me to be inclined to think that there is much more to it than he is letting on, so give me the full version please, and don't leave anything out,' The President demanded.

He spent the next few minutes explaining about Simone, Chandler, Schultz and Ivey. He detailed the money, the money trail and how they had gathered evidence of involvement of the CIA in Sudan. He laid out why the need to get rid of Schultz and Ivey was so important, and that as far as he knew, the new Republican nominee, Harold Howard, had no idea of the events that had taken place. The President listened carefully and did not interrupt once. When he had finished speaking, he was expecting the first question to be about Schultz and Ivey, but the President completely surprised him,

'The British operative who led this mission, tell me about him?'

'What do you want to know about him Sir?' he asked, staggered that the first person he wanted to discuss was Ryan Ward.

'Is he the same man who has evidence hidden somewhere of Vice President Wilson involved in a heinous act?'

The question completely threw him. He would have told anyone with the utmost certainty that Wilson would not have told the President what he had been caught being involved in, in fact, it threw him so much that he dropped his guard and simply said,

'How on earth do you know about that?'

'Wilson is a vile human being and idiotic, but he isn't completely stupid. He told me about it, he had no choice, just like I had no choice but to leave him where he is for now with the elections coming up, but mark my words, if I get re-elected, he will be gone immediately. So, tell me about the British operative?'

'He's efficient Sir. He has the ability to be seven steps ahead of most people all the time. He infuriates me at times because he can be insubordinate, arrogant and can have a total disregard for any political implications of his actions, but we are blessed and very lucky to have him.'

'Where did we get him from, was he one of the ones that you selected from MI6? Would the British Prime Minister be aware of what he does?'

'I doubt that Mr President.'

'Why do you doubt that?'

'Because even I'm not aware of half of the things that he does at times Sir.'

'He sounds like a loose cannon to me?'
'He's loyal and dedicated. I've never known an American as committed to our nation's well-being as much as him in all the years that I have been protecting our country and hiding our secrets Mr President. I think that you should understand that we are very, very lucky to have him.'
'That is what the Russian President said. So, are you confident that he can deal with the two people in question, and you can do what you are held in such high regard for doing and make it look however you need it to look, and there will not be even one single glance that can be aimed at my administration?'
'I can Sir, But there has to be one very specific condition Mr President.' Centrepoint replied apprehensively.
'You sound just like every politician I know Mr McNair,' the President replied and laughed, 'What is your condition?'
'Everything that I agreed with the Vice President stays in place. All of the legislation he passed regarding our accountability, or rather lack of it, and the control of the access routes in Sudan stays under my control only. I don't trust anyone on Capitol Hill enough not to exploit it Sir.'
'I have no idea what you are talking about Mr McNair, but I can tell you that I, just like my predecessors, have no desire or need to change anything. What you do is crucial to our national security and as far as I am concerned, you play an integral part in keeping us all protected, so things stay exactly as you have agreed with other people,' The President replied, putting the emphasis on 'Other People' so that he could claim that

he had no knowledge or involvement in any wrongdoing like a typical politician, even though he had pretty much just agreed to the assassination of two American targets on American soil.
They were all the same The Old Man thought, from the very bottom, to the very top, and he was tired of protecting their cowardly, deceitful actions and presenting a public face full of soundbites and promises that they never had any intention of keeping.
'I need you to do one thing for me Sir?' he said quickly, before he forgot.
'Yes?'
'I know that Schultz is in Washington but I can't find where Ivey is and it would probably make my man's life a lot easier, and certainly leave him less exposed if you could somehow get it arranged so that we know where she is, immediately, so that both parties can be dealt with tomorrow.'
'I'm not sure that I have that much influence over the Republican's, that I can call them and ask them to make sure she is hanging around Washington tomorrow. I wouldn't know what to say.'
'I do Sir,' he replied, a sudden moment of inspiration coming over him.
'Then please share it Mr McNair.'
'I think if you let her know, indirectly of course, that you are considering creating a new committee to look into the use of social media in politics that will comprise of a cross section of party members, it would be feasible that you would not put Senators on the committee but rather other influential people. I'm pretty sure that anyone who made the choices that she made would have a big enough

ego to want to be part of something that could bring more attention to her.'

'That does sound feasible. I'll get my people on it straight away and set the first meeting for tomorrow morning and cancel an hour before, then what happens, happens.'

'Thank you Mr President.'

'Goodbye Mr McNair.'

He let out a satisfied sigh, picked his cell phone up and called Ward immediately. He was surprised to hear him answer,

'Yes?'

'Schultz and Ivey will both be in Washington tomorrow morning, so there will be no surprises of them disappearing. I'm sure that Nicole-Louise and Tackler can tell you where and when, and I'll send you over the details for Schultz when we finish this call. I've spoken to the President and he is fully aware of what is happening and how it needs to end.'

'No lecture?'

'No lecture this time. Just please be aware of your surroundings. There are CCTV cameras everywhere.'

'I'm sure Nicole-Louise and Tackler can fix those easily. So it's agreed no interference from anyone, you included?' Ward asked.

'None at all, you just need to let me know when it is done.'

'Why are you being so accommodating on this, what are you getting out of it? Ward asked suspiciously.

'I told you before; I have to balance everything that happens with what the world sees. This time, believe it or not, apart from some big shoot outs that you insisted on having, this has been kept pretty much off of the streets. Trust me Ryan, for that I am very grateful,' he replied.

'What is it with everyone?' Ward asked.

'Meaning?'

'First Lawson, and now you, suddenly all thinking exactly the way I do.'

'What's wrong with Lawson? And maybe we have always thought like you, we just have other distractions,' he asked.

'Has Lucy Corrigan been in touch with you too?' Ward asked quickly.

'Who's Lucy Corrigan?'

The line went dead.

# THIRTY EIGHT

**The Kremlin – Moscow**

Inside the walls of the Kremlin and deep underground, there are secret interrogation chambers that have been in operation as far back in history to the days of Ivan the Terrible. It was common knowledge that these rooms existed, but not common knowledge that they were still in use today. Inside one of these rooms, a naked General Viktor Zhirkov was tied to a crucifix, but the soles of his feet stood flat to the ground so that his legs could take the weight of his whole body.
Ten feet back and directly opposite him was an empty table with three chairs placed at it. He knew that he was waiting for his judges, jury and executioners to arrive. He had failed Mother Russia and he was resigned to his fate the moment the President had finished his phone conversation with the British agent.
Damn that man he had said to himself at least twenty times in the last two days.
Without any warning, the President had called two guards into his office and told them to take the General to the chamber where a trial would be held immediately. He knew that it would not be a trial but an agreement that he had failed his line of duty. His only wish now was that his life was ended quickly and as painlessly as possible, without the need for torture. He had stood witness to a number of people being tortured to death in the chamber over the years, for the majority of these, he himself had decided the level of pain and punishment that needed to be inflicted, and now it was his turn.

The door opened and the president marched in. The fact that he had changed from his everyday suit to black combat fatigues told him that he would be hearing the evidence as a warrior, not as a friend and politician. The two men who flanked the President were both General's that he had appointed, General's Fedor Fernandes and Daler Zobnin. For a moment he felt a little hope that the rest of his life spent in Siberia could be a possibility, but then he remembered the number of times that he had attended the same hearings with the President and that every single time, before they walked through the door, The President had already decided the outcome and his fate was already pre-determined.
They sat down opposite him, and General Zobnin immediately started reading from a piece of paper.
'General Viktor Zhirkov, you are charged with the grave crime of committing treason against Mother Russia. How do you plead?'
'Not guilty of treason, but guilty of failure,' Zhirkov replied, looking directly at his lifelong friend the President, who refused to make eye contact with him.
'There is one charge, which requires one answer; do you plead guilty or not guilty?' Zobnin repeated.
The President leant to the side and whispered something into Zobnin's ear.
'Be aware that your plea will have a direct impact on your family General. In his good grace, the President will show clemency towards your family dependent upon your dignity and your plea.' Zobnin said clearly and firmly.
There it was Zhirkov thought, the exact same line that he had used on well over thirty victims himself over the

years. Any slight hope of the sanctuary of Siberia disappeared with that question.

'I plead guilty,' he said immediately, the only option he had available to protect his family from harm.

'In the charge of treason against Mother Russia, how do we find the defendant, General Viktor Zhirkov?' the President said.

'Guilty,' Fedor Fernandes said and looked down at the table, clearly uncomfortable with sentencing his one-time mentor to death.

'Guilty,' said Daler Zobnin, unable to hide the excitement in his voice at the likelihood that he was going to be promoted to the President's most senior General.

'Guilty,' said the President to the man who had stood by his side and been loyal for over twenty years while he surged to the top of the pile at The Kremlin.

'General Viktor Zhirkov, you have been found guilty of treason against Mother Russia by a unanimous decision. Our great President has decided to show mercy to your family because of your willing acceptance to your crimes. You are sentenced to death. Do you have anything that you wish to say?' General Fedor Fernandes asked.

Zhirkov had a lot to say, he wanted to plead for his life and remind his old friend of their journey together, but he knew that one wrong word and his entire family would be dead within three hours, tortured and raped, because he had instructed men to do exactly the same many times over. In the end, he decided on saying one short sentence to the President,

'It has been my greatest honour to serve by your side my friend.'

The President stood up, pulled an old looking handgun from his holster and walked around the table and stood three feet in front of Zhirkov.

'Any friend of mine would not have failed me so severely that I had to ask the American President to accept my apologies. You are no friend of mine,' and he raised his gun and fired three shots into the chest of General Viktor Zhirkov.

He turned around,

'You will now take his position,' he said to General Zobnin.

'I will not fail you Sir, ever,' Zobnin replied.

'Then your first task is to be completed within the next hour,' the President said.

'It is my honour Sir, what is it you require?'

'Find General Zhirkov's wife and children and kill them. And then find out who the British man is.'

## 2728 6th Street NE - Washington

Samantha Ivey knew as soon as she received the invitation to be part of a fictitious new social media in politics committee, that her involvement with both Schultz and the Russians had been discovered.

She was at her house on 6th Street North East and she was feeling slightly vulnerable. Her property was a small, two bedroom place that had a small front yard which led up to a neat two story building nestled in the middle of a row of mid-terrace houses. It wasn't grand but it was where her home had been when she stayed in Washington for the last three years.

She hadn't heard anything from Moscow for over twenty four hours and she was aware that Schultz had more pressing matters with yet another sexual harassment allegation being made against him. She knew it was time to get out of Washington. She had frantically tried calling her Russian contact that had put her in touch with the relevant people when she had concocted her plan, but he seemed to have fallen off the grid. She had decided that the safest place for her to be right now would be in Illinois and the first available flight that she had managed to book was at midday tomorrow. She had accepted the invitation anyway with the intention of cancelling about an hour before the meeting was due to start, citing a family illness as her reason.

For now, she would try and get some sleep. She had a feeling that tomorrow was going to be a long day and that she was going to be given some difficult questions to answer.

But she was confident that whoever asked them, she could outsmart them and get them to invariably agree with her.

It was what she did best.

**DUMBO – New York**

Ward had briefed everyone about the plan for tomorrow and told everyone to get some rest. He had called Eloisa and told her that he was going home for the night and she had told him that as desperate as she was for a repeat run in the shower, she was working on a large case and

she would be at work well into the early hours, if she got to leave at all. He had come home, showered and he was feeling hungry so he walked the two blocks to his favourite pizza place and ordered an eat in pizza. He found himself thinking more and more about Lucy Corrigan, and he smiled when he realised how desperate he, and it seems everyone else, was to meet her.
He pulled out his cell phone and called Tackler.
'I was just going to bed,' Tackler answered wearily.
'It won't take long. I just need to know where Schultz and Ivey will be in the morning,' he said.
'We've already done it. The Old Man contacted us and told us you would need to know their movements.'
'So how about letting me know?'
'I thought you might be busy, you know, sleeping in a nice warm bed for once?'
'Tell me now,' he asked, more to keep Tackler from his bed as a need to know right then.
'Schultz has a place in Kingman Park, 1396 C Street North East and Ivey lives on 6th Street North East, number two seven two eight, if you really can't wait,' Tackler replied in such a matter of fact tone that it made him smile,
'You sound tired,' he said.
'Very funny Ryan. I should also let you know that she has booked a flight to Illinois which is leaving Dulles at twelve ten tomorrow lunchtime. Having looked into her diary, she has an appointment at ten thirty tomorrow morning to sit on a new cross section committee. Schultz has nothing booked in his diary and he will more than likely be at home until he gets up. Looking at his calendar for the past six months, he never books

appointments for the morning, so my guess is that he isn't a very early riser, unlike some people I know.'

'You sound a bit edgy,' he said, 'Everything OK with you?'

'I'm fine, it's nothing that a good night's sleep won't put right.'

'Goodnight Tackler, text me the details you've just told me, and to Mac please.'

'Goodnight Ryan.'

He was feeling wide awake, even though he knew that he needed to sleep, and he knew the right thing to do was not call anyone else, let them all get some sleep and so he resisted the urge to call Lawson and ask about his love life.

He read the contents of the envelope that Eloisa had given him, and had been delighted to find that Neil Rourke ran his operation from a small airfield in Washington, so he decided that he would use the visit there to deal with him at the same time. He was going to call Nicole-Louise but decided to text her Rourke's name and asked for an address instead. He still felt energised, so he figured he would call the one person who never slept because he suddenly remembered that he had been meaning to ask him something.

He hit speed dial for The Optician.

'Is that tasty?' The Optician said as he answered.

'Seriously, don't you ever get bored of following me, I mean it is kinda creepy,' he replied.

'Yet here you are sitting in a pizza parlour all alone and calling me. Am I the best you can do?'

Ward laughed,

'It seems that way. I have a question.'

'This sounds serious?'
'Not really, more of wanting your opinion on something,' Ward said.
'I'm listening.'
'I spoke to the President of Russia today, actually spoke to him. Can you believe that?'
'I know, The Old Man told me.'
'He had actually heard of you, can you believe that? Until today, he didn't believe that you existed, but he had actually heard of you.'
'I've heard of him too.'
'I'm being serious. I was wondering what your opinion was of the fact that the most powerful people in the world have all heard of you. I've seen it hundreds of times before. I mention your name to people, some really powerful people too, and also to guys who are specialists in the field that we work in, and literally all of them are terrified of you. How does that sit with you?' Ward asked.
'I don't have an opinion of it. Why should I. They don't know me. Only what I do. Most people are terrified of you, and believe me Ryan, a lot more people have heard of you than you realise, and they all talk about you as some mystical, super assassin who is the smartest guy on the planet, and they are probably as afraid of you as they are me,' The Optician replied.
Ward laughed,
'You want to know one of my favourite things about you?'
'No.'
'It's how completely unassuming you are. You literally have no idea how the world is in awe of you. I know I

have a decent reputation, but I'm nothing compared to you, and yet you can't see it, even when I tell you that one of the most powerful men in the world thought you were too good to be real, and that you were a scare story made up. Does anything impress you?'

'Some things?'

'Like?'

'Maybe one day I'll tell you,' The Optician replied and the line went dead.

He smiled to himself.

He finished up his pizza and took the short walk back home.

Nicole-Louise text him back an address for Rourke, and he was delighted to see that he lived in Merrifield, which was where McDermott had his Washington warehouse. Someone was making things easy for him for once.

He was looking forward to finishing this tomorrow and then taking a few days well-earned rest, after he had sorted out the catholic priests that he knew, without even having looked at the report she had given him, would be abusing young children on a grand scale.

It was, unfortunately, a familiar story.

But most of all, he was looking forward to killing Schultz and Ivey for their involvement with an evil warlord.

# THIRTY NINE

**Washington D.C.**

They landed at Dulles International Airport. The Old Man had arranged for the statutory checks to be bypassed, and as they stepped off the jet, there was a small convoy of four Sedan's waiting for them. Lawson noticed the red Kawasaki motorbike parked a little further back, and was going to mention that it looked like the one that they had seen when they were in Sudan, but as Ward was deep in conversation with McDermott, he chose not to. The drive to McDermott's warehouse was slow because the morning traffic was starting to build up. Before he knew it, they had ground to a stop. Ward looked out the window at the car to his left. It was being driven by a man who looked drained, presumably the father of the two children who seemed to be arguing in the back of the car. He had always fantasised about living a simple life, settling down and being concerned with making packed lunches, as opposed to the complexities of hunting down the bad people. He continued to play out his dream for several minutes in his head as the traffic continued to inch along slowly. It was not long however until these thoughts was disrupted by a boy who didn't look any older than seventeen, pulling up next to their car, with his stereo blurting out a Metallica anthem. Ward did not approve of this, finding it far too heavy for the time of day. However, he smiled to himself at the good taste in music of the young driver. He had mentioned to McDermott when they had gotten off the plane that he just needed to pay a quick visit to

Rourke, and when they checked the address Nicole-Louise had given him, he was delighted to discover that it was literally no more than a five minute drive away from the warehouse.

'Are you OK drawing up the plan for visiting our friends while I pay Rourke a visit?' he asked him.

'Yes. But you will need to be quick, it looks like Schultz hardly ever moves in the morning, but Ivey's movements seem unpredictable. We want to be hitting her place within the next hour.'

That's plenty of time to get to Rourke, eliminate him and get back. Thirty minutes maximum he thought.

## Washington D.C - Merrifield

They were inside the warehouse ten minutes later. They had been here recently but to Ward, it only seemed like yesterday. Regardless of the fact that it looked identical to the one that they had worked out of in New York, Ward had become accustomed to them being the same. It was on an industrial park just off of Lee Highway where it joined Hilltop Road. They turned into the park and Ward saw the familiar 'A & B Auto's sign fitted on the cladding above the reception entrance.

'This looks different,' Lawson said as they stepped inside, the same layout, in the same warehouse, in a different state, but he still felt the need to say it every time they walked into one.

'At least you haven't lost your crap sense of humour,' Ward said to him.

'Thank you Ryan. At least I have one to lose,' he replied, a comment that had McDermott laughing loudly, something that Ward chose to ignore.
'You need to come with me Mike, we have someone to visit,' Ward said, 'OK as discussed Mac?'
McDermott nodded, 'But make sure you are back here by eight thirty Ryan.'
They left the warehouse and climbed into one of the Sedan's,
'Where are we going?' Lawson asked.
'Eight five nine two Dellway Lane,' Ward replied as he typed the address into the GPS.'
'Who are they?'
'It's just one person Mike. A guy called Neil Rourke. It needs to be done quickly because Eloisa didn't explain why, actually, thinking about it now, it was all a bit vague, but as he transports stuff for sick animals, I guess he must have something lined up that needs to be stopped urgently.'
'You and her trust each other more than anything, don't you?'
'We do.'
'Lucy will be here by this afternoon now; she managed to get leave from work. I want you to meet her, maybe have a foursome with your good lady tonight?'
He had found himself thinking about Lucy Corrigan a lot over the past few days, the whole team had, he was even wondering if the Russian President and The Old Man had thought about her because he had made reference to her when they were listening, and he was genuinely excited to meet her,

'I'll see if I can fit it in,' he said casually, for some strange reason, which he couldn't explain to himself, he wanted to sound as disinterested as he possibly could. Lawson laughed.
'What?' Ward asked.
'Nothing Ryan. I just love how you make out that you aren't interested when it's so plainly obvious you want to meet her. It's OK that you are happy for me, I know you like me a lot, I promise not to let onto anyone.'
Now it was Ward's turn to laugh,
'Seriously, you've now got a mountain of intuition and openness to your character. I definitely preferred the old you.'
'Because I made you feel smart?'
'No, because you made me feel that I understood women.'

## 8592 Dellway Lane – Virginia

Rourke's house was on the corner of Dellway. It was a quiet street and there were a lot less people around than he would have expected, it appeared that no one left for work before eight in the morning in Washington. His house was a smart, well presented looking building, clearly cared for like the rest of the street, it was built out of clean red bricks with bright, white window and doorframes which sat well against the colour of the bricks. Outside, there were neat parking bays, defined by clean white lines, and he said to Lawson,
'Pull in right outside Mike, we won't be here long.'
'Does he have a family?'
'According to Nicole-Louise's text, he lives alone.'

Lawson pulled the car to a stop, and without any further discussion, they climbed out of the car and headed up the short path.

Ward knocked on the door four times. He immediately heard noise from inside and then he heard a security chain being removed and the door opened. A wiry, short man with fair hair was looking at him. He looked both inoffensive and very reserved.

'Mr Rourke?' he asked as pleasantly as he could.

'Yes?'

He lunged forward and jabbed Rourke in the throat and he fell back. They stepped inside into the hallway and closed the door.

Rourke was on the floor, clutching at his throat. Ward let him get some air back into his lungs for ten seconds while Lawson walked over him and checked the downstairs rooms to make sure that there was no one else inside.

'Stand up,' Ward demanded when he was sure that Rourke had enough air in his lungs to be able to enter into some form of dialogue.

Rourke uneasily got to his feet, just as Lawson came walking back into the hallway and shook his head to indicate that there was no one else in the house.

Ward pulled out his gun from his waistband and then the silencer from his jacket pocket and started to slowly screw it on,

'Do you know why I'm here?' he asked.

'I have a safe upstairs with three thousand dollars, you can have it, just please don't hurt me,' Rourke replied.

Lawson laughed,

'We're not that greedy,' he said, 'Just half will do.'

'OK,' Rourke replied.
'Do you know why we are here?' Ward asked.
Rourke shook his head. He looked terrified. Ward hadn't even gone into his standard speech about the reason for him confronting him, and yet he looked how most men look just before they die already.
'I'm here to kill you because you have transported vile stuff around the world for animals that prey on weak defenceless kids. There is no chain, no one at the top, no one at the bottom, if you're involved in it; you're involved in it, as simple as that. You are all equally guilty, no matter what part you play,' he said, his eyes burning into Rourke's.
'I have no idea what you are talking about, I run a freight company, I don't understand.'
Ward knew that he was talking to the right person, he had studied the picture that Eloisa had put inside the envelope. But right then, he felt that Rourke was telling the truth and he really didn't have any idea what he was talking about.
He felt a wave of uncertainty wash over him. And uncertainty was something that he never felt.
He didn't like it.
But the one certain thing that he did have in his life was his love and trust for Eloisa.
He would always put his faith in that.
Without saying another word, he raised his gun and fired three shots into Rourke's chest and watched as the force of the bullets knocked his thin body three feet back and he fell backwards, hitting his head on the hallway table as he fell.

'What's wrong with you?' Lawson asked with a frown on his face.

'What do you mean?'

'There was no real speech, but I'm really confused, why didn't you shoot him in the face?'

'Let's go Mike; we have other people to visit.'

He opened the door and pulled out his cell phone. He tried calling Eloisa but there was no answer, so in the end, he did what he always did and typed a message saying, 'It's done' and pressed send.

But this was different.

Something didn't sit right with him at all.

### 1396 C Street North East – Washington

McDermott called on the way back to the warehouse and suggested to Ward that he go straight to Dorian Schultz's house because Paul had been at the house for thirty minutes with Wired and had established that he was inside alone, Fringe and Wallace were having trouble finding Ivey. So he wanted to put his effort into tracking her down. They pulled up behind the Range Rover and Paul stepped out and came and sat in the back of the Sudan.

Schultz's house was the kind of house that was a dream for people like them. It had two large trees which obscured it from the road, a short path that led to a solid wooden door so the person opening it could not see who was calling, no CCTV and even though it sat on a street that had row to row of houses on either side, it was extremely isolated.

'Did you two do whatever you had to do?' Paul asked.
'We did,' Ward replied.
'All OK?'
Ward didn't respond and Lawson looked at Paul and raised an eyebrow.
'He is in bed at the moment,' Paul began, 'Wired broke in and checked everything out and he found Schultz flat out on his bed, snoring like a pig.'
'Is he alright now?' Lawson asked, 'He seemed to get carried away with that machete.'
'He does that now and again, after he calms down, he is fine. I think it's a build-up of stress; he's always been like it. But he's a good guy; you know that Ryan, and a brilliant soldier.'
Ward nodded, 'He is both of those. And I admire the way that you and your dad manage him. Plus all the time he is under your command, he's not in in the civilian world committing mass murder.'
Lawson laughed and Ward looked at him, 'I do have a sense of humour after all then?'
'I didn't think you were joking.'
Lawson's jibe at Ward's humour, or lack of, prompted him to have another dig at Lawson,
'Maybe he wants to find someone to love, then he can turn into man of the year,' he said, and gestured with his thumb towards Lawson.
Before Lawson could respond, Paul said,
'He is in love with someone, surely you've noticed?'
Ward and Lawson looked at each other with confused looks on their faces.
'Wired has a partner?' Lawson asked.

'Not a partner, but he is definitely in love with someone. Honestly, do you two walk around with your eyes closed all day?'

It was the second time that had been said to him recently, and it was starting to irritate him slightly,

'Sorry I retain my focus on the task in hand and don't have time to be an agony aunt to everyone else,' he said defensively in a tone that had Lawson laughing once again.

Paul looked at him blankly, being American he had no idea what an agony aunt was.

'So, who is this mystery woman?' Lawson asked.

'Don't tell me her name is Lucy Corrigan, whatever you do,' Ward said as quickly as he could.

'Who's Lucy Corrigan,' Paul asked.

'It doesn't matter. Who is this woman?'

'Nicole-Louise.'

Ward and Lawson looked at each other and their jaws dropped at exactly the same time.

'How do you come to that conclusion?' Ward asked.

'Poor Tackler,' Lawson said and then laughed much louder than he needed to at his own humour.

'I'm serious Paul,' Ward said, 'How do you know that, did he tell you?'

Paul sighed and rolled his eyes as if to indicate that he couldn't believe how dumb they both were,

'Do you remember that time in L.A. when you had Nicole-Louise and Tackler taken to England so Mike could look after them?'

Ward nodded.

'I certainly do, it was hell,' Lawson quipped.

'You told me and a couple of the others to accompany them there and Wired insisted on being one of the ones who got them there safely. I think you even commented on it. You didn't notice then?'
Ward thought back to it and remembered it. He hadn't thought it was anything more than just Wired being in one of his peculiar zones at the time, but now Paul said it out loud, it was pretty obvious,
'He also jumped out of the car when they got attacked at the motel and started attacking the dead bodies of the guys who had tried killing them. You didn't think that odd either?' Paul added.
It suddenly dawned on Ward that every time the team were all in Nicole-Louise and Tackler's apartment together, Wired was always quiet and reserved which was the complete opposite to what his character really was.
'Well, I never noticed any of that as I wasn't there, but I have definitely noticed that he is quiet whenever he is around her,' Lawson said, 'Don't beat yourself up too much about it Ryan, I'm Doctor Love and I didn't notice it either.'
Ward had the distinct feeling that everyone around him saw him as someone who got so engrossed in what was in front of him that he paid no attention to the people that mattered. Nicole-Louise, Tackler, McDermott and the team, Gilligan, Lawson and Buck to an extent were all his family, yet he never got to know the normal everyday things that made them tick. Apart from The Optician, who he knew that he understood better than any of them, he had never bothered to find out what mattered in the

personal lives to them. He decided to change that right there and then.

'Well now you know. But as I said, we are ready to go, shall we get this over and done with?' Paul asked.

Ward nodded and they all opened the car doors at the same time.

'Who would have thought it, eh?' Lawson said to Ward as they started to head up the path to Schultz's house, 'Wired and Nicole-Louise.'

'You need to do something Mike.'

'I know, focus.'

'No.'

'No, then what?'

'Get a table booked for tonight, I would really like to meet Lucy.'

# FORTY

**1396 C Street North East – Washington**

They walked quietly through the front door to find Wired standing at the bottom of the stairs, waiting for them.
Ward nodded.
Lawson threw the biggest smile at him and winked.
Wired frowned and looked confused.
'He's up here,' Wired said, and promptly headed up the stairs.
They followed him quietly, turning left at the top of the stairs until Wired stopped by an open door and moved to the side.
Ward peered inside.
Schultz was laying on his back on top of the bed, wearing bright blue silk boxer shorts, with his bulging stomach sticking out over the top of them and snoring loudly, his mouth wide open,
'What a coincidence,' Ward whispered to Lawson, 'It's Lucy's ex.'
Lawson threw him a disgusted look, while Ward tried his hardest to stifle his laughter.
Lawson stepped into the room, crept up to the side of the bed, raised his hand over Schultz's midriff, and slammed it down hard. The sound of his hand striking the flabby, pale skin echoed around the room, a noise that had both Paul and Ward giggling at the same time, and Schultz's whole body seemed to jump off of the bed, like Lawson had performed a levitation trick on him.
'Wha.., Who.., what are you doing?' Schultz shouted.

'Sit up and don't say a word,' Lawson said aggressively. Schultz blinked his eyes and rubbed them, when they came into focus, he saw a giant of a man standing over him, two other men wearing black battle fatigues holding handguns and one other man who was just staring at him, studying him.

'My name is Ryan, Mr Schultz, why do you think that we could be here?' Ward asked.

His English accent threw Schultz, like it seemed to throw everyone he came into contact with lately.

'I have no idea. You have the wrong person,' Schultz replied.

Ward moved closer to him and stood at the end of the bed,

'Why did you break up with Lucy?' he asked.

'Very funny Ryan, it's really wearing thin now,' Lawson said.

'Who's Lucy, an intern?' Schultz replied.

'You told me that I never had a sense of humour,' he said to Lawson, 'I'm just demonstrating that I have.'

'Who is Lucy?' Schultz asked again.

'But it's not really a sense of humour, is it?' Lawson said, both of them completely ignoring Schultz, 'It's like you get one funny joke and wear it thin, over and over. That's not humour.'

'You actually don't see the irony in you saying that, do you?' Ward asked, repeating a question that Lawson had asked him just twenty four hours ago.

'Who is Lucy?' Schultz asked.

'Don't you dare say her name fat stuff,' Lawson said and then slapped Schultz hard on the back, the same comical noise echoed around the room.

Ward had decided that their fun had been had, and he dropped his smile immediately and turned to Schultz, 'There are a couple of things that I don't get,' he said calmly and in a soft tone, 'I get that you might have become disillusioned with your party, I guess politics does that to everyone, but why would you turn on your country?'

Schultz looked confused; he still hadn't been able to link these men to what he had been involved in. Ward could see that he genuinely didn't realise why they were there. 'We know about Chandler, you, Ivey, the Russians, Simone, all of it. We broke it down and stopped it all. Even the Russian President has agreed to pretend it never happened. So answer my question?'

The realisation hit Schultz hard.

He had never given a thought to the consequences if he got caught being involved with the Russians, such was his arrogance that he figured at worst, he would be expelled from the party, which didn't matter anyway because the stupid women they were employing now didn't understand how politics was meant to work. It had always been for the benefit of the long serving men, now it was all about equality and power, so being kicked out would have been no big loss. He had calculated that they would never have made his actions public because it would do too much damage to the party.

What he wasn't expecting was to be faced with four men, all now holding silenced handguns in his bedroom. He was suddenly starting to struggle to breathe properly.

'Well?' Ward said.

'It wasn't like that. It was done for the bigger picture, to bring both stability to Sudan and the international stage,' he urgently replied.

'How would that bring stability to the International stage?'

'A friendlier relationship with Russia can only be good for international peace.'

'And the six million dollars that you received helped international relations too?'

Schultz couldn't understand how this man could possibly know about that.

'Well, we've taken it anyway and we're going to kill you, so you really should have put more thought into what you were doing,' Ward said calmly.

'Don't be so preposterous, you can't kill me. This is politics,' Schultz replied, and Ward could have sworn that he smiled as he said it, because he honestly didn't understand the impact that his actions had on other people.

'How many people do you think have died on this mission Mike?' he asked Lawson.

'Let me see, at least twenty in Sudan, at least that many Russians, I'm not entirely convinced that some of the people you wounded, like the Sudanese guys in New York survived, so I would say about fifty. Which in the general count of what you previously achieved, not many? Of course you can probably double that with the amount of Russians and Sudanese who have died by someone else's hands as a result of this, does that sound accurate enough?'

'It seems close enough I guess,' Ward replied, 'the thing is you sit in your ivory tower, not giving a thought to normal people who have to suffer because of your greed and ignorance. I'm sick of it; I've had this conversation a hundred times with people like you. I'm going to kill you, but first I want to tell you your value.'

'OK. Let's talk about this calmly,' Schultz said, some semblance of realism now sinking in, 'I didn't realise what I was getting into but…..'

'Save it,' Ward said, 'it doesn't matter. Normally I have to lie to people at this point, just so they feel worthless, but with you I don't. You have such little value that the President has sanctioned your assassination. They just want you to disappear. You know that's illegal right? But it still didn't stop him doing it, because you are that insignificant and worthless, to him, to your party, to everyone.'

'I'm so sorry, please don't hurt me.'

Ward shook his head. This man in front of him was pathetic. He actually didn't even want to make him feel terrified, he just wanted him gone. He raised his hand and fired two shots into his face, the bullets ripping the bone and flesh apart before lodging into his brain.

The four of them stood still, watching the last grains of life drain out of his body, the last act that Schultz did before he died was wet himself, his blue silky boxer shorts becoming darker by the second.

'We're done then.' Paul said and they all headed out of the room and disappeared in complete silence.

**2728 6th Street NE – Washington**

Samantha Ivey had noticed the black Range Rover drive slowly past her house twice. She didn't get to where she had so quickly without being vigilant and prepared. She had realised that things had taken a very bad turn when she couldn't reach her Russian contact, and the fact that she was invited on a committee that, after making the relevant calls, she had discovered was never going to be formalised, confirmed to her that her involvement with the Russians had come to light.

She knew lying low was the best option for her right now, and that after a few weeks things would blow over, much bigger scandals had been swept under the carpet, and she needed to avoid being questioned over her involvement in the matter more than anything. She had three more hours until her flight left, and after she had seen the Range Rover for the second time, full of Secret Service agents she assumed, she had left her house by the back door and walked the back few blocks to Irvine Street north East and sat in a coffee shop. She thought she would pass an hour waiting patiently and then take a cab to the airport.

She was sure that the only way things could have been discovered was if that idiot Schultz had got drunk and started bragging to the latest intern that he would have been drooling over, and she cursed herself for ever getting him involved in the first place. She now had a list in her mind of at least four people that she should have gone to who would no doubt have been much more effective.

But she wasn't overly concerned. She knew that there was no evidence linking her directly to things and that the Secret Service, even if they had received an allegation, would question her as a standard precaution. The only question that she needed answering was why they drove past the house twice and didn't just knock on the door.

## Washington D.C - Merrifield

Ward and Lawson arrived back at the warehouse and McDermott was talking on the phone. Ward waited for him to finish.
'Have you found her?' he asked.
'No. Fringe said that the lights were on first thing this morning and they then drove around ten minutes later and they were off. So they left it twenty minutes and had a look at the house closer up and it seemed empty and so they broke in and that was him confirming that they can't find her anywhere. Her car is still in the drive, so unless she called a cab, she has walked somewhere.'
'And you've no idea where?'
'They are out looking now.'
Ward pulled out his phone and hit speed dial for Nicole-Louise,
'Hello Ryan,' she answered.
'Hello Nicole-Louise, I need something from you.'
'What is it?'
'I need a location on Samantha Ivey's cell phone; I take it you still have her information to hand?'
'Until you formally tell us this is finished, everything is to hand. Tackler is just distributing the last of Chandler's money to schools and charities,' she replied as Ward heard the faint tapping of a keyboard as she spoke.
'I need it quickly.'

'It will take a couple of minutes, I'll call back.'
'I'll hold,' he said, something that surprised her, and not something the impatient Ryan Ward ever did.
'Are you OK?'
'Yes,' he replied, 'I just thought I could have a couple of minutes catching up with you. How are you and Tackler?'
'We're fine thanks.'
'Anything you want to talk about or share with me?' he asked
'As in what, work?'
'Or personal.'
She started laughing. It was a giggle to begin with, then a loud chuckle and finally a full throated laugh.
'What's so funny?' he asked.
'I get it. Oh Ryan, you can be so sweet at times.'
'You get what?'
'Because I told you that you never took any notice of anyone around you, and you felt upset that Mike had told me about Lucy and not you, then you figure that if you take more interest in our own lives then that will make you a better man, that is so sweet.'
'No, I was just wondering how you were, don't look into it too much,' he replied defensively.
She laughed again.
'Why do you keep laughing?'
'I'm sorry. It's just not you. There is nothing wrong with how you are. We all love you exactly as you are, you don't need to change, so stop trying,' she said, her laughter subsided now.
'I can't win with you lot.'
'I thought you never lost?'

'Give me the location Nicole-Louise.'
He could hear her laughing again. He saw Lawson looking at him and grinning, even McDermott was using his hand to try and cover the smirk on his face,
'If you two don't stop smiling like little kids on Christmas morning I'm going to shoot you both in the face,' he said without the faintest hint of a smile, a comment that made them both burst out with laughter immediately, 'whatever,' he muttered to himself.
'Her phone is at Irving Street north east, there is a coffee shop there, I'll text you the address,' she said.
Ward hung up the phone.
'You two can come with me,' he said to Lawson and McDermott and he strode past them, brushing Lawson's shoulder on the way past and in perfect tandem, Lawson and McDermott gave each other a silent high five behind Ward's back as they followed him out.

# FORTY ONE

**1814 Irving Street NE – Washington**

They were at the coffee shop just twenty minutes later. McDermott pulled the Range Rover into a parking spot almost right outside.
Lawson and McDermott had spent the entire journey laughing, which even Ward eventually joined in with. Lawson did a search on his cell phone for Ivey, and got a picture up and passed it to Ward. He studied it for a few seconds and handed it back.
'We don't really want to take her out inside, although if she mentions one thing to me about my apparent inability to take other people's feelings into account I'll shoot her there and then,' Ward said seriously.
'We'll take her somewhere and kill her,' Lawson said.
'I have a better idea. I'll go in and bring her out, drag her out of I have to, and while you two are waiting, apart from getting to know each other's feelings a bit better, you can determine what the highest, and most easily accessible building in Washington is,' Ward said and stepped out of the car.

He walked into the coffee shop and saw Ivey immediately. She was sitting at a table alone at the back of the shop. She was studying him as he walked in. He walked up to the counter, ordered a coffee, and watched as the waiter poured it out into a gleaming white mug. He handed over ten dollars, telling the waiter to keep the change, and picked up the mug, walked over to Ivey's table and sat down.

'I don't want company so move away to another table,' she said assertively.

'I don't particularly want to be sitting here but you and I are going to have a conversation before I take you to your appointment. Your flight can wait, another one will be arranged for you in due course Miss Ivey,' he lied.

She studied him intensely, his English accent both confusing and intriguing her at the same time,

'You're British?'

'I'm what they call a problem solver. The Republican party have a problem, well I guess the Democrats do because of Schultz, and my job is to smooth things over. The Russian President has apologised to our President and this whole thing needs to go away. I'm sure that you are clever enough, and know how to play the game well enough, that we can't have any of this made public, so they call me in to find a suitable resolution for all parties involved. So, can we talk?'

'You can talk, I'll listen,' she replied snootily.

He actually wanted to pull his gun out right there and then, and for a split second, he almost did exactly that, but there were at least fifteen customers in the shop and a couple of the women had young children with them and his own sense of decency would not allow him to traumatise innocent people.

'Of course,' he said and smiled, 'The President can't do anything about this because one of his senior party members was involved, so any action would result in an even bigger drop in the polls than he is already experiencing, he would ideally like to pin it all on you and your party, but he can't do that without exposing

Schultz, so it's catch twenty two. They called me in and I can only see one viable solution.'

'Which is?'

'We do nothing. Pretend it never happened.'

'Then walk away now and we can all pretend it never happened,' she said curtly.

'They wouldn't call me in for that.'

'So, what did your expertise advise them Mr?'

'Please, call me Ryan.'

'So, what's the answer to my question?'

She really was an arrogant and pretentious human being he thought to himself.

'We need to protect the President, both parties, you and Mr Schultz. To do that, I have arranged for everyone, including the President and Mr Howard, to sign a document, akin to an official secrets document, that you can never reveal any information relating to recent events. It's that simple. You won't break it because that will result in you being imprisoned for life, and it is the extra security that we need to ensure that this incident and any subsequent allegations never see the light of day.'

'That's it?'

'That's it.'

'We are going to the Republican buildings?'

'No, there is a small place that the Secret Service use a few blocks away. We can't be doing this at the home of either party or the White House. Too many people will ask questions. Come with me, we'll complete the document signing, with Mr Schultz and I'll even let you use my private jet to fly you to Illinois. Problem solved.'

He said and leant back into his chair and took a sip of coffee.

'OK. Lead the way Ryan, but I want to be back in Illinois by early evening.'

'I promise you will be Miss Ivey,' he lied.

They walked outside and McDermott already had the engine running. Ward opened the back door and she climbed in and sat next to Lawson, giving him the statutory second glance that every woman who came into contact with him did,

'Well hello handsome,' she said.

He ignored her.

She looked ahead at McDermott and said,

'You don't look like the type of people who are political problem solvers.'

'I can assure you,' Ward replied, 'No one solves problems quite like us.'

McDermott drove down Eighteenth Street and then turned onto New York Avenue; Ward had no idea where he was going until he turned onto I395 South and headed towards South Capitol Street. He knew that there was only one really high building down there, and it was a relatively new apartment block.

'Where are we going?' Ivey asked, 'I thought you said we had to be discreet?'

'We are meeting at Onyx on First Street,' Ward replied, 'We can't have the President travelling too far.'

**Onyx on First – 110 First St SE, Washington.**

Ward knew that the Onyx apartments was probably the tallest building in central Washington, but what he didn't know was that Lawson had stayed there a number of times with one of his many 'Friends', a woman called Alisha. After discussion with McDermott, he had called Alisha and got the entry number for the buildings security system, something that she had gladly handed over after he had lied and told her that he would be visiting her later that evening.

So eager was she to accommodate him, that she happily gave him the access number to her parking bay too, something that was going to make their job a whole lot easier.

As the building came into view, Ward wondered how they were going to get inside, and more importantly, how they were going to be unnoticed.

His fears were quelled when McDermott stopped at the top of the ramp to the parking basement, dropped the window, and punched in a four digit code which raised the barrier immediately.

He never ceased to be impressed with how resourceful McDermott was.

They drove down and pulled into an empty bay marked number one four three.

'They are waiting for us,' Lawson said as he stepped out of the car.

The rest of them climbed out of their doors and followed Lawson to the basement elevator. He punched in another code, and the whirl of the elevator cables could be heard as it kicked into life.

Thirty seconds later, the elevator doors opened and they all stepped in. Ward watched as Lawson hit the button marked 'Rooftop Terrace' and the doors closed.
'It's not quite the circumstances in which I wanted to meet the President for the first time,' Ivey said, 'But I guess he needs my help more than I need his, so I shouldn't complain,' she added and threw a flirtatious smile at Lawson, who simply smiled back.
The elevator stopped travelling and they stepped outside and walked through some glass doors, which Lawson had to punch in a code again to open, and walked out onto the roof terrace.
There were a number of tables and chairs scattered around, one of them occupied by a young couple drinking coffee, who smiled at them as they walked past, and then looked suspiciously at McDermott even though he had now dressed down to standard black tee shirt and combat trousers. They followed Lawson through a small metal gate, walked past the small lap pool which was being used by one older man who seemed too exhausted to even notice them, and through one last gate where the railings ended on the corner of the building.
'This is the best place,' he said casually, 'There is no sidewalk down below and the only vehicles that drive here are dump trucks and delivery vehicles, and looking down there now, they aren't delivering yet.'
Ivey knew straight away what was happening and turned to run, but just ran straight into the solid chest of McDermott, who shoved her hard in her own chest and she stumbled back three feet and fell on the floor to Ward's left.

She started to scream and so he stepped forward and kicked her hard in the ribs. She let out a deep moan and curled into a ball.

Generally, men like Ward, Lawson and McDermott had a code that women and children were always to be protected, never harmed, but they didn't see Ivey as a woman. They saw her as a bad person, who had, in part, been responsible for death on a grand scale in Sudan and on the streets of America.

And their rules were simple.

Bad people were bad people, there was no taking into account gender, race or religion, bad people deserved to be treated as such, regardless of any other factors.

'Pick her up Mike,' he said.

Lawson stepped forward and yanked her up by her hair to an upright position. She let out a scream, which was deep rather than high pitched, and this pleased Ward as he knew the old man in the lap pool and the young couple drinking the coffee would not hear it.

She looked at Ward,

'You can't do this. It's illegal and unconstitutional. You don't realise just how clever I am,' she spat at Ward, 'I have made provisions to deal with this type of scenario, you idiot, if anything happens to me, the information you want hidden will soon become available all over the internet.'

She was trying her hardest to be assertive and intimidate them, like she had managed to do to everyone that she had come into contact with during her rapid rise to the top. Everyone was afraid of Samantha Ivey, and she knew it.

Ward smiled at her.

'I mean it,' she continued, 'Brutes like you have no facility to plan and think, I will repeat, if anything happens to me, information about involvement from both parties and the Russians will go viral.'

Considering Ward was within the top one per cent of smart people on the planet, and McDermott was the most efficient tactical and attack planner that he had ever known, and Lawson was probably not far behind them on either count, the tempting thing was to make her realise how dumb she was. But he felt that equal arrogance would make her feel more insignificant,

'I don't care,' he said.

'What do you mean, you don't care?'

'I mean exactly that. I don't care if the whole world knows about it.'

She looked at him blankly,

'You said that……'

'I said that I was a problem solver. My target was to get you out of the coffee shop with the minimum fuss and away from prying eyes. It wasn't exactly difficult, you are a bit dumb.'

She started to panic; she looked around at all three of them, and noticed that both Lawson and McDermott were looking completely disinterested, like they just wanted the guy doing all of the talking to get whatever he had to do over and done with.

'I can get money, my family are wealthy, my daddy is….'

'Dead,' Ward interrupted, 'Because we assumed that you are so smart and would have a contingency plan, we sent a team to Illinois to kill your parents and sisters, or was it brothers, I can't really remember because it doesn't matter, because if you were going to trust anyone with your back up plan, it would be them,' he both guessed and lied at the same time.

'There is no back up plan, please don't hurt them,' she begged and started to cry.

Now she was where he wanted her to be.

'Too late, and I think it's only fair. You think it is acceptable to play with people's lives; normal people, deprived and poor people in Africa, and don't give it a second thought. The worst thing is that you were doing it for someone else's gain, for Howard. Are you really that desperate that you would do anything to impress your boss and get in his good books?'

She didn't say anything; the tears were streaming down her face.

'I guess we are similar. We are going to kill you right now and we will walk away and never give you another thought, yet you think we are monsters. Looking in the mirror sucks, doesn't it?'

'For most of you,' Lawson quipped.

McDermott laughed.

Ward ignored him.

'Please, I'm begging you.'

'That's not begging. I saw a mute kid being forced to play Russian roulette by the people that you got involved with. He had to beg with his eyes because he couldn't talk. That's begging.'

'Please, I can see what I've done now. I didn't realise, I didn't think of the impact it would have on others.'

'Well you should have,' Ward replied and smiled, 'Mike, throw this crap off the roof.'

She screamed, much louder this time, as Lawson used his incredible strength to pick her up, one hand gripping between her shoulder blades and the other at the back of her thigh's, and he launched her forward, over the railings, it looked exactly like a trash man throwing a bag into the back of the cart.

Both Ward and McDermott leant over the railings and watched her descent until she hit the concrete floor at the bottom, probably at a speed of around fifty miles per hour. She seemed to splay her hands out as she made impact with the floor, almost trying to protect herself, and all this did was leave her face exposed and it slammed into the concrete as soon as her elbows gave way. Even from their high position, they could see bits of bone and blood spray at least ten feet in a semi-circle. For once, they were all happy that someone wasn't dead before they hit the floor.

# FORTY TWO

**Washington D.C - Merrifield**

Ward had called Gilligan on his way back to the warehouse and told him that they had finished in Washington and that he would be in touch soon. He had smiled when he said,
'That's what your mom said.'
Clearly his time with Buck had rubbed off on him. He then called Buck and thanked him and told him that he would be in touch soon, and laughed when Buck said that he was desperate to work with Wired again so don't leave it too long.
When they arrived back at the warehouse, the others had pretty much packed everything up, just the last few weapons needed to be stored away.
He called Eloisa, not expecting her to answer,
'Hello you,' she answered.
He noticed that she sounded a little agitated.
'Are you OK?' he asked.
'It's just work Ryan, I'm fine, what about you?'
'I've just finished something; I'll be home in a few hours. Are you sure that you are alright?'
'Yes. Thank you for dealing with Rourke. That's one less vile human being to worry about.'
'About that,' he said softly, not wanting to agitate her further, 'There was something definitely not right there. It was almost as though he genuinely had no idea what I was talking about. Are you sure that your information was correct, like sure without any doubt?'

'Yes I am. We have tapes here of his involvement and saying that he was increasing the price for certain items, and being very specific. I can send them over to you if you like, if you want peace of mind?'

'That won't be necessary,' he replied as he felt a slight weight lift from his shoulders, 'You've just given me peace of mind. Will I be seeing you tonight?'

'Yes you will, it might not be until about ten, but I will get to you. But I won't be showering at yours again for a while!'

He laughed, as he pictured her sliding around the shower like Bambi on ice.

'Are you sure you are OK?' he asked again.

'I'll be OK if you let me get on so I am not stuck here all night again and I can get to yours at a reasonable time,' she replied and giggled.

'Message received. I love you.'

'I love you too.'

He knew that he had to call Centrepoint. Lawson hadn't bothered calling in a clean-up crew. Ivey would have looked like a suicide, and by the time that the medical examiner would have identified her, no doubt a back story of her depression and anxiety would have been created.

He walked into the reception area and pressed speed dial for The Old Man.

'Hello Ryan. You can't be finished because I have had no reports of carnage on the streets of Washington, so is it a friendly call?'

'Very funny,' Ward replied, 'It has been done, all finished.'

'I know. I'm working on her depression story now.'
He didn't bother to ask him how he knew, because he knew that The Optician would have told him.
'Schultz?'
'All sorted. It will be publicised as a heart attack.'
'What's happening in Sudan?'
'We now have control of the region and I am keeping a team down there permanently to make sure that things don't escalate out of control like they did with Simone. Where is the tape of the Russians killing him?'
'It's safe.'
'You need to give me that tape and the one of Wilson at some point.'
Ward ignored him; he couldn't be bothered to get into a long discussion about them. He would hand them over when he decided the time was right.
'There is nothing on the horizon that needs your attention urgently, so as you have done such incredible work over the past few months, how come you take that week off that you've been promising your good lady for so long?'
He was surprised at The Old Man's willingness for him to take a break, almost suspicious,
'Is there something you are not telling me, you're never this accommodating.'
'No Ryan. Even I know you need a rest, or you will burn out.'
'Have you been spending time with Lawson?'
'Excuse me?'
'It doesn't matter. I will take it, but whether I get to spend time with her or not is a different matter. She's so overrun with work at the moment,' he said dejectedly.

'Do you want me to make a couple of calls? The country owes you, big time, so I'm sure I can get the relevant people to suggest she takes a break.'
'You would do that for me?'
'Yes I would. Just say the word.'
He thought about it for a few seconds, but then decided that if Eloisa found out, she would not be happy,
'Thanks,' he replied, 'but I'll leave it. You're not a bad boss after all.'
'Yes, for an old man.'
For an old man,' Ward replied and hung up the phone.

He looked across the warehouse and saw McDermott studying the boys clearing up. He was almost looking at them with fondness.
Ward knew why.
He walked over towards him and beckoned to the reception area. When McDermott walked in, he closed the door.
'Have you said anything to Paul yet?' he asked.
'You know what I was thinking just then?' McDermott replied, ignoring the question.
Ward shook his head.
'I was thinking how lucky I have been for the past eight years.'
He understood why McDermott would think that,
'I've always thought that. I'm not even sure how you begin to create a team like you have. Their skills are irrelevant. The bond, intuition, loyalty and respect that you all have for each other is incredible. I envy you, all of you, I always have. And you are the greatest warrior I have ever known and you will always be, along with The

Optician, the two people I have always looked up to the most. But you need to tell him so that we can all get our heads around the idea.'
'I know you're right. It was just watching them now, I felt like a father saying goodbye. Not just to Paul, but to all of them. I worry about them. I have faith in Paul but I know Wired in particularly, looks at me as a father figure, his dad used to beat him, broke pretty much every bone in his body when he was a kid. You didn't know that did you? That might give you more of an insight into why he is the way he is.'
He didn't know that. He had always assumed that Wired was what they had always said, not wired correctly, but with McDermott's revelation, his actions, however extreme, vicious and psychotic that they seemed, made a lot more sense now.
'And you took him under your wing from the start?'
'I did as soon as he joined the SEALS. I read his medical report when he arrived for his training, and from his medical file, which was the thickest I have ever seen, I could see by the extensive list of injuries he had suffered as a kid that only one person could have done that to him.'
Ward shook his head, in sympathy, not sadness. Because Wired had found someone to guide, love and make him feel that he belonged to a family in the shape of the great man that he was standing next to.
'After he had become established in our team, I went to see his dad. I beat him to death with my bare hands. I never told Wired that. But I think that is proportionate justice for beating a son of mine, don't you? Because

that's the thing, Paul is my blood son, but they are all my sons now. I'm leaving them.'

'I think from thinking that he had no father in his life, it turned out he had the greatest of them all,' Ward replied and put his hand on McDermott's arm.

'We aren't going to hug are we?'

Ward laughed,

'I'll give you a hug the day you leave but that will be all. What are your plans now?'

'We are going to take a week off, I'll get them over to Los Angeles and let them blow off steam for a week and then I will call them all together and tell them after I have spoken to Paul.'

'But you'll make sure that you come back with me one more time, for old times' sake, to do whatever The Old Man has lined up next?'

'I need the money, so why not?'

The mention of money made Ward think of something that he had always wondered about, so he thought now would be the first appropriate time to ask,

'With all the money that The Old Man has put your way over the years, apart from warehouses and Range Rovers, what have you done with it?'

McDermott laughed,

'What do you think I have done with it?'

He literally had no idea. He knew that warehouses and cars and the best weapons weren't cheap items, but he also knew that at half a million dollars a day, he would have earned well over thirty million dollars in the past year alone, so he knew that there had to be a stockpile of cash somewhere.

'I literally have no idea.'

'Those guys out there are probably the richest guys I know. It goes to them. I have everything I need; every single one of them is worth over ten million dollars, they either don't know, or don't care, and that is why I admire them so much. I give them a few thousand dollars each when we have downtime, but they never mention money to me, ever.'

'Now I see why you are finding it so hard to let go.'

There is one other thing you need to know Ryan.'

'Which is?'

'Every one of them, me included, would work for you for nothing. They look up to you, and I've heard them say countless times that you are the best in every way and they admire you more than anyone they have ever known, but most of all, when you call us in and we are travelling to wherever you call us to, do you know how they refer to you?'

Ward shook his head again.

'Brother Ryan. There is no greater compliment than that to someone who has never been a SEAL.'

He smiled at McDermott. He understood fully how great a compliment that was.

'Just tell Paul and let me know when you have. But let's make this last one that we share, the best.'

And he patted him on his arm and walked out of the reception area.

Lawson was standing in the far corner of the warehouse, engaged in a deep conversation on his phone and beaming from ear to ear. He smiled to himself.

Paul walked over to him,

'We're done Ryan, we are heading over to California, we've made our own travel arrangements, so I guess we'll see you when we see you,' and he extended his hand for him to shake.
'You know the conversation that we had in the car?' he asked as they shook each other's hand firmly.
'Yes?'
'I forgot to tell you something else?'
'What was that?' Paul asked and frowned.
'You and the boys are the most complete unit I have ever known and the fact that you work things with me, and make them so easy for me, is something that I never really thank you for. I respect you boys more than any combat team in the world, you know that, but I want you to know that I respect you all as individuals too. Probably more so.'
'Are we going to hug now?' Paul asked and laughed.
Ward felt a warm glow; he knew that when McDermott walked away in a weeks' time, the team was in safe hands.
Very safe hands.
Her walked around the room and shook hands with everyone, spending an extra few minutes with Wired and joking about his lack of sword fighting ability and his calm nature. It was the first time that he looked at him as just a guy and not a vicious fighting machine, and he liked what he saw. Wired joked about Lawson and Buck and his kind words about how happy it made him to see Gilligan up and about again showed a real human side. He promised himself that he would make more of an effort to engage with them all in future.
After all, aren't brothers meant to talk?

On the way back to the airport in the car, Lawson told him that Lucy had arrived in New York. He seemed nervous, which he initially found funny but then realised the extent of the impact that she had on him, and how it was going to be the first time that they had stood in front of each other for so many years, and he realised that it wasn't funny at all and that it would be a very daunting situation for anyone. He even felt himself getting nervous for Lawson.

'So when do I get to meet her?' he asked.

'I'm going to spend a couple of days with her first, show her around New York and just get used to being in each other's company again. I'll book a table, but you have to promise me that you'll bring your lady with you and none of your trying to make me look stupid tricks?'

'When do I try and make you look stupid?'

'You put me on a sex ban for God's sake, who does that if they are not trying to get a good laugh out of someone and not trying to make them look stupid?'

'It was to keep you focussed,' he protested.

'Which I would have believed if you hadn't of told everyone.'

Lawson had just made a good point he thought to himself.

They reached the airport and the jet was already waiting for them, the pretty stewardess at the top of the stairs waiting for them. It was a woman who had looked after them before, and he knew that she and Lawson had spent time joining the mile high club. They stepped out of the car and Lawson said,

'That red motorbike was over there when we landed; pointing to the opposite side of the hanger it was parked in front of. Ward ignored him and just put the fact that Lawson was talking nonsense because of his nerves. They climbed the steps and took their seats. Lawson completely ignored the stewardess as he walked past her, who looked both offended and upset in equal measure, and they took their seats.
He saw the stewardess say something to the pilot and co-pilot and close the door.
'We'll be taking off now Sir,' she said to him.
'Thank you,' he replied.

Two minutes later, they were airborne, swinging around over Capitol Hill and all the grand monuments and he shook his head. As always, he hated the place and the people who operated in it. He leant back in his chair, closed his eyes and inhaled deeply, and then exhaled slowly.

He would not give Washington another thought.

# FORTY THREE

**DUMBO – New York**

Two days later, and with the recent events in Washington a distant memory in his mind, Ward put down the thick file that Eloisa had given him. He wanted to read it once more before she turned up for their double date with Lawson and Lucy. He had been feeling in really good spirits until he read the file again. The Old Man had been true to his word in giving him time to recharge his batteries, and he had not heard from him since they had spoken on the phone in McDermott's warehouse.
The contents of the file had made him feel angry again. This seemed to be a level of abuse of a different kind because it was happening right in New York and in front of everyone, but those who did have the power to do something about it, were turning a blind eye to it.
Within the file, was the name of two priests, Father Patrick Mahoney and Father Liam Duffy. These were two of the senior priests of New York. Mahoney was in charge of St Patrick's and Duffy St Peter's, which were both prominent churches and landmarks in Manhattan. The Catholic Church carried a lot of political sway in New York due to the large number of residents who were of Irish heritage, and those that had migrated to New York and kept up their Catholic faith. The Mayor knew that if he had the Catholic vote on his side, then re-election would normally be a formality. They also had close links to the unions and this gave them even greater influence.

There was a general perception around New York, as in most cities, that some priests who were affiliated to the Catholic Church committed abuse on young boys who would act as altar boys or belonged to choirs, and as unproved as the majority of these accusations had always been, most people took the attitude that there was no smoke without fire.

There had been a number of allegations made against both men, over a twenty year period, and none of them were proven. It appeared, as he read more into the file, that the NYPD, with their large contingent of Irish American officers, had never investigated the claims as thoroughly as they were obliged to.

But Eloisa had prepared a file full of undisputable evidence. There was even a series of e-mails between the NYPD and the Vatican, which annoyed him more than anything because the Vatican, while being fully aware of the international opinion of some Catholic priests, were extremely dismissive and threatened legal action for slander.

There was also a list of boy's names in the file that had disappeared over the last five years, twelve in total, and he had asked Nicole-Louise and Tackler to find out how hard the NYPD had looked for these boys after they had been reported missing, and their link to the church had been highlighted to the police by their parents. Their response after hacking into the NYPD server concluded that they had not tried very hard at all.

Even if they had, they would not have found them, because he had read two separate transcripts of telephone conversations that both Mahoney and Duffy had with a man called Aiden Francis, about the exchange of these boys for money. There were sickening comments included from both priest's about what sexual acts the boys did well.

Nicole-Louise had told him that they were struggling to find an exact location for Francis, and that he seemed like a ghost, but she was closing in on him and she was positive that he was in New York somewhere and that she would have an address by the end of the day.

Tomorrow, he was going to kill all three of them. He knew that without a doubt.

With Lawson spending all of his time with Lucy, he had already spoken to The Optician, and due to his own past issues, he was itching to help Ward complete the assassinations.

The more he read, the more he felt is should be followed through, and punishment issued to those who knowingly turned a blind eye to such evil actions. He concluded that he would end up having to take out half the priests in the city and too many senior NYPD personnel. But he was confident that if he eliminated Mahoney and Duffy in the appropriate way, then the message would be sent out that there is no hiding place and everyone gets caught up with eventually.

He liked the fact that he didn't have to rush around urgently doing what Eloisa asked him for once, and he thought for a moment that when he and Eloisa start their new lives, away from the world that they live in, in a year or so, he could continue to dish out his type of justice as a hobby.

The apartment door opened and Eloisa walked in. He put the file down and stood up. She noticed the file,

'It's pretty distressing reading, isn't it?' she asked.

'Let's forget about that. I'll deal with it tomorrow, I've got everything under control, let's just enjoy tonight, I'm so excited,' he replied and then kissed her softly on the lips.
'Not too excited I hope, there should only be one woman who excites you,' she said, feigning an angry look.
'There is only you, I can assure you of that.'
'We are going to be late, let's go.'

**Daniel Restaurant – East 65th Street**

They had arranged to meet Lawson at a restaurant called Daniel which currently was considered one of New York's finest and most exclusive places to eat. They arrived and waited to be seated, Ward giving Lawson's name and then they were shown to their table. Lawson had not arrived yet, and he smiled to himself, he had this vision of Lawson making a grand entrance with the love of his life attached to his arm, and every head in the room turning and looking at them.
'What are you smiling at?'
'I'm just thinking how Mike is probably hiding outside until we are seated so that he can make a grand entrance,' he replied and smiled again.
'Now Ryan, it's his night to show off, let him have his moment so he can show his lady what wonderful work colleagues he has,' she said sternly.
'Yes Miss, your instruction is duly noted.'
'What do you think she is like?' she asked.
He had thought about that very same question quite a lot over the last few days. Based on the beauty and standard

of the women that Lawson generally had in his life, he had a rough idea of what Lucy was going to look like. He wasn't generally one for pre-conceived ideas, it was actually one of his greatest strengths that he approached everything with the opposite state of mind, and he really did not warm to shallow people in any form, but he knew that someone very stunning was going to come walking into the restaurant with Lawson.

'I'm pretty sure she will be beautiful. He generally has the pick of any woman that he comes into contact with,' he eventually replied.

'Not this one,' she said and smiled, 'I already have the best one for keeps,' she added.

'But what about her character, do you think I will get on with her? From what you have told me about Mike, I get the feeling that he needs a very, very strong woman to keep him in check.'

'I think you get on with everyone in the world, you're impossible not to like,'

They ordered their drinks and ten minutes later, Lawson had still not arrived.

'I'd better call him,' he said.

'No Ryan, it's obvious why he is late.'

'So he can make a grand entrance?'

'No,' she replied and rolled her eyes, 'It will be because of Lucy.'

'I don't get it?'

'Honestly, you men don't have the faintest idea how women work.'

'Thanks! How about you educate me?'

'Right, listen carefully. It's a big thing for a woman meeting her partner's friends. She will be having a

million doubts, will they think I'm funny, will they like me, will they find me boring, and so on. Understand so far?'
He just shrugged and nodded.
'That's before you even get onto the important part.'
'Do you eat spaghetti or not?' he asked and smiled.
'Do you want to learn or not?' she said, and gave him a sarcastic smile.
'What's the important part?'
'What to wear. I guarantee you that she would have spent the whole day trying on about five different outfits and eventually decided on one, and when she changed into it an hour or so ago, she decided it didn't look right and then has been frantically trying on other outfits, before deciding on wearing the first one that she tried on this morning.'
'I doubt very much she did that. I mean, you never do that, so why should she, and you always look beautiful in what you wear.'
'Of course I do that. I did it this morning. Did you think I just pulled this outfit out of my wardrobe and threw it on?'
He shrugged again.
'But why go through all that? It's just dinner.'
'For someone so smart, it amazes how dumb you are at times.'
'Well, you don't need to impress me, you always look immaculate,' he replied, thinking now was the time for a compliment.
'It's not done to impress you stupid!'
'Then who is it for?'

Before she could answer, he saw Lawson's head towering over everyone else's near the entrance, 'They're here,' he said excitedly.
He was craning his neck, trying to get a glimpse of Lucy. Eloisa did not turn around, she did not want to put any more pressure on her, she was already aware that when she set eyes on the deranged man lifting himself off of his chair to have a look at her, she would be feeling awkward enough.
Ward caught his first glimpse of her, and she didn't look how he had imagined.
She was much shorter than he had anticipated, not much over five feet tall, and while she looked attractive in a 'Girl next door' way, she wasn't what he was expecting. She looked just like that, the girl next door. And while Lawson made the head of literally every woman turn as he walked towards their table, Lucy never warranted a second glance from anyone.
They both stood up to greet them, Eloisa giving Lucy a welcoming hug and Ward shaking Lawson's hand,
'Sorry we're late,' Lawson said, 'Lucy felt the need to change her outfit five times before putting the first one she tried back on.'
Eloisa shot him a knowing smile.
'Mike, you should know that is a woman's prerogative, it's not about making the impression on you. Lucy, you look lovely,' he said and moved forward and gave her a kiss on the cheek.
Lawson looked confused.
Eloisa glared at him.

'I've been really looking forward to meeting you both,' Lucy said in a clear voice, 'I've heard so much about you both.'

'It's all lies,' Ward said and they all laughed.

The longer the evening went on, the more Ward realised why Lawson felt for Lucy what he did. She was captivating, funny, engaging, and intelligent, and he could see as each one of these characteristics became more evident, that she in fact, along with Eloisa, was the most beautiful woman in the room.

She told stories about Lawson which had Ward laughing more than he had in a long time, and had Lawson groaning about the constant ribbing that her revelations were going to induce, and he was happy to see that she and Eloisa were giggling and whispering occasionally, just like two people having a good time together were inclined to do.

Lawson looked at him and nodded, it was an 'I told you so' nod and he smiled back at him in agreement.

They were still laughing and drinking long after most of the other customers had left; there wasn't one of them that wanted the night to end.

When the waiters indicated that it was time for them to leave, by replacing the tablecloths and cutlery on every table around them, Ward walked over to the desk to settle the bill, Lawson followed,

'I'll get this Ryan,' he said.

'No, I've got it.'

'I insist.'

'It doesn't matter; it's probably money I had stolen from someone anyway, so they can pay for it.'

'So what do you think?' Lawson asked eagerly.

'I think she is beautiful and I can see why you feel as you do. You want to hold onto her forever this time Mike, I don't think women like that come along too often,' he replied and patted him on his shoulder.
'I agree. You found one too, so we both needed to hold onto them.'
Ward smiled at him as he punched his pin code into the credit card holder.
'Can I ask you something Ryan?'
'Yes.'
'How did you know that about women not dressing for their man? Lucy said to me when you were in the bathroom that I need to get some advice from you.'
'Mike,' he replied, 'you have a lot to learn about women.'

But it wasn't only Mike Lawson who had a lot to learn. There was a storm coming, the likes of which had never been seen before, and Ryan Ward was going to discover that he knew very little about people, the world that he moved in, and the extremes people would go to in seeking revenge.

And Ryan Ward was going to be caught in the dead centre of the storm.

*To Be Continued…………*

# VOLUME 1

## PART SIX

## Revelation

*He had been in San Francisco for the past four days and not slept. His target was the second person he would kill that day, and he could still smell the smoke on his clothes that had consumed him when he had set fire to his first victim. It had to be that way, because he needed to see them suffer for what they had all done. The only conspiracy was against him and he was fighting back.*

*He was better than them and he had one big advantage. He knew what they all looked like, but to them, he was just a name. He needed to see them suffer and to know that he had beaten them, because everything was about winning to him. He felt strong and in control. He had gotten over the fact that this should be his third kill, and that the One he wanted most should not have got away, but he knew that he would soon be coming for him, and when he did, this time he would make him suffer more than any of them.*

*The second name on the list walked out of his apartment steps and headed towards the underground garage. He knew that it was now or never. He stepped out of the shadows and crossed the road slowly. He would not arouse suspicion by running, and he knew that he had time to spare because he had already disabled the ignition on the victim's car.*

*He walked slowly down the ramp and in the distance he saw the man step out of his car and lift the hood. He was too clever to leave any cables trailing, and had focussed on the electronics. People never checked them; he knew that he had time to spare. He pulled out his cell phone and mimicked talking into it as he got nearer to the man and said 'Goodbye' clearly as he got ten feet away from him.*

*'Have you got a problem?' he asked the man innocently. The second name on the list looked at him and just said, 'I'm good thanks', his crisp English accent biting through his words as he spoke. He knew that by nature the man would not want to engage in a conversation with a stranger in an underground parking garage at night. He would be highly trained and alert. 'Try checking the electronic board, I have the same model, the board comes loose,' he said as he casually walked over to the car. The man looked at him but didn't see a threat. He looked dirty and he smelt of smoke, even from five feet away, the man just saw a guy who was probably a gardener on the way home from work.*

*That was his mistake.*

*As he reached the car and peered over the man's shoulder into the engine, he used his left hand to ram the eight inch serrated blade that he had been holding into the man's kidneys. The victim instinctively threw a punch and reached for his gun which he had tucked into his waistband, but he had already removed it and was holding it in his own hand before the man had even moved his arm.*

*He was that good.*

*The second name fell to the floor on his back, and started to bleed out quickly. He bent down and stuck the blade into his stomach, very deliberately and very slowly, he wanted to cause as much pain as he possibly could. 'Do you know who I am?' he asked as he pulled out the blade and then started to push it into his groin. The second name on the list didn't even look at him. He was dying and he was a coward too, that made all of the things that had happened to him even more insulting.*

*He could see the fear in the man's eyes; he knew he was dying, so he twisted the blade clockwise to make sure he severed an artery. He knew the pain would be excruciating. He moved his head closer to the man's face, 'Do you know who I am?' he asked again, but before he could answer, the second name on the list died. As he lay there on the cold floor, he cut his throat wide open so the blood would drain out of him and flood everywhere. That will warn them he thought to himself.*

*He looked at the body and felt insulted, not only were they vastly inferior to him, they had wiped away any trace of him, and the second name on the list didn't even know who he was. He stood up and spat on the corpse.*

*'I'm Gill Whymark,' he said to the bloody mess on the floor and he turned and vanished into thin air.*

Printed in Great Britain
by Amazon